Untold Tales of Eighteenth-Century Love and War: Martha Root and Elisha Hawley in Colonial New England

By Mary Lane

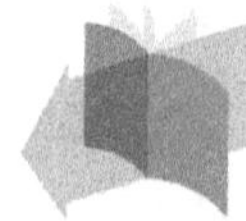

Chapbook Press

Schuler Books
2660 28th Street SE
Grand Rapids, MI 49512
(616) 942-7330
www.schulerbooks.com

Untold Tales of 18th Century Love and War

ISBN 13: 9781948237918

Library of Congress Control Number: 2021919691

Printed in the United States by Chapbook Press.

Table of Contents

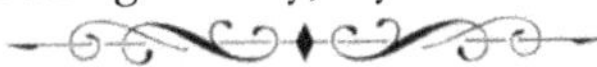

From those before, I learned;
to those behind, I pass on;
and to those along the way, my thanks for everything.

Thank you for undertaking to read my work! I most sincerely appreciate your interest. Of course, you can jump ahead to the stories and return later, but I extend this note of explanation to enlighten you as to the method and veracity of the *Tales*.

This is a work of "historic faction," meaning facts infused with the fiction of detailed imagining of persons, places and things that are no more and cannot be completely reconstructed. I have tried to assemble an understanding of events that occurred through recent philosophic, biological and scientific advances in our understanding of our human natures, as well as based on research and other inter-disciplinary facts; archaeological artifacts; social, economic, political history and documentary and statistical evidence. My methodology is based on solid research left in the historical record, supplemented by investigation of actual quotidian details.

Despite the somewhat limited extent of the directly on-point historical record, I have not deviated from any facts I discovered in more than eight years of intense researching, reading, visiting, discussing and experiencing, but have interpreted those facts/truths. I have provided an extensive list of sources in the Bibliography at the back of the book, organized into two spreadsheets. The historical record as the structure underpinning and fleshed it out with my own inferences but always based on the record of actual events and norms of the time. As proof of this assertion, I offer two extensive background spreadsheets that I have organized to comprehend events:

1.) Timeline of Events for Untold Tales. This spreadsheet of 17-19th Century historical and personal events cites details from the sources about an actual event, where and when it occurred and the source of the information (so that anyone can evaluate its accuracy);

2.) Timeline of Events for Battle of Lake George in Untold Tales.

These two lengthy tables (+1300 and almost 700 kilobytes of plus 280 and 100 pages respectively) of specific events or broad conditions and the sources of factual information can be used to assess my conclusions and interpretations. It is critically important to place everything in its historical perspective to comprehend the mind-sets at the moment. For example, the lack of English troops fighting in North America early in King George's War is coherent due to the Battle at Culloden in 1746. I will make these spreadsheets available on request (to: MaryMLane@comcast.net). Due to the size of these two documents, they cannot be attached or included.

Truth and accuracy to historic reality have been my preeminent goal. In this endeavor I have visited innumerable historic sites, examined historic objects (such as Ephraim Williams' personal effects at the Sawyer Library of Williams College in Williamstown, Massachusetts or original maps at the Clements Library at the University of Michigan) participated in 18th-century tasks, engaged in archaeological digs at the Lake George Battlefield and Fort Edward[1] by Dr. David Starbuck, observed historic re-enactments, attended scholarly presentations (such as the Fort Ticonderoga French and Indian War College) and watched dozens of informative videos. I have quoted extensively from primary source documents. Actual historic texts have been quoted as accurately as possible with only the alteration of superscripts (y[e] to ye) and complete spelling out of no longer commonly recognizable words (s[d] to said). **When I have created a text in the *Tales* that is an imaginary construct, it is based on similar actual documents from other locations of the era and is so footnoted.**

Many of the protagonists in this novella left scanty documentation. Only one signature of Martha Root is preserved. She left no letters, diaries, or other writings presenting her thoughts, feelings, motivations, etc. (None were even mentioned by descendants in the early 1800s. I am one such descendant of Martha.). Unusual for Northampton (Massachusetts) records, even Martha and her twins' birthdates are unknown. Rebekah Hawley also left very little.

We do know the surviving historic record has been deliberately purged by Joseph Hawley III's burning of documents.[2] By doing this, Joseph Hawley attempted to skew historic record or protect the family name and reputation. We know that primary source documents of immense value have been banished or suppressed in collections because they did not comport with the prevailing patriarchal or moral views of the time.[3] Joseph Hawley preserved some of his letters, but not any from his mother or wife and few from his brother.

---

[1] Then referred to as Fort Lyman, as it is called in Chapters 24 and 25.

[2] Trumbull, James Russell. *History of Northampton, Massachusetts, From its Earliest Settlement in 1654. Press of Gazette Printing Company (Northampton, 1898).* Volume 2, Page 542.

[3] For some contemporaneous examples, see Amelia F. Miller, *Romance, Remedies, and Revolution* or Laurel Thatcher Ulrich, *A Midwife's Tale* Complete citations in the Bibliography.

I expected more of Elisha Hawley's letters from the war front – particularly as his war journal was saved and shared (being printed in Trumbull's *History*[4]). While on the Crown Point Expedition, his family knew well that his life was at risk; I expected more treasured last letters in the Hawley Papers (as I did while my uncle was in Vietnam). Many of the remaining letters of Elisha's not burned are not letters *written by* him, but rather *received by* him. None discuss Elisha's response to "ye affair" or Joe's handling of it.

As regards Tiyanoga (aka "Theyanoguin" or "Hendrick") of the Mohawk Nation, his speeches and images are preserved by being "quoted" or pictured in contemporary colonial accounts, although we do not know how accurate these were. Such were often tainted by prejudice and altered by translation. So much must be inferred.

This was the record I had to work with. However, first, I had to recognize it for what it presented and obscured. What is hidden can be as important as what is seen – particularly with women or minority groups who leave few written records or explanations. This limited historic record demands inference of the behaviors and motivations of people that isn't ascribed and can't be documented. This, along with reckoning human traits or biases (i.e., prejudices, predispositions), posits a more nuanced possible picture of these events.

We know that contemporaneous reconstructions, such as witnesses' statements immediately after an incident, differ depending on point of view, motivation, prior experiences, emotional/psychological/physiological state at the time and other factors. Thus, if Martha Root, Elisha Hawley or John Miller were to tell these *Tales*, they would likely forget, re-attribute, re-interpret and contradict their own details and perhaps tell different *Tales*.

I hope I have done this to a fair extent. For example, in the case of Oliver Warner, Timothy and Simeon Root, scholars of Jonathan Edwards have explained them as 'teenage boys,' 'town hoodlums,' etc. without knowing their age, families, occupations or eventual social statuses and occupations. Taking these into account leads to a fuller, richer vision of mid-18th century Northampton. Similarly, I hope to have imagined an alternate Martha Root to those which labeled her as a "village girl," "a woman of the town," etc., as Joseph Hawley implied and which many historians accepted. In this, I am deeply indebted to and grateful for

---

[4] Trumbull. *History*. Vol 2, Pages 254-9.

Professor Kathryn Kish Sklar for first compiling data and stimulating a reinterpretation of Martha and the Root family's status and activities. [5]

Most important is that I have not contradicted known historic facts, rather I let these drive this writing, my conclusions and my imaginings.[6]

Martha, Elisha and the other persons named herein were human beings with 99% of the same DNA and physiological-anatomical compositions as ourselves. I believe their fundamental human emotions and instincts were similar to our own - even when influenced by vastly different social and psychological forces within a physically dissimilar environment. Border collies and huskies still have basic canine characteristics whether in Scotland or Alaska. At a minimum, the book's characters' actions are known - from which their emotions are conceivable (within an 18th century context) - which I hope is what I have done.

Eleanor Roosevelt said, "Great minds discuss ideas; average minds discuss events; small minds discuss people." Discussing people is not necessarily gossip: it can be engaging with reality and attempting to assess what motivates someone. These *Tales* discuss the small minds and stuff of people in order for us to see them as regular people, like ourselves. Historic people enjoyed travel, exploration and

---

[5] Sklar, Kathryn Kish. "Culture Versus Economics: A Case of Fornication in Northampton in the 1740's," *Michigan Feminist Studies*. The University of Michigan Papers in Women's Studies (Ann Arbor, 1976) and "To Use her as His Wife: An Extraordinary Paternity Suit in the 1740s," in *Women and Power in American History*, edited by Kathryn Kish Sklar and Thomas Dublin. Prentice Hall (New York, 2002); Volume 1, Edition 2. Pages 73-91.

[6] Thus, for example, in Chapter 1, "Scenes of a Marriage," these are the recorded facts around which I arranged my narrative: 1. Rebekah Stoddard and Joseph Hawley II's ages at marriage; 2. Esther Warham Mather Stoddard's age at marriage and children; 3. Grandchildren of Esther and their educations; 4. Mary Edwards' care of her grandparents, Esther and Solomon Stoddard; 5. The commonly available foodstuffs, drinks, fabrics, and material aspects of early 18th century life in Northampton are accurate; 6. John Stoddard's biography (ages, age at marriage, titles, occupations, etc.); 7. Early 18th century colonial vocabulary (such as a "thornback old maid") and cultural norms are accurate and utilized; 8. The geography of 1720's Northampton town and area, including the "Red Tavern;" 9. Joseph Hawley II's biography (although I do not know if JHII fell asleep in church, I do know he kept extensive notes of sermons, now at the Joseph Hawley Papers, Bancroft Collection, New York Public Library); 10. The banns for Joseph and Rebekah's marriage were published as noted; 11. Date of their marriage from Northampton records; 12. Details and location of "The Manse" (Stoddard house); 13. Solomon Stoddard's appearance is from an existing portrait; 14. Bess was an African enslaved woman "owned" by John Stoddard; 15. *The Bay Psalm Book* was a collection of church songs published in 1640 in Cambridge, Massachusetts and was well used for the next century; 16. The Hawleys did have forks in their store inventory; 17. Joseph Hawley III owned a Chinese bowl (then called "cheney-ware"), now in the collection at Historic Northampton; 18. Details of John Stoddard, John Bridgman and Thomas Baker's activities in the Deerfield raid are true; and 19. Joseph Hawley II's militia appointment and service are factual.

adventure just as we do. And although formal education was more limited, writing less standardized, people's vocabularies and thoughts were as rich as ours and with surprisingly similar vocabulary. Their accumulated knowledge was different from what is important for us but it was not necessarily less. I have been astonished to learn the myriad types of fabrics available from Elijah Williams' commissary/store in the 1750's in Deerfield, Massachusetts! It amuses me to think that common soldiers stationed at Fort Massachusetts in August 1746 slept on feather beds much the same as is found upstairs in our bedroom. I never heard before that there were "expresses" delivering information and dispatches in the 18th century. Thus, I would add, the past is not dead, it is not even passed. It is our foundation.

I would like to note that I have mostly tried to use historically accurate language. Particularly, I use the word "Indian" rather than "Native American" because it was universally used at the time. I have endeavored to approach these affairs from the perspective of the 18th-century as this is how and why these things happened. Consequently, this is infused with racism and misogyny because it existed (and still exists). I hope that this will be understood and no offense taken. I have tried to recognize and confront my own predispositions, historic prejudices and blinders, as it is not only most ethical but also most fascinating, richly human and useful. I hope that I have been able to view the actors – all of whom were real persons (except Hannah Muchmore) with the understanding and acceptance that each of us is a product of our times and the legacies of our births, families, societies and events that happen to us, around us and by us. Each deserves respect whether or not I like their actions.

Thank you.

Mary Lane
August 15, 2021

<u>Acknowledgements</u>

So many people have assisted me over these years that I hesitate to start naming, but one must offer this small recompense for their generous assistance and support: so… onward! Mere words cannot express my deep appreciation to them.

First, I thank my family and friends who have endured so much tedium, listening to me on this topic obsessively for over eight years now. My husband (Amar Ourchane), children (Tarik, Adam, and Nadia), and their spouses (Lauren, Kristin, and Caleb), parents (Jack and Norma Lane), sister travelers (Ginger and Linda), cousins (Marcella Miller Meyer de Stadelhofen, Carin Krestakos), my editor-helper Jennifer Noyon, friends (Nene Tesija Pocedic, Leslie Adadow), Professor Mary Hieshetter, and others have suffered endless 18th century factoids doled out to them on a constant basis. Of course, they also read pages upon drafts upon versions and they had the combination of kindness, encouragement, and mild correction to allow me to persevere through wondering why I was doing this?

My husband Amar has financially assisted my addiction to 18th century minutiae and the most obscure information. Has anyone ever had a 'helpmate' so true as he?!? Plus, excursions to Ann Arbor, western Massachusetts, upstate New York, New York City, Boston, Washington, D.C. and England, as I tracked down documents and books that no one has viewed in years or decades. Not to mention the piles of my books and papers spread across three rooms and desks!

After the emotional contributions of my closest ones, friends and acquaintances in historic societies, at universities and colleges and those interested in the French and Indian War were indispensable for teaching, guiding and amending. Most important among those who aided me have been Mr. Ralmon Jon Black of the Williamsburg (Massachusetts) Historical Society who commenced this entire journey with his response to my inquiry email: "Martha Root… that's quite a story!" Without Ralmon's reply, I might never have commenced on this topic. I am so grateful to him! His wealth of knowledge was immense and many of us were devastated by its loss in his passing.

Other helpers of historic proportions have been Dr. Kenneth Minkema of Yale University's Jonathan Edwards' Center; "Bloody Morning Scout" aficionado James S. Major of the Old Fort Johnson/Montgomery County Historical Society; Williamsburg amateur historian and hiking guide Eric Weber; Elise Bernier-Feeley of the Forbes Library in Northampton; Daniel Harrison formerly of the Henry Ford College's Eshleman Library; French and Indian War author/reenactor and Robert Rogers expert, Timothy Todish; Vermont history author Gary Shattuck; Clayton Lewis of the University of Michigan's William L. Clements Library; New

York State Archaeologist, Charles Vandrie; title records expert and genealogist Bonnie McCracken; archaeologist/author Dr. David Starbuck formerly of Plymouth State University; Wheatland (New York) Town Historian Barbara Chapman; author Susan Stinson; local children's author Wendy Champney of North Adams (Mass.); author, editor, and local Berkshire historian, Bernard Drew; susan lisk of the Porter Phelps Huntington House Museum; Wayne State University's Purdy Kresge Library; the Sawyer Library of Williams College; the North Adams and Williamstown Historical Societies; and Colonial Williamsburg [Virginia]. Jooyoung Jung read with a real literary analysist's eye. My mother-in-law, Bentali Ghessab, related to me her own experiences of traditional childbirth in an undeveloped village and the practice of midwifery there. Sadia Ourchane translated it for me.

Before this tutelage, I feared venturing into 18th century history as too ancient, abstruse and unknowable for me. I might still not know a rifle from a musket, Colonial Williamsburg (Virginia) from Williamsburg "Burgy" (Massachusetts), Hendrick Peters Tiyanoga from Hendrick Tejonihokarawa, if not for them!

I owe special gratitude to my editor and friend of forty plus years Jennifer Noyon. By challenging and encouraging me, she helped me produce a final product that is clearer, more internally consistent and, I hope, a better literary work. She spent so many hours with Martha, Elisha, Rebekah and the rest that she too feels she knows them personally!

There are undoubtedly mistakes within the work, however, those should be attributed to me.

I am much the richer and better for it all. Thank you so immensely much to everyone!

Mary Lane
July 4, 2021

Chapter Summaries for *Untold Tales*

Chapter 1, Scenes from a Marriage (November 1722). Cranky old maid Rebekah Stoddard marries the eccentric Joseph Hawley Junior. The marriage is celebrated at the Reverend Solomon Stoddard's family home in Northampton, Massachusetts. The bride is escorted to her new marital home (in the same town). In the tavern, the locals drink and dissect the event.

Chapter 2, The Relict Rebekah and her Two Boys (1735-1737). Joseph Hawley Junior, an obsessively religious depressive and father of two young boys, gruesomely commits suicide. The entire town is affected.

Chapter 3, Bad Boys, Bad Books, Bad Blood (March to June 1744). Village young men are discovered reading a scandalous and obscene midwife book. The culprit's names are read out at meetinghouse. A church committee investigates the offense. There is public confession of the misdeeds.

Chapter 4, Off, Away, Under a Flowering Tree (1746). Elisha Hawley and Martha Root become enamored and develop a sexual relationship.

Chapter 5, Martha at the Corners (Summer 1746). Elisha and Martha continue their affair. Elisha's mother Rebekah, Martha's mother and the rest of the town start to suspect its true nature.

Chapter 6, I Seen What I Seen, and I Know What I know (Late 1746). The town's wild girl tells Rebekah Hawley her son Elisha has gotten Martha Root pregnant.

Chapter 7, A Dark Night in Northampton (Late 1746). Martha Root and Elisha Hawley's incipient relationship blossoms. However, Elisha is caught by his mother one night at the house of the Root family. A public fray ensues in the street.

Chapter 8, I Saw the Cloud, though I Did Not Foresee the Storm (1746-1747). The town becomes aware of Martha's pregnancy. It is further discovered that she is carrying twin babies. Amidst the diverse reactions, Martha prepares for the difficult childbirth.

Chapter 9, A Pretty Scandal (1747). Martha confesses fornication before the First Church of Northampton congregation and court. Elisha is shunted out of Northampton by his family to the frontier post of Fort Massachusetts where the French and Indians have attacked, killed, burned and taken captives.

Chapter 10, Twin Babies (Winter-Spring1747). Martha Root endures a long, fraught delivery to finally birth twin baby girls. She avers to the midwives that Elisha Hawley is the father.

Chapter 11, Dying and Trying Times (July-November 1747). Martha Root confesses to the court her "crime," fornication. Epidemics sweep through Northampton and the Valley. Baby Esther and Aunt Sarah Root die of the malady, as do many others.

xiii

Chapter 12, Anne Hawley Lives, John Stoddard's Conundrum (December 1747). Although Lieutenant Elisha Hawley is absent and his brother negotiates in his place, fall-out from Elisha's lack of punishment by the court and church continues to flare in Northampton.

Chapter 13, An Agreement (May 18, 1748). The monetary settlement of £155[7] with the family of Martha Root fails to satisfy Elisha's religious obligation to account to his fornication to the congregation according to the Reverend Mr. Edwards.

Chapter 14, His Foot shall Slide (end May 1748). Martha's father Hezekiah Root meets with the Reverend Mr. Edwards, Colonel John Stoddard, Elisha's mother Rebekah and his brother Joseph amidst disagreements over religious concepts and obligations.

Chapter 15, Excommunication (July 26-August 4, 1748). Pushed by the Reverend Mr. Edwards after the unexpected death of town leader Colonel John Stoddard, the First Church Northampton appoints a committee that finds Elisha Hawley sinful, unrepentant and excommunicates him.

Chapter 16, Nothing Remarkable (at Fort Massachusetts, now North Adams, Massachusetts) (1749). Lieutenant Elisha Hawley commands an unruly company at the lonely fort, far from civilization during the Third French and Indian War. He receives letters from home and reminisces about his old life. Lieutenant Daniel Severance dies in an unexplained incident.

Chapter 17, Hope, Hope, how goes Your Vote? (June 1750). Martha's uncle, Hope Root, fails physically as misfortune and illnesses beset his family. Hope's son Aaron catches the dreaded "throat distemper."

Chapter 18, Dutiful Betty's Prayer (November 1753). Elisha Hawley marries Betty Pomeroy. She fails to conceive and carry a child.

Chapter 19, Marrying Mercy (September 1752-1753). After a protracted courtship and despite his mother's opposition, Joseph Hawley and Mercy Lyman marry. The couple moves into the old Hawley homestead with Mother Rebekah.

Chapter 20, Who is this Lieutenant-Colonel George Washington? (Summer 1754). In the western wilderness, surveyor Elisha Hawley meets up with the Grand Jury investigating road petitions. The men talk current events, including the defeat of the Virginia Lieutenant-Colonel George Washington.

---

[7] The average settlement for child support was 4-6s (shillings) per week, according to Sklar in "Culture versus Economics," pages 35-56, 39. See Sklar and Marsella in Bibliography at end of book. However, per Marsella, "Criminal Cases," the average settlement for child support at this time was 2 shillings per week. Fines were up to £3. In one typical case: "He was ordered to pay two shillings weekly in child support and to post a £100 surety bond with Amesbury selectmen to insure that the child would not become a public charge." Page 37.

<u>Chapter 21, Marrying John Miller (Summer 1754-Spring 1755)</u>. Eight years after her twins were born, Martha Root marries John Miller. Together they have a son Stephen.

<u>Chapter 22, The Crown Point Expedition for which Elisha Writes his Will (June 1755)</u>. Captain Elisha Hawley writes his "Last Will and Testament" as his company marches out of Northampton toward Albany on its expedition to capture the French fortress of Crown Point on Lake Champlain.

<u>Chapter 23, Ephraim's Regiment of the Massachusetts Militia following which He Drafts a New Will (July 1755)</u>. Stopping at Albany on their trek northward to fight at Crown Point, Colonel Ephraim Williams drafts a second will leaving a charitable legacy.

<u>Chapter 24, The Officers' Council in which Brother Long Bow Speaks (September 8, 1755)</u>. At the army camp at Lake George, Mohican-Mohawk chief sachem Tiyanoga remembers land thefts, deceits and relations with the English, French, fellow Caughnawaga Mohawks and the Iroquois Confederacy. In the officers' council at dawn, Colonel Ephraim Williams volunteers to warn the men at Fort Lyman and Tiyanoga boldly proposes to lead the scout of the Iroquois, five hundred Massachusetts soldiers, and five hundred Connecticut soldiers.

<u>Chapter 25, A Bloody Morning Scout (September 8, 1755)</u>. The column of Iroquois warriors, Massachusetts and Connecticut soldiers marches out from the army camp intending to relieve Fort Lyman, near where the tracks of the French and their allied native warriors have been discovered. However, the French General, Baron Dieskau, sets a trap for the Massachusetts regimental commander, Colonel Ephraim Williams and his force. A bloody melee ensues.

<u>Chapter 26, The Devil be Your Doctor (September 11, 1755)</u>. Back at the army camp, the mortally wounded Captain Elisha Hawley struggles to stay alive among others injured.

<u>Chapter 27, Brother-in-law Clarke's Painful Errand (September 13-25, 1755)</u>. Samuel Clarke, best friend and brother-in-law of Joseph Hawley, travels along the Great Boston-to-Albany Road in place of the depressed and hypochondriacal Joseph Hawley to the mortally wounded Captain Elisha Hawley dying at the army camp at Lake George.

<u>Chapter 28, At the Bar (August 28, 1759-February 13,1760)</u>. Martha Root's brother-in-law, Charles Phelps, faces off against Elisha Hawley's attorney brother, Joseph, in the Inferior Court of Common Pleas in a lawsuit against Eben Pomeroy (Mercy Hawley's cousin, the Deacon's son) and his rowdy young customers over "frolicking" of the men and some maids at the White Horse Inn in Hadley (across the river from Northampton).

<u>Chapter 29, In a Name (1766-1773)</u>. Now an adult, "Anne Hawley" is pregnant and marries. Before Anne's name can be inscribed in the Northampton *Town Book*, Town Secretary John Nash travels to visit relatives in Hatfield, falls seriously ill, and dies of smallpox.

xv

<u>Chapter 30, Always a Bed and a Candlestick (April 1792, November 1805).</u> Anne Hawley's mother, Martha Root, the last survivor of her late Puritan generation (of the main characters of the events in this novel), faces old age and death with retrospection and serenity.

<u>The Cast of Characters</u>
(a "cheat sheet" of major personalities in this novel, in alphabetical order by last name)

At the Bar, Chapter 28 The list of named litigants and defendants were real persons in cases at the court then, including "the Informer."

Bad Boys, Bad Books, Bad Blood Chapter 16 The list of people involved is from actual documents of the events at Andover Theological Seminary (Massachusetts).[8]

Hope, Hope, how goes your Vote? Chapter 17 Root relatives named herein and their fates are factual.

Nothing Remarkable Chapter 16 All persons (soldiers, scouts, and cooks) named in this chapter were actual persons stationed at the Fort during this time period. Several of the incidents are factual, some are reimagined based on diaries or other descriptions.

The Bloody Morning Scout Chapter 25 All combatants mentioned were real personalities, as are their fates described therein.

Who is this Lieutenant-Colonel? Chapter 20 The list for the Grand Jury is true, as are the incidents regarding George Washington and Benjamin Franklin.

ALLEN, Betty née Parsons (1716-1800) Northampton midwife for more than 50 years who delivered more than 3,000 babies.

BAKER, Noah (1719-1810) First discovered reading *The Midwife Rightly Instructed* in the notorious "Bad Boys/Bad Books" incident of 1744 in Northampton. Later became a Baptist preacher.

BESS (dates unknown) Black "servant for life" (i.e., enslaved) of John Stoddard. Unable to be traced further by author.

BRANT, Joseph aka Thayendanagea See Thayendanegea.

BRIDGEMAN, John (1674-1755) Uncle of Martha Root, brother of Martha Bridgman Root (mother of Martha Root, main character). Mutilated in 1704 Deerfield Raid. A carpenter. Lived across Pudding Lane from the Hawleys.

BUSH, John (dates unknown) African-American freeman and colonial soldier famous as a superb carver of gunpowder powder-horns. Served at Fort Massachusetts and the Battle of Lake George.

CLARKE, Eunice née Lyman (1728-1784) Mother of Joseph Hawley Clarke ("adopted"[9] son of Mercy and Joseph Hawley III), wife of Samuel Clarke, sister of Mercy Lyman Hawley.

CLARKE, Samuel (1720-1807) Brother-in-law of Mercy Lyman Hawley and friend of Joseph Hawley III, who traveled to care for Elisha Hawley on death-bed at army camp at Lake George, New York. His son, Joseph Hawley Clarke, adopted by Joseph and Mercy. Occupation saddler.

CLARK, Jehiel (1736-1829?) A resident of Northampton during the time period. Private in Elisha Hawley company at Lake George.

COLSON, Hannah (1720-1806) A servant of Rebekah Hawley in some of these years, recorded in the Judd Manuscript at Forbes Library, Northampton (MA) as having many notorious stories of Rebekah that she widely recounted later. Married Lieutenant Timothy Lyman, cousin of Phinehas Lyman (see "At the Bar" chapter).

DANKS, Samuel (1708-1755) Excommunicated for fornication by Reverend Jonathan Edwards June 12, 1743.

---

8 Jonathan Edwards' original fragmentary notes of the "Bad Boys/Bad Books" affair were at the Franklin Trask Library, Andover Newton Theological Seminary, which documents have now moved to the Yale Divinity School.

9 Named "Joseph Clarke" at his birth on October 8, 1749 but later called "Joseph Hawley Clarke" which is on his tombstone. The Massachusetts Adoption of Children Act in 1851 was the first in the United States but too late for this situation.

DWIGHT, Timothy "Colonel" (1694-1771) Trader, surveyor, military officer, supporter of Reverend Jonathan Edwards, Justice of Probate in Hampshire County. Built Fort Dummer in Line of Forts. Justice of Peace for Northampton who officiated at marriage of Martha Root and John Miller. Daughter Eleanor married General Phineas Lyman (attorney who trained Joseph Hawley III).

DWIGHT, Timothy "Ensign" (1726-1777) Son of Colonel Timothy Dwight, Senior (above), husband of Mary Edwards (daughter of Reverend Jonathan and Sarah). Also friend of Jonathan Edwards.

EDWARDS, Esther, Elizabeth, and Mary Daughters of Jonathan and Sarah Pierpont Edwards. Nieces of Rebekah Stoddard Hawley.

EDWARDS, Jonathan (1703-1758) Prominent theologian and author, minister of the First Church of Northampton from 1727-1750; also, Missionary to Stockbridge tribe of Native Americans (aka Mohicans) 1752-1758, President of Princeton College in 1758 at his death from a smallpox immunization. Dismissed from Northampton church due to agitation and opposition lead by Joseph Hawley III and Pomeroys.

EDWARDS, Sarah née Pierpont (1710-1758) Esteemed, educated, traveled wife of Jonathan Edwards., daughter of minister James Pierpont. Mother of 11 children by Edwards. Deeply "enthusiastic" and gifted in religion. Enjoyed certain luxuries criticized by First Church of Northampton congregants.

FAIRFIELD, Samuel "Captain" (1731-1803) Nephew and household member of John Miller. Enlisted in company of Elisha Hawley in the Fourth French & Indian War, where he was injured (extent unknown). Owned Fairfield's Shelter (tavern) in Williamsburg.

FAIRFIELD, Thomas (dates unknown) Imputed relationship to Samuel Fairfield. Unable to trace further. Known to have enlisted in Hawley Company for the Crown Point Expedition; sick in November 1755 at Lake George. Fought with militia also in 1756.

FRANKLIN, Benjamin (1706-1790) Renowned colonial printer and American statesman, diplomat, scientist and inventor. Advocated for "Plan of Union" for American colonies before Albany Congress of 1754.

GUILFORD, William (1744-1814) Husband of Anne Hawley, father of her sons. Farmer and mechanic.

HAWLEY, Anne (may have been called "Anne ROOT"?, married name Guilford) (probably 1727-1818) Daughter of Martha Root and (alleged - but not denied) Elisha Hawley, step-daughter of John Miller. Married as "Anne Hawley" in 1766 in First Church Northampton. Moved to Williamsburg Massachusetts, (probably with Martha and step-father John Miller).

HAWLEY, Elisha "Captain" (also "Lieutenant") (1726-1755) Younger son of Joseph Hawley II and Rebekah Stoddard Hawley, husband of Elizabeth Pomeroy Hawley, with whom he had no children, alleged father of Anne and Esther Root Hawley with Martha Root. Worked as a dealer in skins/furs, surveyor and military officer.

HAWLEY, Elizabeth "Betty" née Pomeroy (1729-1793) Wife of Elisha Hawley, daughter of Ebenezer Pomeroy II, sister of Eben Pomeroy III, 2nd wife of Phinehas Lyman, great-niece of Seth and Daniel Pomeroy. Discovered midwife's book hidden in their chimney, disclosed it, and testified in the "Bad Boys/Bad Books" investigation.

HAWLEY, Esther (aka "Esther ROOT") (probably 1727-1727) Twin daughter of Martha Root and (alleged - but not denied) Elisha Hawley, twin sister of Anne Root Hawley. Died likely of epidemic, same day as her great-aunt Sarah Wright Root.

HAWLEY Joseph I (1654-1711) Father of Joseph Hawley II, grandfather of Joseph Hawley III. Attorney, Northampton town officer. Gory accidental death in May 1711.

HAWLEY Joseph II (1682-1735) Father of Joseph Hawley III and Elisha Hawley, husband of Rebekah Stoddard Hawley. Suicide on June 1, 1735 described in Jonathan Edwards' book *A Faithful Narrative of the Surprising Work of God* (1737).

HAWLEY Joseph III "Major" (1723-1788) Brother of Elisha Hawley, son of Joseph Hawley II and Rebekah Stoddard Hawley, husband of Mercy Lyman Hawley, first cousin of Jonathan Edwards. Chief opponent of Reverend Jonathan Edwards in Northampton in adulthood but succored by Edwards as a boy. Elected official in Northampton. Attorney, Justice of the Peace for Hampshire County. Colonial legislator and activist on Committee of Correspondence in American Revolution. Constitutionalist critic of Massachusetts Constitution, adamant about separation of church and state.

HAWLEY, Mercy née Lyman (1729-1806) Wife of Joseph Hawley III, sister of Eunice Lyman Clarke, sister-in-law of Samuel Clarke.

HAWLEY Rebekah née Stoddard (1685-1788) Mother of Elisha and Joseph Hawley III, wife of Joseph Hawley II, daughter of Solomon Stoddard, sister of Colonel John Stoddard, maternal aunt of Jonathan Edwards. Legendary aristocrat and eccentric in Northampton.

HENDRICK aka "Tiyanoga" (also spelled Theyanoguin). See Tiyanoga.

J. ROMANO (dates unknown) 16-year-old (in February 1755) "Negro boy" and "body servant" (i.e., slave, enslaved man) of Ephraim Williams, Jr., purchased for £53.6.8 and who attended Williams on the Crown Pointe expedition.[10]

JOHNSON, William "General" (nickname "Handsome Billy") (1715-1774) Irish-born British official to the Iroquois League, nephew of English Admiral Peter Warren. Appointed Commander of the Crown Pointe Expedition in 1755 (which resulted in the "Bloody Morning Scout" of the Battle of Lake George). Fluent in Mohawk language and culture. (Unofficially under colonial law) Possibly married to Caroline, niece of Tiyanoga and Mohawk matriarch Molly Brant.

LAWRENCE aka "Thick Lawrence" (dates unknown) Native American (believed Mohawk) scout/tracker associated with Tiyanoga. Mohawk Tiononderoge bear clan leader. Provided intelligence to General William Johnson before Battle of Lake George. Probably Lawrence Sanagaris.

LYMAN, Elizabeth "Betty" née Pomeroy Hawley (1729-1793) Daughter of Deacon Ebenezer Pomeroy II, wife of Elisha Hawley, later second wife of Phinehas Lyman, sister of Eben Pomeroy III. Discovered the "Bad Book" in chimney of their house, reported it and testified to investigating committee.

LYMAN, Phineas "Major General" (1715 or 1716-1775) Son-in-law of Colonel Timothy Dwight of Northampton. Attorney in Suffield, Massachusetts (which became Connecticut); trained Joseph Hawley III in law. Connecticut General; Major General of New England troops, second-in-command to General William Johnson at Battle of Lake George who directed forces upon William Johnson's shooting in the butt. Never acknowledged or credited by Johnson. Died in West Florida after 11 years in England trying to get benefits for veterans from British government.

LYMAN, Phinehas (1725-1792) Second husband of Elizabeth "Betty" Pomeroy Hawley. Cousin of Mercy and Eunice Lyman. Selectman of town of Hadley. Land speculator in Vermont.

MATHER, Cotton Reverend (1663-1728) Brilliant famed Puritan theologian, author and scientist who lived in Boston. Involved in the investigation of the 1692 Salem Witchcraft

---

[10] The receipt for Romano's "purchase" reprinted by Wright in *Colonel Ephraim Williams*. Page 89. See Bibliography for full citation. Romano was not "bequeathed" in the *Last Will and Testament* of Eph Williams although "…all the stock of cattle and Negro servants now upon the place, to be equally divided" between Eph's brothers Josiah and Elijah Williams. Wright. *Williams.* Page 153. Author supposes that Romano would not have gone out on the "Bloody Morning Scout" with Williams and, thus, would have been spared that trauma. It is further surmised that Romano could have been next enslaved by Eph's brother, Dr. Thomas Williams after the Battle of Lake George. Romano is not mentioned in the 1779 probating of Thomas Williams' *Will*, so J. Romano disappears from my historical view.

Trials. Opposed to the "Half-way Covenant" theory of Reverend Solomon Stoddard. Denied the Presidency of Harvard College.

MILLER, Aaron (1708-1779) Brother of John Miller and lived in John's household, brother-in-law of Martha Root, step-uncle of Anne Hawley Guilford. Became a shoemaker after fever incapacitated him from farming.

MILLER, Ebenezer (1664-1737) Father of Sarah, Joseph, Aaron, John. John and Aaron believed to have unexpectedly inherited house upon Ebenezer's and an older brother's proximate deaths.

MILLER, Hadassah (1781-1846) Granddaughter of Martha Root and John Miller.

MILLER, John (1712-1792) Husband of Martha Root, step-father of Anne Hawley. Father of four children with Martha Root (plus still-born). Lived early in Northampton but became a fabled trapper and hunter, then yeoman farmer in the "Hatfield Three Mile Addition," which became the town of Williamsburg, Massachusetts.

MILLER, John (1696-1696) Older brother of John Miller (in these stories). Note: it was a common practice to reuse names after decease of earlier babies in Puritan families (adding to genealogical confusion). Elizabeth Pomeroy Hawley Lyman is another example of such.

MILLER, Joseph (1705-1737) Older brother of Aaron and John Miller. Died unexpectedly, probably of disease, days before their father Ebenezer without sufficient time to change his *Last Will & Testament*; thus, suddenly inheriting Aaron and John of lands and a house in Northampton.

MILLER, Stephen (1755-1834) Son of John Miller and Martha Root., half-brother of Anne Hawley. Revolutionary War veteran.

MITCHEL, Mary (married name Belding) (1731-1783) Fiancée of Aaron Root.

MIX, Elisha, Mary, Sarah, Rebekah Nephew and nieces of Rebekah Stoddard Hawley.

MUCHMORE, Hannah Fictional character (based on Barba of Grbljaba, Croatia and Hannah Hovey of Sunderland in Inferior Court of Common Pleas case August 28, 1759).

NASH, John (1736-1773) First Town Clerk of Williamsburg, Massachusetts.

NEGRO, Bathsheba (dates unknown) African-American "servant for life" of Major Ebenezer Pomeroy II. Northampton church member. Testified in "Bad Boys/Bad Books" investigation.

PHELPS, Charles, Charlie (1717-1789) Husband of Dorothy Root, brother-in-law of Martha Root, represented Martha and negotiated £155 settlement between Roots and Elisha Hawley. Attorney (frequently opposing Joseph Hawley III) in court and church, strong supporter of American Revolution, political activist in Massachusetts, Vermont, and New York. Adherent of Reverend Jonathan Edwards.

POMEROY, Daniel "Lieutenant" (1709-1755) Brother of Lt-Colonel Seth and Deacon Eben Pomeroy II, great-uncle of Betty Pomeroy Hawley Lyman. Massachusetts militia leader throughout French and Indian Wars. Blacksmith, farmer. Had premonition that he would die in Crown Pointe Expedition; his son Justin was born post mortem after Battle.

POMEROY, Ebenezer II "Deacon" (1697-1774) Father of Ebenezer Pomeroy III and Elizabeth Betty Pomeroy, brother of Lieutenant-Colonel Seth and Lieutenant Daniel Pomeroy (second to Captain Elisha Hawley.) Confidant of Rebekah Hawley. Father-in-law of Elisha Hawley. Church deacon during Edwards controversies of 1740s-1750. Civic leader.

POMEROY, Ebenezer III (1733-1801) Brother of Betty Pomeroy Hawley Lyman, son of Deacon Eben Pomeroy, great-nephew of Lt-Colonel Seth and Lieutenant Dan Pomeroy. Implicated in the "Bad Boys/Bad Books" scandal of spring 1744. Innkeeper in Hadley who was prosecuted by Joseph Hawley III in 1759-1760.

POMEROY, Elizabeth "Betty" Hawley Lyman (1729-1793) See Elizabeth Lyman.

POMEROY, Seth "Colonel" or "Lieutenant-Colonel"[11] (1706-1777) Brother of Lt. Dan and Deacon Eben Pomeroy II, uncle of Betty Pomeroy Hawley. Massachusetts militia leader throughout French and Indian Wars and American Revolution. Ardent friend of Joseph Hawley III. Professional blacksmith and gunsmith. Active in civic life in Northampton. Extremely well-liked but reputed intellectual light-weight and ungainly.

ROOT, Aaron (1721-1750) Son of Hope Root and Sarah Wright, cousin of Martha Root. Likely died of epidemic, leaving a *Last Will* drawn up by Joseph Hawley III and witnessed by John Miller.

ROOT, Dorothy "Dolly" (1715-1777) Sister of Martha Root, wife of Charles Phelps. Mother of twins in 1749 (like Martha in 1747). Outspoken and bold defender of husband and sons in Vermont land grant "wars."

ROOT, Hezekiah (1676-1766) Father of Martha, Simeon, Hannah, Joseph Root, brother of Hope Root. Presumed to have been a weaver, as his grandfather. Calculated to be in top 20% of town economically by historian Kathryn Kish Sklar. See Bibliography.

ROOT, Hope (1675-1750) Father of Timothy, Aaron Root, uncle of Martha Root. Presumed to have been a weaver. Believed to be the Mr. Root who complained in May 1744 to Reverend Benjamin Colman of Brattle Street Church, Boston about the new singing of Dr. Watts' hymns by Northampton congregation (which Colman wrote to Edwards about).

ROOT, Joseph (1728-1802) Brother of Martha and Simeon Root. Chorister for church after Daniel Pomeroy. Also married in 1754 by Timothy Dwight (instead of Joseph Hawley)

ROOT, Martha née Bridgman (1690-1759) Mother of Martha, Dorothy, Simeon, Joseph, Hannah Root, wife of Hezekiah Root, sister of John Bridgeman. Married March 23, 1713; oldest son Hezekiah Jr. born January 29, 1713.[1213]

ROOT Miller, Martha (believed 1720-1805) Mother of twins Anne and Esther Root Hawley by fornication with reputed lover Elisha Hawley. Wife of John Miller. Mother of Stephen, Cyrus, John Junior and Martha Miller.

ROOT, Sarah née Wright (1678-1747) Wife of Hope Root, mother of Timothy Root, aunt of Martha Root. Died same day as Martha's twin Esther, possibly of epidemic?

ROOT, Simeon (1718-1753) Brother of Martha, Dolly, Joseph Root, cousin of Timothy Root. A leader in "Bad Boys" incidents in spring 1744. Confessed before congregation.

ROOT, Timothy (1718-unknown but probably before 1750?) First cousin of Martha Root, son of Hope and Sarah Root., brother of Aaron Root. One of chief instigators in "Bad Boys, Bad Books" incident in spring 1744 in Northampton, who then made confession in Church. Unable to trace after about 1748.

---

[11] Although later appointed a Major General (in the American Revolution), Seth fought at the Battle of Bunker Hills as a private. At the time, he was nearly 70 years old!

[12] Presumably not a calendar fluke due to Gregorian versus Julian calendars.

[13] Per *Record of Publishments in the Town of Northampton from July 3, 1630 to 1830-1841*. Marriage record, page 648 of 2680 (recorded as page 110 in upper left-hand corner). Published online: https://www.ancestry.com/interactive/2495/40143_270308_0069-00054/17633503?backurl=https://www.ancestry.com/family-tree/person/tree/4639504/person/6921429320/facts/citation/24081968441/edit/record Hezekiah Junior birth recorded out-of-chronological order, pg 470/2680 (or 48 in script on upper left): https://www.ancestry.com/interactive/2495/40143_270308_0068-00023?pid=7637245&backurl=https://search.ancestry.com/cgi-bin/sse.dll?indiv%3D1%26dbid%3D2495%26h%3D7637245%26tid%3D4639504%26pid%3D6921431460%26usePUB%3Dtrue%26_phsrc%3DBlb5293%26_phstart%3DsuccessSour ce&treeid=4639504&personid=6921431460&hintid=&usePUB=true&_phsrc=Blb5293&_p hstart=successSource&usePUBJs=true Unclear if non-sequential dates of marriage and first birth are dating errors, calendar confusion, evidence of fornication or inability to perform ceremony due to King William's War?

SEVERANCE, Daniel "Lieutenant" (1701-1748) Lieutenant under Captain Ephraim Williams, Jr at Fort Massachusetts.

SHIRLEY, William "Governor" or "General" (1694-1771) Longest serving Governor of the British Massachusetts-Bay Province; later Governor of the Bahamas. Organized effort to take French fortress at Louisbourg, Cape Breton Island in 1745. Headed campaign to reinforce Fort Oswego in 1755, 1756. Succeeded General Edward Braddock as Supreme British Commander in North America at Braddock's death in July 1755. Bitter opponent of General William Johnson. Shirley's son killed with Braddock at Monongahela River.

STEBBINS, Thomas (1689-1752) Famous suicide in Northampton, mentioned in Jonathan Edwards' *A Faithful Narrative*.

STODDARD, Eunice, Mary, Esther, Christian, Sarah, and Hannah Sisters of Rebekah.

STODDARD, John "Colonel" (1682-1748) Older brother of Rebekah Stoddard Hawley, son of Rev Solomon Stoddard, uncle to the Reverend Jonathan Edwards and Joseph Hawley III. Colonial militia leader, Chief Justice of Hampshire County Courts, Representative to Massachusetts House, active in civic affairs. Diplomat to French Canada and Native Americans. Supporter of Indian Mission at Stockbridge. Wealthiest man in Northampton.

STODDARD, Solomon "Reverend" (1643-1729) Highly esteemed second minister of Northampton [congregational] church and originator of the theological membership loosening called "the Halfway Covenant." Father of John and Rebekah Stoddard, grandfather of Jonathan Edwards, Joseph and Elisha Hawley.

THAYENDANEGEA, Joseph Brant (1743-1807) Young brother-in-law of General William Johnson by his common-law wife, Molly Brant. Renowned Mohawk military and political leader, who participated in much of the French and Indian War, starting at age 12 at the Battle of Lake George on September 8, 1755. Allied with the English/Canadians during the American Revolution.

TIYANOGA (aka Theyanoguin), Hendrick Peters or "King Hendrick" (c. 1691-1755) Mohawk chief/Sachem. Uncle of Caroline, reputed first Native wife of General William Johnson. Killed on "Bloody Morning Scout" (the first part of the Battle of Lake George). Prominent in Mohawk-English-colonial diplomacy. Led Mohawks living at Stockbridge, Massachusetts Indian Mission during tenure of Reverend Jonathan Edwards. Celebrated Mohawk negotiator with Massachusetts authorities and at Albany Congress of 1754.

WASHINGTON, George (1732-1799) Noteworthy colonial military officer, investor, and American general, statesman, first President of the United States and planter (slave owner).

WILLIAMS, Ephraim, Jr. "Colonel" (1715-1755) Colonel of 3rd Massachusetts Regiment during 4th French & Indian War, led the "Bloody Morning Scout" at the Battle of Lake George. Captain in charge at Fort Massachusetts (now North Adams, Massachusetts). Appointed Justice for Hampshire County. Cousin of Israel Williams, son of Ephraim Williams, Sr, brother of Dr. Thomas Williams (physician of 3rd Mass regiment and Fort Massachusetts). Well-liked by soldiers. Left his estate to establish a "free school" in Williamstown, Massachusetts that became Williams College.

WILLIAMS, Ephraim, Sr. "Colonel" (1691-1754) Notoriously avaricious "English" settler among Native Americans at Stockbridge Indian Mission in 1737. His family one of four intended to "reside among the Indians to anglicize and civilize them" and teach them agriculture. Father of Ephraim Junior and Dr. Thomas Williams. Cousin of Israel Williams. Militia leader. Adamant opponent of Jonathan Edwards.

WILLIAMS, Israel "Colonel" (1709-1788) Nephew of John Stoddard and Rebekah Hawley. Cousin of Jonathan Edwards (whose tenure he opposed), Joseph Hawley (with whom Israel had a very wary relationship), and Ephraim Williams, Jr (to whom he was a benefactor, but declined to have marry his daughter). Despised greedy despot, a "River

God"[14] of the Connecticut River valley in mid-1700's; also termed the "Monarch of Hampshire." Commander of the western Massachusetts frontier succeeding Colonel John Stoddard. Justice of Hampshire County Courts. Seized by mobs and confronted several times during the American Revolution when he was an unwavering Tory Loyalist.

WILLIAMS, Thomas Dr. (1718-1775) Younger brother of Ephraim Williams, Jr., son of Ephraim Sr., cousin of Israel Williams, Sr. Army physician and surgeon at Fort Massachusetts and on the Crown Pointe Expedition of 1755 (and later campaigns). His house still stands at Historic Deerfield. His family life was inadvertently documented by the diary of his son-in-law and medical trainee, Dr. Elihu Ashley in the book, *Romance, Remedies and Revolution* by Miller and Riggs.[15]

---

[14] The river god families "came to dominate local business and politics, ran the local militias and chose the ministers." For the New England Historical Society's definition and examples: https://www.newenglandhistoricalsociety.com/river-gods-connecticut-river-valley-create-world/ On Northampton's disproportionate land distribution, "When the new settlers divided up land, they did it according to status and wealth. The wealthiest 10 percent along the Connecticut River got between 30 and 40 percent of the land. The poorest 50 percent got 10 to 20 percent of the land."

[15] Miller, Amelia F. and A.R. Riggs. *Romance, Remedies and Revolution: The Journal of Dr. Elihu Ashley of Deerfield, Massachusetts, 1773-1775.* University of Massachusetts Press (Amherst, 2007).

Map of the Events in the Book

A Timeline of Martha Root Miller's Life

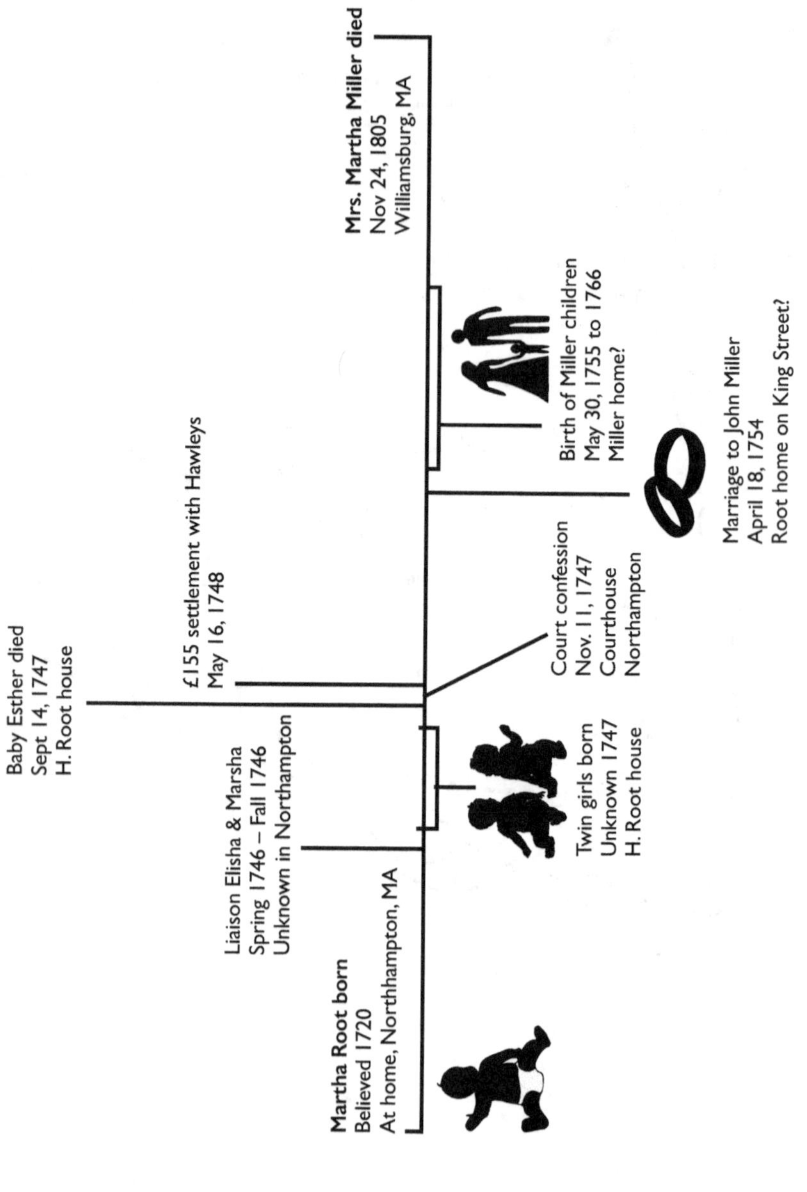

A Timeline of Elisha Hawley's Life

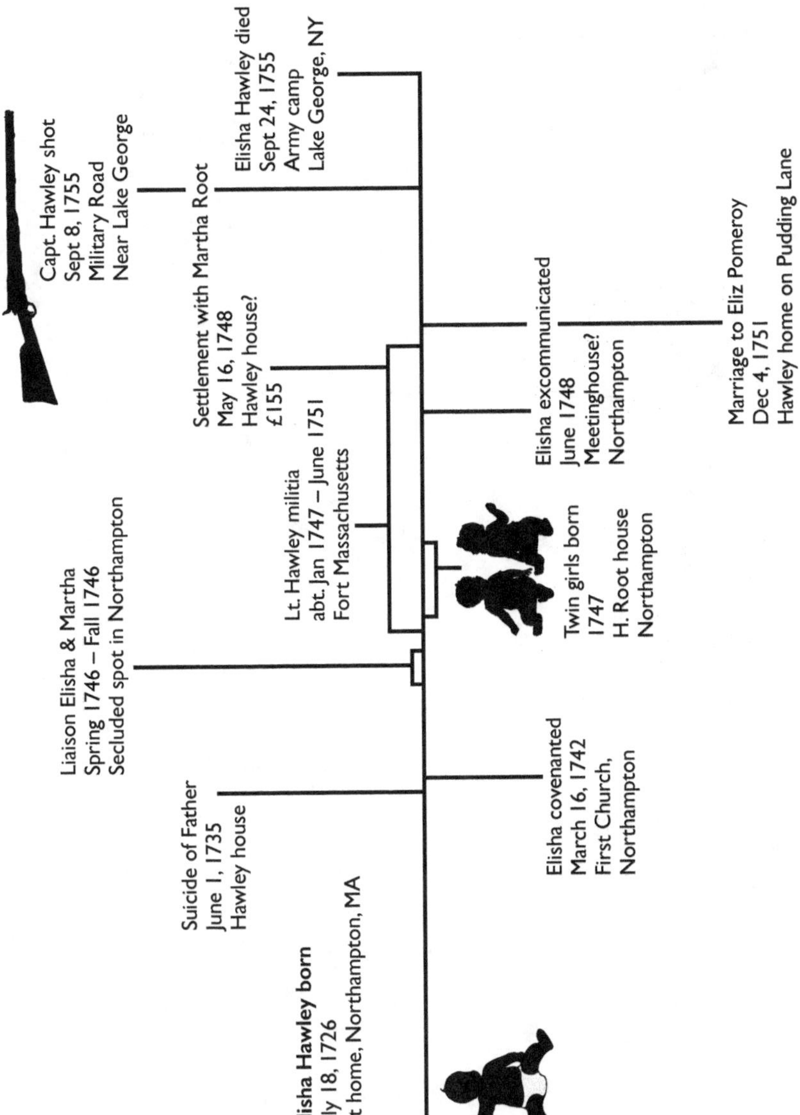

Everyone deemed Rebekah Stoddard to be long past "old" when she finally consented to marry just shy of age 38. Rebekah Stoddard's marriage was a remarkable and providential blessing, at least for a while. But all things mature in time and what they then seem to become is inevitable. The subject of her marriage had been, for years, a severe tension for her frail parents and reproachful siblings. However unnoticed the seamless years had drifted by her, "Spinster Rebekah's" singular status existed within the community as deviance, avoidance of duty or unattended business - perhaps it was even open defiance? No man's hopeful glance had strayed her way across the church pews or rutted cow paths for years.

Rebekah's mother Esther had first married at age 15, birthed 15 babies (ten living children) and was elevated in esteem in Northampton and throughout the province of the Massachusetts-Bay in new-England. In spite of the whispered "curse of insanity" in some branches of their family, virtuous Esther Warham Mather Stoddard was the vaunted wife of two ministers. Like their mother, all Rebekah's sisters too - Eunice, Mary, Esther, Christian, Sarah, and Hannah - had timely and uprightly married prominent ministers and bred legions of educated, prospering progeny up and down the great Connecticut River Valley. Rebekah's nephews (Elnathan Whitman and Elisha Mix) were already enrolling in Yale College. Suitors were calling on Rebekah's desirable nieces, Esther, Ann, Elizabeth and Mary Edwards, and Mary, Sarah, and "little Rebekah" Mix. They might all marry before her! Indeed, time was fleeting and had moved past Rebekah Stoddard.

Years before, eligible men, young and old, had visited "The Manse" house under the guise of consulting her father, the Reverend Solomon Stoddard with the unspoken hope of finding favor in Rebekah's stern walnut-dark eyes. Never one succeeded and never did her father press her to marry against her will. The Reverend took caution from the Isaac and Rebekah Biblical verses - and the taut stretch of daughter Rebekah's sallow lips at the mention of "marriage." Practical and patient in his vision, the Reverend Stoddard recognized that his daughter was too strong-willed and if forced, would extract retribution in her own un-bending way. Granted, as her paternal guardian, he had the legal authority and indeed the moral obligation to select a suitable husband for her.

Rebekah Stoddard had thus tarried years guarding herself against being unsuitably wed. She was far too formidable for anyone in the community to dare a simple curious query within earshot of her family about her marrying. Her multitude of sisters and brothers were years gone to their marital estates and some, even to their graves "as the Lord wills." Yet, Rebekah remained in the noiseless house on Round Hill, minding the needs of her two elderly parents. Twelve years had passed since the last Stoddard wedding in 1710 when younger sister Hannah (then aged 22) had wed. Many townspeople, and Stoddard family members too, said among themselves that "Spinster Stoddard" would never deem any mortal man a worthy enough match for her aristocratic self-esteem.

Time passed as her excuses and objections about suitors petered out. That this one was insufficiently settled. That one was not completely attached to her father's "half-way covenant" theology. That other one was practically a savage himself, that one was well-nigh poverty-stricken, another lived at the edge of the howling wilderness, etc. Rebekah would assess each imperfect suitor, keenly identifying exactly his worst failings. Her assessments were searingly harsh. So sharp that one wondered that her sharp tongue didn't cut her own mouth! Her severity had diminished her community reputation, as she often found herself the object of town gossip and recriminations over her acerbic remarks. Thus, her unmarried state lingered until she was beyond 37 years, with hoary-aged parents and herself growing elderly fast. No more suitors came knocking at the heavy, weathered-gray, oak door.

One brooding autumnal evening as they sat near a fireplace in the hushed house, Rebekah's wise, battle-hardened older brother Colonel John Stoddard set down the most recent documents from Lieutenant-Governor Dummer regarding the local meadow sewer drainage orders and stared into the dancing fireplace flames. He wondered perturbidly how it could be that dealing with younger sister Rebekah could require more careful consideration and caution than commanding drunken soldiers or inveigling with the appointees of His Majesty's Council in Boston?!

John cleared his throat and summoned the resolve to articulate that there would be no more alibis about her unwed state. "Joseph Hawley has agreed to call upon you," John blurted out flatly.

Father dozed beside them in his great-chair with his treasured and smooth-worn Geneva *Bible*[1] drooping looser and looser in his grasp. The mug of

---

[1] The Geneva Bible was the predominant English translation for Protestants, published first in 1560 and predating the King James Version (KJV). The Geneva Bible was carried by the Mayflower Pilgrims when they settled Plimouth Plantation (Plymouth, Massachusetts) in 1620. It was two Puritans who suggested a new translation to King James For these fascinating histories of the Geneva, on Wikipedia:

steaming hard cider with mulled spice sat untouched beside him on the table, as did his white clay pipe stuffed with fine Virginia tobacco. In the back bedroom, mother, in pain from her sciatic nerve, was already asleep on top of the featherbed. Over her were piled thick woven calimanco wool blankets, her prized radiant indigo-blue appliqué quilt, and lastly, the coverlid. Devoted granddaughter Mary Edwards slept with her, should Esther need aid during the night.

Rebekah's ever-flitting hands stopped suddenly, as flapping birds are subdued by the shot of a musket, at the name "Joseph Hawley." Her hands felt cold in her lap, clutching a needle trailing a brown knotted thread. Only minutes before her fingers had darted instinctively through the heavy fabric. Now they felt awkward and unfamiliar, as if her hands posed a danger to prick herself in her distraction. The tracery of blue veins on her hands fairly popped out. The linen breeches she was mending draped limply across her every-day skirt. She sniffed the acrid smell of smoke. Outside, a harsh damp wind warning of winter blew flakes of chill, marking the ponderousness of the moment.

"Rebekah, does thou want to become a thornback old maid?" John asked, driving home his point. "Remember the proverb: 'Women dying maids lead apes in hell!' Do not bring rebuke upon yourself."

After some moments, John breathed again the name of "Joseph Hawley the second," a spindly, peculiar, bachelor Town Clerk of Northampton.

Rebekah shivered at the image of herself surrounded by the ghastly hirsute demons in eternal hell-fires! "All our family have married men of God. Why mother is twice married to a pastor! How can I alone not be?"

Anger laced her voice but tears welled in her eyes. Shame clouded her brain. She heaved her thin shoulders back to squelch her roiling emotions. Her gaze retreated to the far walls of the room and she adopted a cover of pretended disdain and objectivity.

"I am not a pastor. Would you not consider me?" John asked pointedly, underscoring this provocative question with a long pause. "Who to consider then, sister? No ministers in the Valley or Connecticut remain unmarried - except those boys now coming out of Yale College?!"

------

https://en.wikipedia.org/wiki/Geneva_Bible or the King James Version and the banning of the Geneva, see: https://en.wikipedia.org/wiki/King_James_Version

John had the advantage of having debated these arguments with himself, point-by-point multiple times before now and knew he could best her. His arguments were irrefutable.

She herself had heard him disparage the younger Hawley. Thus she sparred back, "You yourself have said that Young Hawley is faint of heart."

"Rebekah, that was during the war! This is different. This is your covenanted marriage! The Hawley family is worthy. They are godly. He is kind, educated. He will build a new house," he paused again for emphasis, "for you."

Of course, she herself must freely consent to marry, but what if she refused? She could be the mistress of a new house on Pudding Lane - or what? "Let us pray on it," John wisely eased out of conversation into reflection. In his mind, the argument had been settled.

This is how it would be, Rebekah immediately realized with unexpected resignation. She gulped down a sigh that emanated from the deepest pool of her personhood so as not to have John hear it. Did she feel suddenly quiet because she had always known marriage was the lot of all women? Or was it the humility of the autumn of her life facing the fearsome coming of winter, old age and destiny?

Of course, elder brother John had been meticulously solicitous and careful, as a well-practiced counselor to the provincial government would be. But to seal his case he intimated carefully that she had almost tarried too long to bear children. She was but one man short of an old age alone with no one to care for her, without the sanctity of marriage, without children, without home of her own. It was clear that one day soon her parents would be gone to their graves in the Bridge Street Cemetery (after all, they were now in their 80's). Brother John too would marry - when his duties to the militia and state business allowed. John would inherit "the old Manse" house and then another mistress would rule here, not Rebekah. Could Rebekah be a second fiddle to a wife of John's? Other children would populate its rooms. Rebekah felt her cheeks flush red-hot as she concluded that John had concocted this for her. How had this day crept upon her so unheralded? How had she not deliberated more upon this? All the old debates and reasoning had been swept aside now. The one man between Rebekah Stoddard and a lonely, grim old age was the socially inept, morose Joseph Hawley Junior. Rebekah gulped hard. She had known Hawley all her life. She had dismissed him, but now she must seriously appraise him.

Joseph Hawley Junior was 40 years old, the oldest unmarried man in Northampton. In point of fact, he was one of the very few known bachelors eligible for her, which was his primary qualification for the proposed marriage. Like herself, Joseph was the last remaining sibling in Northampton with his fragile, eccentric mother. But while Hawley's family line was godly and acceptable (his brothers were ministers). Joseph himself was not impressive. He was not martial, manly, or vigorous whatsoever, unlike her own brother. Hawley Junior had served without distinction as a common soldier under her hardy and valiant brother John during Queen Anne's War. Frankly stated, Hawley was a shirker. He held back until every other man had gone to the fight and it became obvious that he must too. At least, Rebekah reasoned that Joseph Hawley could never muster the fire within himself to mistreat her.

Importantly, the Hawleys did have a respectable pedigree. His father had graduated Harvard College. While the first Joseph Hawley (the father of the proposed suitor) was a merchant, not a minister, he sometimes ministered, periodically assisting in place of Rebekah's own father. The first Joseph Hawley's officer militia commission was purchased and he did nothing with it (except wear it prominently). After he connived for his commission and fought bitterly to keep it, the soldiers of his company nonetheless voted for other officers to replace him. Yet Hawley Senior had held substantial properties, adequate wealth, some of life's comforts, a good regular income. He had traveled up and down the "Great Connecticut River" and to Boston frequently for business. The town had engaged him for their legal business. Then on the 19th of May, 1711, disaster struck when his ox mortally gored him. Several screaming days later, his innards gashed, shredded and oozing, he died.

As the eldest son, Joseph Hawley Junior was destined to be college educated and a place would be made for him within the small Northampton learned group. However, people said he "lacked stamina" and was "prone to illness." Joseph Junior's siblings had already married and moved away. Still, dour Joseph remained a bachelor at home. Thus, he inherited most of his father's property and other assets. His major accomplishment was running the family store adequately without collapse, though admittedly without much profit or renown. At their home-store, one could find him each day with his ever-downcast face reading from the books in stock. It occurred to Rebekah that she had rarely heard his voice. He seemed ever in the background of life observing. Yet he was intelligent and cultured. He had been elected as town Selectman and Clerk. He was dependable and responsible. He was always present at the First Church meetinghouse in the Hawley pew, sometimes weeping, and taking copious notes during her father's sermons. Never did he fall asleep during the three-hour services, as did some deacons! Joseph was devoted to the Lord's word and the salvation of his soul. But he was known in town mainly for his characteristic melancholia and the pervasive gloom that surrounded him like a fog. He surely carried the taint of insanity which ran in their family. Still, he was faithful to his odd old mother, ever solicitously by her side.

Surprisingly, Rebekah Stoddard consented to allow Joseph Hawley to court her for about a month and then publish marriage banns three weeks in a row tacked at the door of the meetinghouse:

> Intention of marriage between Mr. Joseph Hawley and Miss Rebekah Stoddard both of Northampton was entered and published 1 November 1722 in accordance with law. If any of you know cause or just impediment why these two persons - Rebekah Stoddard and Joseph Hawley - should not be joined together in Holy Matrimony, ye are to declare it.

No one countenanced it was a perfect match. Nonetheless, it was the best that could be made for two peculiar souls who were awkward with everything, including themselves. For the wedding sermon the Sabbath before, Rebekah chose the verse from Galatians 2:20.

> "I am crucified with Christ, but I live yet not I anymore, but Christ liveth in me: and in that I now live in the lflesh, I live by the faith in the Son of God, who hath loved me, and given himself for me.."[2]

The morning of November 16, 1722 dawned cheerless across Northampton town. The leaden sky was a cast of grey to white without the faintest glow of insipid sun behind the thick clouds. After completing her morning tasks and preparing herself, Rebekah peered out the window down the hill toward the town where the Great River wound through browned grassy meadows far off. A small gathering of the Stoddard family awaited. Outside, Rebekah noticed two giant crows in front of the house. More seemed to be waiting nearby. A pang seized her heart. She prayed the crows weren't an omen. She hated the graceless birds with their raucous cries, mocking demeanor, beady eyes that peered at humans and searched skittishly for treachery and evil. Beyond the crows, a vast dark cloud of passenger pigeons took wing to sweep as one being across the sky, like a furling, flowing ribbon. Together the flock swept on the wind. Down the path to the town center, Rebekah recognized the skeletal frame of the cheerless Joseph Hawley with this mother climbing the beaten path to the Manse. The

---

[2] Geneva translation according to websites Biblegateway and Biblehub. Several online sources state that the King James Version gradually replaced the Geneva translation.

realization pained her that tomorrow she would be one of those who climbed the hill to the Manse. It would no longer be her home! Henceforth, she would be within the town, not above it. As she steeled herself, her brother John saw the emotion flit across her lean face. He prayed nothing would mar their small festivity.

Once the knot of Stoddard family had arranged themselves around the apprehensive bride and quailing groom in the parlor, her father, resplendent with his thick white mane of hair, led a reading from his brittle antiquarian Bible. Next was a lengthy prayer. The Reverend's starkly white Geneva clerical collar band offset the charcoal color of his button-down cassock.

After somber minutes of introspection with bowed heads and silence, he solemnly asked, "Do you, Rebekah, take this man, Joseph, to be your wedded husband, to have and to hold from this day forward, for better or for worse, for richer or poorer, in sickness and in health, to love and to cherish all the days of your life till death do you part, so help you God?"

Rebekah replied affirmatively.

Joseph stuttered out his, "Yes, I do." Relief spread tight smiles across the families' faces.

They moved to the dining room where each of eight places was set with the Stoddard's finest china, prized two-tined forks and knives, pewter plates, tankards, and blue gingham-check napkins for the wedding meal. Care-worn heads again lowered for another Biblical verse and prayer as Reverend Stoddard thanked Great Providence. Rebekah had chosen her favorite psalm to sing from the *Bay Psalm Book*. All raised a toast of a lightly liquored sack-posset punch.

The African servant woman John Stoddard had recently purchased to cook and aid in the household duties, Bess had placed all the charger-platters of food on the table. There was stewed beef with onions, leeks and parsnip, freshly butchered pork, cornbread and a gloriously formed steamed pumpkin pudding. Bess unobtrusively rounded the table pouring the thick and rich sack-posset celebratory drink, as the Reverend Stoddard launched the group into singing another psalm from the *Psalm Book*.

Rebekah was pleased that her groom had endowed her with six silverware forks and knives from the Hawley store as a wedding gift. Although she wouldn't live in the pre-eminent Stoddard style as one of the town's leading luminaries anymore, she would at least have some comforts. From her brother, she had received two beautiful "cheney ware" (china) bowls from his last trip to Boston.

Her own dowry chest of linens, pillows, and blankets had been transported to the Hawley house on the west side of Pudding Lane, in addition to her spinning wheel with its spindle, flyers and quill, her frying pan, pots, brass kettle and bed warming pan. She was comforted by the familiar carved wooden chest of household necessities, but most of all, she took pride in her looking glass, tortoise-shell combs, box of buttons, lace, ribbons, and silk hood.

After the wedding cakes, hot chocolate and final reading and prayers, Rebekah and Joseph were escorted to his family's homestead as the horizon washed faintly yellow and pink with the descending sun. Following behind, a few former soldiers of brother John's and male friends accompanied the newlywed party as a short "chivaree" celebration from her maiden home to the house where Rebekah would be a house wife. The men were tipped a few copper halfpennies to leave the couple to consummate their marital vows.

The chivaree men sauntered off laughing to the Red Tavern for a robust mug of rum "flip" sweetened with molasses and dried pumpkin. Already inside the jokes were about the noteworthy wedding. "A marriage of two porcupines!" John Stoddard overheard as he opened the door, but the conversation turned into a toast to the newlyweds with the sight of Colonel Stoddard. Across the boisterous pub, John Stoddard nodded at John Bridgman Junior a true common man from the last fighting days with the French and Indians. As usual, Bridgman was displaying his hacked off forefinger stub on his right hand. He recounted his escape from the forced crushing winter trek through mountains of snow from Deerfield on February 29, 1704. The stub of finger resembled the stump of an axed tree, its shape grossly and unnaturally deformed by the hacking. Bridgman's escape and Stoddard's own barefoot race across the snow for help were legends, told a thousand times since in the region. Everyone in Lyman's Red Tavern had heard and even retold the terrible tale at least a dozen, dozen times.

Wordless throughout these exchanges, Colonel Stoddard thought how he enjoyed Bridgman with his simple, rough and rowdy demeanor and ready laugh. Bridgman was regular and uncomplicated, one of the loyal many who could be depended on. While all felt the knot of acidic fear in their stomachs at Indian trepidations and killings, very few had peered so deep, long and hard into the shattering cruelness of extreme fright as John Stoddard and John Bridgman had in that Indian raid. Like Stoddard, Bridgman's soul had stepped back from that brink of screaming, brain-searing terror. Some soldiers broke and became sadists searching to kill and scalp in retaliation for their pain and hatred. Thomas Baker, Bridgman's fellow captive in 1704, had gone on to earn a Captain's commission and £40 bounty by his scalping raids of Wabanaki villages in 1715. Some men grew to enjoy the killing and violence, a deep, unspeakable, incurable sickness.

John Bridgman Jr. and Joseph Hawley Jr. had served together as soldiers under Captain John Stoddard - bawdy Bridgman and popinjay Hawley! John Bridgman had run to volunteer and Joseph Hawley would have volunteered to run! Conversation was almost always easy with Bridgman, but trying and plodding with Hawley. Stoddard recalled the authenticity and bonds of his days among his militia men outside civilized society where each may be forced to depend upon others at any possible second in a dark teeming wilderness.

John Stoddard returned to present thoughts, remembering the groom earlier today. He mused as he downed his mug of flip who to pity more on this cold wedding night, Joseph or Rebekah?

After Stoddard's brief appearance and departure, the jokes at the tavern returned to raucous again. "Bridgman, had you been captivated off to New France instead of escaping, maybe you would have written a book on it, like Reverend Williams's *The Redeemed Captive*," one of his cousins guffawed.

To which another retorted, "It'd a be a miracle upon miracle had John Bridgman ever written anything besides his name!"

"Instead of *The Redeemed Captive, Returned to Zion* the title would have been *The Redeemed Bridge-man, Returned to Northampton!* Wonder if ye governor would have been so anxious to redeem Johnny Bridgman instead of the Reverend Williams?!" chimed in another drinker.

To be sure, Bridgman wondered if a maimed yeoman farmer/carpenter like him would have been ransomed? He'd had little begrudging recognition of his wounding, its effects and his losses by the provincial government in Boston.

"If he hadn't been redeemed, maybe Johnny Bridgman'd be speaking French or Abenaki language today? That'd be an awful thing indeed!"

"Especially since we all know he cain't hardly speak the King's English!"

As the usual toast of the tavern, John Bridgman accepted only so much ribaldry at his expense. The regulars could see he was at that turning point between reluctantly laughing along and becoming ugly tipsy. But perhaps also, the memories of that olden trauma of 1704 flooded back to his mind in November of 1722? Such traumatic memories never left one. Suddenly Bridgman was silent and sullen, burdened by his own ruminating thoughts. Perhaps he remembered facing the penetrating horror of violent death and dismemberment at any moment? Or perhaps he recalled the image of himself being hatcheted, its blinding pain and awful uncontrollable spurting blood across deeply drifted snow? One was always alone with these horrifying images in one's mind. Bridgman wondered if a grandee like Colonel John Stoddard ever woke at night in sweat and tears, as Bridgman still sometimes did?

"Ah well, Johnny, we'd all read your book of *Redeeming* – if you had written it! We'd redeem you from those Papists Frenchies!"

All laughed loudly. The crowd slapped Bridgman's back in the mutual love of camaraderie, to dispel demons and recall him to the safer, warmer hours of the present.

Meanwhile, at the Hawley house on Pudding Lane as the rich golden glow of the bayberry candles was extinguished, Rebekah muffled cries at her groom's bumbling pinches and pokes under the bed sheets. Then Mrs. Joseph Hawley Junior lay awake listening to the sounds in this unknown place which was to be her home forevermore.

"This day is past;
but tell me who can say
That I shall surely live another day."
- prayer from The New England Primer 1727
(after Philip Pain's *Daily Meditations* 1668)

Practically speaking, his death did not change her life except to give some relief. Periodically the immensity of the weight of the care and nurture of their two young boys overburdened her. Still, Rebekah Stoddard Hawley would not allow herself to cry – even in her lonely bed on the blackest night. It was true that she was now labeled a "relict" (widow) of her deceased husband, but in reality she had been alone for a long time. Their marriage had not been a melding of two minds or souls so much as the fulfillment of a contract where two bodies must share too small a common space.

Rebekah Stoddard had known who her husband Joseph Hawley Junior was when she acquiesced to marry him almost 13 years before. His family was educated and comfortable, brilliant - but bizarre. It was widely said that the family was "exceedingly prone to an excess of black bile," which bodily humor produced flammable tempers, violent actions and "the disease of melancholia." Joseph's grandmother was the notorious Elizabeth Tuttle, thrown out of her marriage in a scandalous divorce by her husband of 25 years for her "abuses." Elizabeth's brother-in-law was rumored to have killed himself. Her son had axed his sister to death. One of her daughters had murdered her son with an ax. And three years ago, Joseph Hawley's mother had killed herself. Hawley had inherited a mantle of insanity - a mantle worn in plain view of all.

With the blossoming of religious sentiment in Northampton in late 1734, Joseph Hawley Junior had shed his work-day routine and tasks and focused his every energy on his personal religious studies and devotion. He no longer cared for everyday concerns. He stopped shaving and washing. He cared not at all if a customer came into his shop to buy ribbons or buckles. He might sit staring and muttering for 20 minutes without acknowledging them until they left. If not for Rebekah and the boys assuming his daily farm tasks, the animals would have piled up their excrement until they drowned in it. The animals might never have been pastured if it were left to Joseph. He rarely ate and lost weight from his already skeletal body. His eyes had sunk into deep murky circles. He rarely spoke to people, but more and more had ranted and argued aloud with invisible creatures!

He had even ceased maintaining essential everyday family worship in his household.

What frightened Rebekah most was that her husband stayed awake nights, pacing and arguing with his demons! Everyone grew haggard and was entirely disrupted, reacting with alarm to any noise. Rebekah had removed all the axes in the household to her brother John's house for safe-keeping. She had selected a good sturdy ash wood stick that she kept beside the bed when she slept and in sight at all times as she toiled at her household chores, in case she might need it to defend herself or the boys. The boys mostly tried to escape the household.

While the entire town had flushed "enthusiatical" with religion these days - it was the only topic of conversation in all companies upon all occasions - Joseph's unique demeanor and even more fanatical religiosity often stirred pity and provoked discomfort. His open weeping and note-taking at services was but the unusual start of his eccentricities. An occasional zealous congregant might cry out during the sermon, "How shall we escape the wrath to come?" Joseph obsessed without cease. Soon, he began muttering during their minister, the Reverend Mr. Jonathan Edwards' sermons at the First Church of Northampton. He held his hands over his ears during the singing of hymns. Rebekah could not help but blush crimson across her face and neck with the embarrassment of his unpredictable and peculiar reactions to once routine pieties.

One Sabbath in May 1735 the doors and windows of the meetinghouse were left open for the breeze. Women softly fanned away swarms of insects. Without warning, a pack of dogs, chasing the mangiest among them, ran straight up the main aisle to the pulpit! Fur and blood flew in every direction! The sturdiest, bravest men jumped to the fray, kicking the biting creatures. The tithing man, with his long pole for rapping offenders, managed to clobber one of the deacons, as well as some dogs. Every girl in the congregation screamed at her highest pitch - even the black "servant" girls in the gallery seats who were far from the actual uproar. One of the snarling and snapping animals was actually launched into the air by a kick and flew yelping for a good 10 feet, but it was not before the old town dog-beater was bit and had blood drawn on his leg.

As if this disturbance hadn't been enough commotion for one Sabbath Sunday, Joseph Hawley Junior jumped up and ran following the howling pack of canines out the main door as they careened down the streets and footpaths of Northampton! The most profound mortification was felt by his entire family who promptly left the meetinghouse and headed home without a single word or glance at a solitary person. Mr. Hawley didn't return home for hours. Some said that the Harvard College-educated Joseph Hawley Junior, who was the attorney who drew up the town's petitions and legal papers, had run after the dogs howling himself! Some of the worst gossips in the town opined that he had spent the time arguing with the dogs!

However, it was to get worse! On the sultry morning of the first of June 1735, as his wife Rebekah was turning her cheese wheels in the dairy house and the boys were in the barn feeding the cows, Joseph Hawley Junior extracted himself from a fitful night of almost no slumber. He sat up in his nightgown, took his sharpened straight-edge razor, and did the Devil's bidding. He briskly drew the cold metal edge across his throat, plunging it into the softly yielding flesh of his neck!

When the boys came into the house for their morning porridge and mug of ale, they heard a ghastly unnatural gurgling sound. Older brother Joseph Hawley III peeked around the door of his parents' bed chambers to see his father's protruding, void eyes staring straight ahead. A churn of bubbling blood was spurting out of his neck! Bright red blood saturated all the bed linens! It was pooling darker colored and viscous on the wood planked floor. The musky, loathsome sweet smell nauseated young Joe immediately. It reminded him of the blood-drenched slaughter of a pig or cow with the creature jerking as its life-blood squirted out. Young Joseph vomited out a stream of watery acid and burped. Abruptly, he closed the door and turned to his younger brother shouting, "No Elisha, don't look!"

Young Joe ran out screaming, "Mother! Mother! Mother!"

Still yelling, "Mother! Mother!" Joe burst into the dairy house. "Mother, Father's ...... Father's.... Mother, come! Come!" His voice scraped the hearer's ears.

"Joseph, I'll come when my work is done," Rebekah Hawley replied crisply. Her hands lifted the cheese press as she spun the white bound cheeses around and resituated them on the shelves.

Out of the dairy house ran young Joseph. He ran up toward "Round Hill" heading toward Wolf Pit Swamp to the Reverend Mr. Edwards' and Uncle Stoddard's houses. At the minister's home, his cousin Mr. Edwards' wife Sarah took the pale 12-year-old into her kitchen and sat him down. He cried inconsolably and continued vomiting till he fainted and was put into a bed. The normally sanguine Reverend Mr. Edwards had never before been seen to have run - and wearing such an expression of panic!

Meanwhile younger brother Elisha ran crying across the yard and up the dusty street. On any other day, one would detect the regular rhythm of the pole lathe churning away at a chunk of maple wood for furniture legs from their neighbor, the carpenter John Bridgman's house. As it was a Sabbath, only essential animal chores were being performed there too. "Father's dead! Father's dead! My father's dead!" ran Elisha raising a hue and cry throughout the town. He didn't stop running until he had run screeching through the dusty streets clear to the Great River. Elisha was eventually found sitting with his head in his hands sobbing, past the graveyard, past the schoolhouse, out in the rich alluvial meadow fields past Venturers Fields to Young Rainbow. A townsman carried the speechless boy back home.

At first neighbors up and down Pudding Lane peered out of houses and outbuildings to assess such a commotion on a Sabbath day morn. Soon dozens of men of the town were assembling in the yard and were crowding into the Hawley house with the throng increasing every minute. From every direction more men ran to the catastrophe. Although many of the men had witnessed ghastly massacres in Father Rale's War or the long-ago Queen Anne's War, this scene was more than some could stand. Some men couldn't contain themselves and openly shed tears. Everywhere were the hushed voices of those who were experiencing a flood of emotions. Explanations of what had occurred were being shared, as others added their own recent encounters with the dying Hawley. Of these, some recountings were essentially true. Some were blatantly false. Some were a mix, but most important was to obtain as much information as one could.

"What has come to pass? Someone said there's been a terrible accident?"

"Has Hawley been gored by a steer, like his father? I heard Hawley's dying."

"No, no, he's took his own life."

"What? How?"

"It were clear that he was possessed."

"To commit such an act on the Sabbath is the work of the Devil! Imagine such an act on the Sabbath!"

"Why, I heard him arguing with his-self only a day ago whether to do it! And I says to myself, 'What will he be a-doin'?' But he just kept sayin', 'No, I won't do it.' Then, 'Yes, you must! Do it, I say!' It were the most awful thing I ever saw! And now, there's this!"

"People down this way must be breathing miasmas. You know Tom Stebbins tried to kill hisself too?! He tried to slit his throat, too. He just couldn't do it. He only scarred hisself. Have you seen it? You know he lives just down the lane there. It's bad air in these parts, I tell you."

"Do not draw black conclusions, as we are sometimes apt to do. Remember that God hath told us that he may chasten those whom he loves much."

"It's the devil's work. He's working against the great work of God and religion in harvesting souls, so recently flourishing in our town."

"May God preserve our undeserving souls."

"The Lord will destroy us all!"

"People here are more afraid of smallpox than they are of the devil."

"He was under diabolical delusions and not in his right mind lately."

"His merciless shrew of a wife was no help to him. She is a spiteful old witch."

"That whole family is cursed!"

"May the sun of righteousness shine into our souls. Lord have mercy on us!"

"Things appear most melancholy to me."

On and on went the rising murmuring of the shocked villagers.

With the crowd growing tense, the Reverend Mr. Edwards and Colonel John Stoddard sent the church deacons outside to try to disperse everyone. But as soon as they emerged from the house, the crowd leaned in hoping for some miraculous news. With this great drama being played out, no one would leave and miss this incredible drama. It would be the talk of the town for months to come and everyone would want to be able to contribute what they saw and experienced during the horrible Hawley scene. If they weren't at the event, they would just have to listen to others talk about it. Naturally, no one heeded the request to disperse.

Questions started to come forward from the buzzing crowd. Was he dead yet? What was happening inside the house? Where was the widow – or, eeerrrhhh, aahhh, perhaps not yet widow? Was it true that his wife Rebekah had told him to go to the devil?!? Would there be Sabbath services today? Where was the Reverend Mr. Edwards? Was this the work of the evil forces or something else? What to believe? What to think? What to do?

Then, young men in particular began to quarrel. Some insisted that they must have their regular Sabbath services. There had never been any time – even during the most vicious and precarious periods of the King Philip's War - when the town neglected the worship of the Lord! But others loudly insisted that the devil was abroad in their midst. The Sabbath had been desecrated. How could they go to meetinghouse now?

"It was the will of God that this happen."

"No, no, it was the corruption by vice and we cannot succumb to it!"

"If it had been God's will, Hawley would have had saving grace to withstand the devil's temptations!"

And so on…. and on.

Among the youth, some of whom were crapulously overgone with drink from their Saturday night at the taverns, it seemed they instantly forgot their Christian intentions and scuffles broke out with angry words, shoves and even a few fisticuffs attempted. Two of the most hotheaded brawlers, who had only last night been so ardent in swearing future holy lives, were soon on the ground wrestling, punching and simultaneously still shouting whether it was right to conduct Sabbath services at this time?

Inside the glum house the dying man was propped immobile in his bed. By now he was in a very feeble state and soon to be dead. Many voices were pleading with him to speak. Others were asking what happened, and why, why, why? To the utter dismay of all, Joseph Hawley stared straight ahead, not focusing on anyone - not even his wife - not uttering a single word. Just staring into emptiness.

No adults slept that night in Northampton. At his mansion house John Stoddard lay awake with tears seeping down his face. Trying to dispel the hideous images of that awful calamity, Stoddard thought back to their theological squabbles over God, Satan and the Sabbath. A few hours ago, half the town was arguing whether it was godly for the women to clean up the deceased's bed linens on the Sabbath day? Should Bridgman, the carpenter, build a coffin on a Sabbath when the Bible proscribed work on the day of rest?

John Stoddard remembered past spirited debates among the deacons over whether it could be justified to baptize an infant born on a Sabbath, if it appeared the child might die before the day turned to Monday at sunset? Or the worse monstrous conundrum Stoddard had heard tell of that occurred about 10 years earlier at Yarmouth, when a man fell in and was trapped in a partially collapsed water well, just as the diggers were to cease their work before sundown. Within minutes, it would then be the Sabbath day, which prohibited them from working! Being true Christians, they couldn't violate the holy day! They must hold holy the Sabbath! Why the trapped man himself should be preparing for the Sabbath – even if he was buried in the disintegrating well! But he had been working with them! He was their neighbor, trapped below the ground with little air to breathe! Conversely, God - or the devil? - had chosen this outcome, so therefore…....? There in the lengthening shadows, they contested whether it was lawful according to religious edicts to dig him out on a Sabbath, or whether they must wait until the next day?

John Stoddard sighed deeply in his inviting bedsheets and rolled over again. Even more ominously some of the lurid thinking townspeople said that Joseph had been in the grip of Beelzebub and now was forever damned! His own brother-in-law damned for eternity! The townspeople concluded that Joseph couldn't be buried in the town's cemetery since killing one's self was forbidden. It was a profanity in the hallowed ground!

It was the longest night of Stoddard's life.

Stoddard's dreadful thoughts turned to his sister Rebekah. Yesterday, she had been only "Rebekah Hawley." Tonight she was "The Widow Rebekah" or "Rebekah, Relict of Joseph Hawley the Second." John Stoddard's agitated mind would not stop thinking back over the appalling day - one after another of the myriad perturbing and doleful details. Last was the vision of his sister's pinched and contorted face sending away the kinswomen and neighbor women who had crowded around her to spend the night consoling her. No other woman in the world would have done that. Rebekah was a hard person for others to love. Her brother doubted she had slept one wink through the turbid June night.

John Stoddard decided that, regardless of what his nephew the Reverend Mr. Edwards' opinion was, he could not countenance his brother-in-law Joseph Hawley Junior being buried in the middle of a crossroads (as the people said was mandated for a suicide) and not in the sanctified Burying Grounds. As the town's most prominent citizen John Stoddard, could not countenance any further disgrace!

Almost every denizen of the town - and many from the surrounding communities - packed in and around the meetinghouse two days later to attend the funeral. Almost everyone insisted on being there as a member of the community or in case something else out-of-the-ordinary happened. Most arrived early to try to get the best possible seats or a close outdoor spot.

Once the service commenced, sobbing afflicted every single person there. However, not all were wailing for the deceased. Some were genuinely affected. Some were crying because it was contagious. Some cried in sympathy for the others. Some were crying for themselves or over the fear of death. Many men tried to disguise their crying, hanging their heads low to their chests or with their eyes tightly scrunched. The sobbing would break out and after many minutes die down, only to resurge around the crowd again. Mr. Edwards delivered his usual powerful, emotional sermon, which prompted more sobs and sniffles. The poor Hawley boys stood at prayer throughout the funeral service as long as their exhausted legs could hold them and then slumped down too tired to care about any disrepute or irate glances. Rebekah stood glacially icy.

The funeral cortege stretched back from the pine coffin for a quarter mile, trudging heavily toward the Bridge Street Burying Grounds. Slowly the crowd formed a large circle with the open grave at the center. The etched faces were deeply carved with grief and as still as the gravestones. At this graveside the crowd collectively held their breaths as the first shovels full of dirt hit the top of the coffin. Snivels erupted into sobs again. One after another, the clods of clay and sprinkles of sand thudded and scattered across the wooden box until it piled up to a mound above the ground surface. As the gravedigger and his men tried to push the wooden cross into the fresh pile of dirt to mark the grave (until a gravestone could be chiseled), it toppled over. They struggled, awkwardly attempting to right the cross without drawing attention to a final bad omen.

Within a week, the two Hawley boys were back to sleeping together in the attic. Both still awoke screaming from recurring nightmares of their father's suicide. Rebekah heard them mumble comfort to each other in the silence of the night.

With her stern inherent disposition and a renewed determination, Rebekah prepared her young sons for death, lecturing them daily to be ready at any moment to die. Pray, work, sleep. Die. Life was not for frivolity and vain amusements. "Do not be too much addicted to the world," she admonished. Life was a preparation to meet the one true God from whom frail, undeserving and filthy humans deserved nothing.

"We are children of rebellious Adam and Eve. We are but sinners at the hands of an angry God!" she advised them. At their morning and evening Bible readings, she denounced young people's vanities, especially young men. She warned them to prepare for the day of judgment. "Vain World! False World! Oh, woe! That I had minded this world less, and my own soul more than I have done. That is what all sinners will say at the judgment," Rebekah advised.

But the personalities of Rebekah's two sons diverged completely. So did their reactions to their father's death. Their natures were as different as a sedentary lowland creek spreading wide its shallow waters, trickling almost noiselessly this way and that versus a pulverizing mountain brook, gushing and pushing bed-rock, scouring out its channel. One was a child of contemplation and the other was a child of movement. While Joseph sat at the front of the meetinghouse, younger brother Elisha stayed long in the back with the other rowdy boys, and even some "wildly savage" girls. Many times he was left to his own devices. Consequently, Elisha was Rebekah Hawley's great worry - how and whom to instruct him in some honest calling in life? Each meal together she instructed him, "Keep the Sabbath Day holy. Do not profane it by play or idleness! Pay mind so that God will give you long life and not cut you off in your younger days forever!"

"You should mourn the loss of that time you have spent in useless frivolity, which you should have been sensible to better improve yourself in working out your soul's salvation."

"Mother, I'm not an angel," he quipped once.

"What say you?!?" she almost screeched. "Never ever speak like this again!" Her voice had an edge as sharp as a fresh axe blade.

Rebekah Hawley, head of her now diminished family, observed to herself that a family is a kernel of humanity that can hold every human possibility: from the same parents, one child might become a murderer and another a minister! How unpredictable this life was!

After a long silence she stated with great deliberateness, "Yes, I would rather lose you to death than to sin, to the devil......or to a French Jesuit! It becomes us, as the Elect of God, to staunchly defend the bastion of the true God on earth."

Elisha envied those families where he felt human warmth, even love, in contrast to his own, where worry and guilt ever reigned supreme. Rebekah girdled her sons for battle with the devil. Elisha envied those "red Indians," so free of ceaseless hurry to fulfill their daily tasks. As for him, he found that when one chore was completed, a new one sprouted in its place. The Indians never seemed to worry without end, as the white people did. They didn't constantly invoke the heavens to ask if they were saved? Would the stored crops be enough to tide them through to the spring when they would start to fish or hunt game? Or would this year's harvest be enough? The Indians never immorally cursed the Lord, "God damn it," as the white traders intermixed in every other sentence.

After some years of flailing and inattention to Elisha's prospects, Uncle Stoddard was finally advised, "Young Gentlemen of mathematical bent, who are acquainted with the principles of geometry and who have a taste for drawing, with a few days practice could be a proper assistant for a surveyor." This occupational decision released Elisha to the world of nature, woods and fields – and to less constant observation.

One late summer evening before sundown Elisha walked from the far fields of "Rocky Hill" where he had been helping the chainmen survey with their Jacob's staff and 33-foot Gunter's chain. The crew came upon a "magical" oak tree where the undersides of its leaves harbored hundreds of black and orange butterflies resting. The vibration of their walking by jostled the butterflies out of their roosts to dance noiselessly in the thick and humid air. No one of the men noticed, only the boy who lingered there and fell behind the group. Elisha marveled that he had never noticed it before! He stood in the shade of the burly tree and glowed within himself in wonder at the sight of the dancing butterflies! He decided to lie down underneath gaping in amazement. By the time he arrived home, young Elisha Hawley felt such calm contemplation as to steel him against his mother's harrowed worries.

Meanwhile Elisha's older brother, young Joseph, with his naturally contemplative and somewhat sulky nature, was diligent in his attendance of both the public and his private worship of God. Young Joe kept the Sabbath absolutely, not making his bed or performing any extra tasks. He was industrious in reading the Holy Book and other religious texts with his elder cousin, the Reverend Mr. Edwards. The boy brought to mind the old adage, "A pious child is the delight of God and angels." Mr. Edwards and Joseph's mother adjudged that he was suited to the ministry. He showed no over-attachment to earthly interests, but like Mr. Edwards, was exclusively devoted to God. It was decided young Joe would attend Yale College.

Months passed before the backbiting talk about the death of Joseph Hawley Junior lulled a bit and was replaced by more conventional topics, like the births of babes, planting, the Reverend Edwards and his family, Governor Belcher, the next meeting of the Inferior and General Courts of the County, a new treaty with the Indians, and, always, the weather.

As the mood in the town soured over the suicide of Hawley and the suicide attempt of Thomas Stebbins, the Reverend Mr. Edwards knew he must undertake to explain false religion, unpardonable sin, damnation, good works, converting grace, awakening to true submission to God, heart religion and the roles of "enthusiasm" in one's spiritual awakening. Late into the nights, neighbors and passersby viewed the faint illumination of a sputtering light in the study of the minister's house as he worked away feverishly writing a book on the urgent issue. Jonathan Edwards struggled to communicate to the world the infinite and all-encompassing mercy of God towards penitent, pious and humbled souls. He explained that all their own labors, prayers and tears cannot make atonement for the least sin. And he sought to explain the disconsolate soul who was Joseph Hawley the Second and why he couldn't realize a path to God's mercy. It seemed Joseph had lacked a hoping, waiting disposition. He was like a tree in winter who could not feel the buds of spring on his own branches. He was not of sound mind to have laid violent hands upon himself, clearly, as the coroner had decided. Of course, Jonathan Edwards would never mention Uncle Hawley's name in his book as an abject lesson for the world, but the minister was convinced he must set forth actual particular instances from the work of his ministry to shine a true light for many others to be saved.

Of course, it occurred to Mr. Edwards that everyone in western Massachusetts would infer who it was he was describing. This disturbed the minister but he could figure no other way to get to the essential truths.

One evening as they sat smoking, Jonathan Edwards read a section of his soon-to-be-published book, *A Faithful Narrative of the Surprising Work of God in the Conversion of Many Hundred Souls in Northampton* to his mentor, Uncle Stoddard:

> "In the latter part of May, it began to be very sensible that the
> Spirit of God was gradually withdrawing from us, and after this
> time Satan seemed to be more let loose, and raged in a dreadful
> manner. The first instance wherein it appeared, was a person
> putting an end to his own life by cutting his throat. He was a
> gentleman of more than common understanding, of strict
> morals, religious in his behaviour, and a useful and honourable
> person in the town; but was of a family that are exceedingly
> prone to the disease of melancholy, and his mother was killed
> with it. He had, from the beginning of this extraordinary time,
> been exceedingly concerned about the state of his soul, and there
> were some things in his experience that appeared very hopeful;

but he durst entertain no hope concerning his own good estate. Towards the latter part of his time, he grew much discouraged, and melancholy grew again upon him, till he was wholly overpowered by it, and was in a great measure past a capacity of receiving advice, or being reasoned with to any purpose. The devil took the advantage, and drove him into despairing thoughts. He was kept awake at nights, meditating terror, so that he had scarce any sleep at all for a long time together; and it was observed at last, that he was scarcely well capable of managing his ordinary business, and was judged delirious by the coroner's inquest. The news of this extraordinarily affected the minds of people here, and struck them as it were with astonishment. After this, multitudes in this and other towns seemed to have it strongly suggested to them, and pressed upon them, to do as this person had done. And many who seemed to be under no melancholy, some pious persons, that had no special darkness, or doubts about the goodness of their state, nor were under any special trouble or concern of mind about anything spiritual or temporal, yet had it urged upon them, as if somebody had spoken to them, Cut your throat, now is a good opportunity. Now, now! So that they were obliged to fight with all their might to resist it, and yet no reason suggested to them why they should do it."

Uncle Stoddard puffed his pipe long minutes without responding. He considered all his wife had related to him of the women's gossip in town. Women always knew of and meddled in everyone else's business, hashed it out and then influenced each other to form a general consensus on most affairs. His wife had relayed that Joseph Hawley's burial and gravestone in the burying ground continued to be a topic of controversy amongst them. Many wondered how it could be that he was buried in consecrated ground? How had their own minister not saved him? How had he succumbed to the devil's temptations when he was such a highly educated man? How had he succumbed when Hawley was direct kin to the most illustrious ministers in the Bay Colony?

"Uncle?" the minister questioned lightly, still waiting for a response.

Both men swallowed hard and reflected silently on their own failed attempts to reach the despondent Hawley. Both pondered the ending one's own life - and whether, in any fashion, it could not be one of the gravest of sins? Could it be redeemed if it were the example to save others? How could they deduce that their own Brother/Uncle Hawley was condemned in eternity?!? It tormented and mocked the rational mind.

"You haven't touched upon whether Joseph was saved…" mumbled the elder Stoddard, recognizing the illogic and unorthodoxy of his own point. His voice was cracking as he spoke this short pleading phrase. Both men peered into the blazing fire without another word.

Photograph "View from the Pulpit" of the Sandown Meetinghouse, Sandown, New Hampshire 2007, from the book *A Space for Faith: The Colonial Meetinghouses of New England* by Paul Wainwright. Used with permission.

<u>Chapter 3</u>
<u>Bad Boys, Bad Books, Bad Blood</u>
<u>Northampton, March to June 1744</u>

As early as November 1743, the heavens literally foretold bizarre events. There appeared the most peculiar and frightening vision of the Great Comet of 1744, with six tails fanning out from its radiating head star, and visible for months even in the full sunshine of day! "It's a bad sign," people declared. "Most inauspicious." Further, there had been other ominous, dire occurrences, warning that more misbegotten events would occur. And they did.

Besides the most curious comet there were ongoing earth tremors, which growled a loud rumbling sound across the land! All had happened in the mornings…. What did that mean?!? Would a quake come the next morning? People felt jittery and ill-at-ease at every moment, waiting for troubles and calamities which were sure to come.

Everywhere, everyone expected war throughout the English colonies and New France. Then in March 1744, the King of France declared war against England, which was reciprocated by the King of England. Surely, killings, corruption of body and soul, mayhem and disasters awaited.

Among the young people in Massachusetts, there was "irreverent and disorderly behavior." It seemed all respect and civility were abandoned! In Northampton the many large and small violations clearly showed open rebellion and shocking insolence. There was damage to the school and meetinghouse; fires using the schoolhouse wood at unseemly hours of the night; mud balls hurled at decent people, but the culprits never caught; a leg suddenly stuck out tripping a deacon in the meetinghouse (purportedly accidentally); a hard rap upside the head to a pious gentleman in church (again supposedly accidental); loud mischief by naughty boys and girls during Sabbath services; and numerous other incidents. A spirit of perversion and defiance was ominously growing. "Holy watchfulness" and communal humility were dissolving.

As if it weren't crushing enough that the glorious surge of religious fervor and piety of the "Awakening" had dissipated, next, the Reverend Mr. Edwards was advised of another most disconcerting incidence among the young people of the town. The youth were surreptitiously circulating a base, unclean and lascivious book for lewd titillation!

One March morning in 1744, Captain Moses Lyman stomped over to the house of the Reverend Edwards. For the stern Captain to march over so early in the morning, and in the "mud season" meant he was grievously affected. In fact, the Captain had lain awake all night praying for guidance and worrying about the state of the soul of his nephew Noah Baker. Noah was soon to be married, but perhaps he had anxiety over his upcoming marriage or perhaps he had been led astray by other wayward boys? His Uncle Moses learned that Noah was engaged in squalid, scandalous and outright illicit gazing at Aristotle's book, *The Midwife Rightly Instructed!*

Moses Lyman was informed of the deviance when his brother was told by his wife who had been told by their daughter Sarah Baker. Sarah had discovered the lewd "granny book," *The Midwife Rightly Instructed: or, the Way, which all Women desirous to learn, should take, to acquire the True Knowledge and be Successful in the Presence of, the Art of Midwifery*[3] under Noah's bed betwixt his cot and the lining! Sarah was in such shock at the foul picture of a baby within a woman's body that she dropped the book and refused to touch it! "Malignant filth!" Her mother had cautiously carried the book to her husband as it were the most repugnant offal, who took it to his brother-in-law who transmitted it to the Reverend Mr. Edwards.

Questioning of Noah soon led to many more guilty "boys" who had been similarly engaged in perusing the book and profanely taunting the girls about their "monthly moons!" The list of those boys involved grew with each questioning of culprits! Thus commenced the unraveling of a twisted skein that ultimately entangled a significant proportion of young people of the congregation in Northampton.

At the end of the morning Sabbath services in late March, the Reverend Edwards slowly ascended the steps to the elevated pulpit, where the sounding board above projected his words out to the congregation. Rumors had already flown around the town with the speed of whispers on the winds, so the congregation became completely motionless in anticipation and trepidation. The austere Mr. Edwards announced that he was hereby calling for "an investigation by a committee of church elders of the young men's reading of an unclean book and their contempt of the church and authority." Complete silence reigned as Jonathan Edwards asked noted Elder brethren of the church to remain to consult with him afterwards.

For some extended seconds, the minister fumbled to pull out a worn scrap of writing paper from his pocket. He intoned that the committee would

---

[3] *The Midwife Rightly Instructed: or, the Way, which all Women desirous to learn, should take, to acquire the True Knowledge and be Successful in the Presence of, the Art of Midwifery*, by Thomas Dawkes. J. Oswald Publisher (London, 1736).

require the appearance of these following persons for the investigation. Their names clanged as bell strikes across a hushed, frigid landscape:

Isaac Parsons
Ephraim Wright
Moses Sheldon
Timothy Root
Simeon Root
Eben Bartlett Junior
Eben Bartlett Senior
Medad Lyman
Oliver Warner
Zadok Lyman
Dr. Mather
Dr. Hutchinson
John Miller's wife
Eliphaz Clap's wife
Rebekah Strong
Experience Strong
Lucy Strong
Eben Alvord
Naomi Strong
Elizabeth Pomeroy
Katherine Wright

Among the many similar reactions, the weaver Hezekiah Root's face was ablaze with a crimson glow of worry, shame and dishonor. He felt the hotness of deep embarrassment on his skin. The Roots had long been steadfast full church members (not "half-way" members).[4] However, few in the congregation noticed Hez Root as most all eyes had been lowered, peering at the scuffed wooden floor, as they contemplated the troubles now for someone whose name had been read aloud that they were close to. Mr. Hez Root's eyes registered all those emotions, as well as confusion, smoldering anger and dazed stupefaction. The pronunciation of his son Simeon's name resounded in his ears as if a cannon had been shot off next to him! Even his ears glowered and stung with a scarlet heat.

Except for the children, few felt the urge to eat their lunches during the break before the afternoon services. In truth, most of the adults were stunned into stupor and knew not what to say or do.

---

[4] A great controversy of the time, the "half-way covenant," was a relaxation of church practice by the Reverend Solomon Stoddard, but opposed by more conservative ministers like Increase and Cotton Mather. The covenant allowed church members' family members to join the church without personally professing a converting experience of God.

For weeks contentions over the "bad boys, bad books" stirred the furors within the elder Root brothers' households on King Street in upper Northampton. Brothers Hope and Hezekiah Root had argued for long hours into many nights over the investigation and possible punishment for their respective sons Timothy and Simeon Root. Hope Root resented and was much out-of-sorts, unwilling to accept punishment for his son Tim. Hope had stormed and raged for hours, day after day, almost threatening the Reverend Mr. Edwards and the church committee investigating the whole affair. He called them "a company of blockheads," causing his younger brother, Hez, to immediately try to shush him, grateful that no one else was around to hear such blatant disrespect.

"Damn the Committee! Curse the Committee! Haven't we tolerated them long enough? A pox on them! I wish they would come here now; I would squash them under the treadles of my loom or put them between millstones or under a water wheel! They have no business with this affair! They're such a pompous body of men!"

Hezekiah recognized Hope was venturing perilously close to unacceptable cursing, even in a family conversation, and tried to gently calm his distraught, increasingly feeble and increasingly erratic 70-year-old brother, "Hope, the offense is without precedent. I acknowledge that we, too, were scamps without introspection when young. Yes, yes, they are young.... although they are getting on to adulthood. Although they are unmarried, they are not un-bearded juveniles. Hope, you must admit?"

Hez's voice trailed off as his thoughts flitted over his worries about the unmarried states of the 26-year-old boys.

Hope Root fairly shouted, "But for anyone to say that my Tim was a 'son of the devil'...! Why this obliterates our 70 years religious devotion to the church!"

"Hope, Mr. Edwards said the youth *acted like* children of the devil, *not that they were* sons of devils!" corrected Hezekiah with barely concealed vexation.

Hope replied, "A small distinction, Hez. They are youth without a help-meet to tame their passions. They are but unmarried boys – reckless, frolicking, playing without reflection. Not ravishing scoundrels!"

"Regardless, they have passed the pale of what can be borne by the brethren and the church. It must be conceded," pronounced Hez definitively.

Hope replied bitterly, "Do not all stand equally before the Lord, Hezekiah? Is this not what we are taught since babes on our mother's knee? And are not some herein suffering disproportionate sanction?"

"Yes, I am in agreement, dear brother, that not all are punished equally; some of those guilty are being screened."

The Roots were proudly independent people – some would say independent to brashness. But it sprang unbidden to Hezekiah Root's mind that Simeon had followed Timothy in this as he had in their childhood games. Yes, Tim fed into their crowd of drifting, lazy youth, but neither Tim nor Sim were bully-boys. Those other fellows willingly joined – most particularly Deacon Pomeroy's son. True, they had defied the stale authority of those grandees, the Stoddards, Williams, Hawleys, and others who aspired to constant deference and obsequiousness to their gold watches and powdered wigs! And true that without Tim's lascivious and obscene quagmires - and, worse, audacious defiance during this investigation - Simeon wouldn't be in this awful predicament. Sim was a good boy at heart, thought his father. He can be reasoned with. Timothy, though, was more reckless even to untempered. His own father could not bridle the strapping, rowdy Tim. Everything Tim did was with too much fervor and heat of passion. Once provoked, Tim girded himself with pride, insolence and disobedience. Further, he was imbibing too much flip, rum, beer, grog, cider, punch, sillabub and any other alcohol he could obtain. Hezekiah worried it wouldn't end well.

Actually, Tim and Sim were a mirror of Hope and Hezekiah. Hope forged on his own ways through the human world without a glance around himself - or a care. Hezekiah was as the meaning of his name, strength.

Curtly, Hope retorted, "What about the deacons' sons?"

"Well, their names were called out, as well," replied Hez.

In frustration, Hope scoffed, "Hezekiah, don't play me for a fool! They are being shielded by their fathers! You sees it! The Reverend Mr. Edwards is not calling for the young Eben Pomeroy the Third to atone publicly! Furthermore 'twas he and Captain Lyman's nephew who produced the devilish book in the first place! It was discovered in their homes! 'Twas not our sons, Hez! Thus, who is more guilt-riddled in those acts?"

Hope sat satisfied that his point had been secured but went on, "Truth be told (which I do and will swear to before God and man on the atonement day." Here he shook his open beseeching palms skyward.), it's old "Squire Stoddard" and the deacons whose hands are picking the shamed and those forgiven in this affair!

It's our sons, because they are mere 'commoners,' the sons of weavers or hat-makers, who will bear the brunt! And the sons of deacons will "not remember" their own involvement. Mark my words. Where is Mr. Edwards' truth-telling in that?!"

Hope Root grasped his brother's knee and peered with intensity into his face. "You heard that all the others - every one of them, except Tim and Sim - all claimed they couldn't remember if they had done what indeed they had done! You heard that, didn't you?!? Oh yes, they all "forgot" their transgressions, as the hungry babe forgot its last suckle."

Hope continued, "Yet, of all of them – and there were many, many, Hez… Nay, not many, ALL! All of them! We know that every boy - and many men in this town – and many of the girls, too - have looked at that demonic book! Yet of all of them sinners, it was only my Timothy who spoke truly and boldly, admitting his faults with candor. Alone among all those boys, in all honesty, Timothy admitted that he had full remembrance of his foul expressions."

Hope waited for a silent nod from Hezekiah, then added, "Oh yes, they all claim they could not remember, and thereby they get off without any sanction! Where is our even-handed, brotherly-love justice?! Where is the Reverend's blind judgment – without the taint of favoritism? Where, I ask you, Hezekiah, where?!!"

The distraught Hope Root was speaking almost at a shout. The bowed old man spat a thick yellow clump of spittle into the dust of the yard for emphasis.

Hezekiah responded, "Indubitably true…."

He sighed with his full lungs over the pitiful reality that admitting one's actions guarantees punishment, but willful 'forgetfulness' serves as a guilty escape. He held his long pause for greater effect, "…. but Hope, we are humble - but blessed weavers – truly blessed by the Lord! Many are the blessings the Lord has delivered. We must take what is deserved and what our Lord has ordained."

Hezekiah Root quickly considered on his own and Hope's fates of late. He reflected on how his own fabrics were in such demand in the town for their silky finesse, beauty and combination of colors, while his brother's work had waned. Hez winced at the pain of Hope's deterioration. It seemed that only bad luck and curses visited the house of Hope these days - death, illness, stinginess of food and coins, Indian attacks near son Stephen's farm in Southampton and Timothy's obnoxious rebellion. Was it the Lord's will or Satan's interference? "Dear brother, you must admit, Tim was improvident in so speaking?!? Saying in public that he 'cared not a …a ….'"

Hezekiah Root found himself momentarily unable to mouth the foul words.

"He said he cared not a turd..." Hope spat out. He paused weightily.

"He cared not a fart! That's what he said. Worse yet, he said that those wig-wearing 'dignitaries' are men just like us! He said he wouldn't "worship a wig!" Why they are molded up of God's earth and are nothing more - even for all their gold necklaces, chains, powdered wigs, beaver hats from Boston and fake beauty marks! They are but men, mere mortal men! They are just mere mortal men...."

Hope Root exhaled with a push of stale, dry air, "... just like us."

Again, Hope defended his son, "Yes, Hez, who hasn't so declared? And ain't it truth?"

He waited, then answered himself with finality, "Perhaps even the Reverend Mr. Edwards is!"

Hez gasped audibly and cautioned, "Hope, forbear! Mr. Edwards is a man of God, not a common yeoman! His position as our pastor merits respect!"

Both men let this fruitless conversation die on its vine before Hezekiah continued, "Of course, of course, a hundred times a day perhaps we all think such, but one doesn't say it in the face of the church committee! Especially one doesn't proclaim it before Colonel Stoddard and the Reverend's wife, Mrs. Edwards! Even within hearing of young maidens!"

"The church committee indeed! You mean one doesn't doubt the testimony of Captain Clapp's wife or the deacon's daughter or that black African slave of the deacon."

At last the elder man declared, "Hez, Mr. Edwards cannot punish all the boys of the whole town. And I cannot have Tim excommunicated, thrown out of the church to Satan and the wolves of hell! His future and afterlife destroyed for this youthful 'sporting!' Of which he was but one of many and not even him who produced the book!"

Oppressive anger and profound sadness hunched down the old man's shoulders, "I have a broken and contrite heart. This sin is always before me, but I cannot abide that Tim and Sim will pay, while others not! I cannot, cannot abide it! And will not! There should be consequences for all!"

Hezekiah pleaded, "Hope, Hope, remember the Biblical injunction, as Mr. Edwards has preached, 'lest any root of bitterness spring up trouble you, and thereby many be defiled.' Thinks you that I savor this deepest humiliation of our families, our good name, our standing? Besides you know that there will not be excommunication, rather, a confession to the congregation. Simeon will suffer this fate, too. I will pray that the committee will accept a full confession of their failings before the church. I tolerate it to teach the youth a bitter lesson – one not soon forgotten. And, because a price must be paid for sin even if many others share the sin, but pay not. We cannot sanction them. Our concern must be with our own mortal souls, not with those of our superiors or other persons. God will destine for them what the Almighty wills."

Silence settled between them with only the soft wind of coming summer lilting the air.

"Hezekiah," now it was Hope heaving the deep sigh. "… one teaches a different lesson if one punishes not the powerful amongst the offenders. Then one teaches that power protects – among mammon."

"Hope, as you allude, you and I have truly and rightly placed our faith before our dear Lord Jesus Christ. Thus, we must suffer the indignities and patiently await and earnestly pray for the true accounting on the Final Day."

"Hezekiah, amidst Abenaki Indians who may fall upon our settlers at the frontiers at any time, the French King declaring war against England with murder upon murder," Hope stuttered. "Why, why, why, men and dogs are now being recruited for war! Even that apocalyptic "great comet" with that burning tail in the skies. All of this turmoil in the world and Mr. Edwards tortures the whole town on this matter?! Timothy will take his punishment. But I will have my say with Mr. Edwards…."

"Tim and Sim must repent and confess before the brethren."

Thus another inconclusive evening ended, again, with the air absorbing their passions and the curling tobacco smoke from their elongated white-clay imported Tippett pipes. Their solid glazed red-ware mugs of ale had been drained of every drop but the last wisps of foam at the bottom.

On a brilliant Sabbath day in mid-May, as the Reverend Mr. Jonathan Edwards ascended to the pulpit and was ready to commence his sermon, Hope Root stood up amidst the entire seated listening congregation – without cause or explanation! The old man had plotted his rancorous display with attention for the most hushed moment just as Mr. Edwards was opening his mouth. Hope turned his back full on toward the about-to-orate pastor and just stood noiselessly. Protracted awkward seconds ticked on amid the silence, until finally, after agonizingly stretched minutes, the reverend commenced his sermon.

Hope Root – the one lone standing figure in the middle of hundreds of seated others - let the weight of his disaffection be registered so that none mistook it for anything but strident dissent. After a long enough time for his opposition to register, Hope Root walked out of the public worship service through the main door of the meetinghouse!

"What impudence!" thought many.

Some days later Hope Root informed Mr. Edwards that he opposed the singing of the new psalms of Dr. Isaac Watts in the congregation's services. He, Hope Root, believed in singing exclusively and unadornedly the traditional old hymns, "the usual way of our fathers," "the decent, regular common way of singing," as Hope Root characterized it. He was adamant and unblinking in his rejection, although he said nothing more to the minister and did return to the next Wednesday's service with no further demonstrations.

Amongst the voices of the congregation following the lead of the deacon in the singing, the vibrant tenor of Hezekiah's son Joseph Root, floated as a heavenly pitch. It naturally singled itself out for the ephemeral beauty of its rich clarity. Joseph made no attempt to be heard above anyone else. In fact, he was conscious that he should *not* try to do so. It was his voice which distinguished itself by its clear peal and pitch, as if he were an oriole, warbling away on a branch above a thicket. Anywhere within the church building - front boxes, minister's family pew facing the congregation, main floor, back seating for the wayward youth, and second-story gallery for the poor and slaves - Joseph's voice could be discerned and treasured as uniquely lush, as chestnuts or hazelnuts taste more subtle than clunky, acerbic walnuts or pignut hickories. Singing exhilarated Joseph for the physicality of the lungs pumping as bellows and its sheer beauty in honoring God. Hezekiah Root closed his eyes to reduce his sensory perceptions to only the pure ecstasy of Joseph's silky voice.

The weeks wore on in this fashion until June arrived. The "noise" of old wives' gossip that had filled all the country since the Bad Boys, Bad Books investigation and Hope's stand abated somewhat until the Sunday, June 3rd service which would culminate in the boys' punishments. Most people supposed that there would be public confessions but which culprits would confess and would they demonstrate real remorse?

Joseph, the forbearing younger brother of the now-notorious Simeon, washed his hands off in the leather well-bucket. Young Joe Root took his best fresh linsey-woolsey shirt and "Sunday suit" off the peg behind the door ready to go to meetinghouse for the two Sunday services. He felt within the rabbit-skin pouch tied at his waist to assure that he had packed his fennel seeds to chew and costmary herb leaves which he could put in his Bible as a page marker on the sermon. The numerous Hezekiah Root family walked the mile to Meetinghouse together, including disgraced brother Simeon behind them in contemplation.

As usual, the Reverend Mr. Edwards had carefully prepared his sermon, which he would expound on from the pile of paper scraps with notes in his black robe pocket. He had considered many hours on the exact tenor he must show with his sermon, behavior and voice tone. It must set the right tone. However, Mr. Edwards had only just started the sermon when a low rumble rolled over the landscape! It was another of the earthquakes! Screams of panic erupted throughout the assembly and everyone jumped to their feet to flee out the doors. Amidst this turmoil the church bell rang with the jerky pitching of the earth, although few people noticed it in their haste and terror.

Remembering the 1737 lightning strike on the church steeple that collapsed the gallery of the old meetinghouse, Jonathan Edwards shouted to his frantic parishioners, "Fear not, the Lord of all will preserve! Fear not dying in the House of the Lord! Be not affrighted!"

His words stopped no one from their instinctive frantic flight.

Once outside, the minister attempted to calm those who had fled out the doors shrieking. His wife Sarah moved among the children and the elderly calming and comforting them. The Reverend gathered a crowd around himself in prayer, "Will you turn now onto the Lord?!" he questioned poignantly.

It was obvious that their mighty (but angry) God had preserved them. Someone was heard to remark, "Great is the day the Lord has made!'

Another said, "I am ready to die for my Savoir."

The worship was restarted in the open and the Reverend returned to this sermon. This time the prayers were more fervent than ever before.

"Make thy people sensible of our sins of murmuring, disobedience to superiors. Make us truly penitent."

"Defend us, oh Lord, on every side."

"Revive dying religion everywhere."

"Keep us from ye paths of ye destroyer. Lead all of us in the paths of righteousness."

"Give me power against all vices and corruptions."

When the service finished, it had been designed that public confession of the scandalous sins would be made. Therefore, Timothy and Simeon Root and Oliver Warner approached the gaunt Reverend Mr. Edwards. All stood with bowed heads and abject eyes downcast. Each in turn stumblingly read a confession which begged forgiveness by the brethren and the community.

Simeon appeared to be near physically ill but, in fact, most of the congregation appeared haggard and exhausted after such a trying day. The noon bell had just rung not so long ago. Many wondered if the almighty Lord God would crumble the earth beneath their feet? The tremors had shaken many things besides the ground.

Privately, Timothy Root vowed to swill down a mug of flip at the very soonest opportunity.

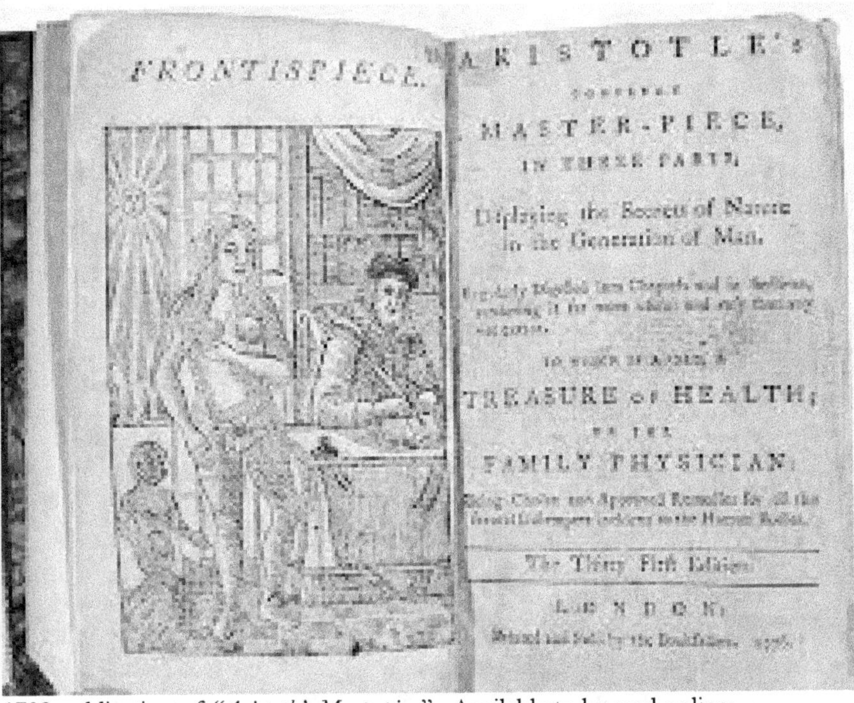

1739 publication of *"Aristotle's Masterpiece"*. Available to be read online:
http://www.exclassics.com/arist/ariscont.htm

War changed the sounds of the world around them. War sounds were the rapid, discordant and loud staccatos of dread, ache and terror.

News came in of distant attacks on isolated farms and settlements, French and Abenaki raids from the north and bloody scalpings by raiding "savages." By order of the Massachusetts Province, all men were required to go about their business armed at all times - even to sacred public worship. Due to its remoteness, Northampton had ordered the building of watchtowers throughout the town.

Regardless of war, young love must have its time. Perhaps it is more cherished when it grows amidst the thorns of violence, fear and hatred, as fruits are sweeter after bitter tastes. Love blossoms even in time of war and perhaps fright heightens the lesser senses of smell, touch and taste?

Thus spring 1746 awakened the promise that life was good and every effort worthwhile for the young, even in times of calamitous ruin and war. Martha Root's heart gladdened and soared when the awakened spring's cheery yellows of forsythia and daffodils illuminated the dull greys, whites and browns of the harsh past winter's landscapes. Her heart had the buoyancy of a gentle breeze. Her eyes were bright with the gleam of someone alive to every possibility.

One day she was surprised to notice a far-off woodlot at the edge of farmed fields where a flowering understory dogwood tree glowed a beguiling pink among the bare branches of the forest behind. Martha Root had walked out there searching for the last of fall's sumac berries and scouring rushes for dyes for her father's weaving, but she failed to notice the fresh radiance of the spring when she moved within it. Later, when the redolent, soul-satisfying smell of late spring lilacs arrived in full force, it made her glow with happiness in every fiber of her being to pull the air into her lungs, holding and savoring every fragrant breath. Her heart and spirits couldn't be squelched, even with war, threat and danger. She noticed the sun glinting on the dewy grasses mornings and felt refreshed and satisfied.

For Elisha Hawley, the late spring brought a relaxing of his mother's clinging fear now that her older son Joe was safely returned home from the intrepid New England campaign to besiege the French-Canadian fortress of Louisbourg on Cape Breton Island in far-away Canada.

Martha Root and Elisha Hawley had been aware of one another for as long as they were aware of people as distinct individuals outside the encircling womb of family. But how or why or when did they really notice each other? Some things are quite impossible to define exactly. They simply exist without being visible or without direct observation of them, as love is perceived but not tangibly visible in the atmosphere. As children, both Martha and Elisha had been schooled by Dr. Mather, the town's doctor and schoolmaster, although as a girl and boy, they mixed little in school and normally only passed by one another. Although the "scholars" gathered and walked together, Martha being some years older paid no mind to younger boys not of her family, who were merely impish annoyances. Yet she knew who Elisha Hawley was, a scion of the Hawley/Stoddard family, but not to be confused with his intensely somber brother Joseph. All in Northampton knew the Hawleys, for their social standing, education and wealth, as well as being descendants of the Reverend Solomon Stoddard. Additionally, everyone remembered the unforgettable suicide of their father and their family's other eccentricities.

Both Martha and Elisha had become full covenanted members of the community of "visible saints" of the First Church Northampton. Both had been ecstatic, impressionable young devotees during the momentous preaching of Reverend George Whitefield, Reverend Jonathan Edwards and the "Great Awakening" that arose (and when fervent hymn singing was introduced into the Church). They had renewed vows of commitment to God and the church before the assembled only a few years earlier. As Reverend Edwards preached from Psalm 144: 12: "That our sons may be as plants grown up in their youth; that our daughters may be as corner stones, polished after the similitude of a palace."

Then came the unfortunate incident of the "Bad Boys, Bad Books" which caught so many in the town in bitter rebukes, punishment and humiliating confessions before the Committee and congregation. Dissention and reproach gnawed at the edges of public and private life. The elders and Church had noted the rising ebullience and disregard over the last years. Reverend Edwards warned, "'Tis a peculiarly lovely & pleasant sight to behold young People walking in the ways of virtue & piety… I dare appeal to those young People that have in a great measure neglected Religion & given the Reins to their inclination & spent a great Deal of their time over wine mirth & those Diversions that are inconsistent with a serious Religion…"

This dissent and disunion dissolved the youths' former spiritual fervor. But in reality, religious "enthusiasm" is an unstable state that cannot last long and must backslide to degenerate, depraved human nature. Thus, daily life slunk back to worldliness, blasphemy, indulgence, gluttony, greed, pride, self-love and all other evil-doings, which constitute the natural condition of humanity. The rule of routine was restored.

The Hezekiah Roots bought cheeses from Rebekah Hawley, whose dairy products were known throughout the valley, and in exchange sold her cheese-cloths and other woven items. Further it fostered favor and goodwill to support a widow, even if a prestigious, haughty and sour one.

One day on an errand to drop off cheese-cloths and pick up a wheel of ripe white cheese (daintily peppered with horseradish, chives, onions and other aromatic herbs), Martha bumped into Elisha Hawley coming around the side of their chicken coop and into the dairy house yard.

Martha barely stifled a startled cry, "Oh, oh! Pardon, pardon. Begging your pardon, Master Hawley, I didn't expect to find but Madame Hawley here."

The slender, comely Martha Root rearranged the stack of cheese-cloths which had become jostled in her arms.

"As I, too, didn't expect you, Mistress Root. Usually your brother Orlando brings them."

Recovering from their mental and physical imbalances, both Martha and Elisha stepped back to pardon themselves and boldly regarded each the other. The air between them emitted a calm pleasantness that tremoloed with gentle excitement and almost existed as an object itself to savor. The surprise and pleasure of the encounter lingered on the senses as a lump of sugar cone slowly dissolves on the tongue and melts happiness throughout the mouth. It startled her to realize that Elisha Hawley's height had surpassed hers and that his face was appealing and no longer an unshaven boy's. A remark of her father's many years ago sprang to mind, "That Joe is a true minister, just like his cousin the Reverend Mr. Edwards with his nose always in a book, but that Elisha is a real man's boy."

Martha regarded Elisha Hawley as if she had never seen him before. He had grown muscular and well-formed from his trading travels on the Great River. His tawny brown hair, heavy and thick as a sturdy rope, was tied back with a black ribbon below his everyday linen cap. The fresh smell of the forest was on him as if he had brushed against pine trees. Was that twinkle in his eyes deliberate or just sunlight playing in her eyes? Martha understood from Elisha's soft smile and mirthful glances that the stunned delight was mutual. "Step inside the cheese-house, Mistress Root, so I can mark on the wall that you have dropped off the cloths and picked up a round?" he invited suggestively.

That luscious moment hung – pendantly, ripely, luxuriantly - in the air. His eyes were a rich, velvety brown, plush as a marsh cattail. Time and breath slowed down and seemed suspended.

The magical moment was broken when his mother shouted out, "Elisha!" from her butter churn in the kitchen. Their bewitched reverie fluttered off in an instant.

"Nay, nay, Mr. Hawley, I must be on my way," Martha Root demurred teasingly. "But do be certain to mark today. We wouldn't want to be forgetting it, would we?"

"Mistress, without a doubt, you can be certain, I will not forget," was the coy reply.

While she had never noticed it before, throughout the early spring of that war year 1746 Elisha Hawley appeared to be everywhere Martha Root was going. As she walked home from her cousin Esther Root Strong's house, he winked one eye and touched the brim of his beaver-felted tricorn hat on the path in passing. As she walked into meetinghouse accompanying her father, mother, brothers Joe and Simeon, sisters Jemima and Hannah and all the younger children, Hawley dawdled along the entrance pathway in no rush to take his pew at the front. He greeted them, "Good Sabbath day, Mr. and Mistress Root. Good Sabbath, Mistress Root." Her mother thought his eyes appeared to flicker with playfulness and tapped her elbow into Martha's side whispering, "Young Mr. Hawley in a right jovial mood this day. Don't you think, Martha?!"

Next door down Pudding Lane from Martha's Uncle Bridgman's clapboard house, Elisha Hawley stood outside discussing his fur-trades with some other young men and laughing boisterously. Was she dreaming it or did his eyes seem to follow her down the lane? Another time, at the corners of Bridge Street and Schoolhouse Lane, he was chatting with friends and reached out to hand her a fingerful bouquet of lily of the valleys with a bold "Good day, Mistress Root." She tucked them into the neckline of her dress with affected care. "Why thanks indeed, Mr. Hawley."

The crowd of friends around him laughed and joked, "Oh look at Hawley: quite the *gentille homme*, he! His manners good enough for the Court of the French king and his ladies!"

"Raleigh draping down his waistcoat over the muddy puddle for Good Queen Bess was never more gallant than this Gentleman Hawley!"

"Fellows, since when does a gentleman smell of animal furs or a tannery!? Me thinks this one does reek too much!"

They all gave great belly-laughs and slaps on his back. Martha Root fairly felt her feet dance on the path with all the male eyes delighting upon her. She knew her own supple form to be "winsome," as her aunties had told her so. Her own eyes were bright with flirtatious gamboles and her heart felt carefree and entranced by the soft spring season.

Had he always been there in the background of her life as the moon always traverses the sky whether or not she consciously remarked on its light? Bird song always filled the mornings, even when she didn't bother to distinguish the chickadee's insistent "dee-dee-dee'" from the raucousness cry of a blue jay. Had Elisha Hawley always been where she was or was it pure happy serendipity that she was seeing for the first time?

One Sabbath Martha felt a heat settle on her as she sat amongst her kinswomen at meetinghouse. Her mind had been emptied without pondering any specific thoughts. Then without understanding why, she was conscious of feeling afire and sensed her cheeks becoming beet red and glowing as the sun on a summer horizon. A wave of unsettledness swept over her. What was it? Why this reaction? Nothing seemed to have happened. Martha gazed around discretely. She felt guilty for not minding the sermon in the background, where the voice of the Reverend Mr. Edwards continued his exhortations to the assemblage, "Christ is the great medium and head of union with God in whom all elect creatures are united… in the divine Transactions and dispensations relating to men's salvation, Christ, and Believers are considered as one mystical person…"

But for Martha, something wafted on the air that seemingly touched only her; she felt as one mystical person in harmony with another world. She wondered that life seemed to be normal for everyone else, oblivious to the deep vibration that reached her? From whence this force emanating? Was it a spirit affecting only her? It felt as a cool wind soothing a hot face. She sensed a silent beckoning across the cold space of the stark, cavernous two-story wooden meetinghouse and raised her bowed head to lock eyes directly, shockingly and unexpectedly with Elisha Hawley. There was no questioning what it was. It was an unseen power pulling between them. Hawley gazed calmly at her with no care to disguise his unhurried contemplation as if it mattered not that his gaze was so frank and uncovered! His eyes invited her. Martha marveled that no one else seemed to notice their looks which seemed charged with the energy of lightning, as if eyes locking could explode the air around them all!

But others had observed the gaze. Hovering mothers miss little as concerns their broods. "Big Martha" Bridgman Root, Martha's mother, clucked quietly to herself in satisfaction as she adjusted the lace-fringed mob cap that

secured her twisted-up cord of brown hair (now with its touches of grey). She
mentally inventoried the statuses of her offspring. Hez Junior married and settled
on his own place in Cold Spring. Dolly and husband Charlie Phelps up and
coming at Hadley. And three living grandchildren, Elisha Root, Solomon and
Charles Phelps Junior. Boundless thanks to the Great Provider for these smiles of
Providence upon her family. Halleluiah! God had showered his blessings on them.
Although she was a miserable unworthy daughter of Eve, born of sin and
depravity, Martha Bridgman Root was eminently grateful and happy, while trying
not to surrender to the sin of "self-pride."

In the front pew Mother Rebekah Hawley gritted her teeth and vowed to
take heed. Elisha gazing at girls and philandering was not part of her plan for her
sons, which plans definitely did *not* involve such vanities or frolics! At long last her
dream of a minister in her own little family had been achieved with Joe Junior's
appointment as chaplain to the Louisbourg Expedition. No longer would she feel
an inferior failure amongst the Stoddard/Williams clan of clergy. But Elisha off
playing with lesser sorts of people was not to be tolerated! This flirtatiousness of
Elisha's would have to be watched and, if necessary, curtailed. Soon.

Yet a force had budded and swelled between Martha Root and Elisha
Hawley in the spring and into the summer of the war year 1746. The blossoms and
fruit were set and would ripen in due time. Within the Hawley household clouds of
malaise darkened the cheery skies.

"Elisha, Uncle Stoddard's wife Prudence informs me she's seen you
conversing with ye Root girl at the schoolhouse corner by the bridge this fortnight
past," grimaced Mother Rebekah Hawley in a poorly feigned aside.

The lean, straight-backed woman smoothed down her walnut brown linen
skirt and white apron with calculated disregard, although there had never been
casualness in the bones of Rebekah Stoddard Hawley for even a minute. Her mind
spent every waking second – and many semi-sleep minutes - lying awake fretting
for hours in the deepest night. Many minutes of her days she spent thinking,
thinking, thinking. Her thoughts raced fulminating, shrewdly calculating, gauging
movements and motivations around her. She tried to connect her eyes with
Elisha's as she placed the steaming, smooth wooden trencher bowl of porridge and
a pewter mug of ale before her second son.

"Keep a close eye on that milk," Rebekah admonished the hired girl at the
bubbling kettle in the fireplace nearby. The scalding milk was close to curdling.
Soon they would soon be straining off the whey for Rebekah's cheeses. Not only

were the cheeses her source of income, but additionally, they were a point of justifiable pride and accomplishment for her.

Elisha restrained himself strictly, remembering that he must contain himself. He must display dispassionate manliness in the face of Rebekah cunning and domineering. He must ever remember how to comport. He shook his mother off with his usual defensive fleetingness to her clawing concerns.

"So, said Aunt Prudence? Which Root girl would that be that she referred to? You know there's so many Roots and many of them girls. When did she remark upon that, Mother? Of course, you know the family be good customers. Seems I just got an order from one of ye Root girls for buttons and ribbons. Let me remember…"

Elisha's exaggerated pause and deliberately obvious forgetting showed he, too, could scheme and connive. "Oh, yes, it was old Goodwife Mrs. Hannah Root who sits amongst the first rows at Meetinghouse. Me thinks she ordered buttons. And needles, too…." he trailed off dismissively, using the archaic grammar and terms to distance himself from the present.

His mind flashed with the thought of comely Martha. Her figure was lean and lithe. Her skin as pale, smooth, and creamy as a fresh pan of cream or as the peeling bark of a sycamore tree, luminous in the scarcest light. He remembered seeing her, off and away, under a flowering tree at a woodlot's edge. His thoughts raced on to the petals of a pink rose as it snuggled comfortably in the tie of a white cotton shirt's neckline, the sinuous curves of breasts below... He remembered the surreptitious pleasure and racing excitement of stealing away from the village in an opposite direction, to double back on his tracks. He saw himself pulling Martha Root down in a quiet glade and how easily he lifted her skirts to the white shift under-garment beneath. His hands quivered as he tried to unbutton the front flap of his breeches. He had been introduced to the heaven of bodily satisfaction and it had captured him! Martha, of the ice blue eyes, held him in thrall.

He felt himself radiating heat and desire but quickly quashed the thought and regained control, so as not to betray himself with his mother. He pulled his casualness defense around him like a suffocating wet woolen blanket.

"Elisha, we've talked on this before. You must be vigilant about the family name and honor! We are Stoddards and Hawleys. They are a low-born inferior sort. They are nothings and will always be nothings. Our family line is righteous and educated for many generations, a family of distinction. My father, your grandfather Stoddard, the eminent…."

Elisha and brother Joe had heard this oration many times before and he instantly tuned out of conscious hearing of it again. Elisha hesitated and added tentatively, "The family Root was among the eight "Pillars of the Church" back to the founding days of Northampton."

"That was in 1654. Bah, meaning nothing now!" she sniffled. "That was the mere fate of their earlier arrival. Conversely, our family has education, erudition and an accumulation of history, connections and wealth."

"Mother, we are richer but by a single cow more…" scoffed Elisha.

"Elisha, we are the accumulation of generations of values, experiences, education and advances. These are the treasures a family line works over generations to hoard and amass."

As Elisha resumed his facade of bored, worldly man, Rebekah retreated back into the hard Madame Hawley that the village knew. She felt sodden with worry and frustration for the inability to make him comprehend. She added darkly, "Ye women, such as these, will lure good men down the path to flirtation, frivolousness, frolics, fornication and marriage by force of necessity! They have unrestrained appetites! How many have had to confess such rashness before the congregation and court! We are not as such. We trust in the Lord to strengthen us to resist temptation. They are not for you! I know these people, you do not. I have seen so many disreputable cases. Nothing but problems and rebellion. Remember those boys and the Bad Books? Appalling! Shameful youthful carnality! And Deacon Pomeroy himself mortified by Eben partaking of that naughtiness, due to those rowdy tempters!"

Warming to the topic, she continued to feel a bubbling outrage, "I remember that Root man standing up with his back to the pulpit over the hymns! Unimaginable, such shocking insolence! Who is he?! A weaver! Nothing but a mere common weaver! And not even the best weaver at that! Granted that I, too, am not in agreement with the singing of those new-fangled hymns. The psalms were song enough for our fore-fathers. Such levity and disrespect would never have been tolerated before! Never!"

The color was rising in her cheeks as she reinvigorated her tirade. "And the bonnets those women wear hardly covers their hair at all! Locks of hair falling out of their caps in meetinghouse! It is verily, too convenient to be happenstance. I suspect the deliberate allure of the loose and lowest class of women! With their airs, finery and colored ribbons! Where has proper decorum and place gone to?! I

declare that Biddy Root must have four church gowns! Such wastefulness!
Flaunting and triviality! Such women will lead to nothing, nothing, nothing but …"

"Well, Mother, the family are weavers and gownmakers. So of course,
they've excessive much clothing. They make it, of course," trailed off Elisha
lamely.

During their exchange, brother Joe had sat pensively avoiding eye contact
with either Elisha or Mother. His fingers mindlessly stroked the red-checked
cotton napkin as he stared into the blackened cobblestone fireplace across from
him. Around it, the cooking implements were tainted with its carbonized burn. A
few of the cinders spilled out onto the red-brick hearth. His eyes wandered over
the slotted spoons, toasting iron, roasting spit, hanging crane, skillets,
"salamander," pans, cast-iron pots, kettles, andirons, bellows, trivets and more.
The chimney flue drew up the sooty gray smoke. Without his summoning it, the
image of a coal-tar bucket sprang to mind. That ooze seemed to enjoy sucking
other life and light into it, engulfing it and extinguishing it, as did the fireplace. A
quicksand of evil, as years ago his father's inability to escape his demons leaped to
Joseph Hawley's mind.

"Eternal blackness and damnation! One thousand years in hell! Black
devils!" he recalled his father shouting.

Father had often ranted and paced the house in those turbulent days and
tortured nights. His wild eyes were unseeing of this world, but clarions direct to
the fires of hell. Young Joseph had softly sobbed alone at night in bed listening to
father try to shout away his demons. Where was Mother?! Little Elisha slept
soundly beside him. In the end, the devils told Father to slit his own throat. The
devils and the darkness had prevailed.

Joe still sometimes woke at night in terror, sweating and aching. Joseph
Hawley the Third shivered as a drop of sweat trickled down the indentation of his
backbone. He struggled mightily to banish the remembrances and force himself
back to the present. But again unbidden, he pictured the Pomeroy's blacksmithing
shop with charcoal dust descended on everything that wasn't fire itself. This was
Joseph's image of eternal damnation – darkness no light could penetrate and
blazing orange-to-red flames at the center, the hell that awaited those who were not
saved by the true religion.

Across the table, Joe furtively scowled at Elisha who (it seemed to Joe),
glowed with far too much self-satisfaction. Joe felt pangs of surety of Elisha's guilt

from the empty pit in his stomach. He worried about Elisha's casualness and the disregard of the state of his eternal soul.

From a glance shot aside at Mother, he noticed the age lines etching her face in apprehension. In them he saw the depths of her worries. If only Elisha was as concerned, and cautious as Joe himself was. But Joe realized that their mother's many apprehensions must disturb her such that she would stew over her suspicions for days or weeks. Sadly, if one anxiety were relieved, a new disquiet would appear and propagate in her churning mind. She always seemed to discover another. He wished to shelter her from her gnawing concerns but was powerless to do so. Her sons were helpless to relieve the self-imposed disquietude.

Elisha avoided conversing about the worries that plagued her and attempted to keep his activities from her. Accordingly, he was out the door and down the path to the road as he yelled back, "Sorry, Mother. I must meet Miller who has some beaver furs for us and they're harder and harder to come by these days. He'll be waiting at Broughton Brook, so I must hurry to get there!"

As he ran out to the road, he turned to shout back, "Oh, and Mother, since I'll be trading with Tim Wright later, I probably will stay tonight with him."

Rebekah Hawley's face started to register a surprised scowl, "Elisha, take some victuals for later…"

It was too late as the gate was already slamming shut with a clap of finality. He wouldn't be hungry for victuals…. Rebekah leveled an angry glance at Joseph as he quickly and silently finished his breakfast, weighed it all and scurried out, too. "Aahhh, Mother, I will take mid-day break with the Lymans. Don't plan on me. We've many General Court sessions to transcribe today. I've much work to do."

Rebekah Hawley stood beside the table and benches. Her hands were still clutching the delicate creamware bowl with the inlaid pattern of wheat sheafs on the rim. This season's maple syrup that had warmly topped the porridge was congealing now. She realized her strategy - like an iridescent soap bubble floating on a gentle drift of air - had suddenly popped.

Before its official start on March 25, 1746[5] had been a year of paralyzing, overwhelming apprehensions that approached near-constant panic in the English colonies. Despair and rumors of attacks, killings and captures proliferated weekly. There was the frightening news about the expanding "French War" and its consequent desolation by unleashed "Indian trepidations and captivating" of frontier settlers. There had been intelligence for months that the French intended to attack Boston. Then, on September 24, 1746, the alarming news reached the Connecticut River valley of a French invasion fleet.

Intensifying all, there was widespread sickness. Each family consulted their most trusted "physician and surgeon" for preventative and curative medicines. Mortality settled like a fog upon new-England.

There had been public fast-days for Providence's intervention to save the Bay Colony. There had been sermons and most earnest prayers for months, such as the Reverend Judd's from 2 Chronicles 20:12: "Neither know we what to do: but our eyes are upon thee."

Northampton's response to the drum-beat of war and the crescendo of deaths was to build watch-towers around and within the exposed town of 1,000. Every family was on alert and every man was subject to immediate militia call-up and defense.

Besides these threatening preoccupations, personal worries possessed mother Rebekah Hawley. She lay in wait for Elisha within the secure confines of her house at the warm stone hearth, where she toasted waffles on an iron over the licking flames. Occasionally she stirred the great kettle boiling with the evening's supper. As soon as he entered she blurted out, 'Elisha, what know you of this Root woman?"

He wondered did she smell alcohol on him?

She wondered had he passed by the tavern?

He replied dully, "What Root woman, Mother?"

---

[5] For information on the Julian and Gregorian calendars used herein, see Wikipedia or: http://www.history.com/news/6-things-you-may-not-know-about-the-gregorian-calendar

Elisha pulled off his twisted and trod-down boots and shook the day's soiling off. He sat down at one of the ladder-backed chairs. He had walked a good twenty miles plus today and felt its nagging ache in his sinewy muscles and pinched feet. After the morning farm and animal chores were done, he had gone from stopping by the Red Tavern for news, down to the ferry to find Tim Wright, over to Phineas Lyman's Law Office to consult with Brother Joe, to each one of his distant fields and back home.

"What? Well, Mother…." Her son's confusion was not totally feigned, as he was indeed trying to guess what she might have heard or seen. "Can you describe her? I've hardly time for girls talking at the street corners."

"The one who is fair. With the bright eyes. Her hair seems always to being falling down out of her mob cap… rather capriciously, I would say, or as my esteemed father would note, 'It has something of …. Aahhh…. being 'unclad.'" She paused, deeply embarrassed at the word implying "nakedness."

"I know she was brought up in learning. She seems to know her "Good Book" verses well. She must be serious, studious."

This last was a lie because Martha was more sprightly than somber, but Elisha knew he was playing a dangerous game to show any evidence of noticing any unsanctioned woman. He dared not take such too far with his mother.

"Brought up in learning?! Hah! Simply because she attended the town school and listened to her catechism? I think not. Now, one truly brought up in learning - and piousness - is the deacon's daughter," Mother Hawley corrected.

Elisha pictured in his mind a vision of Deacon Ebenezer Pomeroy the Second's daughter Betty (there was only one daughter). He had not wanted to contemplate the Deacon's daughter with anything but a casual glance and subsequent dismissal. Hmmm, he summoned up images of the girls of the town… Yes, there was Betty Pomeroy, inseparable all through the "Bad Books" investigation and religious meetings from her friend Kate Wright in the young women's seating gallery of the meetinghouse. By the end of that Bad Books fury, even Deacon Pomeroy's eldest son, Eben (the Third) was embroiled in it and was beaten with a heavy stick for his stealthy perusal of the obscene book.

"Yes, the Deacon's daughter Betty now there's a fine, virtuous young woman. As it sayeth in the Book of Proverbs, 'Charm is deceptive, and beauty is fleeting; but a woman who fears the Lord is to be praised.' True wisdom."

An image flitted to Elisha's mind of the Pomeroys' blacksmithing works. He pictured fine, silty, grey ash settling therein thickly coating everything like a funeral pallor. For some reason, Betty Pomeroy's squarish wrists and broad shoulders reminded Elisha of her sturdy male gunsmithing relatives with their muscular arms, dripping sweat and bawdy masculinity. Such robustness was admirable in his friend Seth Pomeroy but revolted him in Betty. Was it his imagination that Betty always exuded the smell of smoke and sweat?

Rebekah Hawley wondered if she glimpsed a recoil or revulsion roll across his face? His answer convinced her she had seen some truth beneath his placid obscurity.

Some seconds later he wanly objected, "Mother, the deacon's daughter is not what one terms "becoming."

Rebekah's anger was laced with righteous indignation and fright. "Becoming? Becoming?! As in comely?" Scorn was clearly visible on her distorted face before she continued on this tirade. "And what is a pretty face? Nothing! I tell you a comely woman is nothing but bubbles, empty shadows and idleness! She is nothing in God's judgment! A temptation only! Harrumph! Imagine if only attractive girls married!"

Rebekah paused for a breath, then stormed on, "Your charge is to converse with God alone. Seek the divine grace and comfort, the least drop of which is more worth than all the comeliness, riches, gaiety, pleasures and entertainments of the whole world."

Elisha's distrait mind drifted to the remembrance of May blossoms and their perfumes. He thought of Martha Root's mass of hair flopping out of her mob cap and into his surging hands. Of her richly ripe apple-dumpling bosoms. He couldn't help but think of his own wide-awake and hungry privates, to his tongue licking every inch in her mouth like a cat preening itself, of his fingers following the beguiling curve of her hips, supple as a green willow branch…. It could hardly be suppressed inside him: he felt as if he were fighting a demon to silently contain it. Every part of his being exalted!

Elisha Hawley reluctantly admitted to himself that he was enraptured by Martha Root. He felt joyous to glimpse her - in church, along a path, at a youth Bible study, as she went to her Uncle Bridgman's, with her friends. Everything about Martha ignited his true soul. Her body kindled his desire. Her conversation sparked him. Her personality captivated him. It harmonized with his own: their spirits were kindred. He thought of her every unbusied moment. He journeyed to her in his dreams.

Conversely, he was realizing that he was not his own true person in the confines of his mother's house. Was anyone ever their own true person - except when in their own imaginings, alone or in the woods?

"Low estate, low station," he thought with irony that dripped vinegar, remembering Rebekah's prior remarks. He sneered to recall that Rebekah's real and personal estate had been assessed at less than half Hezekiah Root's in the last town tax assessment. Then he instantly understood the import of her caution. She still controlled his own "hereditament" from his father. He was nothing. He had nothing.

There followed silence, as Rebekah in her preoccupation burned the hasty pudding. Brother Joe would soon join them. They would put the cows to barn, feed and water them, check their stalls. When their farm chores were completed, they would read some Bible verses, say their evening prayers, and retire exhausted for the day. Joe would stay awake by tallow candle light reading law books.

Meanwhile, across the sprawling and irregular town, at the homestead of Hezekiah Root, daughter Martha felt nauseated and lethargic working at the hearthside beside her mother. Young Martha noticed "sour belching" and felt lethargic and woozy. She felt conflicted as she had not had her monthly bleed. A pot hung from the cooking crane over the fire, while an iron spider sat on the bricks below warming the cornbread. These days were busy with their steady preparation for winter, pressing and boiling apples for cider and sauce, preserving currants and plums, storing pumpkins and turnips in the cellar.

Mother Martha could not help but peer at the family night-slop jars for signs of young Martha's bleeding or surveil the frequency of her visits to the outhouse. Big Martha reminded herself, "sometimes it flows too soon, sometimes too late, they are too many or too few, or are quite stopped that they flow not at all." The younger Root girls had had their "lady days," but young Martha's did not come. When Big Martha questioned her, young Martha admitted that her monthly bleeding "purgation" hadn't come for two months now.

Her mother urged her to eat. Big Martha suspected she recognized her daughter's fickle infirmity, "Don't worry, my dear. It's the curse of Eve to bring forth a living child in pain. Your sickness is but the precursor of motherhood." Big Martha sensed that Martha was in a family way by Elisha Hawley. "I know you're upset but everyone will come to their senses with this, if it truly be. Then, he will marry you. After the travail of childbirth, they will come around. They always do."

"No, Mum, they don't always these-a-days. Remember Tom Wait? He refused to marry Jemima Miller, and he is even saying that poor Jemima's baby was not his! Even with her swearing during her travails that Tom was the father. And she swore it to the midwife!"

"Truth be told, my dear Martha, people have no morals today. These men have been raised up with no conscience before God or the church. They have no care for even their own blood or kin." Mother Martha paused in confused reflection. "Although I do know Tom Wait's sister, Betsy. And she is the dearest soul…. I don't understand, I don't understand…. What kind of man is it that don't own up to their using a girl!? Some young folks today have no hearts or fear of God's judgment!"

Mother Martha Bridgman Root knew well that true justice eluded mere mortals here on earth, but she had some faith in her town, her minister, her church. Northampton was a city governed under the highest laws of God and country. Still, Big Martha could push her logic no further, acknowledging that justice sometimes fails. Her husband had been accused of not governing their son Simeon properly during the "Bad Boys, Bad Book" controversy. Some said Hezekiah Root had "failed to keep the youth from disorder." Mother Martha returned in her mind to the complaint of "misrule and disorder… reveling in indecency… contrary to law" that Rebekah Hawley had loudly expressed outside the meetinghouse during the nooning between church services. Mother Martha blushed deep ashamed and angry to remember Madame Hawley peering at her with a cutting malice, remarking within hearing of the other women, "Alas for their frolics and dances! How shall they remember their foolish trifles when they are in hell?"

That was how Rebekah Hawley uncharitably judged others before! Wait until the disdainful Madame confronted the reality that this time it was HER son who would be snagged by this trouble! Big Martha was sure that Rebekah Hawley did not know yet, but once she was confronted with it, Martha would surely hear an earful of it!

Big Martha was thoroughly seeped and saturated in her abiding love of her children. Although she knew in her mind no one could be assured of eternal salvation merely by their own attempts at good works, she could never countenance that her beloved sons and daughters would not be counted among the saved. She judged, "Twill be that time when our dear Lord of Salvation shows his great love to us, undeserving degenerate sinners."

As Madame Hawley had strutted away that day, Big Martha cursed quietly at her back, "Base old whore! Even she has to obey the laws of God!"

The question burned into Rebekah Hawley's brain since Hannah Muchmore, that "distracted person" had spoken on it as she shepherded her cows past the Hawley homestead on Pudding Lane. The addle-brained Hannah had ambled up the lane. Once again Hannah was singing gibberish and laughing in an imbecilic fashion aloud to herself. As she glimpsed grim old Rebekah Hawley, Hannah Muchmore called to her cheerfully, "Even's tidings, soon-to-be-Grandmother Hawley."

She laughed her bizarre, unnerving laugh. Rebekah Hawley felt as if she had been scratched across the face with the grating sound of Hannah Muchmore's cackling. Although Hannah was a pitiable person of no consequence – dismissed by most persons - yet she irritated Rebekah exceedingly. The sight of the scruffy, disheveled girl disturbed and unbalanced Rebekah.

"What say you Hannah Muchmore? What said you there?" the stern matron Hawley demanded from her yard where she was throwing kitchen scraps out to her handsome Nankin and Dominique breed chickens.

Rebekah Stoddard Hawley was used to respect from the regular Northampton folk, but no one got any from the deranged young woman. Even a minister in the pulpit got scant deference from the waif Muchmore. Hannah said the most amazing and outrageous things on the worst and most curious occasions. As the entire congregation sat in peaceful contemplation, Hannah might jump up and yell something inappropriate and jostle everyone's nerves. Other times in the meetinghouse she unexpectedly rose and shouted out her twisted notions. One Sabbath she decried, "Gentlemen with hair as women are condemned by the light of nature, and the laws of God. Next will they take up a mobcap and petticoat?!" On another occasion, "Sabbath-evening dissipation and mirth-making dooms this brethren! Damnation for debauchery!"

She was reported to have barked at the moon! This girl conversed with animals! One day she ejected a pile of spittle onto the floor as the Reverend Edwards walked by. Another morning she cuffed Deacon Pomeroy about the back of his head then calmly walked out. The dimwitted, filthy girl dared stare Rebekah straight in the eye, as no others did.

At the question posed this day by Rebekah as to what she had said, Hannah threw back her head (which was constantly unkempt) in her own private, crazy glee. She laughed and laughed to the wind. Rebekah did not believe in superstition, but who knew what spirits the girl had intercourse with!?

"Says I, knows you lullabies for a baby, Granny Hawley? Them chickens'll be a fending for theyselves - soon as you have a grandson."

"Where on earth did you hear such an outrageous thing? As impossible that is as to bridge the Great River! And contemptible defamation further! Contain your unruly passions! Don't you cast foolish aspersions, you young tart!"

"No, no, Grandmother, not I. But I seen what I seen and I knows what I knows. And I knows Mistress Martha Root is growing big in the belly with the baby of Elisha Hawley," offered Hannah. "You'll be Grandmother Hawley next spring."

Hannah laughed again to her imagined friends and muttered more incomprehensible, garbled trifles to herself, sounding more like guttering candles than human speech.

"What? What? What unpardonable blasphemy! How dare you advance such an accusation! How dare you?" shouted Madame Hawley in stunned disbelief at the boldness of both the manner and the dissoluteness of the accusation.

The accusation itself was literally blinding to Rebekah Hawley! Her heart thumped wildly as she trembled, aghast with fear and shock. She grabbed at the fence to steady herself, then struggled to compose herself before the urchin Muchmore. How dare this doddering fool-child spread such slander about her family, thought Rebekah! Or – or might it be so?

"How dare you speak so about the Hawley family!" menaced Rebekah. "I'll not have you filling the town with useless noise and tittle-tattle! You'll not spread falsehoods about your respectable superiors!"

"Nay, nay, Grandmother. These eyes seen 'em. I does all my own seeing and all my own thinking, too," replied Hannah proudly. "Even an idiot, like me, knows what I see and what I think. I seen Gentleman Hawley with his breeches down at his boots and Mistress Martha petticoats up to her waist - there off in the woods off toward the hills. I seen it with my own mind! Indeed, I did."

Hannah pointed off up the town hill to the northwest where banks of puffy violet clouds, saturated with rosy pink undersides scuttled along the evening skyline. They glowed against the golden sky of an early winter sunset.

A loud gasp escaped the stoic old lady, while her mind was set on a blinding whirl! Outrageous scandal! Never had anyone ever articulated such a notion aloud! She grabbed at her ears to have heard such dreadful words uttered aloud. But Rebekah Hawley began reexamining in her mind Elisha's behaviors over the last weeks and months. She felt a blaze of heat searing across her brain and face. Hannah Muchmore was startled to see Rebekah Hawley collapse in a dead heap in the dust of the homelot yard.

Hannah gazed over at the lump of clothes that was Rebekah Hawley's inert form in the yard outside her buttery building and said aloud, "Well, Goodwife Hawley, take that as you may, but it's as true as Northampton is far from Massachusetts! I swear on the minister's powdered head - or wig." She gazed off to think deeply. Then she continued, "Or powdered wig-head, and all else under and above. Oh well… Mistress. The cows head home. I can't tarry. Good day, Granny."

Hannah Muchmore walked off following the cows home. "Hhrump, indeed, Granny Hawley! Gloating and bloating, but your supper's all parsnips!" scoffed Hannah. She hoped there would be something good for her supper tonight, not all parsnips.

After she was long down the road, Hannah Muchmore heard an ear-splitting howl from the Hawley home-yard, "Elisha-a-a-a!"

As she turned back to look, she saw neighbors run down Pudding Lane to the Hawley farm.

Had it started in the spring of 1746? Even though it was a time of dangers and hazard everywhere, nevertheless, nature had re-wakened with the promise of new life. Spring spawned hope, beauty and joy even in the middle of a war time. Especially, these live among the young, whose senses are always so keen. Because terror and desolation every moment might bring death and destruction, sentiments were concentrated with fire and passion.

It was in this caldron that an encounter between Elisha Hawley and Martha Root kindled smoldering embers of regard, affection and yearning. Each meeting intensified the next. Thus, a chance glance became a deliberate look. A look became a gaze. A gaze became words exchanged which then became an ardent conversation. Then, in the moment of a casual gesture, bodies brushed. Next, a hand deliberately touched and fingers explored. Skin tingled. Mouths found each other and drank in kissing. Like warming soil in the spring, once a seed is sown, a plant must grow.

Martha and Elisha managed to steal precious time away from their daily drudgery to sneak off and unite. Martha purportedly was picking field herbs (for her family's dyeing, she knew many different plants than he), visiting or picking up something from relatives. Elisha excused himself from home under pretexts of meeting distant fur traders for business or etcetera. Else, he snuck out in the dark of night to the Roots' house - to reappear early the next morning before cock-crow and his mother might discover his absence.

The Roots made "bundling" easy and natural. Innocently, Elisha and Martha stayed awake talking and laughing one pleasant evening over a mug of hard cider-jack until all the rest of the family was going to sleep. The company of a lively house, full with younger siblings and extended family coming and going especially gratified Elisha. He had never experienced the give-and-take of a large boisterous group such as the Roots. One night, Mother Martha told Elisha it was too late to be walking home on the treacherous, rutted, undetectable or shadowy wagon roads. He might fall into a hole and break his neck! She suggested that he should just stay and they would make him up a place to sleep.

Martha's ten-year-old brother Orlando so admired Elisha that he snuggled up close to Hawley's warm body. Their mutual heat felt like a blacksmith's forge. Of course, it was impossible for Elisha to sleep. He laid awake afire with Martha's nearness. After more visits, rather than bed down with one of the younger Root boys, the Root parents allowed the couple to lie down in a "bundling bed" and talk with a heavy pine board separating them. It didn't take long for Elisha and Martha to be side by side with no bundling board between them any longer....

After their trysts, Martha Root and Elisha Hawley coveted each other more in the time apart. Martha was enchanted by Elisha's obvious infatuation with her. She felt respected and desired. He seemed to trail her everywhere: she had never noticed him before near the Edwards' house, yet there he was (and watching her!). Of course, she volunteered to bring in the cows from the commons more often; and there he was again over in a nearby field! Martha wondered if Elisha Hawley might be the best opportunity for her to establish a home and family?

But it was no longer enough to simply see the beloved. Elisha became obsessed by the memory of lying with Martha under a lilac bush in flower and coupling with her. It evoked glorious pleasure, just to think of the curve of her ankle as she dabbled her feet in the brook or his bumbling with the two buttons of his front breeches flap - and afterwards, ecstasy! He had been drugged by the sweet satisfaction of sexual consummation with someone delightful. It invigorated every aspect of his life. Martha was bewitching to him. The scents around them, the feel of aliveness of his hot skin on her coolness, her taste on his tongue, her whispers lingered buzzing about his ears day and night.

He was all a-flame with her: eclipsed by her, enthralled with and engulfed by her. She was the purest water-well that he returned to gulp and dowse himself in. Once tasted, the elixir of love was irresistible, and insisted that it be tasted again and again. He was helpless to resist her, for they were both ready and ripe for this love-making. So, he persisted in being with Martha, only increasingly more surreptitiously with his mother's suspicions aroused and her growing scrutiny of his every move.

Inevitably, the duck only evades the fox for so long. Such passion, like light, is hard to obscure completely. Thus, Rebekah Hawley was informed not only by Hannah Muchmore but also by Aunt Prudence Stoddard who noted Elisha's increasing interactions with "a certain young woman."

Her suspicions growing with each piece of information, one night with a luminous full moon, Rebekah lay awake to set a trap. She retired early but lay down fully dressed. She had nagged older son Joe that he should sleep early, purportedly to preserve his eyesight from reading law books long into the night and wastefully burning the supply of tallow candles. Reluctantly Joe was hustled off to bed.

This early in the season there were no crickets or high summer noises. Careless and impatient, Elisha waited for the human sounds of deep sleep as a signal to rouse himself. Like his mother, Elisha had reclined fully dressed and ready.

Rebekah had planned to intercept him in the yard or down the streets. However, Elisha's highly-tuned and practiced instincts were second nature to him, so he was onto Pudding Lane before his mother realized his noiseless departure. With her advancing age (61), she was no match for a 21-year-old male. Her mind was engrossed with evil creatures of the night. Nighttime was the province of the "prince of darkness," not a place she ever wanted to frequent with bats, hoot owls, or other nocturnal beasts.

As she set off after him, the dread of venturing into the blackness outside their house rose up as a tight knot constricting her throat. Madame Hawley had never been abroad in the town alone at such a time as this! Night-walking! Not only were there the unhealthy humours and miasmas in the night air, but she realized of-a-sudden that she could meet the night watchmen of the town! What if they snatched her from behind? She struggled to encourage herself and calm the panic that wanted to creep in to her pounding heart, "Why, those watchmen never catch anyone!" she scoffed. "They are practically useless! They are never around when any perfidy occurs. All one ever hears is how thieves are forever getting off in the night! Fear not, Rebekah!"

She had no idea what she might confront, but her natural brashness and disparagement combined with her maternal instincts to compel her forward. Her family's future was at stake! She paused for her racing heart to abate somewhat in which time she lost Elisha's shadowy figure far-ahead. However, that didn't matter, she knew where they both were headed.

Once again, her timing was faulty. She failed to catch Elisha before he entered the Root house which was glowing with the light of pine-knot candlewood. She despaired. Her vigilance had been to no purpose! She had not stopped his lurid undertaking despite her best efforts! No matter. What must be done must be accomplished, even if tongues would clatter and harsh judgments would be made against her. As she stood out on the horse and wagon-pounded dirt of King Street, Rebekah Hawley listened in despair to the light-hearted laughter inside the Root house. There inside was her son being ensnared further! She had already decided she would confront him. This was no time for a failure of courage. Mother Rebekah Hawley shouted aloud in the thick, murky summer air, "Elisha Hawley, come out!"

The sound of her voice shouting clanked in unnatural dissonance in the sleepy village! Shocked and affronted herself by the shattering of the peace, she urged herself on her mission. It required forcefulness of voice and nerve, but she continued to call out his name, piercing the Northampton night air, with a determined forcefulness. "Elisha Hawley! Elisha Hawley!" Come out here right now! Elisha, I demand you come out here this moment!"

Inside the suddenly silenced house, Elisha cautioned mother and daughter Martha, "She is not to be trifled with! I know. Stay within."

The fray in the street as an enraged Rebekah batted at Elisha became legendary, repeated by townspeople thousands of times until everyone was current of every small detail of the sordid affair. Although there had been fist-a-cuffs in Northampton, no one had ever experienced anything quite like the domineering, tall and grand woman swatting at her dodging son as she chased him back home in the dark!

Some elderly neighbors thought at first that the Indian alarm had been raised, "Is it war?"

"What's the ruckus about?" other neighbors called out open windows.

"Call the sheriff! Call the night watchman!"

"Confounded Hawley woman screaming, disturbing the peace!" other neighbors yelled out.

The entire humiliating scene had been broadcast by neighbors to friends, cousins, aunts, uncles, and elders all over town within hours. The quiet but determined public censure obligated all of the extended Stoddard and Hawley families to meekness in demeanor they had never professed before.

Uncle John Stoddard pocketed his gleaming gold watch and would not draw it out as he usually floridly did. For the time being, he spoke less at meetings or outside. Aunt Prudence wore her "meanest clothes" to Sabbath services and tamed her normally majestic sweeping entry into the meetinghouse.

All the Hawley relatives shunned contact with the Roots, the many Root and Bridgman relatives, the Reverend Mr. Jonathan Edwards and his family.

Rebekah avoided any relations or social intercourse. She rarely spoke to anyone these days and her cheese sales plummeted. (Consequently, she, Joe and Elisha ate copious chunks of cheese with every meal.) She forbade anyone to speak to her of it. Many mornings Joe and Elisha noticed her eyes red and her face blotchy and creased.

As for Elisha, his meagerest hope to convince his mother about Martha lay wrecked and demolished. He felt his heart pounding and hot blood racing to recall the night.

"Not that I didn't advise you," Joe railed at Elisha. Elisha, still in shock, demurred.

Joe took lessons from his great unease with Elisha. His own infatuation with Mercy Lyman (who Joseph was secretly "visiting" and who, too, was unacceptable to the Mother Hawley) would have to be deferred for the time being.

<u>Chapter 8</u>
<u>I saw the cloud, though I did not foresee the Storm</u>
<u>Northampton, 1746-1747</u>

Martha Root dolefully carried on her daily life (without her lover's presence, which had been curtailed by his family). The secluded days and nights of their merry-making together in fields, the Inner Commons, at Hunt's Tavern, and Halfway Brook abruptly ended. While Elisha was forced to hunker down, close to home and constantly surveilled by his brother, mother, or cousins, Uncle John Stoddard hastily negotiated to find him an appointment to a distant military post away from Northampton.

The sudden cessation of her cheery rendezvous' disconnected Martha from what she thought could have been a promising future. Her heart mourned the death of their love. Her mind and body ached to be held, caressed and loved but that comfort and pleasure had now vanished. It seemed to the restless Martha that each day clung on and refused to cede to night. Time hung heavily over her. The Roots observed sadness, confusion, and lethargy in Martha. She dragged about her daily chores with a depressed, sodden sluggishness that dragged down her usual blithe spirits and slowed the passage of days.

Night was no shorter. It meant lying alone and awake for interminable hours - when she once had had excitement and joy. Martha ticked off in her mind that another day had come and gone - without her monthly blood. (Older sister, Dolly, had surreptitiously whispered to Martha a few of the furtive mysteries of a woman becoming with child.) Martha observed sisters Jemimah and Hannah tying their linen pads into their girdles, knowing it had been more 35, 42, and then 54 days since her cycle. Both mother and daughter's conclusion that young Martha was in a family way was solidified the morning she awoke and puked into the slop jar, overflowing it.

"It looks like the "green sickness," stated her mother factually. "Yes, me thinks so. It results from gross, vicious and rude humors in the womb."

Soon young Martha was carrying a bucket with her all the time on her household duties.

Martha unintentionally revealed her secret to the town when she could not remove herself quickly enough from the morning service at the meetinghouse one Sunday. She expelled a strong stream of vomit into her towel (which had been discretely hidden under her apron). With sisters Jemimah and Hannah at her sides, Martha staggered out the side door trying to quell her violent retching. The spray of puke sprinkled the widow's seating box at the south side door as the sisters hustled out. Meanwhile the sorority of every woman in Northampton who had ever experienced a pregnancy clucked to herself thinking, "Hhmmh, Mistress Root appears quite indisposed this morning; I wonders what illness that might be? She doesn't appear to be feverish…."

Sister Hannah's face colored a bright scarlet of abiding shame at their visibility before their minister, the Reverend Mr. Edwards, and the entire town. "I'll never marry," Hannah swore to herself. "Never ever. And, I'll never lie with a man – ever!"

In the weeks that followed, as Martha Root's belly bulge became discernable, the matrons of the congregation gossiped ceaselessly on the topic, unless there was war news to divert their attentions. Mother Martha Bridgman Root made no effort to deny it or tamp down talk that daughter Martha, an unmarried woman, was with child and the offending father was none other than "gentleman" Elisha Hawley. "It has filled all the country with noise." Why should Big Martha try to refute the many times Martha and Elisha had been seen throughout the town as well as the notorious incident of Rebekah Hawley loudly confronting her son in front of the Root house?

For the elders of the First Church, Martha's fornication was an affront to the morals of the church which had to be rectified. Martha Root was a full member of the Calvinist congregation - and a fornicator. Of course, she must publicly confess and be brought to court for civil action.

However, the church deacons were leery to ask her to publicly name the father, if (as was believed probable) she would name Elisha Hawley, the grandson of their deceased esteemed minister, nephew of the current minister, nephew of the church elder and Chief Justice of the Court and son of the most fearsome woman in the entire Great River valley.

For weeks the Hawley family insistently ignored the controversy hoping it somehow might disappear. They were somewhat insulated by their prominence but eventually, the clamor among the lower levels of society became too boisterous. Widespread tensions were arising. As civil and religious leader of the town Colonel John Stoddard knew from his wife Prudence of the expanding ripples of murmurs about Martha Root's growing bastard child and the women's' endless vituperations toward his recalcitrant nephew Elisha Hawley. The controversy over the rightful punishment flared even within their own extended family as some Williams cousins (in whispered voice and _not_ before the family patriarchs like "the Colonel") argued over what was honorable, family honor (and status) and Elisha's conscience.

Meanwhile, Colonel Stoddard felt increasingly crushed under all of the demands on him. Deep into the night he thrashed and rolled back and forth in his bed, tormented by contemplation of potential invasion by a French fleet - even possibly up the Great River! It was a calamitous time. It was war and ruination! It was a life and death struggle! What might be next? Certainly, there would be more raids down the upper reach of the River to the far-flung Massachusetts settlements, where Abenaki warriors might kill, slash, maim and burn at will. They could strike down into the heart of the western Bay Colony settlements of Deerfield, Hatfield or Northampton itself. With worries of official war, being perturbed by the petty foibles and faults of a lustful young man was an unnecessary aggravation for the old man.

The Colonel felt as if he had heard all the deepest terrors and sorrows of all the Valley towns confided in his ears. Finally, he concluded it best that the frenzied turmoil of King George's War would present an opportunity to absent Elisha on a military commission at the frontier until his controversy abated. Colonel Stoddard could then silence his frenetic, caustic sister Rebekah.

"He can be removed from the outcry and then she can marry someone of her own "station." Perhaps she'll take a sudden fright and the womb will expel the creature?" Rebekah speculated.

And yet the Root family appeared oblivious to the fact that Martha should get married – to someone, if not Elisha Hawley! Week followed week, but there was no news of a bridegroom for Martha with her appearing as big, bulging and healthy as a sturdy ox. However, due to her "showing," the stays of her girdle had to be loosened. Next, she disappeared from services at meetinghouse. She left their house and yard rarely and felt isolated. She missed the comfort of sitting amidst a congregation of fellow believers and friends.

Like every woman, Martha Root felt full of concern for "the dreaded apparition." (As poetess Anne Bradstreet had written about her own child birthing, "death may my steps attend.") Martha considered on the deaths of her cousin, Martha Root Hannum, and other women she knew or had heard of who had died in childbirth travails or shortly afterwards. It was possible that no one could help her during that trial. Only she herself would do the sweating, enduring, remaining conscious, holding back urges to bear down (or not), pushing and wailing. She knew that every woman present would stroke her skin with the tenderest and deepest love and concern. Every woman at the birthing would walk beside her as she paced the room, would hold her standing up. But, of course, no one could physically be her.

Even with her larger than usual contingent of wise women attendants, Martha alone would walk through the "valley of the shadow of death." Every woman shuddered at the risk of death in childbirth, but Martha had hers doubled! Twin births in Northampton only occurred once a decade or so, and there had already been one almost two years ago, Martha and Mary Searl. What did it mean that there might be another? Many said, "Twin babies will likely be wan and may not even survive." True to that sage old adage, tiny baby Mary Searl had already expired at three months of age.

It was also rumored that twins conceived in sin could be born conjoined. Martha Root worried that she could give birth to a malformed "monster." Sometimes God punished sinful women (such as the dissenter Anne Hutchinson) by giving birth to horrible creatures that weren't even completely human! Some such babies were born covered in hair, like a wild beast, or with other ghastly deformities! As the day drew ever nearer, Martha Root's nights became restless and nightmares awakened her, drenched in sweat.

As her time approached, Martha tried to calm herself with the small comfort that her devoted mother and older midwife, Mindwell Parsons and younger midwife-in-training, Betty Parsons Allen, who lived across the fields on King Street, would be with her. So close was she that Betty would be able to run to be at Martha's side as soon as the "grumbling pains" progressed. Martha prayed that no other woman would also be laboring at the same time, as had been the case on December 19th when two different Clap families had babes delivered.

Martha prayed morning, noon, and night - and in between as well. She earnestly entreated God to see her through as a "living mother" of "a living child," although she acknowledged that her sinful nature deserved nothing but hell-fire and sulfurous brimstone. She admitted to herself that the Madame Hawley and Elisha's brother Joseph would probably be as earnestly praying for the baby's decease in the passage to life, to resolve their "difficulties" with her. Perhaps they prayed for her own death in the laboring fury to come?

Ten births had occurred at Northampton that winter 1746 to spring 1747:

December 19 Phineas Clap to Samuel and Mindwell Clap;
December 19 Rhoda Clapp to Jonathan and Submit Clap;
December 21 Daniel Kingsley to Moses and Mercy Kingsley;
December 21 Ephraim Wright to Ephraim and Miriam Wright;
December 23 Martin Clark to Ezra and Martha Clark;
December 25, 1746 Solomon Strong to Ichabod and Mary
    Strong;

January 7, 1746/7[6] Supply Kingsley to Jonathan and Rebecca
    Kingsley;
January 24, 1747 Oliver Wright to Aaron and Miriam Wright;
February 5, 1747 Nathan Clark to Daniel and Experience Clark;
May 12, 1747 Isabel Strong to Ezra and Miriam Strong.

It occurred to Martha that this condition of being with child unfolded as unhurriedly as a spring with its long waits for buds to unfurl but which then proceeded apace once started. As she grew heavy faster and farther beyond the norm for a woman with babe, Martha's "wise women" confirmed by gentle examination poking her belly that she was carrying not one but *two* babies, a rare and perilous event!

Thus, she would need to prepare for her looming travails faster and harder than other woman in her condition. Sisters Jemima and Hannah would help spinning yarn, weaving it, sewing it into cloths, clothes and bandages and preparing the foods, soap, candles, etcetera. The Root women had prepared the sick room off the kitchen in anticipation of Martha's lying in there. The door keyholes and latches had been stopped up with cloth for privacy. The Root men commenced spending much time at the nearby home of their close relatives, the Hope Root family to avoid interfering with the women's affairs of childbirth. Mountains of food had been cleaned, cooked, prepared and stored in the cellar in anticipation of the extra women who would be needed to help with the delivery of whatever babe(s) arrived. The usual "caudle" spiced wine had been bought for the new mother's recovery. There were stacks of swaddling cloths, diapers, towels and soap, straw for the floor to sop up blood, sweat, urine, excrement or vomit and bandages all had to be at the ready anytime.

Midwife-in-training Betty Allen, too, struggled with her own preoccupations about helping at the travails of twin births. It would be the first twin birthing in which she was an important part. The mother and daughter midwives had prepared their herbal concoctions and medicine bags for the call to attend Martha's birthing (as well as their darning and knitting to keep themselves occupied during the long waits). Betty begged her mother, Mindwell Parsons, to consult with old Dr. Mather about these special difficulties of delivering twins. Would these twins present properly in Martha's birth passage or might they be entangled together? Would one be born head first – as normal - with the other unable to get into position in the womb they shared? How long would it be between their births? Too long? Would their "birth strings" to their mother be

---

⁶ The Julian calendar rendering of the January to March part of the year. January 1st was referred to as New Year's Day, although the year numbering started on March 25. See "Year numbering" and "New Year's Day" on https://en.wikipedia.org/wiki/Julian_calendar

tangled together or around each other's necks and one's birth strangle the other in utero? Would there be two "afterbirths" to be sure were expelled or only one? Might Mindwell have to reach into Martha's womb to feel if there were two? Would they both be born alive or would one die in process? Would one be too small to survive as was frequently the case? If so, would it die soon or struggle days or weeks to live? Would Martha herself have the strength to push through two births? Of course, she could hemorrhage or die of exhaustion…

New midwife Betty Allen knew she was facing her greatest test to date. She earnestly prayed that her own experiences of birthing seven living children herself would help her judgment in this trial. There was so much to remember to do and to be wary of. There was much to worry about. Further, although they would pass hours upon hours watching, waiting, fretting and bustling about, when the moments of decision came, they might appear all-of-a-sudden without time for reflecting or assessing much. Complications could happen without warning! She did not want to face a dead mother or child! Betty's instincts would be on their highest alert until the afterbirth was safely expelled, the mother safely resting, the baby washed and swaddled in its special soft, warming blanket. Then, she (and the attending women) could relax and enjoy the accomplishment of ushering in a new life, if it were to be God's will.

Most importantly for the authorities, should the mother survive, the midwife would be required to testify before the Court of Common Pleas on the child's paternity.[7] As the law stated, the unmarried woman must be questioned in her travail who was the father of the child? Betty Allen and the other witnesses at Martha's birthing must question her as to the true identity of the father - in the deepest depths of the worst trial of the mother's life. Whose name would Martha Root scream out in her pains?

Of course, Betty Allen knew Martha's accusation that the father was Elisha Hawley. Would she shout aloud Elisha's name? Or might she name someone else? Would she continue constant in her attestation against whomever? Betty must be ready for everything.

---

[7] If the normal process were followed, a constable would have filed a presentment for Martha Root to appear on the charge of fornication before the Hampshire County Inferior Court of Common Pleas. However, it is not known that such documents have survived in this case. See the Hampshire County (Massachusetts) *Inferior Court of Common Pleas and Court of General Sessions of the Peace.* Lib D, Volume 5. 1746-1757. A scanned copy of the actual book can be read online at: http://credo.library.umass.edu/view/pageturn/mums704-i4657/

Finally, if Martha did shriek Elisha's name would she, Betty Allen, have the temerity and honesty to testify against the Hawley family and their powerful relatives?

Rebekah repeatedly, furiously and noisily denied the babies-to-be expected by Martha Root were Elisha's. She had marched out of the meetinghouse with Elisha and Joe in tow at Martha's confession of fornication before the First Church (although Martha confessed fornication only by herself). For that stomping departure, Elisha was relieved, as he sat scorching in shame as the Reverend searingly sermonized. Elisha could find no neutral site upon which to stare his dull eyes, as Martha Root stood in the middle of the church, facing the congregation, head slunk down till her chin rested on her slender neck collar.

She read,

"Tho I have experiencd much Enlightening & humbling and been encourag'd by this assembled brethren, yet I have had great Concern & been in great Trouble where I must thorowly humble myself before God and this Church, …

Upon the whole, I humbly ask forgiveness before God, among You, and whosoever anybody whom I hath hurt at any Time, or who has been amiss with Me, I earnestly ask their forgiveness of, and I desire humbly to put myself under the Government of this Church requesting your kind and faithfull Watch over Me at all Times; and I ask your Prayers for me that I may walk agreeable to these solemn Engagements; and that I may not only return to Membership of the visible Church here, but that I may at last sit down with Abraham, Isaac & Jacob in the Kingdom of Heaven, and drink of that Wine that is ever New with God in Glory…."[8]

Worse still, the Hawley pew (up at the very front - in full view of all the church - next to Reverend Edwards' family) sat directly facing Martha's father Hezekiah Root's pew. This meant that both families sat percolating in frigid cold fury each two-to-three-hour Sabbath and mid-week service. Every Hawley reaction - sneeze, cough, twitch, blink, slouch, flushing of face, eyebrow cocked, nervous hands, sweat, tear, feigned disinterest, etc. was on full exhibit to the assemblage and it was then the subject of endless gossip, whispering and conjecture. Elisha sensed how Rebekah had grown to detest the sight of Martha, sitting so unmoved and unbowed, so ripe with her babies to come and so damaging to Rebekah's designs

---

[8] As noted in the Introduction, the author has relied on actual documents as much as possible. The Reverend Edwards is known to have inked several confessions before the Northampton congregation. However, this is not the exact confession read by Martha (which is not known to exist) but is based on similar ones in other parishes.

for her son. Throughout all, though, Rebekah sat with erect backbone and head high as proud and dismissive as a queen. If she willed it, Rebekah could probably ignore bees stinging her face! Her inner resolve and self-command were like granite.

Elisha hated himself for his silence, indecisiveness and his own horrid profaneness when Joe broke the news that Martha Root was pregnant, yet he felt he could do nothing. He was frozen between his primeval, crushing fear of his mother's wrath: he couldn't hurt the only parent who had stayed by him and Joe, and the diametrically opposed interests of his mother, his brother, his minister, his family, his lover, and the generous Root family. He had been shocked that she was expecting, but told himself that at least it meant that she had pleasured in it, as it was a well-known fact that a woman could not conceive a child unless both parties did pleasure.

Elisha Hawley relievedly observed that Martha shed no tears. Her back was stiff and unbent as the tallest old white pine. Elisha entertained a faint wish that Martha didn't hate him, which quivering thought vanished swiftly from his mind. He questioned if she was in utter remorse over him? In a rush of sorrow, he dared wonder if she regretted everything of their liaison and naïve love? Did she despise every thought of him? Did she cuss hexes at him in the night? Quickly, he banished the thought, bolstering himself she would understand this wasn't his fault. Elisha dreaded the thought of Martha's weakening and collapsing before the congregation.

In the beginning, he had nurtured a frail hope that things might work themselves out. Of course, he and Martha were not the first or only such sinners in the court books:

> "Jemima Miller of Northampton Confessed before this Court
> that She had been guilty of the Crime of Fornication, ordered
> that She pay a fine of twenty five Shillings to his Majesty. Cost
> paid. November 11, 1746"

> "Gideon Clark and Rachel his Wife Confessed before this Court
> That they had been guilty of the Crime of Fornication Together.
> Twenty five Shillings money each. Cost paid. November 11,
> 1746"

Only two years before, Sam Danks and Tom Wait had denied paternity of children and refused to marry the mothers of those babies. Danks and Wait were now excommunicated incorrigibles. At the time of their shames, Rebekah had railed against Danks' and Wait's rebellion against the Church and society, their "gratifying a lust of lasciviousness" and "their unruly passions." However, Danks and Wait were not of the first family of town as Elisha Hawley was. He was the grandson of the Reverend Solomon Stoddard, a nephew of the esteemed civil and military commander, Colonel John Stoddard, and a close nephew of the Reverend Mr. Jonathan Edwards!

When Martha's mother heard of Madame Hawley's repeated loud denials of Elisha's paternity, she snorted, "That old vixen! What is she to have us believe? That the bundling board [that was placed between them in the night when Elisha slept over at the Roots' house] put Martha with child? Ha, not likely!"

Mother Martha Bridgman Root reassured young Martha. Big Martha knew of many, many such indiscretions – too many to name, and even more that were suspected. Life was just like that: it just happened. Yes, fornication was a scandal in the eyes of the church but had become so common. Repentance must be shown and then forgiveness sought. It was then fixed. Life went on. So, Martha Bridgman Root assuredly, "Not to fret. This sort of thing happens. You shall see, the great Lord always works things out. He always does." She counseled patience, the queen of virtues.

The philosophical, placid and accepting Hezekiah Root said little. He accepted all as God's will - not for a humble weaver, like himself, to question - but simply to acquiesce to - with grace.

But Mother Rebekah Hawley was the converse of Mother Martha Bridgman. Instead of simmering down, her fire was stoked. As time wore on Mother Hawley softened none to Elisha's halting, tentative comments. Tensions mounted between them and within the community. In ignoring a communal feeling that there must be a penitent act and rebalancing, outrage grew. Still, Rebekah dismissed any public profession of guilt by her son. "Never, never!"

The Reverend Mr. Edwards, ever enthralled with the goodness of God, had believed, too, that there would come an acceptable solution. In this, he relied on guiding Providence, the wisdom and gravitas of the Church and Colonel Stoddard to dictate a compromise that all would ultimately yield to and comply with - even if begrudgingly.

> "We live in a day wherein God is doing marvelous things; in that respect we are distinguished from former generations. God has wrought great things in New England, which though exceedingly glorious, have all along been attended with some threatening clouds…

"And therefore, a wise God has so ordered it that love and fear
should rise and fall like the scales of a balance, when one rises,
the other falls, as there is need; or as light and darkness take
place of each other in a room, as light decays, darkness comes in,
and as light increases and fills the room, darkness is cast out; so
love, or the spirit of adoption, casts out fear, the spirit of
bondage."[9]

Slowly, the Reverend began to view Rebekah's unbending defiance and refusal to any sanctions as repudiation of the authority of the church. He had counseled from the Old Testament verse, "Tis utterly unfit that men should think to put away at their pleasure, those when they have seen cause for their pleasure, thus to unite themselves to." But she substituted her own judgment for that of her minister.

It was Brother Joe who was most tormented by the mounting rock wall of criticism and social ostracism. Most of the townswomen turned their heads each time Elisha, Rebekah, or Joseph Hawley walked by on the trodden streets. The common men grew stone silent with the approach of any Hawley. Martha's brothers, neighbors and cousins, with whom Elisha had shared drinks and laughs, mumbled low insults as he walked by and all refused to meet his eyes. They brokered no excuses, no forgiveness without confession. Likewise, the Root women were positively venomous to Rebekah making a point to have their taunting remarks overheard, "The crazy Hawley family, too superior to own up to their own sins."

Or "Oh, Hawleys, they thinks they don't have to obey the laws of God or the church."

"Them Hawleys can ruin a girl with no care whatsoever, 'cept for themselves. Good Lord forbid!"

Even the consummate diplomat and problem-solver Elisha's uncle Colonel Stoddard could find no other solution but to commission Elisha to the militia and send him far from town and talk to the frontier. The Colonel had written to the Governor,

"I recommend him to any Civilities in your power to show him
which may contribute to his Ease and Satisfaction…. as a man
of quality, a gentleman."

---

⁹ *The Works of Jonathan Edwards.* Vol. 1, i, xii. Jonathan Edwards *Religious Affections*, Part 3.

The slightest stab of guilt pinched him as he admitted to himself, "Aaaahhhmmm, not completely the true definition of a gentleman - somewhat of a rogue and philanderer - but a gentleman rogue of the good family of my sister." So naturally, it had cost extra for the commission as Elisha did not qualify as regenerated without a confession in the church. Colonel Stoddard saw that nephew Joe was a true Hawley descendant who hated the military life during his chaplaincy with the troops at the siege of Louisbourg in 1745. Elisha, on the contrary, might have a penchant for it. He was tall and powerful, not awkward and contrived in each movement. Their differences dated from their youth when Elisha was always outdoors tagging along with the other boys while Joe obediently attended his books and prayers with his cousin the Reverend Mr. Edwards. Uncle Stoddard also carefully weighed the church's judgment, his nephew the Reverend Edwards' theological arguments, versus the need for militia men in this crucial time of the French War.

Thus, for this pretty scandal the Hawleys paid out some pretty shillings to hurriedly buy the commission and outfit Elisha as an officer. Uncle Stoddard easily convinced Captain Ephraim Williams Junior to accept Elisha as a Lieutenant under his command or militia scout at a distant frontier fort. Thereafter, Colonel Stoddard leaned on his Boston contacts for the commission papers and acceptance of his 21-year-old wayward nephew under "Captain Eph." Although the gregarious Ephraim readily agreed - in deference to his great benefactor, Colonel Stoddard, and in seeming real fondness for Elisha - the usual slow bureaucracy in Boston delayed the actual official documents (as Commander of the Western Frontier the Colonel had some leverage but the official commission would have to come from the Governor). Regardless, Elisha was immediately ordered to station on the "Line of Forts." Not long after the first snow squalls had menacingly gathered, new "Lieutenant Elisha Hawley" was enlisted in the Massachusetts militia.

In the end, Colonel Stoddard had had to carefully write to Massachusetts Governor William Shirley to cajole an official appointment:

> "North Hampton March 1, 1747/8
>
> Sir:
> ... There are forty able soldiers posted at Fort-Massachusetts
> and I was in expectation that Capt. Ephraim Williams would
> have taken the charge of that garrison, but home affairs have
> hitherto prevented him. We could at first get no better officer
> than a sergeant, afterwards I gave a Lieutenant's commission to
> Mr. Elisha Hawley, who is the only officer there at present. And
> it is vain to expect that suitable persons can be obtained for that
> service so long as their wages is so contemptable, unless we can
> find some persons out of business."

Fortunately, in time of war, there is always a need for men and officers. And, of course, money flowing from commissions and other profiteering was welcome.

Subsequently, equipment was needed to shift Elisha's former occupation trading animals' skins and running the family store to marching off to mortal combat. Besides a new more martial waistcoat of a bright red broadcloth with 20-some brass buttons to befit a commissioned officer, Hawley needed a cooking kit, better-quality wooden canteen, bigger hemp canvas knapsack, heavier knee-high black leather boots (well-oiled with thick bear grease), spatterdashes, several more pairs of fuller hose stockings, four more white linen shirts, gloves, a bullet mold, one pound of lead to pour bullets, one pound of gunpowder and a dozen flints. Most expensive were the newest model firearm, cutlass, sword and tomahawk hatchet from the Pomeroys' blacksmithing gunsmith shop.

The glint of the shiny metal in the sun consoled Elisha with relief from his miserable ostracism and the expectant thrill of a test of his strength and martial valor. He recalled the promise from the de Lamont military duties manual: "The art of war being the noblest of all the other arts."[10]

Elisha carried in his knapsack his notes from Uncle Stoddard's copy of the Colonel Humphrey Bland's famous book, *A Treatise of Military Discipline: In Which is laid down and Explained the Duties of Officer and Soldier.*[11] Elisha was reviewing its recommendations for his future martial conduct as an officer and a gentleman, remembering "honor above all else."

On the day of Elisha's departure out of Northampton Uncle Stoddard inconspicuously slid into the palm of his right hand a gleaming brass surveyors' compass with a built-in sundial. It was the newest model produced by the mathematical instrument maker Thomas Greenough of Boston. Hawley recalled his previous service on a 66-foot-long Gunter's chain for a surveying crew of Uncle Stoddard's. He judged that as a surveyor he could become a valued member of the forts' personnel. As he trod along the military supply road, Lieutenant Elisha Hawley periodically fingered the heft of the compass in the rabbit-skin pouch at his

---

[10] *The Art Of War, Containing, I. The Duties Of All Military Officers In Actual Service; Including Necessary Instructions, In Many Capital Matters, By The Knowledge Of Which, A Man May Soon Become An Ornament To The Profession Of Arms* by Monsieur De Lamont, Town-Major Of Toulon.

[11] *A Treatise Of Military Discipline; In Which Is Laid Down And Explained The Duty Of The Officer And Soldier, Thro' The Several Branches Of The Service* by Lieutenant-Colonel Humphrey Bland. (London, 1734).

waist. He admired the beauty of the compass' precision. He figured this had been charged against his increasing debts in the Hawley *Account Book* (their tradesman's book of accounts) by his mother. He pondered how much he would owe to his Uncle Stoddard?

As a Colonel and his commanding officer, Uncle Stoddard fully expected the new lieutenant to report valuable information about the "Line of Forts" candidly to him. He also carefully instructed Elisha to keep a tight lip among the other soldiers, "Provoke no problems up there. There are disorderly, spirited men among them and you will need keep your wits. Say little and listen much. Although you may think you are far way, remember, everything will get back to the commanders at Hatfield, the commissary at Deerfield and Northampton!" he warned. His dark scowl advised Elisha there had better be no future problems.

A moment later Uncle added, "And lend no money to the enlisted men…" He paused, "Or to anyone!" He could have added, "Especially not to gentlemen!" And he might have added, "Like some of your cousins." But, of course, he didn't say it. With that, Uncle Stoddard was gone.

Elisha was hustled out of town with a militia supply convoy traveling up the road to Hatfield and then on to the Deerfield-Albany Road to his new life on the frontier at Fort Massachusetts before Martha Root delivered her babies. He supposed he would just have to think of Martha no more…

Brother Joe would handle Elisha's legal and ecclesiastical affairs in his absence. Joe's current legal training with attorney Phineas Lyman and Yale College theological training would suit well. The Hawleys - with the concurrence of Uncle Stoddard - thought it best for Elisha to wait it out there on the fringes of society at Fort Massachusetts until Providence would bring resolution to the matter.

The year 1747 brought the bustle of preparations to the Hezekiah Root household for young Martha's "time of travails" and the prayed-for safe delivery of twin babies. Most of the Root males were staying with other family more and more, away from the "female absurdities." The windows, key-holes and door latches were stoppered up against prying eyes and to ward off evil. A vat of soap had been boiled and was at the ready, along with various medicinal alcohols (like brandy, caudle spiced wine, "groaning beer"). Beneficial herbs, such as dried mugwort, betony, ergot, chamomile, tansy, hyssop and pennyroyal hung from the ceiling rafters for use when needed. There were piles of first aid (bandages, rags, towels) and food necessities (fresh butter, honey, wine, "groaning cakes," broth, eggs, toast, marmalade, boiled pork, turkey pie and tarts) were stocked in the Root's cellar hole.

Although all the preparations were at the ready, no woman can ever be truly ready for the delivery of a new child into the world! Every delivery is unique. Every delivery is hard – even after 12 pregnancies (and eight living sons and daughters), Mother Martha Bridgman Root felt it hadn't grown easier! Every successful delivery of a mother and child is one of the greatest events of a lifetime – magnified in intensity by its risks and rewards. Knowing how unpredictable and potentially dangerous every delivery was, Mother Martha Bridgman Root was on edge and irritable in the days before young Martha's travails. Big Martha had attended and aided at many babies' births, her sister-in-laws', her cousins', her nieces' and those of her daughter Dolly's and son's Hezekiah's wife. These taught her that Providence should never ever be taken for granted. She was in high anxiety over young Martha, particularly as her daughter's would be a twin birth with double the perils.

In her prolonged agitation Big Martha shouted irritably at the younger children if they played nearby. She yelled at her older sons Simeon and Joseph when they sat down in the kitchen to rest. She snapped at her husband Hezekiah for asking discourtesily to pass the pickled root vegetables and baked beans. She prayed every quiet moment for her daughter's and grandchildren's safe delivery in the days to come.

The tedious months of waiting enabled everyone to know the plan with the first signal of the "sanctifying afflictions" of childbirth. Everyone involved in any fashion by the "lying-in" knew their roles, such as running to fetch the midwives, keeping the fire burning, drawing water and heating it, preparing a cordial or broth, washing or holding poor dear,Martha; encouraging the laboring woman, walking her around the sick room before the toasty hearth fire to be sure she didn't get cold, holding her upright during the grumbling pains, heartening her to hold back when she was needed *not* to push, cleaning out the blood-soaked straw of the room, swaddling the new baby/babies in warmed up new linen, putting the new mother to rest, burying the afterbirths and other "garbages" and finally - celebrating - if God wills it!

Because there would be *two* babies to deliver, more nearby female relatives and neighbor women would attend. Since it might well be a prolonged travail, all the women brought those portable household tasks to busy their hands in the tedious slow hours of waiting: their sewing, mending, darning, knitting, quilting, embroidery or other small jobs. Mother Martha Bridgman Root would direct the laboring with the midwives. Young Martha was grateful and felt reassured by her mother and the older, experienced women's presence and comfort to her.

Both midwives Mindwell Parsons and her daughter Betty Allen would be attending. Both had many personal experiences of child birthing – including almost 20 children born between them. The common wisdom was 'Physicians and midwives, like beer, are best when they are old,"but young Martha felt relieved in the knowledge that Betty would attend her. In spite of her relative youth (for a midwife-in-training, 31 years old), Betty's call to midwifery engendered confidence in the other young mothers in Northampton. About male physicians and surgeons, people said, 'Occasionally nature gets the best of the doctor and the patient recovers!" or "God heals, and the doctor takes the fees." However, these were not the general feelings about Betty Allen. Betty had been preparing both young Martha and herself for a twin delivery for weeks. Martha marveled with gratitude for the kindnesses of so many around her and her own undeservedness. "Kindness is not a straight line," she concluded. It doesn't necessarily spring up from where one expects it but it is always to be found somewhere.

Most marvelous for young Martha was the sense of the babies' independent movements she felt as her babies rolled, kicked and squirmed inside her belly. These children were indeed their own new lives in her body. They would be healthy and feisty.

In addition, Martha had visited her pastor the Reverend Mr. Edwards who had counseled, prepared and prayed with her in the event of her own death, should it be the will of God. Mr. Edwards reminded her of the advice of the great Puritan sage the Reverend Mr. Cotton Mather who wrote, "No midwives can do what angels can!" Martha drifted off to sleep every night praying for mercy, forgiveness and strength.

As she walked outside one afternoon, Martha noted a hemlock tree along the path that had split into two leader top branches from a single trunk about 15 feet off the ground. She stopped to regard it and wondered if this was what had happened within her belly? Was a seed within her somehow riven into two babies?

Late one evening Martha Root adjusted the "stay" that was supporting the bodice of her dress when an unexpected torrent of liquid flowed uncontrollably down her legs. Even though she had never seen such a flow before, she understood that her babies' delivery time was here! Soon, Betty Allen and the other women were arriving, scurrying along the path to the Hezekiah Root house from every direction.

In the enclosed house, the fraught Martha felt ripples of agony squeeze and spasm across her huge, pendulous belly, coming consistently now every few minutes. While Martha paused to relax in a moment of inaction, Betty set to work gently smearing and soothing Martha's private "woman parts" with fresh butter.

Hour after monotonous hour passed on into the night. For long minutes, Martha could not even identify where the pain commenced. It obliterated and numbed her entire body and brain! She could not think and only knew she existed in the world because there was the arresting, stupefying pain. In the beginning, she could regroup herself between the tormenting contractions, but they came harder and closer together till it seemed as if every part of her was wracked with agony. Poor tortured Martha tried to get into a comfortable – or less painful – position by pacing, crouching, kneeling or sitting down over every inch of the room in the intervals between her bearing pains. Sometimes Martha was unable to endure what a moment before she had begged for. Sometimes she begged for someone to rub her back but then she would seize up and exclaim that she couldn't stand to be touched! Whether she stood paralyzed with pain or walked back and forth, a stream of prayers alternated with yelps, howls, screams and heavy breathing from the laboring woman. All of her women helpers cooed softly to Martha how strong she was, how her travails were progressing well, how she could endure the pains, how she must be strong for her babies, how they had all lived through this, too. One of her helpers would pace with Martha across and around the room, then another would take over. One would support her leaning weight, followed by another when that one grew tired; each in their turns. As the hours wore on Martha's strength waned. She sweated profusely with every move.

Her midwives checked for her stretching and the opening of her birth passage as well as Martha's discharges of bile, vomit, excrement, blood and mucus. The first baby was descending to present itself to life!

"Oh, dear God! Oh, dear Lord! Now I know what hell is!" screamed Martha through her pains. Her rhythmic sobbing pants – "Awh, awh, awh, awh, awh, awh, awh, awh" - sounded like the bleating of an animal caught in the teeth of its killer.

Mindwell and Betty had, naturally, considered on how they would get Martha's testimony of paternity during her travails. Mindwell must ask at the absolute worst contractions squeezing across her body and at the moment of most insupportable pain, when Martha was close to presenting the first baby's crowning head and when most of the helper-women were close at hand to listen well as witnesses. Mindwell would ask repeatedly with the warning to Martha that she could die during the worst pangs and should never leave behind in this world a false accusation! They must press her to speak truly and at her worst extremity what man had had his way with her? This happened as the morning was lighting, after they all had been at the work all the night.

"Martha Root, name the man who is the father to these babies! Martha, tell us, who fathered these babies?"

Martha was being held by her women under her arms as she leaned on a ladder-back chair grunting fiercely and crying, "I can't, I can't take any more."

Her eyes looked dull and dreary. She was clearly exhausted, but the deepest recesses of her brain knew that she must name "Elisha Hawley" – firmly and without any hesitation or reservation. Aunt Sarah Root wiped her perspiring face, while Mother Martha coaxed the young Martha to answer, "Martha, you must answer and you must answer in all God's truth!"

"Martha, who is the father of these babies? Name him – and only him – who is the very true father thereof!" Mindwell Parsons continued to prod her.

Across the stirring farm fields, where lifeless corn stalk stubble littered the clumpy earth, at the Hope Root house, Martha Root's scream "Elisha Hawley! Elisha Hawley! Elisha Hawley is the father!" could be heard in the dawn lull of inactivity.

"Martha Root, do you swear on the *Holy Bible* to the truth of what you have just said?"

"Yes, yes, I do I do, I do, I do, I do..." her voice trailed off weakly.

"Martha, do you swear and affirm before God and all here that Elisha Hawley is the father of the babies? Martha, are you well and truly certain?"

"… yes, yes…"

"Martha, do you swear, on penalty of death on the Day of Judgment that what you have told us is true about the father of these babes?"

With her mind long past rational thinking, Martha Root muttered some assent and wept with her aching. She was too tired and twinged and twisted with hurting to shout any more. Mindwell gently continued the questioning a bit longer to satisfy everyone beyond any doubt as to Martha's testimony during her travails. Now the midwives could attest before the Justices of the Court that Martha Root had named Elisha Hawley as the father of her babies: no one else.

The hours of Martha Root's delivery dragged on terribly and agonizingly protracted. It felt as if one was postponing the longest possible stretch to draw each and every breath. No one could be diverted from thinking on any other topic. They held hands and prayed, hummed or softly sang hymns for many hours.

But the last minutes before the first babe pushed its head through the mother's passage dragged on - as time always decelerates in the most severe and intense events. Her women felt suffocated as they waited with their nerves tingling. Every heart was galloping. Every attention was focused on the task at hand. Every woman felt the anxiety of this highest drama and was completely immersed in and exhausted by it. The midwives were now fixated on the crowning of a ball of tousled and slimy hair ramming its way into the world as its beleaguered mother panted and rolled her eyes back. Martha felt she was at the absolute end of her endurance.

"Yes, Martha, yes! You are almost there, darling Martha! Easy, easy. Your baby is almost here. Your baby is almost born, Martha. Be strong, Martha."

How miraculous that something as delicate and ephemeral as a word could instantly overpower, empower and absolutely change one's perspective! Mere words! That Martha had felt she could not endure a second more of this torture and just begged God to let her die, then straightaway, her mind was stripped clean and transformed by the shout, "Your baby's almost here! Here comes your baby!"

It was as a ray of sunlight shoots through a dark bank of storm clouds. It was like lifting a gauze of linen from one's face to sudden clarity!

With a blessed squirt of sudden relief, the struggle of a bruised baby, hovering between life and death had battered her way into the living world! Every heart paused long seconds as they waited for the cry of the infant's first breath.

Midwife Mindwell handed the glazed lump of humanity to one of the assistants to hold and wipe down with warm wine and fresh water, as Mindwell unplugged the mucus smeared across the baby's nose and mouth. Working with the quick skill of many prior experiences, Mindwell carefully glided the baby's dark, throbbing navel string next to her mother's thigh. When a gasp for air broke forth into a full cry, all the women felt overwhelming true elation and gushes of tears erupted! Big Martha sensed her soul rise to heaven with the most exquisite joy and gratitude! Hallelujah to her Lord and Savior! A powerful cry burst forth which quickly dissolved into an unrestrained deluge of blubbering. Of course, none felt more so than the new mother of a "living child" who was gratefully stunned by the cessation of the interminable birth pains! Water poured out of her haggard red eyes as she gasped and panted.

"Is it alive? Is it a perfect living child?" gasped the new mother.

With the baby's cry accomplished Mindwell Parsons would now be able to tie off the naval cord four fingers' width from its little deep-red, wrinkled body. Immediately, a cozy swaddling cloth was tenderly wrapped around her and the newly-born girl was set on her side next to her mother's leg.

"Martha, Martha, you've borned a perfect, lusty baby girl!" crowed her overjoyed mother with deep appreciation. Martha Bridgman Root felt such a powerful rush of emotions flooding over her that she streamed tears of joy. After caressing young Martha's hair, Big Martha staggered into the arms of Aunt Sarah Root (her sister-in-law) who hugged her with indescribable tenderness. The grandmother Martha's entire body tingled with the most profound relief. Every one of the attending women felt jubilant!

Once the next twin was delivered, Mindwell would make sure all the afterbirths had detached from Martha's womb within and the great dangers would then be passed - assuming nothing untoward happened...

The helper-women waited patiently for the second twin to present, powered by the knowledge of the first successful delivery. Previously, they had chattered inconsequential "noise" to distract Martha and themselves. Now, however, all grew serious in their awareness that the midwives could not let too much time pass with no activity. The women were growing nervous, but feigned to show no fear. They urged the lagging Martha to continue walking, squatting, and moving to bring the baby down into the birth passage. Velvety words of encouragement were murmured as they stroked her back.

Every few minutes the midwives stroked Martha's immense globe of belly to feel the position of the second baby. (No one could remember such an enormous protrusion as Martha Root's gut.) Mindwell would try to lay on hands to align the position of the babe within. The day was wearing on from morning to afternoon. As lightning hides within dark thunderous clouds of storms, so here emotions were crackling below visibility in the sick room.

Just when the second baby's head crowned and seemed to be ready to come into the world, it slid back into her mother's birth passage! "Oouuhh!" all crooned. This baby was being born upside down which then caused its nose to catch on Martha's tailbone and slide back inside! This baby must be born and it must happen before too long! The midwives focused intently on the second twin's position and if its naval cord was entangled. Another time the baby reverted, sliding back in again.

"I just want to die," pleaded young Martha.

The poor woman's moans would have made stones weep and splinter for sorrow. The only way for the rest of them to not dissolve in pity for her unbearable pain was to resolve to carry her through this peril. It weighed on every woman's mind that they could yet lose her in complete exhaustion or a baby stuck in the passage.

Martha Bridgman Root's eyes were a mix of terror and determination. Big Martha struggled with herself to push the terror of such a possible loss to the back recesses of her brain. She must do this for young Martha! She fought the thought that her daughter could peter out and die here before her. Her eyes were pools of watery anxiety. The Roots' world was their love of their family and their religion. These were Mother Martha's first concerns every morning and last thoughts every night as she swooned off liltingly into ephemeral sleep.

If it was God's predetermined plan for Martha to die in childbirth, then it would certainly be. They had been taught that all of their efforts together or anything one could do herself would not avert God's true plan for the world. BUT if it was not young Martha's destiny to die in this childbirth, then her mother must marshal all the strength within her daughter to fight to live and deliver this second baby. Her mother grabbed young Martha's face with both hands and glared into her wan eyes with enough willpower to fire up the younger woman. "Martha, my dear Martha! One baby is here. One baby is already borned! You must endure this and bring forth your other baby. It is God's curse on Eve, on all women. You are strong, Martha! This baby is almost born. It's almost here. You must push out this baby!"

As Big Martha instilled the strength to carry on in her daughter, she guided young Martha onto the lap of a helper seated nearby. They reached under her arms to hold her in place as she pushed down. "Push Martha, now! Push!"

Mindwell Parsons lightly slithered her fingers and hand up into young Martha's birth passage toward the stuck baby! It was a life-or-death moment! This baby must come! "Bear down with everything's left in you, Martha! Push down against me! Now!"

The laboring mother howled "Nooooooooooo!" in blaring anguished suffering. Young Martha had never ever experienced or imagined such excruciating agony! Nothing else seemed to exist in the world, except this blinding scream of pain, which seemed to growl forth from the center of the earth itself! The yowl of insufferable agony was awful to hear – and so much more to exert it! It used up all the air in Martha's lungs! It cleared away any cloud of doubt about the painful cost of these births. But by some miracle, Mindwell must have caught the intransigent squirming baby and now pulled it out to life! Midwife Betty was at young Martha's side to catch the afterbirth and the blue string attached to it. Betty grabbed more hands full of guts and garbages that spewed out. The new mother was insensate and had collapsed gasping with her body almost in fits.

The second baby – another red, wrinkled and squawking girl – had been born! Relief swept across all the women, as a large wave crashes a beach. Sighs and happy utterances filled the room.

"Martha Root, brought to bed and delivered two perfect living twins! Hallelujah!"

"Martha, with God's good graces, you've done the work of two mothers!"

"Praise the Lord, who has preserved our dear Martha!"

Before the celebrations could begin, Mindwell and Betty were at the last tasks. "Dear Martha, we know you're tired, but you have to get up and walk a bit now," Mindwell told her.

Martha Root was debilitated with fatigue. So tired was she that she did not feel Betty applying compresses and bandages to her abdomen and thighs (a cold draft could cause a flux to a new mother). Her scarlet face was a flood of tears and pulsing veins. "We got to clean up your bedding and it's time we get some hearty nourishment into you, Marthie."

As they lifted and tenderly walked her about, the ecstatic group of women cleaned and fondled the new mother of two "perfect living children."

"You're a true mother now, Martha! Twice at once!" congratulated Aunt Sarah.

Whimpering, Martha allowed her mother and cousin to raise her up from where she had been sitting on her cousin's lap.

"That's it, dearie. Come, come, a little more. In a bit they'll have the "groaning meal" for all the ladies and the feverfew tea ready for you, dear one. After we all refresh ourselves, we'll all rest and sleep here a bit. The large group of overjoyed, but exhausted, women were all gathered around. "Just walk a little more, precious darling."

Before the end of "sitting up week," the twin babies should be named. Traditionally, the mother or grandmother's name would be selected. In such a case, that name would be "Martha" for them both but the Roots were not traditionalists, and young Martha was a determined, non-tradition-bound Root woman.

The Biblical story of Mary and Martha at John 11:21-26 occurred to her:

"Martha told Jesus, "Lord, if you had been here, my brother
would not have died But even now I know that God will give
you whatever you ask him."
Jesus told Martha, "Your brother will come back to life."
Martha answered Jesus, "I know that he'll come back to life on
the last day, when everyone will come back to life."
Jesus said to her, "I am the one who brings people back to life,
and I am life itself. Those who believe in me will live even if they
die. Everyone who lives and believes in me will never die. Do
you believe that?"

The import of the verse disturbed young Martha. In the tale, the Biblical Martha had continued sweeping the floor and was distracted in the face of a great miracle.

"God has truly favored me," sighed young Martha feebly. It struck her that the name "Anne" meant "God has favored me." Thus, it was decided for the first and bigger of the twin girls. Meanwhile, as her mother hugged and caressed her with relief, love and joy, she whispered to her daughter, "Every Christian should readily and cheerfully venture his all to serve the people of God when a time of distress and danger calleth for it,' so wrote the Reverend Mr. Cotton Mather." It had truly been "a time of distress and danger."

Like the Jewish queen "Esther," the second of Martha's twins had been "the hidden one." Mother Martha Bridgman Root and new mother Martha liked Esther in acknowledgment of undaunted courage and also that Queen Esther was said to be beautiful. They knew well too of their pastor, Jonathan Edwards' strong-willed daughter Esther, named after her grandmother and great-grandmother.

"Anne Hawley," pronounced Martha aloud. "And Esther Hawley."

"Beautiful," clucked Martha Bridgman Root. "God be praised for his mercies."

The news spread quickly through the community of Martha's safe delivery of twin girls. At the Hawley household on Pudding Lane, this reminded Rebekah Hawley of her own older sister Esther, "the beauty," (mother of Jonathan Edwards) with whom she had always feuded. Rebekah thought to herself, "Esther and Anne, what puffery to name the daughters of a weaver's daughter after queens!"

But now - beyond the Roots' earlier verbal allegations that Elisha Hawley was the father, there would be the actual legal proof of the midwives' testimony before the Inferior Court of Common Pleas. Should Martha Root appear and name Elisha as the father of her bastard children and be examined under oath, the midwives might then be called to testify. Mindwell and Betty could affirm that Martha Root had accused Elisha in her travails.

Martha Root would be lying-in for a month after the births to receive congratulatory visits from friends and relatives. The Root family felt deep gratitude to God for young Martha's blessed deliverance. Soon they would ask for prayers by their church brethren and for the baptisms of the baby girls.

Some days later, at the tense frontier Fort Massachusetts, Lieutenant Elisha Hawley received a letter that began,

"Burn this letter immediately once you have read it…."

Chapter 11
Dying and Trying Times
Northampton, July-November 1747

"Oh, sorrowful world!" breathed mother Martha Bridgman Root. "Dear Lord, only you can save these towns from ruin! Preserve your undeserving people!"

The sturdy matriarch Martha Bridgman Root's hand fluttered to her heart with overwhelming emotion as tears flowed down her face: Mother Martha was relieved to have her sons Joseph and Simeon home in Northampton, back from scouts out in the wilderness woods. Every eligible man was being sent out to patrol and detect incursions by the French and their Indian allies. Once returned the young men told terrifying tales of people pitilessly attacked: farmers hacked to death while harvesting a wheat field or walking an isolated path; "praying Indians" (friendly to the English) betrayed by greedy whites; militia men shot at or soldiers' fighting hand-to-hand in dark forests; chasing Indians down with dogs who shredded their bodies to pulp; scalpings; kidnappings of children; barns and crops torched; and other most dreadful mayhem.

Men carried their guns to the meetinghouse by order of the Governor. It seemed the world was aflame with danger, killing, death, grievous injury and senseless destruction. Daily this calamitous war brought rumors and reports of more disasters for the English colonies. As a mother, Big Martha welled with tears at each account. Her own family, neighbors or dear friends might be a next victim, which caused her to dissolve sometimes in crying spasms. In fact, Martha Bridgman Root's cousin, Jonathan Bridgeman,[12] had died miserably in a Quebec prison only a few months before. Mother Martha was a tough woman, but it was hard to sleep some nights. Days were draining with their endless worries. She was always on a jittery nerve edge. Everyone felt at the ready to hear a scream of, "Run for your lives!"

Beyond the drum beat of violence, an epidemic raged as well! As God's will would have it, the summer of 1747 brought a scorching measles epidemic which consumed many by fever accompanied by its garish red, pus-filled welts. The dread of infection slowed commerce as well as social life. Daily routines were

---

[12] This is not a spelling error. Although first cousins, their names were recorded differently in documents. Martha's father, John's name is spelled both Bridgman and Bridgeman within his last Will and the Probating of it! (He is the same man in chapter 1.) Similarly, Jonathan's name is recorded both ways but is "Bridgeman" in John Montague Smith's *History of the Town of Sunderland, Massachusetts, 1673-1899*. Press of E. A. Hall (Greenfield, Mass, 1899). See page 118.

84

upturned. Fright underwrote every action. For example, most people wouldn't walk by the house of an infected family for fear of the bad air there. The Reverend Mr. Jonathan Edwards called for "holy lives and Christian practice" from his parish to offer for "the great mercy of God." Surely, every member of the First Church congregation offered personal prayers. Many fasted for relief.

Laudanum being unavailable, Doctor Samuel Mather prescribed bloodletting, cold bathing, pukes, purges and potions of willow bark, henbane, pennyroyal or the shiny black berry of nightshade for his patients to ease the burning throats and bodies.

The remains of those who had died of the disease were carried to the Bridge Street Cemetery at night by way of the meadows, avoiding the town center. To ward off contagion, every victim was buried in a tarred sheet rather than a burying cloth. Further, they were buried without ceremony in the middle of the night. How terrible it had been for the lifeless corpses to be carried to the cemetery without the proper Christian mourning!

People recounted that a baby born with six fingers in an up-river town had died soon after its painful birth; probably it was connected somehow. Some said that a pesthouse should be built by the town. Others said it was enough to avoid the night miasmas and humors. Everywhere were heard lamentations, "Oh mournfulest day that ever mine eyes saw!"

"These are wearisome and tedious days."

"Oh, the vengeance of the Lord is mighty!"

"The Lord punishes Massachusetts Bay for its neglect of religion!" or "The Lord punishes Massachusetts Bay because its people violate his Commandments."

"God has had a great controversy with the country for many years. Woe to new-England!"

A minister in one of the country towns had proclaimed, "Forasmuch as it hath pleased God to visit the capital town of this province, and other towns within the same with a contagious malignant pleurisy, and putrid fever in some places, measles, which hath proved mortal to great numbers of persons…. Thus, partly by the smallpox, fevers of one kind and another and the throat distemper, we are wasted away! The Lord of vengeance reaps among us for our wickedness and our turn away from his laws."

Measles struck Northampton hard. In June, Benoni Wright lost all his children to the disease. One after another came news of families infected. In August, Lieutenant William Lyman's wife and daughter, both named Rachel, died, as had both Lieutenant Nathaniel Phelps and Samuel Phelps' twins, both sets dying.

At the homes of Hope and Hezekiah Root, when Aunt Sarah and Baby Esther both began coughing, mother Martha Bridgman Root sternly instructed daughter Martha to stay away from the sick room, "I'll care for Esther and Sarah. You're needed for Anne and the rest of the family. Stay out!"

Big Martha ate, slept and never left the sickroom except to use the outhouse (when no one was already out there and she took a path around the far side of the house to get there). Husband Hezekiah, Uncle Hope, Aunt Sarah's daughter-in-law and young Martha murmured in through the door every few hours to ask for news. It broke their hearts to have their dearest ones begging for relief, yet they could provide only prayer and counsel the sick to prepare to "meet their maker." It was a dying time with the women of almost every family in the town frantically caring for someone miserably ill and quarantined in the back rooms of their houses.

As it would be, the smaller weaker of Martha's twin, baby Esther, died pitifully sputtering and wheezing her tiny lungs out. Aunt Sarah Root cried and screamed that her throat was scalded - when she drank a sip of cold well water! After all their sufferings, Aunt Sarah and baby Esther expired with soft, whimpering exhales the same day, September 14, 1747.

The dead baby and old aunt lay as stiff as logs of wood in the sick room. That night the grieving Root families would hold their own double funeral attended only by them, lacking the wailing as they were all too depleted to weep and wail.

The thought of precious baby Esther and dear old Aunt Sarah, who had assuaged Martha in her childbirth, carried to the grave without "decent Christian burial" troubled her soul. Martha's thoughts vacillated wildly. Sometimes she was unable to concentrate to read her Bible. At these moments, she simply sat and stared ahead. She contemplated that she must sink entirely under this yoke, "How evilly I have walked in God's sight. Yet the Lord still showed mercy to me and upheld me, and as he wounded me with one hand, so he healed me with the other." Young Martha could not sit still, but rocked herself for hours. At other times she walked and paced back and forth, grieving and lamenting her profound loss. Her heart felt slashed. Abysmal sorrow lay upon her spirit. She had suffered everything for her babes and now, one was gone and the other was listless.

After the feverish deaths of baby Esther and Aunt Sarah, poor baby Anne developed colic and distress. Would she be the next to burn herself out with the terrible fever? New-mother Martha cooed and cooled her forehead, singing lullabies to the agitated infant,

"You become what you love, and you were born to love and be
loved.
"You will be loved, you will be loved… and You will live in
love…"

The heavy days sluggishly unwound and Anne healed, but there was no return to before for Martha Root. Her social standing felt unnatural and outside the laws of God and the church: she was neither a young girl, nor a respected matron in the community. She. was not a "goodwife" of her own domicile. Although not a maid, yet she was no one's wife. The father of her babes and the man who she had hoped for as a husband, Elisha Hawley, was gone - shunted off to the frontier without a glance of sorrowful or pensive goodbye.

In her loneliest moments, Martha sobbed silently, clinging to baby Anne with the love that had deepened from knowing loss. Every cough or gurgle out of Anne seized Martha's heart with panic and gave her shivers for Anne's life. But even nights when Martha lay exhausted in their warm homespun sheets and rolled over to nurse, she was grateful to be reassured that Anne was still alive, another day, in spite of all. Martha nuzzled her baby's silky pure skin and fuzz of hair, and shed tears like raindrops.

Miles beyond Northampton's verdant valley farm fields and pastures, up the sloping woodland hills rising up to the rocky mountainous frontier, Martha knew Elisha Hawley too rested his head in the same mysterious expanse of night. Under the same moon, stars, and sun. He existed in the same serene and evocative lull. He was gone. Did Elisha lie awake and think of her? Ever? Did he imagine gazing upon their favored daughter Anne's face? Martha treasured gurgling baby Anne as a unique and exquisite being, but what did Elisha feel? Anything? Had he forgotten their loving hours together? Did he merely put her and Anne away in the farthest recesses of his mind without a backward glance? Heavily laden tears streamed from Martha's groggy eyes. Just asking herself these questions made her heart feel cruelly ravaged and smashed, stripped bare and shamed. She had experienced love - and pitilessly lost it.

In the midst of these vicious times, tiny Anne's fight for life empowered Martha to carry on each day. Big Martha told her daughter, "Acknowledge as a favor of God that Anne remains alive, Martha. Know that God lays upon us less than we abominable sinners deserve. Remember that comfortable Scripture from the Psalms, "I shall not die, but live, and declare the works of the Lord. So that all, that are both far and near, may see his mighty power." What shall I say, my beloved daughter? It has pleased God to take your precious child Esther," said her mother. "Learn by these awful strokes to number our days, my dear. Ye time in this life is short. Soon we will be taken out of this world but how and when, only God knows."

"God hath added grief on top of my sorrow," replied her daughter resignedly. "I know it becomes me to hold my peace."

The deaths were recorded in the town book, *"Register of the Deaths in Northampton"*:

> Sep^t. 14, 1747 Sarah Root wife of Hope Root died
> Sep^t. 14, 1747 Esther Root daug^h of Martha Root died it being
>   one of her twins

The Root family informed Joseph Hawley, who had been elected as Town Clerk, that "Esther Hawley died on September 14, 1747." Joseph, however, had inscribed it as "Esther, daughter of Martha Root" and refused to write "Esther Hawley."

"Know you that under the law a fatherless child is 'filius nullius' or 'no one's child' under the law. As no marital union exists between my brother Elisha and said Martha Root, the child cannot be named "Hawley" under the law," stated Joseph blandly.

His face was taut and his voice harsh, as the entire issue of the twins' conception and birth severely discomposed him. He wanted to say nothing at all on the subject, because as a barrister, Joseph knew that even a "no one's child" was entitled to the support of the parish or the alleged father, if he were proven to be the father. Joseph Hawley felt a weltering rage, combined with alarm, inside when confronting these troublesome Roots. He thought (although he did not speak it), "Insolent upstarts."

For Martha Root, it was another bitter disgrace. She had – sadly mistakenly - trusted Elisha's professions of love and prospective devotion to her. Together they had been "awakened" in the "Great Awakening."[13] Together they had "owned" Reverend Edwards' covenant in 1742. They both had declared their

---

[13] The Great Awakening was a powerful religious revival (mainly) of the mid-1740s. See: https://en.wikipedia.org/wiki/Great_Awakening or
https://www.britannica.com/event/Great-Awakening

"covenants of grace" for full church membership.[14] With their church admission, they had both sworn their allegiance to walk the straight and narrow path of the Lord. They had slipped in that upright walk (in their fornication outside of marriage), yes, but submission could restore them to the fellowship of the faithful! Yet, here was Elisha apparently disavowing the truth of their lying together, discrediting their promises to each other, denying the town, history and even their church morals! Could she ever believe a grandson of "the Divine Stoddard" would lie to the Court and church?! How could it be that the daughter of a weaver would be more devoted to their church and the "One True Saving Religion?!" Had he not truly been "converted?" Was his conversion one only of convenience?

What a dismal slap to her beliefs! She felt utterly destroyed.

Her mother tried to comfort her, "Martha, dear Martha, listen to me. Life is what matters, not what is written on paper. That base villain Joseph Hawley can refuse to write the babies' true names in the book, but everyone knows they are who they are. They are fathered by Elisha Hawley! It is written on the babies' faces. They are adored and beloved, your beautiful babes. Just as you are, my Martha. You are strong, Martha. Gather up your fortitude and believe in your mighty God. Fall on your Rock and Salvation, Martha!"

"How ignorant and undeserving am I," murmured young Martha in assent. She resolved that she must use this mortification to examine, re-examine, regenerate and re-dedicate herself to God.

Then in the blustery chill of late autumn, the court sent a summons for Martha Root to appear before the Hampshire County Inferior Court of Common Pleas on the charge of "fornication." She must answer for her crime of unclean lascivious behavior outside of marriage, both a civil and ecclesiastical crime. Dressed still in her somber mourning clothes for the deaths of Aunt Sarah and Baby Esther, the young woman appeared at the Northampton court-house on November 11, 1747. She was accompanied by her father Hezekiah and her extremely tall, red-headed brother-in-law, Charles Phelps, husband of her older sister Dolly. As the crowd of court attendees sat on planks at the back of the unheated building, the six justices of the Court filed in with their curled and powdered wigs and black robes.

'Oyez, Oyez, silence is commanded in this court while his Majesty's Justices are sitting. All manner of persons that have business to do with this court,

---

14 For a comprehensive explanation of the theology, see Alan D. Strange "Jonathan Edwards and the Communion Controversy," in the Bibliography.

draw near and give your attendance. If anyone has any plaint to enter or suit to prosecute, let them come forth and they shall be heard. God save the King," announced the Justice's Assistant.

The 12 men constituting a trial jury and 16 grand jurors sat at the front ready to be called for specific cases. Chief Justice John Stoddard, tall and distinguished, had each case called up to stand before the justices and plead to the charges against them. First,

"Israel Williams versus Samuel Wells"
"John Pegilly versus David Smith"
Nathaniel Downing versus Joseph Owen"
"Samuel Smith versus Thomas Mather"
and on…

Just as Martha was called for her confession, baby Anne began to whimper and fuss. Martha frantically attempted to quiet the infant, but brother-in-law Phelps whispered, "Sister Martha, let the babe cry if she will. I see that it disconcerts Esquire Joseph Hawley and Chief Justice Stoddard. Let them hear the cries of the babe their kinsman has fathered but neglects to acknowledge."

Charlie Phelps considered it odd that Martha's was the only fornication case called at this court session. Normally, there was a string of fornication cases. The flamboyant and peculiar Charlie Phelps sat in obvious satisfaction, lightly smiling and staring at the justices as Anne's cries grew. Attorney Hawley (the Court Assistant and acting as Elisha's lawyer) and Chief Justice John Stoddard (Elisha's uncle) shifted uncomfortably in their seats. Chief Justice Stoddard demanded impatiently, "What is the disturbance in this court?"

To which Charles Phelps jumped to his feet and answered with thickly slathered sarcasm, "Begging the court's pardon, your most esteemed and honorable honor. It is the bastard child of Elisha Hawley by spinster Martha Root, here attending."

In the crowd at the back, both gasps of shock and snickers were squelched (but still heard). An irate John Stoddard hammered down his gavel thunderously and ordered, "Remove the disturbance!"

Hezekiah Root's backbone stiffened and he stood inflexibly next to his daughter. Brother-in-law Charles, aiding Martha to rise, mumbled softly to her, "Remove yourself and the babe, Martha - but be in no rush."

Justice Stoddard bent over to a fellow robed justice and breathed, "I know the old man: that's the weaver Root, but who is the younger man there? The red-haired one? Is that the son of Lieutenant Nathaniel Phelps, recently deceased?"

"Yes, Colonel, it is," replied the justice. "He's the husband of the fornicator's sister."

"Hhhhmmm, indeed," uttered the Chief Justice with unconcealed anger on his lined face. A glistening drop of sweat hung at the end of his nose in a suspended state of inanimation for several long seconds. The justices stared at it, waiting for it to drop.

Joseph Hawley seethed to himself with cold fury in the front row seating, He thought that this, Phelps, is not Shakespearean theatre. This is a court of law. But you are only a bricklayer and, you, obviously, know no decorum! The more I see of the representatives of the people, like Phelps, the more I admire my dogs!

Although it was end of the court session, Chief Justice Stoddard saw that the crowd at the back of the court house had not diminished. "These damnable voyeurs want to hear all the delectable details," groused the justice to himself with a combination of denunciation and erupting embarrassment.

Mistress Martha Root was called back into court to return and plead. She walked slowly to the front and stood staunchly erect with her father behind her. "Spinster" Martha Root mouthed the necessary formulaic words to confess herself guilty and stopped abruptly. The attendees questioned if this had been practiced? The sentence's finish had been loped off.

The audience sat in unmoving silence to catch every moment, gesture and word. Sneering in their minds, the rabble thought, "Not one of these justices will question *this witness* in *this case* about whether she wore "enticing garb" in luring *this male fornicator* in his "carnal knowledge" or whether their "unclean behavior" was done in the Middle Meadowland, the Root's back acres, or in old widow Hawley's cheese house itself! Ha! Those old dissemblers!"

In contrast to the court audience, the other gentlemen justices at the front and nervous jurors averted their eyes from Chief Justice Stoddard, defendant Root and Esquire Hawley in the greatest chagrin. No one wanted to express the slightest indication of any abnormality or seeming interest. Absolutely no one budged as everyone prayed for someone else to break the silent spell over the room. Finally, the court recorder wrote:

"Martha Root Confessed herself Guilty of the Crime of
Fornication ordered to pay a fine of 25 shills of ye last Emission
and Cost. February 9, 1747/8"

Nonetheless, for the court, there remained the unfinished business of
Elisha Hawley's role in the fornication. As even the most naïve schoolboy would
recognize, it took two persons to fornicate. Some among the townsfolk were
already expressing "murmuring thought" over Elisha's apparent dearth of
repentance and punishment.

"That rascal, that immoral fellow, Hawley has fled righteous punishment."

Although - strangely - Elisha Hawley's name was omitted from the record,
he would be required to appear at a future session of the Court on May 17th of the
next year. Indeed, it took two to fornicate!

The engorged cumulous clouds in the early winter sky were washed with a rainbow of delicate highlights of the sunset, but the Chief Justice did not notice either the lumination or the nipping hard cold. Colonel John Stoddard walked vigorously to his home the Manse from the town court house with sparks firing in his dark eyes and thunder knitting together his eyebrows. The court session had not gone well, disavowing him of the notion that things had been discretely arranged by his nephew Joseph Hawley. Instead, the court cases had almost all been heard, when that pettifogger Charles Phelps had stirred the hot pot of trouble by goading on that irksome fornication case among the people there. The countryside would be all a-twitter with it.

The door slamming alerted Justice Stoddard's wife Prudence that the Colonel carried sweeping anger and piled up worries home with him today. He tossed his elaborate periwig of powdered curls and his crimson judicial robe at the table with choler. "Fornication, drunkenness, filthy dalliance, breach of Sabbath…" he fumed. "It's all so tiring, wife."

"Without a doubt, husband," she replied cautiously.

"These fornication accusations have become as common as petty offenses like illegal dancing, idleness, cursing, smoking on the Sabbath. It fatigues me much, I tell you, you've no idea how tiresome that mob of countrymen at the sessions courts are."

"Without question," Prudence tried to uplift him.

"But worst of all is dealing with my own…" he spat inadvertently through his teeth. "…my sister."

Prudence Chester Stoddard gasped, "Sister Rebekah didn't appear in the court house, did she?"

"No, thankfully, no! I did warn her to stay away and that she did. However, it's her refusal to accept my counsel and forbear and hold her tongue in the town. She flatly refuses to understand that there must be some …. some… consequences for her wayward rake of a son. And he can't skip the few shillings fine for fornication, while the woman pays. She confessed in court today but the family created a ruckus in doing so."

"How so?"

"Phelps, the brother-in-law of the Root woman, had to cry out my nephew's name – as she was approaching the bench. He feigned to make it appear innocent but it was anything but that, I can assure you! He wanted to be sure to remind that rabble of dumb dogs of young Hawley's departure from the town and avoidance of sanctions." The colonel paused, "And he managed to stir up half a riot, doing so – particularly amongst the rabble women."

The aristocratic Stoddard smirked and continued, "As my father repeatedly observed, 'We have no reason to think that Christ would entrust the government of his church - and this town - to men so incapable of governing.' But of course, Phelps wanted to implicate me with Hawley's dodging it all."

Prudence discreetly declined to continue the conversation, but the spring of her husband's ill temper was wound up so tightly that he continued in his exasperation. "And, as if my vexatious and prideful sister weren't enough for even the patient Biblical Job, nephew Edwards also refuses to moderate his stance an inch whatsoever! The learned-but-impractical Reverend intones the punishments as if we live in the days of the Israelites, not as modern-day Englishmen of the American colonies! Yes, he is brilliant with the Scriptures but impossible with living men."

Stoddard sighed in weary exasperation, "It all almost makes me crazy."

As she served her husband a mug of "small beer" and pewter plate of roasted vegetables with venison, Prudence Stoddard noted that he appeared battered and bent by the wear on him. His back seemed more bowed.

He mumbled sullenly, "There is over much self-conceitedness, tricks everywhere and excessive pride throughout the land. Each yeoman considers himself worthy to opine on *my* decisions - no matter how well-considered! I do declare I haven't encountered such simplemindedness since that fellow swore an oath that he was swearing an oath! I tell you, wife, a time of war is a time of lying!" He calmed slightly. "They aver to the worst clankers of outright, obvious lies. Not that there isn't a sprinkling of truth even in thse worst lies and times. Without doubt though, these harrowing times are the worst of times!"

His eyes glazed while staring at the beer foam. "Then, here am I, between two immobile rocks. I only seek to resolve. I have no sinister end to serve - yet harvest all the blame!"

"Husband, no. No, you are beloved, even by Sister Hawley and Mr. Edwards. They simply bluster. You alone can find a path between them," counseled his wife. She hated his cranky moods and this one appeared likely to endure to the end of the day.

Prudence Stoddard knew this meant that Sister Hawley, her son Joseph, and the Reverend would be seeking the Colonel's counsel and intervention in the near future, even with all his responsibilities in this long, brutal war. There was so much work… It would be more burdens, more visitors and less peace in her home. Each night John Stoddard sat awake into the late darkness, writing militia orders or missives to officials in Boston by candlelight.

Joseph Hawley, cousin Israel Williams and the Colonel had been analyzing the complex personnel and command issues at the colony's remotest outpost, Fort Massachusetts in the "Line of Forts." Captain Ephraim Williams Junior (another of his more distant cousins) was in command there. It was paramount that Lieutenant Elisha Hawley continue to insinuate himself with the Captain, who was a regular visitor in Boston had his own contacts and favorites among officials, such as Uncle Stoddard's business partner, Colonel Jacob Wendell. There must be daily scouts out of the fort against the French and Indian enemies. Food was short. Severe weather had prevented resupplying them many times throughout the winter. Further, men had to be pressed into service which was very unpopular and most irksome.

In addition, as Commander of the Western Frontier, John Stoddard had to consider the political factors at the colonial capital in Boston and even the crown government in London's acquiescence to the way things were being run in the Great River Valley. Their Williams cousins and nephews had their interests too. All of these had to be balanced and counter-balanced. For example, there were the ceaseless land thefts and absorptions by the Ephraim Williams Senior clan at the Stockbridge Indian settlement which mission had wealthy and important supporters in London and Glasgow. There were endless quarrels between the Indians and the Ephraim Williams family over civil governance and land proprietorship at Stockbridge, both of which groups had their own connections to the powerful. There were unending acrimonious wranglings. Should the last town meeting's decisions be voided because a selectman called the meeting in Stockbridge to order instead of a constable? There was also John Stoddard's own request for 1000 acres of "unimproved land" (Indian land). There was the granting of liquor licenses to other Williams cousins…. and on and on.

Joseph Hawley had winced to think of how their Williams cousins in Hatfield and Stockbridge were benefitting from the Colonel's influence while he and Elisha were being left out. Joe vowed that he and Elisha must also do some land speculating in the future, that was where money was being made, not trading animal skins and leathers. "An emolument to our own private fortunes, or greasing the skids, as they say...." he thought.

Soon after the court hearing and Martha Root's fornication confession, sister Rebekah Hawley, nephew Joseph Hawley and the Reverend Mr. Jonathan Edwards (Stoddard's nephew, Hawley's cousin, and minister of their First Church) met with the Colonel over what to do with the court case, the church discipline and the lingering effects in the town.

Normally, a minister should meet privately to interview the parties in such a religious controversy to guide the miscreants to the right path. Although Mr. Edwards was meeting with Martha and the Roots, the minister had not met with Elisha, as Rebekah and Joe could never seem to provide a time when Lieutenant Elisha Hawley might be available to meet the minister.

"I'm afraid my brother is simply too occupied guarding the security of this colony to be able to give a date when he might be available to you, Mr. Edwards," Joseph insolently informed his minister cousin (once his idolized mentor). "He must tarry at the Fort for the present. We simply cannot state a precise date when he will be relieved from pressing duty in the king's service for this colony."

Joseph Hawley glanced slyly at his Uncle Stoddard to gauge his reaction. Uncle Stoddard was a close confidant of the Reverend Mr. Edwards on church matters, as the Colonel was to Joseph on civil and military affairs. So, Joe tried not to show hostility to Mr. Edwards. "One cannot hear Mr. Edwards talk for two minutes without hearing him preach," grumbled Joseph Hawley silently.

Although it was Jonathan Edwards' fervent resolution and wish not to involve himself in personalities and the petty day-to-day affairs of life, he could not help but observe that cousin Joseph Hawley had grown to detest him. Joseph's scornful expression was unobserved by Uncle Stoddard, who had turned away. Mr. Edwards chose to ignore it as was his usual custom with displays of emotion.

The Reverend Mr. Edwards worried about his wartime physical safety (his house had already been fortified) and the payment of his minister's salary. But the main urgency for him was the spiritual state of his flock and "reproving public sins" as enjoined at Timothy 5:20: "Them that sin rebuke before all, that others also may fear."

He intoned, "The censures of the church are appointed by Christ for the preventing, removing and healing of offenses in the church; for the reclaiming and gaining of offending brethren; for the deterring of others from the like offences; for purging out the leaven which may infect the whole lump; for vindicating the honor of Christ, and of his Church and the whole profession of the gospel; and for preventing the wrath of God…."

The lanky churchman stopped abruptly and turned toward his cousin, "Cousin Joseph, indeed I sincerely lament that the youth of this parish have been - many of them - much addicted to night-walking, and frequenting the taverns…even to lewd practices, wherein some by their example, have exceedingly corrupted others."

His high-pitched but somber voice paused, "Sadly, it has been their manner to get together both sexes, for mirth and jollity, in what they call "frolics." Some even have spent the night - without any regard to order in the families they belong to or indeed without any regard to family government."

Obviously, Joseph was well acquainted with this fact. It was the minister's talking down to him that Joe hated. He thought what a real bagpipe of a talker the Reverend was.

Reverend Edwards was droning on, "Where this frolicking has taken place, there have been the most frequent breakings out of gross sins," there was a lull as he delivered his verdict: "There has been fornication in particular."

Jonathan Edwards allowed a few moments of silence to absorb the import of his message.

"Cousin Hawley, children of the Church who are 'under scandal' must submit to the appointed ways of discipline that believers are ordained…" the somber clergyman felt shocked and startled by the evident disregard of his kinsman to the authority of the clergy and church. He had encountered flagrant and open dismissal of authority, of course, but from a kinsman!? Mr. Edwards' mind wandered over memories of public confession of scandals, admonitions and even excommunications in his twenty-plus-years as pastor. Excommunication!

Why, such a case had just last year presented in Northampton by Jemima Miller and Thomas Wait. Although accused in the customary manner, Wait (bull-calf of a wanton fellow that he was) denied the validity of the usual proofs and continued to insist he was innocent!

Joseph observed drily, "Fornication was a sin committed frequently in Israel."

"And seemingly in Northampton among this indolent and contemptuous youth," inserted Uncle Stoddard slyly in a low tone. "Further… if your brother Elisha was not the offender with the Root woman, then whom?"

Joseph's heart seized up with panic, but fortunately, he did not have to answer.

Jonathan Edwards recalled his cousin Joseph's reputed entanglement with liberal "Arminianism"[15] at Harvard College but advised simply, "The words can't be reasonably understood otherwise than that 'he hath humbled her and taken the liberty to use her as his wife,' and as 'tis proper none should use any woman but a wife; therefore, 'tis fit and suitable that she should indeed be his wife.'"

Joseph Hawley retorted, "She has been a person of grossly indecent character. She enticed him!"

But with pure unemotional logic Reverend Edwards responded gently, "Cousin Joseph, whatever the difficulties one meets with, how many or how great, how extenuating or inculpating, the punishments are clearly prescribed." After a brief pause for breath, he began quoting John 20:23, "'Whose soever sins ye remit, they are remitted unto them; and whose soever sins ye retain, they are retained.'"

"Mr. Edwards…" Joseph Hawley tried to interrupt.

"The punishment is Christ's, who is the sole head of the church," the Reverend intoned. "Cursers, swearers, blasphemers, all whoremongers and fornicators and adulterers, all drunkards, ranters and profaners of the Lord's Day must be punished and acknowledge their sin. As Christ commands at Matthew 18, '…if he shall neglect to hear them, tell it unto the church: but if he neglect to hear the church, let him be unto thee as an heathen man and a publican.'"

Joseph Hawley finally realized that he could not out argue Jonathan Edwards on Scripture. It would be best to ignore his interjections, but his Uncle Stoddard inserted himself next.

"Joseph, admittedly, there is some basis for the accusation. It is the common fame in the community that Elisha has been seen repeatedly with the Root woman far beyond the norm and in-and-out of the ordinary places. I have it on good source that he was seen conversing very familiarly with this young Root

---

[15] Arminianism was a liberalization of Calvinistic theology by the Dutchman Jacobus Arminius early in the 1600's. Arminius advanced the free will of man in their salvation, as opposed to Luther, Calvin and other Protestant Reformers who believed in divine predestination and election. For more, see: https://en.wikipedia.org/wiki/Arminianism

woman as she brought in the cows one evening. My own wife has noticed them both crossing paths frequently over on Schoolhouse Lane. She noted them conversing very closely. He was said to be standing up close to her - his face to hers!" interrupted the older man.

A long minute of silence ensued in which the men listened to the noises of Colonel Stoddard's wife and young children in a room nearby. The Colonel and Joseph Hawley sweated profusely. Reverend Edwards appeared sublimely content. Joseph thought resentfully that the Reverend must enjoy levying justice and punishing transgressors. He bit his lip.

"Have you not noted that the Root woman visits her Uncle Bridgman across from your homestead often?" queried John Stoddard. In truth the Colonel was dissatisfied with the entire younger generation of descendants, except cousin Israel Williams. They were capable enough but exhibited little self-restraint in most matters according to the Colonel. Not like the vaunted days of old…

"You yourself know that Elisha was at the Root house. Your mother confronted him there that night," reasoned the colonel. (It was unnecessary to specify which night as the incident was of universal fame throughout the town. It was an incident of deep embarrassment to the Colonel). "Has he denied it?" asked the Colonel acerbically.

Joseph's silence hung as heavy as a prisoner's rusted iron ball and chain, as his uncle blazed on, "Perhaps you should ask him? It does seem pertinent, doesn't it, Mr. Edwards?"

Colonel Stoddard then turned away from his nephew, the Reverend Mr. Edwards to nephew Mr. Joseph Hawley. "Nephew, I should have thought with your legal readings you would have read the 1692 Acts and Resolves of this Colony?"

After clearing his throat, Uncle Stoddard continued, "Particularly on point would be the chapter on the 'Punishment of Criminal Offenders …. as in 'Fornication.'"

He turned directly to stand before Joseph Hawley and demanded, "You have read the 1692 statute, haven't you, Esquire?"

The interview was becoming more unsettling and unwieldy with each ticking second. "Besides, the townswomen absolutely will not cease in their prattling on about it…" added his uncle with further displeasure.

"Those Roots are troublesome, impudent, low-class upstarts trying to move above their stations in life," muttered Joseph under his breath.

"Without a doubt, nephew, but I cannot have continual uproar and contention in the town. As Commander of the Western Frontier, I must conserve the peace within the town," stated the Colonel flatly. "We are at war! And this public infamy engenders disunity and dissent. The women jabber constantly over it. Every Sabbath and evening service, the Root woman comes to meeting as an unmarried spinster with a bastard child! There are inflamed remarks to my wife at every Sabbath service! It cannot be sustained."

With the thought of his mother's unequivocal instructions on his mind, Joseph peeped out rather feebly, "Uncle, the Root woman cannot prove her absolute virginity."

"Clearly the current evidence is against her…" said his uncle with obvious sarcasm. "… which she has confessed."

"Sir, I mean, she cannot prove her absolute virginity *at the time*," Joseph corrected himself with acute humiliation.

"Then it should be no problem to produce witnesses to so testify, shouldn't it?" retorted his uncle. "And, of course, your brother can stand as one of the two required witnesses to the fornication and her lack of virginity." Joseph now began to doubt the friendliness of his uncle to his brother's cause. "Bring your witnesses, Joseph."

"Or, of course, she can simply marry any other man," pronounced Joseph faintly.

"Fine, then have her do so," determined John Stoddard. "…if you can," Stoddard paused to offer wryly. "Just realize that the town will not likely undertake the bastard's support in order to release your brother from it."

Joseph Hawley fumed inside. "Payment, which I consider far too much! Particularly considering what risk there is of ye child's life. It is weak and wan and probably unlikely to survive. I have, therefore, thought it best to tarry a while longer. I plan, before the next court session, I shall accommodate ye affair upon easier terms," explained Joe Hawley, squirming inside.

The topic was disquieting and distasteful in the extreme. "Those Roots engage in loud complaints as pure foppery to extract the maximum possible payment from my brother," said Hawley indignantly. "They appear very odious."

"If a man entice a maid that is not betrothed, and lie with her, he shall surely endow her to be his wife," quoted Reverend Edwards softly. He was ignored by the other two men whose attentions were locked on each other solely.

"Joseph," said the older man with impatience now. "The family could appeal the case if they believe it is unjust or return to court for the Root woman to name the father - most especially if Elisha suffers no sanction whatsoever. Then, she could call in the Parsons midwives to testify for her." The colonel exhaled a punctuating breath. "I will not have an 'Anne Hutchinson case' of revolutionary dissention in my court room. Ye affair must be concluded," replied his uncle tartly.

"Uncle Stoddard, I believe it best to do nothing in the Root matter. The one babe has died and, I hear, the second one is sickly," pleaded Joseph. His mother's reaction to all this made him feel physically ill. She would undoubtedly interrogate him the instant he stepped in their door.

"Nephew Hawley on inspection of the entire matter, I am of the opinion that it is consonant and agreeable both to law, justice and the church that a reputed father can be convicted by the oath of the mother of a bastard child, provided the oath be taken as the law requires and that the midwives attest to said oath under travails. Under the practice of English law, the reputed father shall be convicted and shall suffer such punishment as the laws do provide." John Stoddard's dour tone brought to an ending the conversation for the day.

"Nephew, sickly though it is, one babe lives. Relay to your mother that I forbear for the present on the issue, but there must be some resolution to this 'fillius nullius' soon!"

Joseph Hawley noted the Reverend Edwards distractedly peering out the window with a look of wonderment. Perhaps he sees "a divine and supernatural light?" scoffed Hawley ironically to himself.

John Stoddard exhaled with profound disillusionment and irrepressible angst as he now gazed off. It struck him that the families Hawley and Edwards were opposite and irreconcilable magnetic poles. Or one might think of them like water and oil that could not mix. There could be no reconciling people so conflicting with each other. Where was the path forward?

Colonel John Stoddard was weighted down by the burdens of two years of crushing and debilitating war throughout the Massachusetts western frontier. He was drained down to the marrow of his very bones. The colony's defenses were on his mind day and night. He worried, lying awake late into the early morning hours and dreamed of grisly massacres or bewildering and heartlessly cruel "ambushments."

Besides his militia responsibilities, John Stoddard himself was besieged. His mansion-house was no respite from the endless stream of petitioners, pleaders and favor-seekers. In this time of violent turmoil, everyone wanted the great man's aid and intervention in one thing or another. They stopped by his house on the hill at all hours - so that sometimes he avoided his own home for a bit of peaceful solitude! Even at meetinghouse, those wanting to confide in him and ask for help would approach him. He felt he couldn't even pray without interruption!

However, this didn't mean that he saw much of his own council (and nephew) the Reverend Mr. Edwards, who was similarly persistently distracted and absent much of the time. Jonathan Edwards was alone in his study writing his latest treatise, *An Humble Inquiry into the Rules of the Word of God, Concerning… Full Communion in the Visible Christian Church*. John Stoddard missed the solace of time with his minister and spiritual confidante.

Like all the other advice-seekers, petitioners and supplicants, Stoddard's sister Rebekah and her son Joseph were regularly calling at "The Manse." John Stoddard felt beyond the current limits of his endurance for both of them. However, in Joseph's case the two men were often joined by others, discussing and analyzing military affairs and the conduct, which urgently had to be done.

Conversely, at the sight of the pinched visage of his sister Rebekah, the Colonel suffered an immediate grating irritation, as with the ceaseless wail of a feverish infant that instantly and unavoidably unnerves. Stoddard heaved a heavy sigh to hear her strident, "Brother, brother…" knowing that she would again want to talk about something else in the case of her errant son Elisha.

"Sister, your son and dozens of other good men are in daily mortal danger. The enemy are destroying our people and their substance! It is that I must focus on."

Stoddard clenched his jaw hard. As a woman, she had no business interfering in any military affair or arena. Yet she went so far as to actually question him and forward her own ideas in military, political or economic issues! She continued at it in spite of his gruff rebuffs – and far too frequently! He thought back to his honored father's exhortation to "train women to love their husbands and children, to be sensible, chaste, domestic, kind and submissive to their husbands, that the word of God may not be discredited."

Rebekah Stoddard Hawley held their deceased father, the Reverend Solomon Stoddard's opinion to be indisputable, and held other women to the Reverend's injunctions - but for some reason, she didn't apply them to herself! She had refused to consider remarriage after her husband's suicide and ran his store and leather skins business dealings herself. She directed her sons' daily activities. She had raised her sons without a manly presence in the house. Neither did she keep her feelings, schemes, critiques or religious interpretations to herself. She inserted herself incessantly in all kinds of affairs! She felt competent to question and critique their minister as well.

"And thinks you that Sarah Edwards' gold chain furthers her on her road toward heaven, as the Reverend claimed?!" she spat out derisibly. "He keepth not his own council to forswear the trinkets and temptations of this world!" Rebekah's tone was sharp and caustic. "For this, he hath not the complete love of the brethren of the church with him."

As often, her insight was stinging – and accurate.

"Small wonder her husband took his life," John Stoddard grumbled to himself, knowing it was not truly fair. He knew from his wife Prudence that she blamed the Reverend for her husband Joseph Hawley Junior's excessive religious zealotry and enthusiasm. His own wife Prudence was plenty headstrong but no other woman even closely compared to Sister Rebekah for domineering. She defied the laws of God, nature and the weaker sex.

"Sir, the danger of eternal damnation is far more critical than death on this earth," his sister had informed him simultaneously coyly and defiantly.

From this approach, John Stoddard knew this conversation would be on the outcome of Lieutenant Elisha Hawley's still unsettled fornication case and the church's discipline thereof, now that the required appearance before the Inferior Court of Common Pleas had been discharged yesterday at Springfield. Colonel Stoddard glanced over her head to the enlarged eyes and cautionary expression of her son Joseph. Stoddard immediately realized that this would be a prolonged aggravating discussion. He would not be able to sleep early tonight and would probably lie awake for hours rehashing arguments with her in his mind.

"Madame, as a deacon of the church, as well as Chief Presiding Justice of the Court and Commander of the Western Frontier, I am very well versed in the perilousness of all of these at this junction," he replied curtly. Never did one feel as a "prophet without honor in his own country," among his own kin, and in his own house as a man of expertise before this doubting sister! He hated her scolding him as if he were a youth of no experience! He was the elder of the two siblings - besides being the man! She was maddening! Absolutely maddening!

"I frequently paint in my mind images of those embattled soldiers at that woe-begotten post, Fort Massachusetts…" Rebekah began. "I sincerely and unfailingly entreat our Lord and Protector to preserve good health to them and to save ye soldiers from falling into the vicious clutches of our mortal Papist enemies. The aspect of the war is undeniably gloomy at present. I doubt not that the French and their Indians possess all the advantages in several late attacks."

"I thought your great concern was the spiritual danger, sister?" John Stoddard asked drily. "But as was said in the Good Book, sister, 'And Abram said unto Lot, let there be no strife, I pray thee between me and thee.'"

She ignored his sarcasm and the Biblical injunction. She knew he wanted no broil. After a pause, she continued, "Certainly, my son cannot be spared from the frontier to appear before the Court or in the church at present?"

"As the commanding officer, it is without doubt," agreed the older brother while her son Joseph nodded happy for some assent amongst them.

"And you will be pleased to know that Joseph has, at long and labored last, and in spite of the worst kind of contention and argumentation from them, concluded an agreement with the family of that woman," Rebekah said. She did not attempt to conceal her deeply furrowed frown.

"So, the matter should now be terminated," the unhappy woman closed decisively with a scowl of pure acidity on her wizened face.

One of the most powerful and respected men in the colony flushed red across his scorching face as if he had been slapped by his bold, defiant and presumptuous sister. Why, the complete impudence of it! John Stoddard turned to glare at Rebekah and face her full-on. All he could eek out momentarily, over the hard knot in his dry throat was, "What did you say?"

"Joseph has been in negotiations with those Root people," she paused to swallow. "He has finally concluded an agreement with them, as I said. It is more money than even they demanded in the beginning."

The entire concept that Elisha Hawley was hereby free and clear of his fornication case with the Church was anti-Scriptural, anti-Biblical, contrary to the principles of rapturous religious observation as a City on a Hill on which the Bay-Colony was based! Sheer antinomianism! It reeked of Popishness or Rome-ish Catholic "indulgences" and dark secret "inquisitions," to suppose a sinner could buy off his sins with high state or church officials! Preposterous! What about an obligation to the town to conserve the peace and order?! Youth today were overturning society. There was no respect, no authority! Outrageous and preposterous!

John Stoddard wanted to bore his furious eyes thru Joseph Hawley, but the younger man had turned away to peer out of a night-darkened window. Stoddard understood that while he had been preoccupied and attending to the defenses of the colony, he had not controlled these negotiations with the Roots, thereby leaving his sister and nephew exclusively to them. Now they were informing him of their version of the needed results. They had stunned him with their £155 agreement with the Roots witnessed by Joseph, and Martha Root *herself* (but not by her father, and with a drunken uncle of Joseph's female friend, Enoch Lyman, and that loud-mouthed upstart Phelps)! The old man pitched and reeled with the sudden outflow of tradition, esteem, regulation and lawfulness in this move. It washed over his mind as a crashing wave pushes sand and rocks to the shore!

The Colonel blurted out, "Well, aahhh, has Elisha counseled with Mr. Edwards?"

Instantly, he regretted the question for appearing indecisive and faint, as well as already knowing the answer. He realized, of course, that Elisha had been at Fort Massachusetts the entire time and could not possibly have been counseling with Minister Edwards. Besides which, Jonathan Edwards had been consumed by the death of his beloved protégé, the missionary minister to the Indians, David Brainerd, and his most favored daughter Jerusha, flower of the Edwards family, both within the last six months. The Reverend had buried himself alone in his study at home, unavailable to almost everyone while he was maniacally writing his latest book *An Humble Inquiry* on some topics. Colonel John Stoddard growled to himself with the thought of his nephew, the Reverend, dazzling and inspiring in his preaching of the "excellency of Christ" but inept in his handling of his flock as followers. An involuntary groan of agony escaped the old commander. He felt as if he were reeling from shock.

"And what sayth Mr. Edwards?" he asked, steaming in his heat and trying to quickly assess it all.

Then, a thunderbolt of a realization struck John Stoddard. Was his nephew refusing to acknowledge his fornication with the saucy young Root woman? Why, there was law! There were the 1692 *Acts of the Province*,

> "… if any man commit fornication… he that is accused by any woman to be the father of a bastard child, begotten of her body, she continuing constant in such accusation, being examined upon oath, and put upon the discovery of the truth in the time of her travail, shall be adjudged the reputed father of such child, notwithstanding his denial, and stand charged with the maintenance thereof…"

Stoddard wondered if Elisha was doing as Thomas Wait had done with Jemima Miller, almost exactly one year ago?! What if this became a practice amongst young men and women - then what of town morals?

Was Elisha intending to refuse the mandatory confession before the church brethren and congregation? It appeared as if Rebekah would not concede even admonition or censure! And for this, an indubitable sin! Was Elisha contemplating defying the authority of the church? It was breath-stealing, the brazenness! John Stoddard's mind wandered fleetingly through times past to imagine how the brilliant, acerbic Reverend Cotton Mather (a distant step-relative by marriage through his mother) might fulminate and denounce it! Why he would positively thunder! How his father, the Reverend Stoddard's unquenchable critics would have inveigled against the hypocrisy of it!

But Stoddard's eyes turned his distracted thoughts to the point at issue. Was his own nephew, Lieutenant Elisha Hawley, actually considering the unabashed rebellion of that infamous and now-excommunicated reprobate, Thomas Wait? Mere payment of the King's sterling would not dodge the spiritual discipline the church fellowship was entitled to enforce on its covenanted members! How could he ignore the sanctioned "Modes of Evidence" and "Rules of Law" of the Root woman's attestation under oath to the midwives at her delivery? As if such social taboos were simple civil infractions and nothing more! Would the grandson of one of the most famous ministers in Massachusetts Bay defy the edicts of the colony's Cambridge and Saybrook *Platform of Church Discipline*, which elucidated the purpose of censures:

"The censures of the church are appointed by Christ for the
preventing, removing, and healing of offenses in the church; for
the reclaiming and gaining of offending brethren; for the
deterring others from the like offences; for purging out the
leaven which may infect the whole lump; for vindicating the
honor of Christ, and of his Church, and the whole profession of
the Gospel and for preventing the wrath of God."

Colonel Stoddard's head was a-swirl with thoughts of what his father, the
venerated Solomon Stoddard, would say of it all. He would shudder to dissolution
to know that the most resolute full church members would demand and receive no
sanctions for such outrage! How could they tolerate the debauched amongst their
visible saintly membership with hardly a peep, much less without "holy watching"
of their brethren?! Why if Solomon Stoddard could but see his own daughter
Rebekah and her son Elisha refuse Biblically ordained punishment! As if the entire
affair of Elisha's fornication wasn't horrendous enough! Now this!? In the days of
the "Old French war," there had been some respect and obedience to authority.
Commoners tipped themselves in a modest bow when the Reverend Stoddard
entered a room! And he himself, Colonel John Stoddard, too, had deference.
People rose when he entered a room. (The irreligious newspapers in Boston,
naturally, were ceaseless critics, such as when that printer Franklin mocked his
father's criticism of shameless dress.[16]) The group grew silent when John Stoddard
cleared his throat to speak. All movement – even breathing - ceased.

"We shall meet with the Reverend Mr. Edwards without any delay –
tomorrow!" he commanded Rebekah and Joseph as a massive pounding settled
upon his tormented brain.

---

[16] James Franklin, older brother of the illustrious Benjamin, printer of *The New-England
Courant*, parodied Stoddard's published pamphlet, "Hoop-Petticoats Arraigned and
Condemned by the Light of Nature and Law of God" in 1722. Sarcasm toward religion,
morals and ministers has a long history even in the Puritan state. See Horton in
Bibliography.

George Pynchon of Springfield in the County of Hampshire
Gentleman Plt vs Ebenezer Taylor of sd Springfield husbandman deft [Pynchon vs Taylor]
In action of the case as of this writt on file is fully set forth — The deft Taylor
being three times called made default of appearance as sd
Its therefore considered by the Court That the Plant shall recover
against the deft the sum of £18:7:11 d In Damages and
£1:1:6 Cost of suit — after all which the deft by his Attorney
Mr Cornelius Jones came into Court and appealed from
the judgment of this Court to the next Superiour Court of
Judicature to be holden at Springfield for sd County on the
fourth Tuesday of Augt next and Recognizd himself &c
as the Law directs for the Appellants Prosecuting his appeal
with Effect and Recognizance on file appears —

Elizabeth Corse plant vs Joseph Bartlet deft This action was [Corse vs Bartlet]
Continued by order of Court to the next Inferiour Court —

Elizabeth Corse plant vs Joseph Bartlet deft This action was
Continued by order of Court to the next Inferiour Court —

Isaac Ellen appellant vs Ebenezer Marsh appellee The [Ellen vs Marsh]
Court ordered that this appeal be dismisst and that the Appellant
go without day —

Hall appellant vs Roberts appellee This appeal [Hall vs Roberts]
was Continued by order of Court to the next Inferiour Court —

Ball appellant vs Lenox appellee The parties agreed [Ball vs Lenox]
to refer this Case the appellt chose Thomas Ingersoll the Applt
chose those Jones and the Court appointed Seth Warriner who
are to hear the parties and make report as soon as may be and
the action is Continued in the mean time —

Samuel Smith appellt vs Peter Roberts Appellee in four [Smith vs Roberts]
actions which were all continued to the next Inferiour Court
by order of Court —

Jemima Miller of Northampton confest before this Court that [Jemima Miller]
she had been guilty of the Sin of fornication, ordered that she
pay a fine of twenty five shillings to his Majesty & Cost paid

Gideon Clark and Rachel his wife Confest before this Court [Gideon Clark and]
that they had been guilty of the Sin of fornication within
before marriage ordered that they pay a fine to the King
twenty five shillings money each & Cost paid —

Hampshire County Inferior Court of Common Pleas and Court of General
Sessions of the Peace book, Lib D, Page 2½ (volume 5, page 12 from cover).

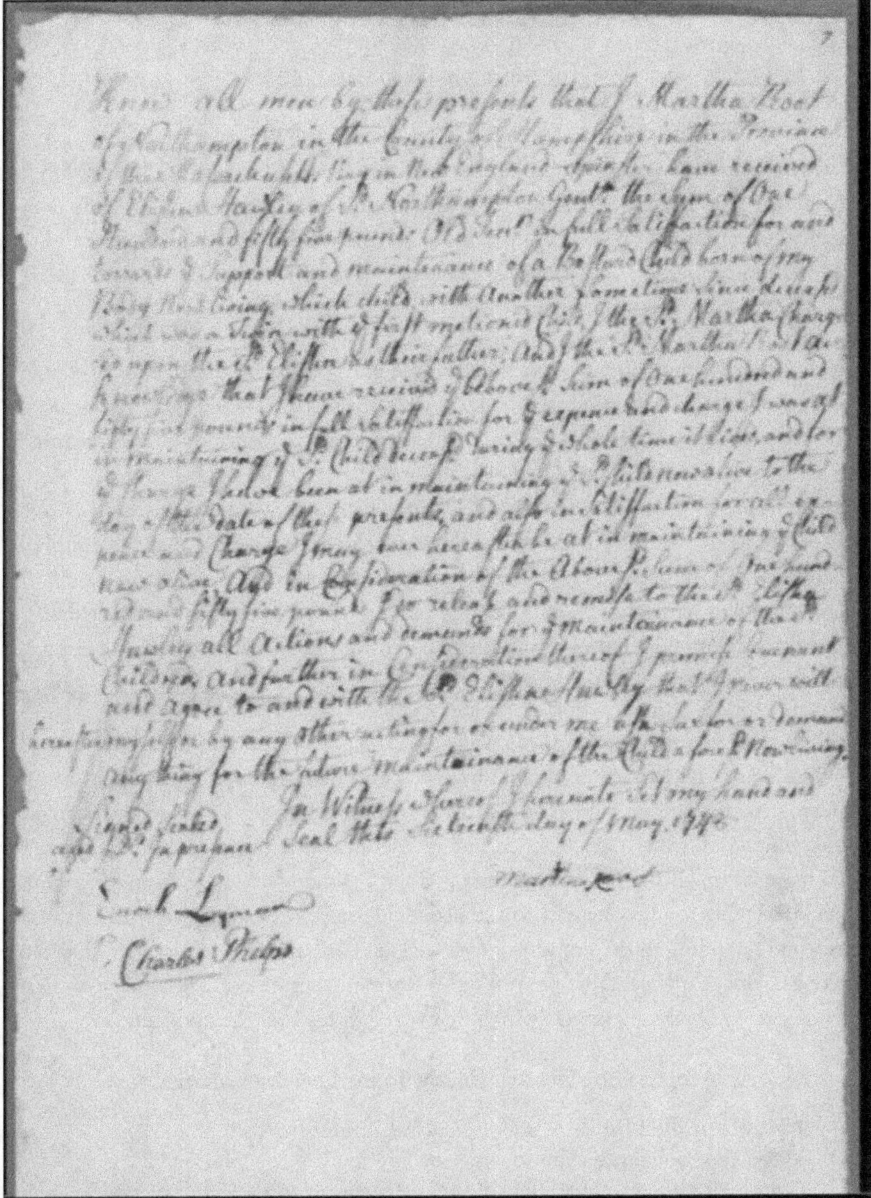

Untitled financial arrangement of May 16, 1748 signed by Martha Root and on behalf of Elisha Hawley, probably drafted by Joseph Hawley in Joseph. Hawley Papers, George Bancroft Collection, New York Public Library, New York City, NY.

"The pretty scandal" which had upended Elisha Hawley's prior Northampton life manifested in the mammoth bulge of Martha Root's belly and his refusal to marry her in the late fall of 1746 through early winter of 1747. Rebekah Hawley had summed up the family's response when she shouted in a desperation pitch to John Stoddard and Jonathan Edwards, "He will neither confess nor marry her! Never, I say! Never, never, never!"

Back when Elisha Hawley had revealed his amorous interest in Martha, the Root family had been pleased. The couple appeared to be genuinely smitten with one another. They had been out walking and talking for weeks, even months. Perhaps soon, the Roots imagined, Martha and Elisha could walk into the meetinghouse in proximity to each other, once Elisha had brought his mother over to it? The Root parents, "Big Martha" and Hezekiah, had judged that the couple could be good "help-meets" to each other through life as the elder Roots themselves had harmonized their lives together. As the weeks passed Elisha had seemed to feel at ease and comfortable in the Root household and with their ways. The Root family liked Elisha Hawley.

Before Madame Hawley's notorious street screaming in the night, Hezekiah Root had considered what he could endow on daughter Martha as a dowry, attractive and suitable enough for a groom of Hawley's stature and which would enable Martha to establish an independent productive household of their own in comfort (as the Roots had already done for older sister Dolly and brother Hezekiah Junior). Of course, it would also evidence Hezekiah Root's prosperity, surety and standing in the community as well as the family's love for their charming maid, Martha. On a scrap of paper Father Root had scribbled "*An Account of Things to Endow to my Daughter Martha*" which he carried in his breeches pocket:

"An Account of Things to Endow to my Daughter Martha" [17]

1 Newly printed Bible from S. Kneeland Printer Boston
1 Bed-tick Bolster & Pillows
6 yards of choice "china" fabric for curtains (including
    curtain trim, headcloth, curtain rings)
Shalloon for a bed quilt

---

[17] This list is my fictionalization of one similar made in the diary of Samuel Lane of New Hampshire; it is not an existing document. See Brown, Jerald E. *The Years of the Life of Samuel Lane, 1718-1806: A New Hampshire Man and His World* in the Bibliography.

Homespun Ticken & bolster & pillows. About 10
        pounds of feather for same
1 yarn Coverlid
2 wool blankets, 1 rug coverlid for bed
2 pair of bed sheets
1 oval Looking Glass
2 pewter platters, 4 plates, 1-quart pitcher 2 porridgers, 3
        spoons, 1-pint pot
1 iron pot & pail, iron kettle, frying pan, fire tongs
        toasting iron, trammel & hooks
Curtain rods, candle sticks
Chest with a draw & lock, 2 kitchen chairs, 1 great Chair,
        1 small table, 2 bedsteads, 1 spinning wheel, 1
        wooling wheel & spindle, 1 loom
1 butter Churn, 2 pewter mugs, 1 wash tub, 2 pails Black
        & yellow platters, earthenware pans, case of knives
1 Cow
2 sheep

These were not all actual expenditures, of course, as the family produced
fine-quality, supple fabrics. They had already raised the livestock themselves. Like
every young woman of respectable family, Martha must immediately accumulate
her "marriage portion" of essentials for a new household's establishment (even if it
was only for a private room in a parent's house). The list had not been completed
as Father Root waffled between expressing magnanimity and ebullient confidence
versus cautious economy since Martha's younger siblings Simeon, Jemima, Joe,
Hannah and Orlando too, would eventually be readying for marriage dowries and
farm lands. Thus, it would have to be sufficient for the prestigious Hawley family
but not too, too much…

After the street scene, stalling at the court, refusals to submit to church
discipline and ultimatums of Rebekah Hawley, all realized there would be no family
negotiations and no marriage banns posted for Martha and Elisha. Finally,
Martha's father consulted with the Reverend Mr. Edwards. A genuine, contrite
confession before the congregation would bring forgiveness for her sinful lapse and
restore her to good standing as a church member. It would not, of course,
legitimize her pregnancy.

Thus, instead of marriage banns on the church doors, she found herself
standing before the congregation.

Yet the Hawleys took no action. Elisha, with his lieutenant's commission
absented himself to the distant frontier post of Fort Massachusetts before the
babies' births. Weeks of no reply from the Hawley family to the Roots' insistent

queries dragged into months. Neither Rebekah nor Joseph could state any time when or what Elisha might plan to do.

After months of futile attempts at negotiations and inconclusive answers from the Hawleys, Hezekiah Root decided to approach the Reverend Mr. Edwards to arrange another meeting with Elisha's Uncle Stoddard and the minister. Though it was contrary to decorum for females to be present, the widow Rebekah Hawley insisted that she would attend the meeting with brother Joseph as Elisha's representative. "She is a most determined and unusual woman," recapped Hezekiah Root, who dreaded the thought of encountering the Madame Hawley.

"She is an unnatural she-devil who will enjoy biting your head off and viciously defaming our Martha," replied his wife Big Martha Bridgman Root.

At the beginning of their meeting that clear but chilly April day, the Reverend Edwards had earnestly asked for the Christian brotherly love of those gathered there. Then the Reverend prayed for God's guidance, after reading Exodus 22:16, "And if a man entice a maid that is not betrothed, and lie with her, he shall surely endow her to be his wife."

The lanky Reverend commenced their meeting with prayer and a reading, entreating God to guide them,

> "In that night did God appear unto Solomon, and said unto him,
> Ask what I shall give thee....
> Give me now wisdom and knowledge, that I may go out and
> come in before this people: for who can judge this thy people,
> [that is so] great?
> Wisdom and knowledge [is] granted unto thee; and I will give
> thee riches, and wealth, and honour, such as none of the kings
> have had that [have been] before thee, neither shall there any
> after thee have the like."

Then the Reverend prayed for the reformation of sinners (and, in his own mind, for Elisha to submit to God's sovereignty and do his duty to relieve the community of this enduring anxiousness). The Reverend John Williams' (and a cousin of Elisha's and Mr. Edwards') exhortation sprang to mind, which Mr. Edwards repeated, "The line of (God's) election runs in the families of believers. The high privilege of being descended from "Godly Ancestors" and the consequent important duty and responsibility of such descent, are so privileged as to demand nothing short of the most faultless conduct. Our duty is to exalt the God of our fathers by our every thought, word, feeling, and daily conduct."

In his usual esoteric manner Mr. Edwards argued as if this were another exposition from his height in the meetinghouse pulpit that the sanctions must be guided by the Lord's Word. "Law and institutions are given to the general good and not to avoid every particular inconvenience…."

From life-long acquaintance, Mr. Edwards did not expect his Aunt Hawley would be anything but formidable. The Reverend had most cautiously probed his Uncle Stoddard on the best, irrefutable, convincing arguments to marshal with Aunt Hawley. Jonathan Edwards had prayed and pondered many hours on how to convince her - but reached no definitive conclusion.

The Reverend Mr. Edwards had only just launched into his exposition when Aunt Hawley commenced a lecture of her own (one not infrequently heard in the Hawley household) on their own unique and special place in the First Church's community of "visible saints" and the venerable history of their Puritan ancestors' flight to the "Next Coming." Rebekah knew the adulation and undying love his people bore for her father the Reverend Mr. Solomon Stoddard and their family's preeminence and exceptionalism in Northampton – indeed throughout all of Massachusetts. She reminded the Reverend Mr. Edwards of the parents' obligation for the right selection of a help-meet of the right social standing and 'estate' for their sons and daughters, and the sons' filial duties to honor and obey.

"Mr. Edwards, I need not remind you that Elisha is not an unconverted person. He is descended, suffused throughout his lineage, and bred on sanctifying grace," she added.

"Yes, Aunt. However, we are all sisters and brothers under God. God's law applies to all his children. Even male and female are declared to be one in Christ."

Mr. Edwards had replied softly to his Aunt Hawley's diatribe. "At Corinthians 5:11, the Lord hath said, 'But now have written unto you not to keep company, if any man that is called a brother be a fornicator…' Drawing in a deep breath he resumed, "'If a man ought to marry a woman, the sin would not be so great in the sight of God as it would be if he did not…'"

Jonathan Edwards hesitated hopefully to assess his impact, quickly glancing at her hardened face for any trace of melting. The minister paused, "Aunt Hawley, visible saints in the Church may become visibly wicked and guilty of the common failures of humanity, the daily short-comings of the best of men. We naturally argue," he summarized, "that they cannot remain impenitent in their sins. We use proper means to reclaim them from gross sin. In such a case, a visibly wicked person may be cast out into the wicked world. This is divine instruction. There must be strict and proper discipline of the gospel. But obstinacy and contumacy in gross sin commands censure …"

Again, Mr. Edwards paused to deliver the hope and redemption of the church. "… until Grace is appointed and the sinner is reclaimed by penitent public confession before the brethren. Then follow the path prescribed by God."

This line of reasoning and consequences was well-known. It had been applied to Samuel Danks and Thomas Wait just months ago who had refused to comply with the church's authority and defied the church's disciplinary edicts. As a result, they were excommunicated from the church. As recently as at the February 9, 1748 Inferior Court of Common Pleas session, meeting in Northampton, a-dozen-or-so fornication confessions were recorded of belatedly married couples or soon-to-be-married pairs with babes at the suckle.

New attorney Joseph Hawley, had accompanied his mother and had been sitting unobtrusively but sharply attentive in the background. He gritted his teeth at the thought of his cousin Edwards' arrogance toward them. (Naturally, however, this attitude did not extend to Colonel Stoddard, whom Joseph practically worshipped.) The younger man knew of his cousin Mr. Edwards' estimation of Joseph's own religious views as radical "Arminian." Joe Hawley clinched down his teeth at the thought of the Reverend judging him. Joseph reminded himself of his cousin's constant demands for annual salary increases by the town. And yet, the minister did little of his own farm labor. In addition, his wife hired girls like the young Root women for household help. He and his mother didn't do that!

Rebekah Hawley reprimanded simultaneously both the Reverend and her powerful brother Colonel Stoddard by referencing Scripture and openly challenging them, "Anathema! Remember that there is the perseverance of the saints." In other words, since Elisha had already been "saved," nothing mortal could change God's design for him, regardless of his conduct. "Besides," she continued, "as written in Proverbs 12:4: "A virtuous woman is a crown to her husband: but she that maketh ashamed is as rottenness in his bones.'"

Jonathan Edwards sat stupefied. Was Rebekah defying the authority of their church?!

Goodman Hezekiah Root could not believe he heard rightly: "What?" Root asked himself "What? What?" in the stupor of sudden, startling insult! His brain seemed to plod on slowly questioning and deducing. Was Madame Hawley saying that his Martha, a devout full church member who never neglected to attend the twice-weekly services, who had humbly submitted to the church discipline, that Martha was not observant because of a common temptation like this? Or was she not among the elect because of her lesser lineage? Did the widow Hawley deem herself so virtuous - although cruel and judgmental? Why, how mean and un-Christian! Or were only those Christians who never faced temptation - consigned ministers' and deacons' daughters who sat imprisoned in their houses all the day, and never went to bring the cows home, fetch from a store, etc.? Yes, of course, ministers had enslaved "servants!" Therefore, those ministers' daughters had no opportunity for frivolity or enticement (and no naughty young males – like Elisha Hawley! - chasing after them). (The Edwards' fine and virtuous daughters excepted.) Were these the only virtuous ones? The widow Hawley esteemed herself and her son far too highly!

Since God had created the world, since the beginning of time, since the days of the ancient Israelites, "indiscretions" and sin had routinely occurred! It was man's nature to be pathetic, tempted and to succumb to sin… "Carnal relations" before the Inferior Court of Common Pleas were becoming as common as tea in China! Indubitably, there were even many unacknowledged incidents, such as those couples caught behind haystacks or in barn attics evidenced. Everyone knew that those couples who were discovered rectified the indiscretion by submitting to humiliation, confessing to their failures and taking matrimonial vows. As the old farmers whisperingly advised with a wink, "Don't buy the cow without first tasting her milk!"

"Mr. Edwards, I'll not be told what is written and what is not. If my son were predestined to marry that woman, then they would be married and my opposition would be for naught and I could not prevent it. But, since they are not married, then it is clearly not so fore-ordained," Rebekah announced with biting finality and her own unassailable reasoning.

"Be that as our Savior wishes," replied the weaver Hezekiah Root. With his own logic, "…as a perfect living child has been borned, our Lord must have preordained it as well. No one can deny that."

"Nay, nay! If it were pre-ordained that they were to be bride and groom and that were to be the will of our Lord, they would be married when this, this…" the indomitable widow commenced to stutter in her cold fury. ".. when this catastrophe happened, but as that is not the case, it cannot be God's will."

"Only what has not yet occurred is their marriage. A babe has come. My daughter has been brought with child, Madame," the hard-headed weaver paused for emphasis, "and, and…" He let his words hang in the air before pronouncing,

"… and she avers on our family Bible that it is your son Elisha who has brought her here."

Root looked at her with the satisfaction of having a quiet final retort and added calmly, "And the midwives also have witnessed her testimony during her time of travails. They can attest to it. In court, of course."

They all knew that Root was correct in this being law and the legal proof was on his side. So silent was the house that Colonel Stoddard's glistening gold watch could be heard ticking away within his pocket.

The Reverend swallowed hard at the very thought of the weaver and the obstinate woman interpreting God's preordained plan since the creation and man's innumerable multitude of millions and millions of volitions within mankind's history! It pained and disgusted him to hear them argue proof of God's sovereignty from a context of the sinful human behavior of his two young parishioners – both of whom he himself had instructed. The Reverend visualized the devout but strong-willed Martha and the popular but mischievous Elisha. Was Martha Root a Northampton version of *Pamela* (of the popularly circulating novel of the times)? He pushed those two youths out of mind - but his own daughters Sarah and Jerusha and their courtiers came to his consciousness. His distractions were abruptly halted by the shrill voice of Aunt Hawley.

"The blasphemy of the desperate, Mr. Root. All know well that talk is cheap," announced Rebekah Hawley. With her own dramatic pause, she finished, "Talk is cheap - but it takes money to buy a farm!"

Especially now, in times of treachery, war, death and danger everywhere - young blood rises, thought the weaver Root. Hezekiah Root felt his blood boil with outrage at the callous judgment of his pretty sprightly daughter by the unfeeling and arrogant Rebekah Hawley. His family had welcomed Elisha Hawley and had raised toasts with him. They had worked and laughed with him. Had conversed and confided in him. Elisha Hawley had needed no pleading or convincing to come into their house, eat their food, lie down on their soft, warm beds. He had given small tokens of affection to Martha. He had made promises to her. Hezekiah had seen levity and spirit light up his eyes when Elisha saw Martha. Now "Gentleman Hawley" had used Martha and wanted her flung away in her dire hour of need and sorest trial?! No, it was not the way of the church! Giving all due deference to Hawley's blood, worldly goods, learning and superior social standing, Root couldn't help tasting the sourness of choler to Rebekah Hawley's reaction. Hezekiah Root's nascent boldness rising from insult against the weight of traditional respect and intimidation for the Stoddard family seemed like a butterfly struggling to rise on an updraft of breeze against the pull of gravity. He felt the sharp sting of Rebekah Hawley's condescension, and sat silent wondering, "Is this the Christian brotherhood of church members? Is this the behavior of visible saints? Elisha didn't even have to voice repentance? Money payment sufficed?"

After a long pause, widow Hawley blurted, "My son will not marry down with this low strumpet - or any other such - regardless of what base accusations any woman forwards. He was ignorant of such sin before her. He knew not this temptation before her. Why it was she who I have seen repeatedly on our street and coming to our shop! Whereas, why…. her family is the epitome of it!"

"What say you?" Root responded in disbelief. "Say you that SHE (strongly emphasizing this word) lured him to lie down with her?!?"

He paused in astonishment, then blurted out, "I say *not*, Madame!"

"No, sir, I say not only that but, further, that you *too* lured my boy into your house for him to play about!" retorted the agitated woman.

There was an audible intake of breaths at this impudence! Root jumped to his feet as if he might attack this woman of poisonous, reckless words. "Spiteful old witch!" he thought. How dare she speak so scandalously!

Colonel Stoddard, too, rose stiffly between them to keep them a-distance but he could find no soothing words in his blank brain or dry mouth. Ever the man of answers, "Squire Stoddard" could find none now.

The audacity of her charge had stilled the tense atmosphere until Mr. Edwards quietly held up his hand to Root and turned to reason with Aunt Hawley. He thought, when Satan has tempted the church must rectify. Aloud he said, "the Lord has commanded at Corinthians 7:9, "'But if they cannot contain let them marry, for it is better to marry than to burn.'"" He paused finished, "Elisha has not denied the charge against him."

"Mr. Edwards," Rebekah replied drawing out her tense words. "Elisha Hawley is not Sam Danks or Tom Wait. My son has not been excommunicated. Elisha Hawley is a full church member. My son has not denied the authority of the church. Election, that is the difference here," she closed with irrefutable finality.

Joseph inserted, "Mr. Edwards, no church can censure and enforce a matrimony, where ye absolute virginity is unproven and where ye man was enticed…. Why, sir, this would be a yoke even beyond the Jew yoke of old…against which Saint Peter declared that neither they of old nor their fathers before them …"

Jonathan Edwards' blood surged, pulsing through his temples in a hot throb. He groaned audibly at the affront of his young cousin's reasoning in the realm of Biblical dictates' application in daily life: he who had rejected the ministry! It was indubitably the conceit of Arminianism, man's contradiction of the Holy Ghost's teachings!

"We must interpret the Scripture by itself, God's pure words themselves, not by the dictates of our own hearts or man's reason," replied the Reverend coldly, close to complete shock. This was haughty contempt of man's smallness and low state before the Almighty! To believe that man's reason superseded or interpreted doctrines of divine revelation was preposterous and sacrilegious! God's will or the devil's?

Although of a prodigious intellect, Rebekah Hawley ignored both her nephew the reverend's religious injunction, as well as her son's "enlightened" analysis. Unquestionably she would not argue further (as Joseph had) interpretation versus the application of doctrine from Scripture in their lives with the clergyman and her brother. Therefore, as if jetting out a wormy piece of apple, she added dully, "He denies the child."

"Aunt Hawley," stumbled on the now-flustered minister with the change of focus, "but do you know…. do you know (again, a long pause hung in the still air) …"

"…for an irrefutable fact, (another pause)"

"…an absolutely irrefutable fact, (pause)"

"…that none under God heavens can deny"

"– and can you swear on the Holy Book, it to be true? True… true under God and the church…."

Without any hesitation, Rebekah Hawley returned, "Sir, it is as true as I know that I am alive and here at this very moment."

"True. And you aver that it is the truth without any scintilla of a doubt?"

The deadly silence felt as another living force pushing amongst them. It was the longest yet, hanging there between them for minutes in the crisp air, during which time the minister's face changed from open bewilderment to obscure confusion.

Speaking with the utmost somberness and in an unhurried tenor, the Reverend intoned broodingly, "Aunt Hawley, as minister of this precious church, I have sought paths through the sterile darkness of our contentions across many years: the accusations, the testimonies and councils, the sanctions, confessions and even excommunications…"

"Excommunication," the pronunciation of the most dire word of the ecclesiastical vocabulary resounded off the wooden floor and walls of the chilly room. The Reverend Mr. Jonathan Edwards waited patiently for the echo to ripple off to nothingness before he would continue.

Rebekah Hawley blanched.

"Of course, a committee has not been called…."

Heavy at the end of the Reverend's sentence, she could imagine the unspoken word "yet" - just like a cannon ball is momentarily suspended in the air before it crashes cripplingly down. Somewhere away in the cold house a clock ticked as loudly as if it were a pealing church bell directly overhead. The silence was so tense that the reverberations of the clock chime could be heard until the last gentle fading to the faintest sound vibrations. Tight muscles yearned to move, but held locked rigid and motionless. Joseph Hawley noticed that Rebekah had her hands balled up into fists so tight that the skin's surface could be seen pulsing with strained blue veins. Everyone's clenched jaws felt as if they had locked and rusted into immobility.

With his terse statement, the Reverend Edwards had elucidated a potential future direction for the church that might surmount the current tempest if it could not be averted.

Excommunication! Dread squeezed her heart so as to palpitate wildly in her narrow chest.

"Calm, Rebekah, calm. Steady yourself," she counseled herself mentally. She emptied her eyes of emotion and then focused afar. "Remember even Good Queen Bess was excommunicated by that Anti-Christ Pope…. Think clearly, Rebekah. Do not weaken."

She continued aloud, "Well, Mr. Edwards, predestination and perseverance of the saints is God's promise to the faithful that – regardless of whatever the pathetic efforts and actions of humans – those chosen by the Savior for salvation will ultimately be saved.”

No one spoke as all retreated to the privacy of their own minds to ponder and muse on what and how events would flow onward now.

After many noiseless minutes, Rebekah Hawley blurted out, “I tell you, it is not his child! Absolutely.”

That girl baby could not be his child, she thought. It was common knowledge that conception of a child requires both persons involved to “delight” in the act. She glared into their eyes giving Hezekiah Root a sidewise glance permeated with the red blaze of anger even into the whites of her eyes. “My son has been failed,” she fairly shouted.

Indescribable sadness filled her being. Emptiness pervaded her heart. Rebekah Hawley’s lifetime of crushing solitary worries flashed before her. She saw an image of herself standing at the foot of the bed where her husband gaped at an invisible devil as he bled to death. In his final days on earth, he had talked only to his devils. Even in his last moments on earth, Joseph Hawley Junior had said nothing to her or their sons. The gaping hole in his throat stole the breaths that his lungs struggled to take. His eyes screamed anathemas which lacked air and thus, had no voice to them. He would have died cursing, but nothing came from his thin, tight blue lips. “Eternal Hell is the only place where the miserably unhappy can be happy being unhappy,” she mourned to herself alone. “As he was.”

Rebekah’s indictment of lack of male guardianship by her two kinsmen bit fiercely at Jonathan Edwards and John Stoddard. Edwards had mentored the boy Joe for years. He pictured their many mature, earnest spiritual conversations, their hours of prayer and Biblical readings together. The Reverend Edwards had urged Joe to the ministry, which he had been poised to enter. Edwards’ family had loved and nurtured Elisha, too. Reverend Edwards thought immediately of his own payments for Joseph Hawley the Third’s Yale College tuition at a time when his wife Sarah was constantly trying to stretch their family’s budget.

Mr. Edwards winced with a flash of guilty sentiment over how he had removed himself from much social interaction over the last half year in his grief over the deaths of their dear daughter Jerusha and his beloved protégé, David Brainerd - and his nearly frenetic writing of his latest publication, *The Life of David Brainerd*. He had been emotionally dead to the townsfolk in his own almost unappeasable sorrow. He had just been living as if he were performing empty motions.

Next the Reverend thought of the horrifying illnesses sweeping through the surrounding towns and into Northampton itself. Although he and Sarah were calmly facing this "frown of Providence" upon their own family as upon so many others, Sarah was becoming overwhelmed with the endless laundry and care-giving demands by the sick children. In the midst of all these personal trials, for his Aunt Hawley to accuse him of lack of concern and apprenticing of the Hawley boys was insulting and crushingly hurtful!

Conversely, Rebekah's verbal rebuke ignited a burning ember of anger in her brother John. Colonel Stoddard considered his urging of the provincial Governor to have her son Joseph appointed Chaplain to the Louisbourg Expedition last year, despite the rumors of Joseph's Arminian theological tendencies during his brief stint at Harvard College. After all, Colonel John's efforts for Joseph's commission, the youth was faint of heart and stomach. He was "convalescing" in his tent for practically the entire Louisbourg siege. Fortunately, Joseph's tent-mate had been the stout-hearted Seth Pomeroy who had watched over him and kept Colonel Stoddard advised.

John Stoddard's mind thought back to the provisions he had made for his sister and her family, his watchfulness over and protection of them for years. The extended family secretly debated over the culpability of the frolicsome Elisha and the agitation of the young radical Joseph. (In times past, Rebekah's brother John, too, had debated with their father Solomon over his intransigent sister Rebekah. John had urged her, "The women should keep silence in the churches. For they are not permitted to speak, but should be subordinate, as even the law says. If there is any thing they desire to know, let them ask their husbands at home.")

Now with the war on the French and their Indian allies, John Stoddard was so weighted down with duties and demands on his time and energy, he never had time to rest. There were so many pressing disquiets with the war, like the recently rumored invasion of Boston by the French (which had not proven true, "Praise God."). There were attacks on the frontiers north and west of the town. Men, women, and children had been scalped and their bodies despoiled! Babes' brains were smashed against walls and trees! Buildings and animals burnt. English towns on the frontier set aflame! Every day brought messengers from Boston and remote parts. Every day there were new orders from the Governor and petitions by remote settlements for the protection of stationing of soldiers at their small farms in the untamed infinite woodlands. Panic seemed always perched above their heads, but amidst all the turmoil and devastation of war all that mattered to Sister Rebekah was that brother John hadn't watched over her wayward son carefully enough!

The demands on him were ceaseless! His own wife was packing his bags for his trip, soon, to Boston for the session of the Great and General Court. "Damnation! Damnation!" he cursed to himself with a serious pang of guilt in his heart…

John Stoddard fidgeted in depthless fury, discomfit and anxiety. How would it all end? It was less volatile to negotiate with the French governor of Canada than his family and church brethren! He could see no peace between the towering cliffs of resolution that were Jonathan Edwards' dogmatisms that Elisha must atone and Rebekah's refusal to admit his culpability. Besides, there was young Joseph's dangerous infatuation with that radical Harvard religion. Where was the path between them all?

Stoddard despaired to realize that no one could be rational about a matter of passion or about their own family. The Roots' insistence (perhaps with Elisha's secret bolstering, as his sister alleged?) that the Hawleys follow the laws set down could not find compromise with his sister's doggedness that her son was apart from the rest of the community. Stoddard had tried to patch it over with a face-saving compromise with Hezekiah Root. Why couldn't those damnable Roots accept the various proposals he had advanced? Once Root had agreed, then it was his own nephew (through his mother, of course) who wouldn't broker "an arrangement."

But a moment later, Stoddard was forced to retract his own conclusion. Actually, there was one person who could be dispassionate in applying God's laws, even to his own family. This was his nephew, the Reverend Mr. Edwards, who viewed human beings detachedly. While other mortals had deep wells of emotion and passion, the Reverend's was shallow and he quickly depleted his. He was passionate about God but not much about humans. Perhaps he only truly experienced unfathomable emotion for the Lord, his wife Sarah and their children? Jonathan Edwards paid scant attention to the trite day-to-day dramas that occupied normal people, like a neighbor's fallen fence, cows in the corn or the volatile Northampton weather. This was Mr. Edwards' problem: he didn't feel and act as other common people did. He didn't think their daily thoughts of shoveling manure, feeding oxen morning and evening, plowing clods of hardened earth, harvesting the beans in good time, relocating the "necessary" (privy), etc. It was hard for him to comprehend others' deviousness and darkness. Jonathan Edwards contemplated daily thoughts of God's plan, the beauty of God's creations, divine light and the life beyond. He was ever distracted from earth to heaven. Why Jonathan Edwards forgot to eat his meals - the first thing on most men's minds!

And then there was further the rest of the church members to contend with. The women of the town unequivocally sided with the young Root woman and against Rebekah, Elisha and - even he himself! His wife had been telling him for weeks of the "women's farces" that were occurring outside of his view. Cutting remarks made within her hearing, harping on the slights against her, how all the young women who had worked household tasks or spinning and sewing for her were supposedly no longer available, their household cows' inexplicable escapes, the burning looks in their direction at church services, how young men no longer picked up something she might have dropped and the quiet hissssss sound they made when any Hawley or Stoddard family members walked past.

John Stoddard suddenly felt the weight of age and time burdensome upon him. He desperately wanted peace and rest, yet was endlessly badgered by these paltry misfortunes! "Tarnation!" he silently cursed to himself. This business of the incautious Elisha had caused weeks and months of agonizing, endless talking, crying, debating, disparagements! These irksome, unsavory fornication cases came before the court every single session. But in this case the entire town knew – and chattered on - many of the sordid details of their coupling! His own wife Prudence had reported to him long ago that she observed the two of them standing face-to-face in the "Venturers Meadows!"

Stoddard realized that Hezekiah Root and the Reverend Edwards were looking at him expectantly, so he shook off his contemplations and countered with legal guidance, "Sister, the young Root woman appears not to dissemble. Root here declares that she is ready to appear before the church committee, the court or a council. He states that she has sworn on their Lord's Book that she spoke truth in her time of trials. Remember too that it is written that 'The just man walketh in his integrity; his children are blessed after him.' If her accusations are true, Elisha, like all church members, must account now and on the Day of Reckoning…."

Stoddard's voice trailed off as he knew not how to bring compromise to these uncompromising persons.

"I care not for the opinion of others. As our own esteemed Father has said, ""We have no reason to think that Christ would entrust the government of His church to men so incapable to govern,' if they cannot see the truth of this!" Resorting to the authority of their deceased father settled the entire matter for Rebekah. It was beyond comprehension that he too might have been human. "I will not have my son so abase himself…."

The air hung heavy, motionless and electrically charged. It felt as if they might be struck by lightning if they budged even one cell of their bodies! Widow

Hawley added, "Our esteemed and beloved father would have blazed a path through this Valley of the Shadow of Death for my son, if he were alive."

The Reverend Mr. Edwards glanced quickly at his Uncle Stoddard who motioned for Edwards not to speak.

The blue veins in her brother's neck bulged as if they would pop and spew the blood of his wildly oscillating anger at any single moment.

Hezekiah Root felt his jaw slacken, as his mouth hung open, empty of words. Root's wife had been prescient. Dealing with the Widow Hawley was as dangerous and unpredictable as dealing with a savage war party!

Being a weaver, Hezekiah Root had always been braided within a social web of dealings with his town-folk. He constantly had visitors to the loom room in his house - showing them colors, yarns and threads with which he could produce various fabrics for them, taking their orders, small talking, and negotiating over price and time. He was eminently comfortable in the hurly-burly of Northampton's busy market life and with his own secure place therein.

But Root had been naively optimistic and hopeful. Madame Hawley was now making it abundantly clear that she had no intention of negotiating or even moderating her stance on any potential responsibility for her son. It occurred to Root that she had the nature of flint: cold as a stone in the depth of winter, but upon striking became a spark that grew into a raging fire. Now struck, she had become that raging fire before which even her brother Stoddard, the preeminent man in all of western Massachusetts, and her nephew the Reverend Mr. Edwards, theological luminary and accomplished author, shuddered most impotently!

Weaver Hezekiah Root could only peer on, wondering how he had ever thought to be generous and imagine settling a new couple, Martha and Elisha? His face burned with the surging crimson rage of suppressed response to insult. Her dismissal and scorn tasted like bile bubbled up from his churning stomach. He vowed henceforth to fight the condescending Hawley privilege and rejection, no matter what! Root vowed to oppose her in every way possible in the future. Be this the case, Martha must name Elisha Hawley to answer for "fornication" in the context of the church.

Did Colonel Stoddard note a new resoluteness evidenced in Hezekiah Root's jaw compressing down hard? "Let us pray on it and seek God's will," resolved Colonel Stoddard with a burp of acid in his mouth and a tightness at his chest.

Hezekiah Root knew this was the end of yet another attempt to discuss and settle Martha's unsettled state. She had appeared before the court, she had confessed before the church, while Elisha had left town with a military commission in a gorgeous, bright new uniform! Root himself had woven the broadcloth! Yet nothing was done in regards to Elisha. Would anything be done by his minister if the Roots themselves didn't act? Why did his son Simeon confess before the congregation on the Bad Books controversy but about the far worse Hawley's fornication offense nothing was publicly said? The Hawleys had stalled even on paying for the support of little Anne.

The weaver Hez Root jumped to his feet and shouted, "I don't care if I myself go to hell, just so that I am able to see you there, Madame!"

With the scowling Root's stomping out the door of the Reverend Mr. Edwards's house, this interview was done.

"May I never see her face again until the Final Resurrection!" cursed the weaver Root as he stomped up the muddy road toward his own homelot.

Upon her husband's return home, Root's wife was sitting at the hearth table slowly inscribing in the family's small leather account book of debts and credits as he clomped furiously in the door. She scanned his demeanor and within a second guessed the outcome of the encounter at the Reverend's. Big Martha Bridgman Root could see that the Hawleys would continue ignoring and procrastinating, since denial was no longer credited by anyone.

Finally, after months public silence, Big Martha could not restrain her rancorous recriminations. Within hearing of Rebekah and Joseph Hawley and everyone else present on all occasions, she grew direct, loud, bold, boisterous and impatient with strings of dire invectives when entering and leaving the meetinghouse, at the nooning between the morning and afternoon Sabbath sermons, in the streets and paths of town, when the women gathered in groups for their tittle-tattling, at the women's quilting bees or corn huskings or similar assemblages. "A dog shows greater conscience than that hellhound Hawley! God defend us from ye depredations and insults of the heartless, corrupt and shameless," she cursed.

On another occasion an animated Big Martha said, "May he die alone and crying for a child! May the seeds of the Hawley line shrivel up and die out forever. O Lord, rebuke the unrepentant!"

"May their blood lines curdle and thicken like sour milk in their veins! Not treasuring children, like tiny, little Annie, may they never have any! May their family lines die with them."

And, "May that old hag Rebekah Hawley die alone, while my Anne caresses my dying hands."

This provoked audible gasps of shock from her listeners. All remembered the local farmer John Adams Junior who had been brought before the Court and fined five shillings for cursing Colonel Stoddard as "a cursed, lazy devil" after the destruction of Fort Massachusetts in 1746!

"Them Hawleys have the blackest of hearts!" raged Big Martha.

"May they all die unmourned and unremembered! Such are the vengeances of the Lord."

While the widow Rebekah sloughed off Big Martha's curses without acknowledgement, the words echoed and lingered in Joseph's head again and again. The poisonous words may have ricocheted off Rebekah, but Joe woke throughout the night haunted with anxiety and melancholy. In one nightmare he awoke with an image of Big Martha shrieking out curses and offering him a straight-edge razor, urging him to slit his throat and end their plagued family lineage! His heart was racing and sweat covered his face. His skin tingled with itching. Many a time, he trembled to imagine how the whole ugly affair was being taken by Mercy Lyman's family, especially quiet, meek Mercy herself whom Joe had been listlessly "seeing" for years. Joseph Hawley blanched at the sight of Big Martha in town and her dreaded profanities and turned to walk in any other direction.

The Reverend Mr. Edwards grew more deeply troubled about the inaction of his nephew, the now notorious Elisha Hawley. Not only were the Biblical injunctions well-known, but he himself had counseled the committees which had excommunicated Samuel Danks and Thomas Wait for their fornication and sworn disavowals of paternity or marriage. Thus, the Danks and Wait families, too, waited to see what would be the church's actions against Elisha Hawley. Feelings of tension and hypocrisy leered down upon the congregation every Sabbath as Rebekah and Joseph Hawley promenaded to the front of the meetinghouse.

Then one day in the meetinghouse at the end of May 1748 just two weeks after their meeting, Martha Bridgman Root pressed a prayer request into the Reverend Edwards' hand. It read:

"The families of Hezekiah and Hope Root request the prayers of God's people for the souls of their dear departed Wife and Mother Sarah Root and granddaughter, Esther Hawley, and grateful thanks to the almighty and righteous Savior for sparing, in ye great mercy, the life of Anne Hawley from the Malignant pleurisy."[18]

Suddenly after a spring season of being engrossed in his writing on theology, Reverend Edwards was faced with another earthly aggravation. He gulped hard to read the names "Esther Hawley" and "Anne Hawley," not "Esther Root" and "Anne Root." What if he read the prayer request as it was written? What would be the reaction of Uncle Stoddard and Aunt Hawley would be if those names were read aloud from the pulpit! He could change the names, but he did apprehend that the Roots would force the issue and could not be put off much longer. In the meantime, he prayed for direction and assured Mother Root about Elisha, "His foot shall slide in due time."

To which Big Martha calmly replied, "Mr. Edwards, me thinks the due time is now."

---

[18] As with Martha's church confession earlier in this book, this is not an actual document but rather one this author created based on other such received by Jonathan Edwards and published by Edwards's biographers. The 99 original "bid prayers" are housed in the Jonathan Edwards Center at Yale University Divinity School. One such of the Ebenezer Miller family (brother or father of John Miller?) sewn into sermon notes of October 29, 1748 is contained in Ola Elizabeth Winslow's *Jonathan Edwards, 1703-1758*: "Ebenezer Miller & his children desire prayers of Gods people for his wife & their mother that is bereaved of her understanding that god would restore her understanding to her a gain if it be his will if other wayes fit them for his holy will." Stephen J. Stein believes this would have been Ebenezer Miller Jr. but author wonders if this date might be wrong, could be different as Winslow believed? Could it have been a bid from Ebenezer Miller Sr? Thomas Wells, Joseph Bascom and Daniel Strong were among those giving thanks for the safe delivery of babies in the bid prayers. See Stein, "For their Spiritual Good," page 280, 270, 279, 282, 284 in the Bibliography at end of this book.

<u>Chapter 15</u>
Excommunication
<u>Northampton, July 26-August 4, 1748</u>

After months of waiting to see if the infant Anne would die or not, Joseph Hawley advanced a proposal in early 1748 on a scrap of paper to Martha's brother-in-law, Charles Phelps (who was representing the Root family). Elisha Hawley would pay the Roots £10 to pay for Anne's care through the age of six, at which time she could be put to work for her own upkeep. The proud and determined Roots replied with an abrupt rejection, delivered by the tall, blazingly red-headed, capricious Phelps, "Completely unacceptable."

The Roots initially wanted a marriage of Elisha and Martha. However, the Hawleys dismissed that with Joseph Hawley saying, "Impossible! Think you, Phelps, that my Uncle Stoddard would consent to such? Think again, man!"

Hawley further prodded Phelps, "Be realistic about this business. How long can you wait for a settlement? How long can you continue this impudence?"

Phelps retorted with his usual provocative mannerisms, "We will not consider anything less than a substantial payment with public confession."

"It is not your place to mandate punishments, Phelps."

In spite of his duty to Christian charity, Joseph had to admit that he despised the man deeply. His gut acid increased at the sight of Phelps, and then started up his throat. Phelps constantly stirred Hawley's distaste and disdain. Hawley hated to be in the same physical space as the giant, domineering, galling man.

Hezekiah Root declared to his wife, "I have no more faith – neither in the Inferior Court, nor … nor… maybe even … in the Church!" He breathed in deeply, "That Hawley has borne no sanction for his ways, none at all! Such immoral misbehavior has never been allowed to stand before in our church. Why the brethren and Mr. Edwards have done nothing! Nothing! His family surrounds him like a smothering pillow, trying to silence all justified criticism of that scoundrel! The Devil wouldn't even take those dissembling Hawley hypocrites, that 'Court of Injustice', or even the brethren of the Church! Even Satan doesn't want their company in hell!

"Husband, hold your tongue from foul curses!" gasped his shocked wife, who turned away to stifle a snicker. "Even the Devil won't take 'em in hell… imagine," she repeated in a low breath.

It was a state of quavering tension and strife near explosion when Colonel John Stoddard departed for the Provincial General Court session in Boston on a bright and promising day late in May of 1748. He left behind the rumbling cauldron that was the town of Northampton boiling with controversy, and grievances multiplying. Like rabbits breeding, one begat more. Stoddard was struggling mentally with finding a practical compromise, as his father, Solomon Stoddard, had accomplished many decades ago with his "Stoddardean System" or "Halfway Covenant" for church admission.[19] Only the immense stature of the Colonel could quell the competing forces within the town factions and compel compromises among people so at loggerheads. The Colonel departed to Boston with these cares and worries heavy as an outbound peddler's load.

Within only a few weeks came the dire and shocking news of his death! Colonel John Stoddard collapsed on a street in Boston, lingered awhile, and then died. His rotting corpse (stinking well outside his hardwood coffin, covered with a black shroud) reached Northampton on a horse cart in procession with the Reverend's wife Sarah Edwards on June 24th. It was truly "an awful judgment of God upon his people" that the one moderating influence in Northampton had been "rendt asunder and is to be greatly lamented," pronounced the minister. None felt the sting and ache of loss more so than the Reverend Mr. Jonathan Edwards.

Over the next days, the town truly grieved through the process of Colonel Stoddard's funeral and burial at the Bridge Street Cemetery. The meetinghouse was thronged for the funeral. Many more mourners sat in the churchyard outside. Out-of-towners had brought their noon dinners and the Old Red Tavern did a brisk business both before and afterwards. The sobbing of distress over their eminent leader's death made it impossible at times to hear the actual words of *"God's Awful Judgment in the Breaking and Withering of the Strong Rods of a Community,"* the Reverend Mr. Edwards' sermon on the death as a critical judgment on Northampton itself. Only two persons shed no tears in public: Rebekah Stoddard Hawley and the Reverend Mr. Edwards. A deep gloom hung over the people of the Connecticut River valley as thick, inescapable and oppressive as a steamy summer day with a thundershower barreling down on them - even over those intransigent youth unconcerned with the community's standards and behavior.

---

[19] The "Halfway Covenant" was a theological adaptation for partial (Congregational) church membership which did not mandate a public profession of conversion or covenant of grace. For a comprehensive explanation of the "Halfway Covenant" of Reverend Solomon Stoddard (Jonathan Edwards' grandfather and predecessor), see Strange "Jonathan Edwards and the Communion Controversy," in the Bibliography or less extensively on Wikipedia: https://en.wikipedia.org/wiki/Half-Way_Covenant

As soon as the funeral was over, the exhaustion of being amidst the throngs of people sent Mr. Edwards fleeing for the solitude of his study. He needed seclusion to reflect on the church's admission policy, on which he was giving four public lectures at the meetinghouse. Should it be expected that those persons seeking admission to the church fellowship of God's "saints on earth" testify to their conversion? Or should anyone already a member be granted the right to have their family members admitted without any statement whatsoever of the proposed members' actual beliefs, even if they made no attempt to true godliness and were adjudged profane? The Reverend's mind was so distracted by these profound religious questions and away from the trivialities of daily life that he frequently left the drinks and meals brought to him by his wife and daughters untouched. His already gaunt face appeared further strained and aged.

In the annals of the church and the mind of the Reverend, not only was there the communion controversy but the Hawley-Root affair remained alive as proof of the self-deception of those who profess to believe but falter and falsely justify their morality. The Reverend struggled with how to explain and finesse the explanation of the pitfalls of free grace versus good works or excessive "enthusiasm" for common people? How to distinguish for the unrefined mind pure, true religious rapture, such as his wife Sarah's visions and trances, from those fanatical "New Lights" whose wild dreams, jerks and interpretations took flight from the actual Gospels?

In the Root family's seating box on the front left before the pulpit sat the unmarried "spinster" Martha Root twice a week at services. As Reverend Edwards had counseled her, she confessed publicly before the church membership, had been forgiven and returned to the communion of the church.

Meanwhile, Elisha Hawley the reputed father of Martha's babes had suffered no discipline. He had not been named in court by Martha on November 17, 1747 when she confessed to fornication. Then, the Roots' obtained the £155 financial payment. Thanks to Uncle Stoddard and Elisha's attorney brother, Elisha had had no sanction before the Hampshire County Inferior Court of Common Pleas. Martha's case had been dismissed with her paying a fine of 25 shillings. At the insistence of his Uncle Stoddard who had still been thinking on a palatable solution, nothing had yet been done by the church. There had been no confession by Elisha before the church. For Elisha to remain unsanctioned by the church in a matter of such egregious moral gravamen was unprecedented and unthinkable. Something must be done, but Elisha would absolutely not own up to his sins in spite of Martha's constant accusations during her travails and the midwives' witnessing. How could the order and piety of the church allow a member to so seriously breach the laws of God without any discipline? It stood as a mockery before all!

Reverend Jonathan Edwards had prayed, pondered and reflected on the Hawley-Root matter extensively. The Roots were universally openly naming Elisha Hawley as the father of Martha's babies. Everyone in the town and valley had heard that midwives Mindwell Parsons and Betty Allen could testify to the legal proof that Martha Root had truly cried out the name "Elisha Hawley" when questioned who the father was during the travails of her babies' deliveries.

Although deeply troubled by the hypocrisy, Mr. Edwards insinuated, but had delayed in calling for an investigating committee of the church brethren to be appointed. He and Colonel Stoddard had prayed mightily in the confines of the pastor's study, falling to their knees in earnest prayer. They had begged the Lord for wisdom and guidance. 'Lord, I pray that I may thank thee, pray to thee, groan to thee, weep to thee…Oh let me, my family and our town turn unto thee.'

Elisha Hawley, like so many of the constant "back-sliders" Mr. Edwards had dealt with over the long years of his ministry in Northampton, had owned the covenant of the church most recently in the 1742 awakening. Elisha had ardently accepted Jesus Christ as his savior. He had sworn that he had been and hoped henceforth to be a "saint" in the church. He had owned that he was in brotherhood with the church members. Yet he had fornicated with Martha Root in "gross and open scandal." The Biblical verse at Job 40: 4 sprang to Mr. Edward's mind, "Behold I am vile; what shall I answer thee?" The pale minister prayed that Rebekah and Joseph Hawley would adopt the Biblical response at 2 Timothy 2: 25, 'God … give them repentance to acknowledging the truth.'

Alas, the Hawley family preferred that the Roots place their hands upon Martha's mouth and not accuse Elisha. They advanced that she had enticed him in her dress and frequent appearance on his street. Therefore, the public censure should remain only with her. Mr. Jonathan Edwards regretfully concluded that Rebekah and Joseph Hawley cared most to preserve their status and wealth. They expressed no moral qualms over the authority of the church, the fate of the Root woman or the living child born of the liaison. Per the clergyman, they were guilty of the first and worst causes of error: spiritual pride and self-deception. Rebekah and Joseph's interests were not first and foremost God's laws, but rather the Hawley standing/prestige, power, and wealth. It was a thunderclap to their cousin, the Reverend!

The worst of all for the clergyman was defiance of the church's authority and discipline by a full church member. Here Elisha stood in step with his mother and brother, unregenerate before the community, unregenerate even upon the presentment of his shame by Martha to the church brethren! How could a minister accept such? Every saint of their church must live "in a godly way." They were encouraged to "holy watchfulness" of each other as church members. Mr. Edwards remembered the exhortation of the ancient Reverend Increase Mather, "our hearts are so deep that we cannot see to the bottom of them; there we may see one deceit under another, and another still under that ... so that we have need to be much in searching our hearts." The esteemed Mather had urged his people to "labor to find out this evil in your selves, and mourn under it." Were the brethren failing to watch each over each other?

Unhappily, Jonathan Edwards concluded that if the unregenerate could not find the evil within themselves, then simply, the church must exclude and expel them. "Mankind are by nature proud and exceeding envious and ever jealous. This we know. It exceedingly irritates and affronts 'em. Decent and natural modesty is what is needed." A great sigh escaped him as he concluded, "One cannot retain spiritual pride before the eternal laws of God."

However, Reverend Edwards' irrefutable logic seemed to harden the Hawley against him and their insistence on Elisha's purported innocence. He knew also the elders of his church and Elisha's Pomeroy supporters were entrenching. Deacon Ebenezer Pomeroy had long been Rebekah Hawley's trusted confidante. Deacon Pomeroy's son, Eben the Third, had been one of the "Bad Boys" that the Reverend had investigated in the spring of 1744 for reading the bad *Midwife's Book*. Now with Colonel Stoddard dead, Deacon Pomeroy replaced Stoddard's moderating influence within the town and church with Pomeroy's own stridency and unabashed hostility toward Reverend Edwards.

Numerous false rumors and "janglings" were circulating among the townspeople, such as that the Reverend was trying to "ensnare the church." Imagine! Or that their minister was acting out of "sinister views, from stiffness of spirit, and from religious pride, and an arbitrary and tyrannical spirit" or that he — even though their ordained spiritual leader — was trying to force everyone to comply with his opinions! But this was not a matter of personal opinion. These were God's laws as enunciated in The Good Book! A poisonous mistrust infected the town. No one paused at the doors of the meetinghouse in Christian fellowship any longer. Each group looked past the other with feigned indifference as they took their seats. Few words of greeting, fellowship or communion were spoken.

After the sudden death of the Colonel, Mr. Edwards could procrastinate no longer. The fornication had occurred almost two years ago now. The situation was so hypocritical as to excite open defiance and disrespect within the church and

outside. The solemn clergyman had started his lectures on his theology of
admission to the church and the necessity of a member to pronounce his or her
own personal experience of saving grace, while the infamy of the Hawley-Root
wound festered unresolved before them all. Among the congregation, some
quaked in blushing awkwardness. Others quietly chortled with the satisfaction of
seeing the high and mighty squirm. A growing number grew restive and resentful,
as the culprit was the minister's and the colonel's own cousin. Where lay justice?

Beyond summer's stupor breezed rumors of peace talks far away in
Europe between England and France, alternating with news of vicious attacks and
killings here in the colonies. There had been many deaths in Northampton town.
A stifling heat hung over the Great River valley. The Reverend felt ill at ease and
of stomach. His head throbbed at the temples each time he thought on what
actions the church must take in regards to the fornication by full church member
Elisha Hawley. Who should head a disciplinary committee, with Uncle Stoddard
dead? Who should the pastor ask to be on such a committee?

It was against practice to for the brethren of the church or congregation
(most of whom were women) to vote. Reverend Edwards noted that it was
common sense that the multitude should not judge every case or decision. A
committee of sage and deliberating brethren would be appointed. Since Colonel
Stoddard was no longer alive to head such a church committee, Mr. Edwards
countenanced that it wouldn't be like committees in the past. The Colonel was no
longer there to moderate hot feelings, such as by some deacons or relatives. A
committee of just the three deacons would be a disaster. Deacons Ebenezer
Pomeroy and Ebenezer Hunt were notoriously allied with young Joseph Hawley
and biased against the minister. Mr. Edwards decided he must call a larger
committee of elders.

The pastor grimaced to recall that in the past the Hawleys had been
furious when he had alluded to Joseph Hawley Junior's mental instability in his
book, *A Faithful Narrative of the Surprising Work of God in the Conversion of Many
Hundred Souls in Northampton*, although it was all true and had been discretely and
gently written:

> "… he was of a family much prone to melancholy… he grew
> much discouraged… till he was wholly overpowered by it…"

Sarah Edwards believed that Aunt Hawley had felt publicly dishonored
and shamed by it. Above all Rebekah Stoddard Hawley valued her public stature.
Never had any word been openly spoken on it, but Jonathan Edwards had sensed

her virulent dislike of him ever since. In the future he would try to avoid public shaming of his aunt.

At the end of services Sunday, July 24th, the church was absolutely noiseless and motionless. The congregants could hear distant noises of the world outside as Mr. Edwards' steps clapped across the wooden floor in the rising heat. He mounted the pulpit, cleared his throat, and announced that he was appointing a 15-man church committee to investigate the "order and purity" of the church. It would stand in "trial and judgment" of violations. (Jonathan Edwards would not make the same mistake that he had in 1744 when he announced the names of accused and accusers in the "Bad Boys/Bad Books" incident.) The Reverend asked the three church deacons, the two town doctors, Colonel Timothy Dwight, Major Timothy Dwight (son), Captains Clapp and Baker and six other select men of "distinguishing ability and integrity" to assemble in the meetinghouse two days later on July 26th.

Joseph Hawley's face wore a stretched grimace of the fury that smoldered inside him. He sat in the Hawley family box at the front of the church behind the Reverend, unbending with suppressed wrath knowing that he would not be involved in the committee. It was clear that most of the committee members were men favorable to the Reverend Mr. Edwards.

"Of course," Joseph fumed, "the only case of pending order and purity for trial and judgment before the First Church at the present time is that of Elisha!"

More pertinently, Elisha would not have time to get news of these proceedings, come to town and defend himself.

Joseph and Rebekah Hawley trudged home from services without a solitary word spoken between them. It occurred to Rebekah that she had spent half her adult married life walking uphill from the Hawley homelot near the riverside as a supplicant of the favor of her brother, the Colonel or her nephew Mr. Edwards. Then, she had spent the other half of her life, walking downhill after receiving their biddings. She bit her lip until she could taste her own blood, and bit beyond that. Glancing at her, Joseph saw an insipid, drawn and deeply-carved face with spots of crimson-red at the drawn line of her lips. Her eyes stared straight ahead blinking only after long pauses. Joe dared say nothing the entire half mile walk home. Dark thoughts enveloped them both.

Over the past two years, Rebekah had spewed freezing and steaming torrents of invectives over Elisha, "his heinous wickedness," "gratifying his lust of lasciviousness," "the scandalous sin," how he was "obscene" and "a wanton person," until the overwhelmed Elisha had frequently retreated with a bottle of rum to the meadowlands along the river where he sat drinking and staring, and refusing to speak. Finally, he was packed off to Fort Massachusetts. This heavy July evening, after Joseph had led his mother in Biblical reading and family prayer, Rebekah turned to the issue of the church committee. "He hath always obeyed the law and performed his militia duty," she rationalized.

Joseph nodded in assent and mumbled something.

She added wistfully, "Let him only be admonished. Let him be suspended from the Lord's Supper. He hath already privately repented...." Her voice trailed off, crackling in emotion.

After long minutes of silence, her voice changed to one of blasting criticism, "That Root father did not control her! Why, that family is ever repugnant!"

She continued, "Certainly, it was she who was desirous of seeking his company! Why, I have seen her here on Pudding Lane at least a hundred times! I have seen her at the corners where ye paths met... over at Pudding Lane and Main Street or at Bridge Street and Schoolhouse Lane.... It was obviously her desire!"

The agitated old woman drew a breath, "Indeed, I would say that she enticed him." She paused, "Actually... she did entice him with her bright ribbons and silk scarf, her loose mob cap and jaunty attitude!"

Rebekah paused as if she had discovered a deep proof to present, and blurted out, "She seeks to benefit from her lewdness and marry up from her rude station in life."

"Aahhh, Mother, I don't know that she has benefited from the child. She has by necessity had to care for and nurture it," reasoned her cautious lawyer son.

"Joseph!" Rebekah hissed out in anger. He could see that she continued on her scheming over the Committee. "I will tell them.... I will tell them I will not support it! I will never countenance it! Never!"

At this, her son blanched in fear and mortification at what she might do before the men of the committee. She would not be gentlewomanly. There was no predicting that she would not insult the committee, ignore 'em, curse 'em or stomp out. Once again she, rather than the committee, might end up being the object of the town's gossip.

"Mother, aahhh…" he grasped for ways to mollify her. Marshalling his most authoritative lawyer voice and gravitas, he asserted, "I will appear before the committee on the 26th."

With only a second of contemplation, Rebekah (thankfully!) agreed, "You must appear before the committee for him. Yes, you must speak your mind and be heard! Firmly!"

Joe Hawley winced. "Yes, Mother, of course."

He paused thoughtfully before adding, "But there is the matter of following the Scriptures…." Both of them remembered the excommunication of Thomas Wait only last year with a chill of dread wicking down their spines and raising the hairs on their forearms.

"Mother," began Joseph cautiously, "I have thought a great deal on this affair from the viewpoint of civil law, unlike the Reverend Mr. Edwards' ecclesiastical vantage. No church could enforce a marriage between such non-consenting parties…" Here Joseph Hawley audibly inhaled deeply, "… unless the absolute virginity of the female and the enticement of the man are proven."

He felt satisfaction at the beauty of his legal prowess and savored it for a moment before continuing on, "This burden of proof, beyond all dispute, should lie wholly with either the woman or the church, not with the man. I should have no regard at all to anything the committee or the church pretends to do in regard to matrimony. Nor would I attempt or labor to prove anything against her, since the burden of proof beyond all dispute lies wholly on either ye woman or ye Church."

"There'll be no matrimony," replied Rebekah sourly. The choler of her emotion was rising, as was her voice, till she was at a scream in the hushed household. "Most absolutely, there'll be *no excommunication! No excommunication!*"

This night neither Rebekah nor Joseph Hawley slept till shortly before the dawn. They went about their chores the following day lethargically and with nary a word between them until the evening prayers. Both slept fitfully that next night with recurring nightmares of appearing before God's throne of grace with the word "excommunication" echoing endlessly out across eternity!

Joseph felt the ghastly word excommunication ringing through his mind as he trudged uphill to the meetinghouse on the morning of July 26th. Again, and again, the awful word clanged throughout the committee meeting. Joseph Hawley sweated profusely, scratched at the sopped and damply clinging cotton of his blue checked gingham shirt. He had suffered so from his head throbbing that he thought he might vomit several times during the proceedings and had to guide himself to calm.

Afterwards as he plodded grimly down Meetinghouse Hill, at a point along the path where he could not be observed, the young lawyer stepped behind a large chestnut tree to bawl. Even though he was wearing his best Sabbath suit pants and great-coat with vest, he sat directly on the ground holding his head in the palms of his hands, as if the weight of his thoughts was too much to uphold. The utterances of the committee meeting hung in the air before him as if they could be physically plucked and examined, as if they existed like the nascent apples ripening in his orchard. Without warning his sensitive nature welled up and puke spilled out of him so quickly that some splattered drops on to his best breeches.

Joe's tears flowed freely as he recalled the emotionless voice of his first cousin and minister, Jonathan Edwards, who had commenced the committee's excommunication proceedings with a long prayer and an injunction from Proverbs 1:7, "The fear of the Lord is the beginning of knowledge, but fools despise wisdom and instruction." Soon after, the lanky Mr. Edwards had intoned, "Every church should exclude and expel the wicked. This precious town of Northampton was established as an errand in the wilderness, *for God*, which must be preserved. If every leaf on every tree, every bird on the wing, and every spire of grass matters *to God*, then we can deduce with complete veritability that so does each human soul and action. Our dear Savior commands each soul to live in a godly way, to honor God with each of our actions...." He droned on as if it were a Sabbath day service, laying out his case, as Joseph Hawley seethed in a stew of anger, self-righteousness, denial, jealousy and rancor.

Finally, the minister was summing up, "If a man find a damsel that is a virgin, which is not betrothed, and lay hold on her and lie with her; and they be found; then the man that lay with her shall give unto the damsel's father fifty shekels of silver, and she shall be his wife, because he has humbled her, he may not put her away all his days."

Stretching for Hawley's acknowledgement and assent to his logic, Mr. Edwards pleaded, "Dear cousin Hawley, mankind is by nature proud and exceeding envious and ever jealous: this we know. It exceedingly irrates and affronts 'em. Decent and natural modesty is what ..."

Joseph had interrupted, "Mr. Edwards, you need not instruct me in a child's catechism." Hawley replied prickly. "... Is any man eminent in holiness?"

"Nephew, if the powerful and prominent do not abide by God's laws, the weak and faint-of-heart will be unable to. It behooves Elisha, as a community leader …"

Joseph Hawley acknowledged that licentiousness had greatly prevailed among the youth of the town but he justified to himself that a payment of £155 had been made to the Roots. That should settle the most unfortunate matter. The nagging question of whether Elisha had truly and uncategorically repented bit fiercely at Joe's mind. Elisha was contrite, yes, but truly repentant? The closest person to Elisha, his brother Joseph, did not truly know, but that was between Elisha and God, Joe analyzed. Aloud Joseph Hawley insisted, "He repents and hath indeed reformed his ways."

But the minister concluded faintly in fierce and irrefutable logic, "Reformed or truly repented? We have not examined his conscience together. He hath not evidenced repentance."

Mr. Edwards waited a moment for this load to sink in before adding, "There must be vindication of the Name of God, the Honor of Jesus Christ, the great Head of the Church, and the Holiness of our Church. There must be obedience to the church's demand of confession. Obstinacy and contempt of the authority of Jesus Christ in the Church cannot stand." The minister paused unhurriedly, but then added, "Our brother Elisha has not acceded to the church's authority as is the path to repentance, as has been expected of all others; therefore, excommunication is the church's rod of discipline but we need not pick up that rod …" He breathed in audibly, "… if there is *confession*."

It was terribly sour to Joseph and Rebekah Hawley that the only return to salvation through the church for Elisha lay through the minister and accession to *his* demands for the church. The lawyer in Joseph reflected on all the suffering he and his mother had endured. Some of the worst of that, such as this, could be attributed to Jonathan Edwards. "I'll never allow this to stand," he swore to himself.

It was quite impossible for Joseph to know how long he had remained along the path home from the meeting with the words ringing in his ears, reliving that most awful humiliation and shame. However long he had sat there, it was not enough to erase the red cast out of his eyes.

His mother read the results of the committee decision from the stoop of his frame and his glowing face the moment his figure came into view on Pudding Lane near their homelot. Across the Lane, at his house front where he stood fixing his fence, Captain Orlando Bridgman glanced quickly at Hawley's hunched posture and grasped that the committee had reached the inevitable conclusion that Elisha Hawley had fornicated with his niece Martha Root and he had been adjudged the father of Bridgman's grand-niece Anne. Now finally he had been adjudged guilty of it. Bridgman remained outside for many minutes to listen if he would be able to hear if Rebekah Hawley would pierce the air with screams, invectives or retain her normal ice-cold exterior. Before long the answer came in the sound of smashing of ceramic and glass. Rebekah Stoddard Hawley did not take the verdict well.

Following the verdict of excommunication, the town of Northampton became practically an armed camp, not only because of its war footing with the French and Indians, but more so because of the division of the townspeople into those who adhered to their minister versus those who followed the Hawley and Pomeroy camp in their opposition. Was the issue hypocrisy and public morals in a town founded and centered upon God's true religion or was the minister infringing upon the independent conscience of each soul or the congregation? Was this abiding by ancient Biblical laws or a tradition of compromise to worldly frailties?

Reverend Edwards succinctly announced the decision to excommunicate Elisha Hawley at the morning service of July 31st. The entire town was awash in most of the details of the meeting already. Still, it was announced.

Outside the meetinghouse venomous words were exchanged, "Sir, the church must conserve the morals upon which the entire peace and good order of our town depends."

"Caution, yourself! We have many friends and you could find yourself in problems not just with us, but others as well."

"Meddle not in matters not for yourselves."

"They are but yeomen, like us. It's presumptuous to think themselves better."

"Under God, none is above another."

"You will never buy anything in our store again! Your credit may be called in… Further, I think your farm is lowly taxed. The town should investigate it at the next Town Meeting; I think I'll suggest it!"

"Your conscience should not feel comfortable. The final day approaches!"

"I warn you that you will regret proceeding further."

"I warn you that the laws of God and the Law of Moses are greater and you will much more deeply regret disrespecting them!"

"None but the most shiftless crook would marry a woman of such lascivious carriage! Likely she'll never marry!"

After enduring two weeks of such poisonous vituperation, an express runner brought the jolting news that Fort Massachusetts had been attacked by hundreds of French and Indians. This was beyond their own personal dramas. Additionally, there was the news via the military command at Hatfield that a scout out of the Fort had been attacked! The scout attack had been foiled without any injuries but reports from the war front were abysmal. Soldiers were low on bread and all other supplies. French Indians were seen in the forests surrounding the Fort. Both the officers and men at the Fort were terrorized and near mutiny. There were men dead and injured in the attack on the Fort, including Lieutenant Elisha Hawley!

Surprisingly, there was no wailing and gnashing of teeth at the Hawley house. Rebekah decided to order her tombstone carved immediately. It occurred to her that she had lived in everyone's shadow, unrecognized for her sacrifices and her intelligence. She thought to herself, "I have the body of a feeble woman, but the mind and heart of a fearless man – indeed a King! At least I can have the honor of an eternal sleep of satisfaction and honor on my tombstone." She decided that her stone would be larger than her husband's. She would not demur as her mother-in-law had in buying a smaller slab of stone. She instructed the stone mason to carve upon it (besides the dates):

Earth's highest station ends in here he [sic] lies,
And dust to dust concludes her noblest song.

The defensive "Line of Forts," of which Fort Massachusetts was the primary, lay at the brink where the boundless untamed void beyond met the march of English empire. It was where forest met frontier. It was the most remote and exposed of any place under the provincial government of the Massachusetts-Bay.

One cuttingly cold morning in the winter of 1748/9, steam rose off the Hoosic[20] River and immediately formed into snow crystals in the icy air, and then fell back upon itself. It was a haze of snow crystals hovering over the changeling waters with dazzling miniature rainbows of colors visible disappearing and reforming each instant. The day before a snowblasting squall had swirled and blown wicked all across new-England. The day's faint yellow orb of sun had been so insipid as to allow one to stare directly at it (when one could see). It abated begrudgingly during the night. Snow had swirled in curls and churns. The earlier incessant wail of the winds had calmed to the occasional howl and bluster.

Outside the barracks of Fort Massachusetts, a solitary figure hurriedly piled firewood in his arms to haul inside. An officer crossed the parade yard to survey the narrow Hoosic Valley from Fort Massachusetts's twelve-foot-high "good commodious blockhouse" watch tower. It was Lieutenant Elisha Hawley who gazed out to the starkness of the glinting white snow etched against the black and gray bark of skeletal hardwood trees and dark green-needled evergreens. He knew this pastel blue cast of twilight over the snow indicated a clear starry night of numbing cold. Within an hour this would all fade as gradually as grains of sand sliding to unmitigated blackness. Fort Massachusetts would kindle the sole light in a boundless immensity of wilderness. It stood sentinel in a minute circle of man-made commotion around the white English men who had invaded the vast, northern forest.

Lieutenant Hawley climbed up the ladder to the northwest corner blockhouse and pushed open the trap door to the second story to survey the cannon and gun loop-holes across the majestic narrow Valley. When he had first viewed it, Hawley was stunned by the never-ending nothingness here, just trees and trees and trees forever. Not a single sign of civilization. Nothing anywhere within

---

[20] The spellings of the locations and the geological attributes of each feature (river, mountain, road, valley, trail and tunnel) varied at the time: Hoosic, Hoosick, Hoosuc, Hoosuck, Hoosuk, Hoosac, Hoosack. I try to use the most common current geographic spelling, but will use the current name variants for some features so that they can be searched. "Hoosic"/"Hoosac" meant "place of stones" or "the beyond place" in Algonquin.

view. Not a trail over the mountains; not a house; not a farm; not a meetinghouse steeple; not a rich meadow; not a cow, sheep, or pig, not an Indian village. Just eternal forest forever and ever.

The valley was hemmed in by "Pine Cobble" and "Bald Mountain" facing them to the north. "Hoosac Mountain" loomed up from the valley to their right. Behind them was the Grand Hoosac Mountain, what the soldiers called 'Captain Williams' Mountain," the closest to their view. Although he had heard it spoken, Lieutenant Hawley could not recall the difficult musical Mohican name (which by usual Indian custom described its feature) and the Ragged Mountains.

Peering out at the unending march of the billions of bare deciduous and needled evergreen trees assuaged him, as wave after wave, to the horizon till they shrank to indistinguishability and met the sky. He gazed across the bleached winter landscape, devoid of sounds, smells, colors and joy. It was a landscape of deadened paleness, a landscape of white, gray, dull browns and black.

Beyond the Hoosac Mountains, others of the Taconic range stretched out as a great and terrible wilderness of hundreds upon hundreds of miles all the way to New France, without known end. It was an ocean of mountains and trees. George Quaquid, a Mohican scout, informed him the Indians pronounced it "Taghkanic" or "Taughannock" which meant "in the trees." It was truly in the trees! Billions upon billions of massive towering trees. The fresh snow covered nearby Furnace Hill to the "Indian ledge" obscuring everything. He marveled how the Hoosic River's water could one day be a sparkling, clear blue babbling over pebbles in the sunshine, but today appeared as a deep indigo blue suffused with the ruminating dark grey of a storm's menace. Hawley's heart had accustomed itself to this awe-inspiring beauty.

Lieutenant Hawley inquired whether the sentry had seen anything?

"Nothing at all, Lieutenant. Nothing moving anywhere. No, sir."

The huge pine logs of the rebuilt blockhouse still oozed that strong acrid resin as if the trees themselves refused to surrender two years later. On the cut logs glistening drops of solidified resin retained their droplet shapes and tar-like stickiness. The astringent smell tweaked his nostrils. His every step echoed hollow in his ears.

His spine tingled as he realized these were the interregnum moments between day and night, the best and clearest time to think, sense and feel. Like its twin, dawn-light, twilight was the physical world's version of that human time between sleep and waking. It was pregnant and full. Hawley did his best thinking at this time. It was that perfect twilight time when the sun has just disappeared behind the irregular mountainous horizon, but the darkness has not yet obscured all. It was the gloaming time, that divine period of the day when seconds were suspended and drawn out slightly longer. He had never felt the earth's beauty as intently in Northampton as here at the edges of the English people. A sermon from Reverend Edwards about the sweet delight in contemplation of God and creation sprang unbidden to mind:

> "… when we behold the fragrant rose and lily, we see his love
> and purity. So the green trees and fields, and the singing of
> birds are emanations of his infinite joy and benignity; and
> easiness and naturalness of trees and vines are shadows of his
> infinite beauty and loveliness; the crystal rivers and murmuring
> streams have the footsteps of his sweet grace and bounty."

"The Reverend Mr. Jonathan Edwards,'" observed Lieutenant Elisha Hawley with resignation. "… the cause of my exile."

Where the sky had been that deeply rich, bright cobalt blue of day (heightened by the stark whiteness of snow), now the twilight depleted it of harshness until both the sky and snow were blended to a supple matching pallid, artic blue. Gentle blue snow and sky. Suddenly, he recollected Martha Root's brilliant blue eyes. Her eyes were the color of juniper berries, the tinge of everything in the ascetically fresh snowy world of these gloaming moments. He realized her eyes were the color found in the mountains, water or winter. They were as luminous to gaze on as pools of sapphire ice water.

Inside the barracks, the laundry and cooking women had kettles of dried peas furiously popping with salt-pork, onions, squashes, pumpkin and turnips in the immense stone chimney's fire. This smell would have been relished by empty stomachs, except for the fact that these were the only provisions the men had eaten for weeks. They had eaten it for their noon-time dinner, then their evening supper and probably would tomorrow twice more again. At least tonight there was enticing hot bread in reed-and-grass Indian baskets. The Indian meal and ground chestnut bread tasted of the slight fustiness of the woods and acorns. Still, the smell of food beckoned. Lieutenant Elisha Hawley would slather his bread with the remaining butter mother had sent up to him. (With the bitter cold outside, he didn't need to store the butter in the water-well as during the summer's heat. It was stored in his chilly room.) And there was the added luxury of whortleberry pudding tonight!

But except for the whortleberries, it was another day, week and month in which nothing remarkable happened. Nothing at all, just the common ordinariness of life in a picketed fort on the edge of an endless howling wilderness.

Once back inside the barracks, Hawley was given a chair at the center of the hearth, most ideally situated to the monumental fieldstone fireplace within the half circle of indolent officers. Surrounding the Lieutenant were most of the lower ranking officers, including the loyal Chapin brothers (Caleb and Elisha), ambitious and miserly Isaac Wyman, and trustworthy gunnery sergeant John Hooker. Each sucked languidly on the long, thin white-clay pipes and sipped their mugs of warm rum-laced cider apple-jack. They stared into the lulling flames in the great fireplace but roused to greet him crisply, 'Lieutenant, all well?"

All the other soldiers and even the lesser-ranked officers at Fort Massachusetts came from the small collections of crude log huts and primitive sheds that called themselves "new towns" but were really only outposts of hardened picketed buildings. Lieutenant Hawley was the only man at the fort with real culture: a few books, quill pens and some fine writing paper.

A haze of blue tobacco smoke defined their circle in the raw and cold quarter-house. The smokers' circle puffed, each one absorbed in his own ruminations. None would be so bold as to intrude into another man's quiet by too many questions or mere jamblings. Besides, there was no news to mull over until the next snow-shoe scout or delivery of provisions came in - which might be a week yet with the deep snow everywhere.

However, at the opposite end of the building before the other hulking stone hearth around a plank table sat another circle of men, a larger rowdier crowd. These vulgar soldiers were laughing, smoking and guzzling tankards of rum flip into which hot-toddy irons (a 'flip-dog') had been jammed to produce a steaming, effervescent foam of liquor. Some men had whole flagons of cider sitting in front of them to chug. The warm alcohol and spices had heated up the conversation and spirits as well as the bodies. At the center was a game of 'hazard" with a pair of wooden dice and a crowd gathered to wager.

'Holy Jerusalem!" cussed a losing soldier. As he jumped up, he flung down his copper half-pennies and wooden chips, one of which then rolled from the plank table to a gap in the flooring where it was lost below.

"Oh, curses! You deliberately lost my winnings! You come back here and pay up like a right, decent man!"

"I'm done. Ain't coming back and you ain't gittin nothing more from me… 'les, I get another mug of rumbooze from someone?" the loser spat back. While jumping up his step had landed on one of the scruffy, mottled brown fort dogs who limped away yelping to a slightly colder but safer spot.

"Right impossible, you dog-booby! Next time, we'll give 'ya nothing but that chatter-broth the lovely ladies swizzle!" piped in an observer. The rest of the men guffawed heartily.

"You owe me another farthing!"

"And what, you miser? Like one little half-copper is gonna make or break ya?"

"You're just afraid to lose, ain't ya? Can't take no more?" returned the gibe.

"Tired of the company!" came the retort.

An empty olive-green bottle, which had just been drained of its last gill of rum was hurled into the stone fireplace by the now-unhappy winner. "Whooa, whooa, whooa," his watching colleagues chorused as they tried to smooth over the rising spat. The cooking women grew stern with the intrusion of the flung bottle toward their boiling kettles of tonight's stew. No one wanted any disturbance to the cooks! This had to be controlled and indeed, the other dice players stepped between to block and mollify the besotted parties.

But the loser, a formidable hand-to-hand fighter, leaped to his feet and grabbed the long stick he always stacked near-by. He was a throw-back to the English peasant of olden stories with his ferocious style of body battling. All the men had seen him use his long stick to strike, thrust, and even impale an Indian once, so an awed hush instantly fell over the spectators. He was loosening up for close combat.

"Now, now, gentlemen…" soothed a lower ranking ensign. "Let us amicably settle this squabble. Why, this is nothing boys…. Come, come now."

As he crooned to the agitated fighter and distracted him, his fellow soldiers grabbed his arms from behind and tried to swamp the fire of anger.

"There, there, my lad, you've just gottin' a bit cherry merry, but we'll all squelch this disagreement for a bit o' supper now, won't we boys?"

The tense crowd breathed a sigh of relief over a tiff that had been doused. The officers reminded themselves that this soldier, while a formidable fighting machine, could turn too quickly against his own side. He was one of those men who must be constantly monitored. Hawley wished Phineas Forbush or one of the other soldiers might bring out a fiddle so that it would be an uneventful night without any real bedlam to necessitate the Lieutenant intervening between drunkards, stanching serious injuries, or ordering any discipline tomorrow. The last thing Hawley wanted was one soldier to seriously injure another. One of the worst tasks for an officer was dealing with men so drunk they couldn't find the way from the table to their beds across the room - or worse yet who might fall asleep too near the fire, slump face down in the snow, accidentally discharge their ancient rifle, or otherwise endanger themselves and everyone else.

It was even more dicey when the sodden drunkard might be a commander, which also happened (and not so seldom as one might imagine). His mind jumped to the stories told by the soldiers at Fort Dummer of Colonel Hinsdale so precariously tipsy as to endanger everyone, but mostly himself. On repeated occasions he had been so drunk as to leave his wife in charge of the fort! One night he stumbled away from a scouting party's campfire to relieve himself a few yards away in the woods and didn't return for a half an hour as he "got turned around," lost within hearing distance of his men! When a search party found him disheveled, scratched, and fallen down off the side of the trail, some leagues away, he recounted a story of a terrible encounter with a giant who had surprised and assaulted him! After a long struggle in which he was beaten and injured, the colonel told them, he had finally prevailed against the herculean villain. The next morning the colonel's hatchet was discovered embedded deep within a mighty oak tree just over the hillock.

Another day the sodden colonel walked into the Great River trying to see the boat they would be crossing in. Once in the boat, he reeled so violently from side to side that he fell in and had to be fished out - repeatedly. Further along the road the old tippler fell off his horse several times and would have killed himself but for the three poor sentinels that kept clear heads to safeguard him.

The group of Hawley's soldiers tonight had, as usual, brought out their alcohol with their homemade wooden dice. The fact that they still had part of their rum ration remaining and were not yet down to their spruce "small beer" cautioned Hawley against being overly optimistic for a night without some kind of rout. It didn't require much for fist fighting, scratching, tearing out handfuls of hair and black eyes to break out among drinking men and they would soon be surrounded by a cheering crowd to watch and wager on who would win and who would be bested. Hawley was reminded of the adage, "When wine and beer, punch and eggnog meet, instantly ensues a quarrel."

Hawley knew for certainty that his mother would be shocked at the complete intoxication, combustible passion, lack of manly control and lack of Christian virtue that he dealt with daily at Fort Massachusetts. Against the endless drub of quotidian life, the soldiers were constantly and actively making disorder. It was amazing the zeal and effort the soldiers devoted to brewing their spruce beer. Three hours of boiling down the bright-green spruce branch tips; mixing the bubbling brew with the thick, sticky, exotic molasses; straining it into any cask or barrel or container they could secure; setting it to cool – and then immediately drinking a couple of quarts as soon as it cooled. Of course, it was the drink of last recourse after their gills of rum, punch, wine, brandy, flip or apple-jack.

It occurred to Hawley that this would be a good moment for the women to serve up that stew for supper, "Mrs. Taylor, isn't that stew ready yet?"

It was the salted pork, peas and pumpkin again ("… and no complaints 'bout the cooks, 'else ya not git that!"). Hawley quickly prayed it would be edible, not the bottom of that last hogshead barrel which was mostly spoiled rotten and wretchedly sour.

At the announcement of supper, all quickly retrieved brown or red-glazed earthenware bowls, pewter and every other sort of eating vessel along with their spoons, two-tined forks, and bone-handled knives. Before long the conversational tenor at the enlisted sentinels' table again grew shrill as the usual beetle-headed chaps argued a new wager, another war, and everything else.

"Yes, for sure as I'm a sitting here, your Majesties in England and France will have us back at it. And even more, we's scalp-bait them savages can't resist, just sitting out here at poor old Massachusetts Fort with too little powder, too little lead, too little food, no reinforcements, few scout patrols watching, too little pay, too little of everything, 'cept misery! We got plenty of that! And I guarantee youse that they'll all be out on the war-path again before a year's out and we'll be the ones whose hair will be cut!"

"You know they say them Indians never forget an injury. Oh, right sure, they'll be back here again for the spirits of them we killed last August."

It was true that there was no forgetting in this land – with the Indians, the English or the French. At some places, a rock pile marked where a woman was hit in the head with a stone by her husband and was never the same again. In another spot, a tree was twisted to show where someone was ambushed but escaped. Every settlement and half the countryside were littered with sites at which someone experienced a traumatic event. Usually these were recounted at each passing by.

At the periphery of the Fort soldiers' eating circles, the company's Indian scouts Conawoca Delow and John Harmon silently studied the others and nursed their own mugs of flip and bowls of mushy stew. They were acknowledged masters of the forests and reading even the minutest signs therein. Delow and Harmon rarely spoke, although Hawley was unsure why.

It was the same with the African men Moses Peter Attucks and John Bush. Bush sat slightly afar, carving another of his exquisitely detailed oxhorn gunpowder-horns with his prized sharpened jack-knife. Hawley wondered who Bush was selling this one to? He wondered what these non-white men really thought of their oft unruly and oft belligerent cohort? They seemed ever wary of their white military "brothers." "Wary with good reason," Hawley thought. How often they must have heard statements about the "beady Indians," the "lazy African nature," "the caprice of an Indian is of all caprices the most capricious," and how "they can never be trusted," although Attucks and Bush rarely said anything about their fellow rank sentinels.

"Well, when the next war do come - in a month, a year, or maybe so - I wouldn't be surprised it be you gets scalped with the way you dozed at sentry, night before last!"

"Hey no, I just closed my eyes for a second and 'twas near the end of the shift whilst waiting for relief from you! I, for sure, hain't ever fall asleep at post!" The soldier paused then spat out, "And I hain't done nothing like shooting a lieutenant in the back!"

Brusquely the conversation ceased. Lieutenant Daniel Severance's death had occurred only a few weeks ago, December 15, 1748. Everybody went stiff. Their visages hardened with jaws locked down on their teeth. Every man listened to the suddenly audible sound of breathing and their own hearts pounding inside. Eyes looked down or away.

Every man at the fort had sensed that something was wrong with the scout of men that came in the day after Daniel Severance's death. They spoke little and repeated the same exact explanation of "the terrible accident of the Lieutenant" standing up without warning in the line of fire when the scout suddenly came upon a large group of Indians on the trail that fired on them first. The French, Indians and English were officially at peace now and patrolled only as a watch. The soldiers knew they were not to provoke bloodshed, only to defend themselves in compliance with the new Peace Treaty of Aix-la-Chapelle. No one seemed to know who had fired. They said only that Severance had been killed - accidentally.

Lieutenant Hawley had found it implausible. How had a man whose second nature was ambush and bush-fighting, a man who had lived his entire adult lifetime in the active militia, placed himself directly in the line of fire? Indeed, who had fired the fatal ball? Besides these, Hawley had a few more questions he didn't want to ask. He worried about what answers he might hear. He had always felt disturbed by Severance and recalled his uncle's Stoddard's advice, "Provoke no problems up there. There are disorderly spirited men among them and you will need keep your wits. Say little and listen much."

Yet Hawley considered it odd that the rest of the men in the barracks only feigned mild surprise and asked no probing questions about what had transpired out in the rough vale…. Was it that everyone just expected Daniel Severance to die suddenly in a blaze? It was true there had been countless times that Severance vowed to all that he would only die in vengeance. There had been many times that aggravated other men had sworn to kill him! That the scout 'buried him where he fell" instead of bringing his body back to the fort's burying ground deviated from protocol. Hawley worried about the reactions of Captain Ephraim and Colonel Israel Williams. But to his amazement, his superior officers, too, displayed no shock or exhaustive inquiry. The awkward lack of inquiry indicated something peculiar.

About a week after the scout's return Hawley overheard whispers that "Lieutenant Sev" might have been shot by his own men as he threatened to execute one of the Indian group they had encountered. Hawley recalled Colonel Oliver Partridge's warning to Severance years ago that "if he should do such a thing in time of peace, he must go on trial for his life." Hawley recalled Severance's oath that he would willingly pay with his life. Severance's 'black designs" for revenge were known by all. Therefore, Hawley sensed that it would be best not to ask any more questions about exactly what had happened and who did what in an obscure twilight on the Indian trail footpath on the banks of the Cold River, dozens of miles from the Fort or the nearest log cabin. For himself, Lieutenant Hawley admitted that he did not really want to know what had occurred or think on it anymore. His Indian scouts had cautioned him, "If the devil had a son, it would be Dan Severance."

Old Lieutenant Dan Severance held one of those impenetrable hearts of hate and meanness since one October day a quarter century before in 1723, when Dan had watched helplessly from a field as his father Ebenezer was shot dead and scalped bringing in the last of their family's corn harvest. Most pitifully, the father had been warned and was careless.

By the time Daniel and other village boys ran to the aid of his father, the Indians had fled like deer bounding off into the woods. Dan could only race up Grass Hill in time to hold his dying father and demand stupidly, "Father, who killed you?"

He hated himself the minute the words escaped him, not only because it was foolish, but also because he had just told his bewildered father that he would soon be dead! To which his father gasped out the useless reply, "Indians."

That day's harvest of hatred seared the soul of Daniel Severance, so much so that he feared no living person and no possible outcome – except he was afraid only of dying before taking his revenge. Dan had sworn to avenge his father's heartless killing on all Indians generally, but especially on the Waranoke and Abenaki warriors of Chief Sachem Greylock, whose warriors had so brutally dispatched Ebenezer Severance. Daniel Severance had declared that he would 'kill every damnable Indian if I have to, to get to ye Indian that scalped my father!"

Thus, Daniel Severance practiced his hunting and shooting skills dreaming of the day he would stand face-to-face with "Old Man Greylock" and split his head open with a tomahawk sunk in to the middle of his skull! It was said that Dan could load his musket on his back, roll over to his belly, and get off five shots with deadly accuracy in one minute! Caleb Chapin confided to Hawley, "Maybe Dan's breathed in too much turpentine spirits and it corroded down his soul… Maybe he's just born to grow up a hard man, or maybe he's got a pact with the devil over his father's disfigurement… I don't know, but I can tell ye that he's been like this all these years and he ain't a-goin' to change now. Take care, sir, 'cause there's no predicting what Dan might do. They's why he got moved from Fort Pelham to Fort Massachusetts. No predicting what might happen with Dan…."

Chapin exhaled deeply, then added, "And, take care, Lieutenant, don't put any of our "praying friendly Indians" in front of him, 'cause some kind of accidents happen in fights way out there in the woodlands and some of the dead men are found later shot in their backs! Lots o' odd things can happen when they's skulking about in ye dark woods."

Then, after four long years of war and the months of rumors about it ending, late in the fall of 1748, the garrison was informed of the signing of the peace Treaty of Aix-la-Chapelle between England and France.

As the year 1748 and the war closed, peace brought new habits, different thinking, adjustments and changes to the soldiers' way of life. There was much conjecture among all the militia about reductions in forces they heard rumored would be in for the Line of Forts. Forts Shirley and Pelham probably would be reduced down to one soldier and his family. Fort Massachusetts would retain some sentinels, but not all of its war-time strength. Into the winter of 1749, soldiers had been gradually leaving their posts at Fort Massachusetts. The Mohican scouts, George Quaquagid and Connewoonhoundelo Savage, and 23 sentinels were released from service. Sergeant Adonijah Atherton and Corporal Ebenezer Gould were discharged.

The peace had presented an opportunity for Elisha Hawley to resume his civilian life in Northampton. He could return as a heroic officer, one who had been gallantly wounded in service King and country in the skirmish at the fort's gates on August 2, 1748 with the French and their Indians. Fortunately, Lieutenant Hawley had only an ugly scar and slight limp in his left leg. Now was that chance he had so desperately yearned for when he was first exiled out of Northampton and overrun with melancholy and longing. But two years later Hawley felt strength, accomplishment, a sense of adventure and freedom. In civilian life, he supposed he could work with brother Joe and his mother trading and store-keeping. Other prospects might exist to survey new towns opening for settlement.

But there remained the quandary of the pending appeal of his excommunication before the Hampshire Council of Ministers and his cousin, the Reverend Mr. Edwards' insistence that he atone for his sin. The minister continued to insist that Elisha confess publicly to his fornication with Martha. It would revive the all-consuming blabbering. Joe wrote sharply to Elisha in a letter on December 23, 1748,

> "I believe it best for you to Come down as soon as you Can
> with any Convenience!

> "I have thought a great deal of your affair., ... No Church on
> earth Can by their Censures inforce a Match in Such Case, until
> ye two points viz Absolute virginity and the enticement on ye
> man's Side are pretty proved; ...in ye particular of matrimony,
> nor would I attempt or labour to prove anything against her
> Since the burden of proof, beyond all dispute lies wholly on
> either ye woman or the Church."

> "But more than all this there, the woman declares against taking
> you, in ye form ye Church talk of, as also her father and mother.
> ...offer them a proper Confession and rest ye matter. As to
> matrimony, I would Do what I knew ~~God~~ was right in

Conscience and before God, by if there was anything I knew of,
that was particularly binding that, No body else knew of …"[21]

On January 16, 1749 Joe wrote again to Elisha on the turbulence besetting
the First Church Northampton,

"The dispute between Mr. Edwards and ye Church is very much
unsettled, the peoples' minds seem to be calmer that they were
before ye Council[22] which lately sat here…

Joe's letters prattling on about some claptrap or intrigue in town evoked
only distant disinterest or disgust in Elisha. Here in the wilds, he had earned
respect. There in the town, he was the object of scathing criticism. This life was
the world of his true nature. Thus, of the choice between the tangled intrigues of
town versus unintrusive forest and fort, Hawley preferred the company and
affection of his tiny isolated band of comrades-at-arms in the howling wilderness to
the dishonesty and fopperies of town society.

With the onset of peace, their scouting patrols might range out to explore
the curious warm sand springs down from the ox-bow meadow of the Hoosic
River where the fort sat, or the gleaming white marble wall and gorge up Beaver
Brook, "the cascades" falling down a tight crevasse of great "Greylock Mountain,"
north toward the Ragged Mountains, "Big Nose Mountain," the Taconic Hills, or
down to the foreigner Dutch settlements at Albany and Kinderhook with their odd
"Yorker" eccentricities and flavors. Hawley savored some peaceful exploration.

Anyway, his soul lived mostly alone in its own society.

Elisha Hawley caressed his fingertips across the beautifully grained and
oiled maple-wood lap-desk feeling not a single rough splinter, imperfect spot or
friction. The sensation at his fingertips evoked the times he had drawn those same
trembling, warmly pulsing fingertips across the milky, cool skin of Martha Root.

---

[21] To remind readers, authentic documents are interspersed throughout these *Tales*.
Documents are exact, including strikethrough's, grammar and punctuation, except if
footnoted otherwise. This letter is contained in the Joseph Hawley Papers, Bancroft
Collection, New York Public Library. See Bibliography for more information.
[22] A Council of Ministers was convened on June 17, 1749 "to determine a dispute between
the First Church of Northampton and [Elisha Hawley]." Another Council of Ministers met
on June 19, 1750 about dismissing the Reverend Edwards from the Church (his ministry of
about 25 years). The date of this letter would seem to indicate the former Council, although,
the context seems to indicate that this could be confusion over the Julian calendar system
which may not record "1749/50." Alternatively, it could be another Council? Note that the
letters that Elisha Hawley wrote in response to his brother (or others) have not survived,
probably due to Joseph's destruction of them. Read more in the Epilogue at back.

He felt drunkenly giddy - without drink. Her smell invaded his nose and his man-part jumped in anticipation. "Hell-fire damnation!" he cursed quietly at his own reaction. He would now be stuck again with the hardened knot of penis in his breeches screeching for attention.

Hawley stared off at the mud-chinked wall of rough logs commanding down his desires. The more he tried to avoid such thoughts, the more they re-visited him. He knew it was devilish vileness to long for that most pleasurable sin of fornication but the reminders of Martha and their luscious couplings bounded into his thoughts often in unexpected ways. While plopping down on a bower of white pine needles out on a supply trip up toward Cold River (that so-called "river" that was 90% rocks and gargantuan boulders and very little river water), he remembered lowering himself into the downy bundling bed at the Root house. His body stirred again with semen at the ready. It made him catch his breath to remember another liaison when they surreptitiously met down toward the Great River and hush-laughed in quiet throaty giggles or trotted across fields. Around them in the semi-dark/semi-light of sunset, layer upon layer of insect noises had resounded. He remembered breathing in Martha's smell of flowers and berries for dying. Martha Root had been the most unique woman he had ever known: she was assured and intelligent. She had taught him to truly feel.

That single phrase from Joseph's letter clanged again in his ears and stabbed as a pick to a block of ice, "the woman declares against taking you."

"The woman declares against taking you."

Probably he would dream of her again tonight, every part of his being exalt with sensual pleasure, and then he would wake up with his undershirt wetted, as usual. Oh, how suddenly the heavenly warmth of a dream of his manliness sliding among her petticoats and open-bottomed, cotton undergarment to her warm, engulfing womanliness and coming inside her, coagulated to a sleep-stirring chill that awoke one in the night solitude. It took but an instant for the deep satisfaction of the dream to evaporate leaving a gelatinous slime in his shirt and under-drawers! Shame! He had defiled himself again! Oh shame, he felt ashamed of where his 'uncontrolled youthful passions" led him. But it did feel exhilarating and was a tremendous release. He dreamed of lying with her almost every night - and then awoke to find himself alone, aroused, aching and longing.

Later that night as Lieutenant Hawley lay awake, Whiskers his tabby cat soothed herself by licking her fur smooth and clean. She curled atop his chest, keeping herself and Hawley extra warm. Hawley wondered why being together seemed to more-than-double the heat that they produced? Could any creature epitomize true contentment more than a warm, well-fed cat sitting on its owner's lap being gently stroked?!

At the foot of his rope-bed cot were piled cozy two militia regulation-issue white wool blankets, featherbed, sheets and three other types of coverlets/bed rugs. Hawley's dog Hunter, ever a faithful companion and best alarm, lay close by, growling occasionally and flinching in his sleep.

Elisha Hawley waxed poetic picturing the mountains that rose up to the sky with every greenish hue around their miniscule fort. He felt his soul lifted with the multi-colored ribbons of sunset. He gazed at the ebullient stream of the Hoosic River that wandered all the way to the great sea. Prosaically though, he reminded himself that tomorrow he must clean out his magnificent new model "Brown Bess" musket. He must also check the padlocks to the fort's storeroom (repaired by blacksmith, Captain Seth Pomeroy) up from Northampton. Hawley hoped there had been no significant pilfering that he would have to deal with.

Elisha Hawley fervently wished that he could feel the caress of a woman's touch sliding across his skin again. Oh, that was what ecstasy is! He had never experienced anything better. A profound sigh escaped his depths. He wondered, why had her sensation been so singularly marvelous? It was a shimmer across lucid waters. It was a breeze rustling feather-like through his hair. It was cool water gurgling down one's throat in the height of a stifling drought. Why didn't the touch of his own hand on his own back, thigh, or stomach tingle doubly special – particularly since he was experiencing it from two of his own nerve sources? He wondered if it had felt more intense in the autumn's crispness or spring's suppleness? Whichever. He had lain awake many night hours listening to the indoor breathing of other men or the outside howling of forest animals as his spirit roamed the night world of thoughts and memories.

Hawley exhaled another poignant sigh.

Reconstructed Fort Massachusetts from Williamstown Historical Society, with permission.

Hartwell Tavern, Minute Man Road, Lexington, Massachusetts
© Copyright 2019, Todd Atteberry, all rights reserved. Used with permission.

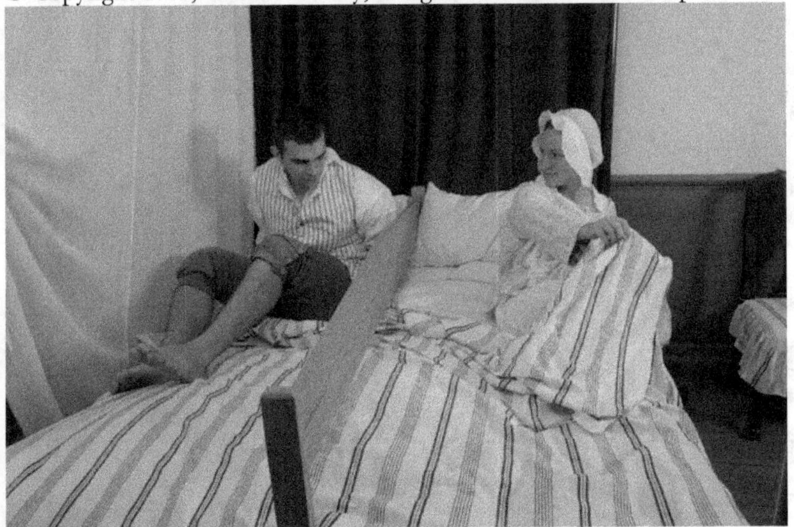

Bundling. Photo from Colonial Williamsburg, used with permission.

Photo from Colonial Williamsburg, used with permission.

Mrs. Elizabeth Clark Freake and Baby Mary, artist unknown.
Portrait in the Worcester Museum of Art. Use in the public domain.

"Royal" by Slabcity Gang is licensed under Creative Commons BY-ND 2.0

Fort at Number 4, view, Charlestown New Hampshire. 28 April 2018. John Phelan Creative Commons Attribution-Share Alike 4.0 International license

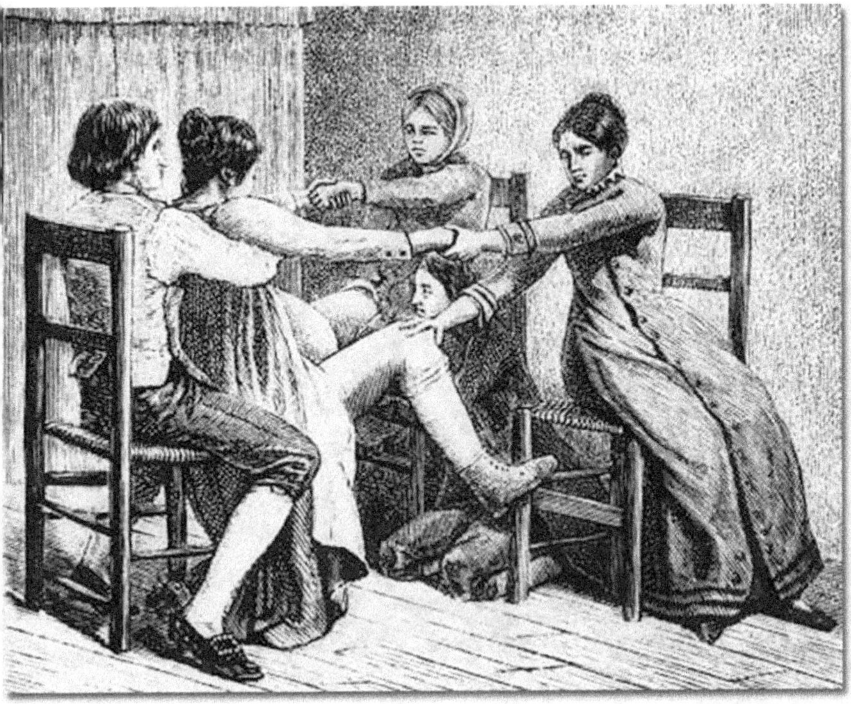

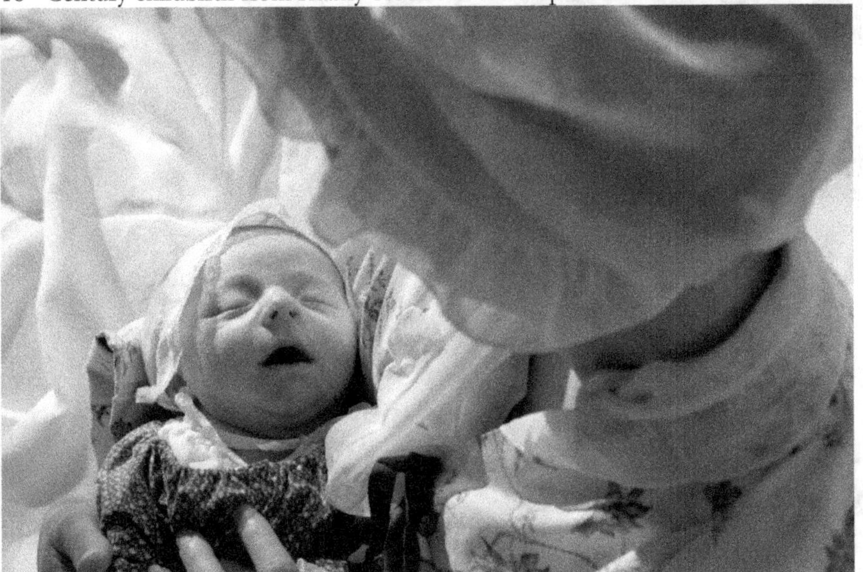

18ᵗʰ Century childbirth from Alamy Stock Photos. Reprinted under "fair use."

Colonial baby from Colonial Williamsburg. Used with permission.

William Hogarth, The Bench (1758)

Jonathan Edwards. Portrait in the public domain.

Photo of colonial cooking at Mount Vernon by Fiona Keyes on www.Flickr.com
Use under Creative Commons attribution license.

Tavern at Blandford, Massachusetts. Photo by Mary Lane.

Photo of outhouse at Historic Eastfield, New York by Mary Lane.

18th century hearth at Historic Eastfield by Mary Lane

©Paladin Communications. Used with permission.

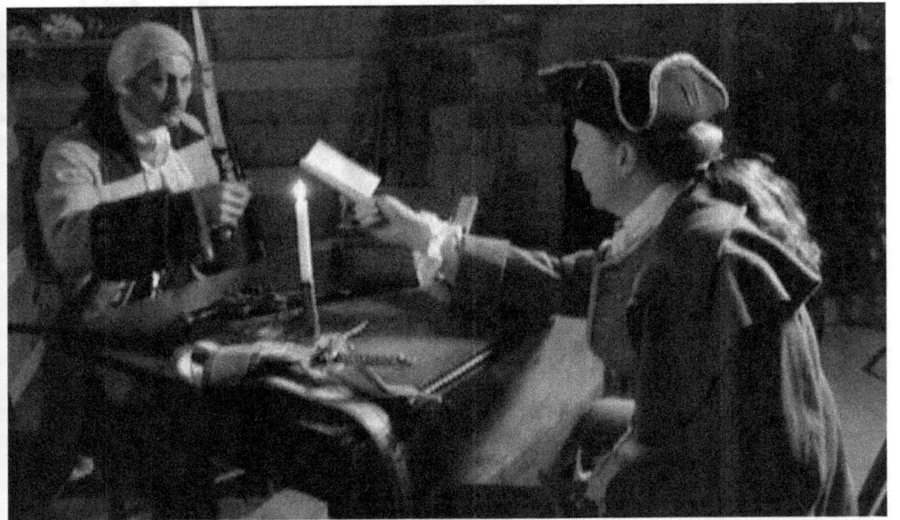

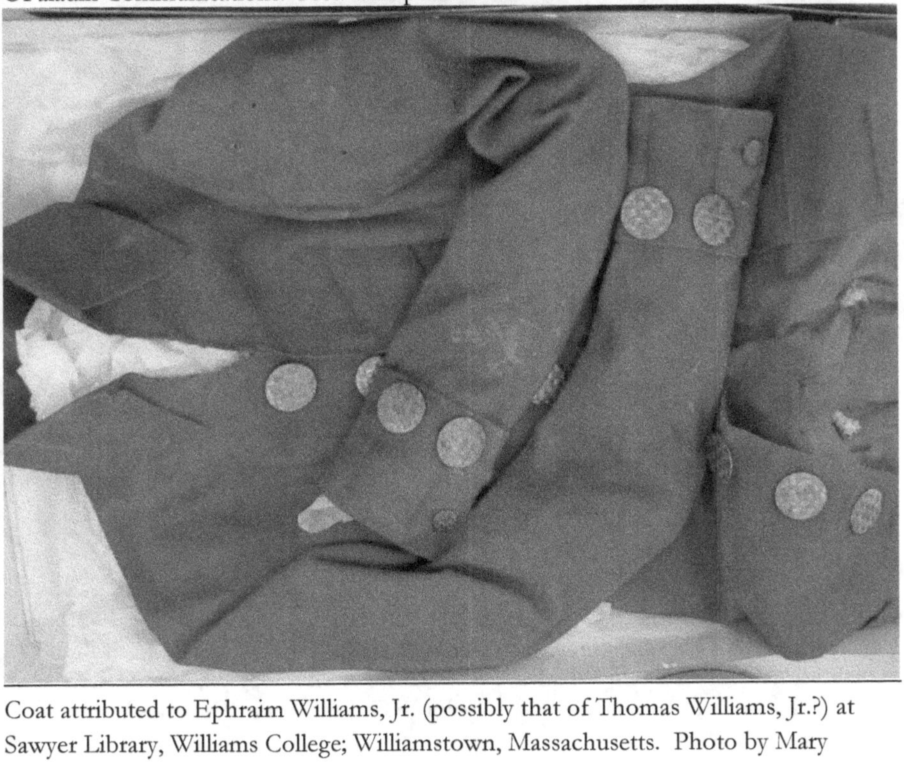

Coat attributed to Ephraim Williams, Jr. (possibly that of Thomas Williams, Jr.?) at Sawyer Library, Williams College; Williamstown, Massachusetts. Photo by Mary Lane.

"The Brave old Hendrick the great sachem or chief of the Mohawk Indians", a hand-tinted engraving of Mohawk leader Hendrick Theyanoguin, published in London in 1755, based on an earlier lost portrait. John Carter Brown Library. In the public domain.

The Bloody Morning Scout by Carin Krestakos. Used with permission.

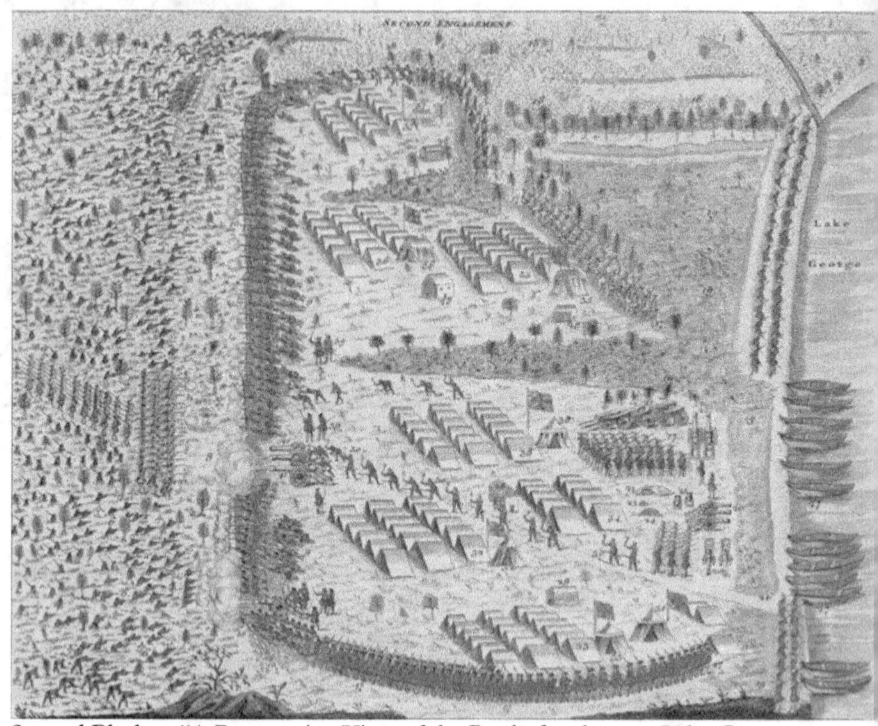

Samuel Blodget "A Prospective View of the Battle fought near Lake George, on the 8th of Sepr. 1755, between 2000 English with 250 Mohawks, under the command of Genl. Johnson: & 2500 French & Indians under the command of Genl. Dieaskau in which the English were victorious captivating the French Genl. with a Number of his Men killing 700 & putting the rest to flight." Published Boston, December 1755. Image in the public domain.

On the Albany Boston Road by Carin Krestakos.

The operation, by Italian painter Gaspare Traversi c.1722-1770. Oil on canvas, 77.5 x 103.5 cm, c.1753-1754. The Staatsgalerie Stuttgart Germany.

Courthouse at Colonial Williamsburg [Virginia] Used with permission.

Hampshire Court of General Sessions, May 15, 1759 at Springfield. Public record.

Hearth candlelight http://passionforthepast.blogspot.com/2016/09/candles-light-at-its-brightest.html Used with permission.

It was after he returned to his family home in Northampton from a courtship visit to Miss Mary Mitchel at Deerfield in late February 1750 that Martha's first cousin, Uncle Hope and Aunt Sarah's son, Aaron Root heard the horrifying news that "throat distemper" was abroad and multiple youths in Deerfield had taken to their sick beds with it! The dreaded throat distemper was known as "the strangling angel of death." In the last epidemic to strike New England in 1735, the disease had killed half of those infected! Its course was heart-breaking, wiping out entire families. In some towns in New Hampshire, four children had to be buried to a single grave.

Aaron Root's heart raced and he could think about nothing but the worry of the throat distemper. Had the dear Miss Mitchel been among those who contracted it? Was she protecting herself from breathing "bad air" and getting the disease? He shuddered and experienced heart palpitations. His temples pounded with surging blood, as his entire body shuddered and flared up. He thought of her pure face, blushing the color of pink hidden deep within a rose petal's core. Throughout the day, he whispered prayers that she would not be afflicted. He knew it a temptation not to submit to the will of the Savior but he begged in his own mind. "Dearest Lord, I implore you to spare Miss Mary Mitchel in your great mercy," poor distressed Aaron silently prayed.

Meanwhile, the daily chores of feeding the cows, sheep, pigs and chickens demanded immediate attention, as did the shoveling of manure out of the barn and onto the garden, but Aaron found himself missing the feeding trough as he distractedly poured the slop for the grunting sows. Nearby in the barn yard, his elder brother Stephen peered quizzically at him with worry and asked if he was a-right? At the unheated meetinghouse for the Sabbath services instead of hearing the Reverend Mr. Edwards' powerful, emotional sermons, Aaron heard nothing but imagined Miss Mary in bed with the throat distemper. He lay awake for hours at night.

Unfortunately, Aaron Root had prayed for Miss Mary, but he hadn't prayed for himself to avoid the throat distemper. It was while the reduced Hope Root family sat at supper meal that Aaron acknowledged the first tinge of wooziness and fatigue and some slight unnatural heat come over him. Then he began to notice soreness in his throat. Overnight and into the next day, he realized that swallowing was torture. As if he was stuffing a sausage, he had to consciously force food and drink down his throat which had grown scratchy and red raw. His family could see that Aaron's tonsils had swelled. It was a struggle to clear his throat of the thick pus-laden mucus that stuck like honey. Soon the dreaded white spots and gray membrane were appearing at the back of his mouth, tongue and throat. He could but sip cautiously at warmed water and ate no more.

Doctor Samuel Mather was hurriedly called to the house and prescribed various concoctions to make Aaron puke up any occult or disturbing substances within. After that, the doctor completely purged his intestines. He prescribed a honey drink and sassafras tea, with a plaster of ungientium dialthae to be applied to his neck.

As his illness continued, the sick man would raise himself up on his bed momentarily, gesture or mouth what he wanted from his sister Hannah Root Strong, who had come to aid her elderly father Hope (as there was no longer any woman in the household after the death of Hope's wife Sarah in September 1747).

The next day when Aaron grew aquiver thrashing on his sleeping cot, the doctor returned to bleed him of a goodly amount of blood from his arm (in Boston some doctors thought it best to bleed from the vein under the tongue first). A day later, on February 28th, the once-robust, handsome and hearty Aaron could not croak out any comprehensible words. His sister noticed his neck seemed to be puffed wide and swelled with fluid, while his cheek bones had become haggard enough to stand out sharply on his constricted face. He commenced coughing up smelly chunks of thick yellow-green mucus. Now when sister Hannah peered into his mouth, she was horrified to see his throat appeared black as dark night! Death was creeping up over him from his innards! Aaron understood from their unnerved reactions and tone that his family was worried, struggling with their faith in a vengeful God, and believing he might soon die.

His elderly father Hope and sister Hannah averted their eyes to cry copious tears when Aaron struggled to express his death wishes. Only five days before he was a living, working, vital man! So suddenly was he smote asunder! Cruelest of all to Hannah was addition of yet one more to the pile of losses to the Hope Root family's many severe losses in such a few years. Dead were their brother Elias, sister Martha Root Hannum and her son Joel, their Mother Sarah, sister Esther Root Strong, sister Sarah Root Southwell and five of her seven children, brother Timothy… Only Hannah, Stephen and Eleazar remained of Hope Root's once-numerous family!

Still, Aaron's mind was alert and consumed with the details of his funeral, grave and last wishes to provide his love, Miss Mary Mitchel, with the best mourning outfit. She must have the best gown, a fan and gloves and a mourning ring …. yet he labored with his inability to breathe, speak and even gesture as his life was evaporating in the face of the raging heat of the black throat distemper. Hope and Hannah sat for hours on chairs pulled beside Aaron's rope-bed, piled with the comforting linens woven by their father's hands many years before. As Aaron labored to give them instructions, Hannah gently but haltingly read Bible verses from Psalms, Corinthians or Revelations:

> "He will wipe every tear from their eyes. There will be no more death' or mourning or crying or pain, for the old order of things has passed away."
> He who was seated on the throne said, "I am making everything new!" Then he said, "Write this down, for these words are trustworthy and true."
> He said to me: "It is done. I am the Alpha and the Omega, the Beginning and the End. To the thirsty I will give water without cost from the spring of the water of life."

Then later,

> "The Lord is my shepherd; I shall not want. He maketh me to lie down in green pastures: he leadeth me beside the still waters. He restoreth my soul: he leadeth me in the paths of righteousness for his name's sake. Yea, though I walk through the valley of the shadow of death, I will fear no evil: for thou art with me; thy rod and thy staff they comfort me.
> "Thou preparest a table before me in the presence of mine enemies: thou anointest my head with oil; my cup runneth over.
> "Surely goodness and mercy shall follow me all the days of my life: and I will dwell in the house of the Lord for ever."

Besides Hannah, his close Root cousins Simeon and Joseph shared some care for Aaron. Family had gathered at his side to faintly sing psalms. Knowing their uncle Hope's opposition to the new hymns, they sang only old-time psalms – nothing newer by the popular Dr. Isaac Watts.

With his deep faith and stark reason, Aaron Root understood that in some days he could be dead of this world but he bravely hoped (in spite of his repeatedly, humbly acknowledged unworthiness) that he might be admitted to his Savior's glorious heaven. He allowed himself some cautious, joyous thoughts of the afterlife….

As he lay on his bedding and tried to ponder what could be the results of his death, he realized that one person's death (his own) would destroy many relationships in this world (such as the friendships with the young men of the town and with the Reverend Mitchel's family at Deerfield). It would set into motion a series of consequences, many of which upset him. He could imagine Mr. Edwards delivering his funeral eulogy. In a state of half dream/half wake, he knew the mourners would be stifling their sobs and sorrow for him. Would Mary Mitchel be amongst his mourners? How could he patiently wait for her arrival in Heaven? It then occurred to him to wonder if she survived, would she later marry another man? How could she still be committed to him - after he died? What if she had children with another man? No one will carry my name, he choked sadly.[23] Maybe no one will remember me? How would it – could it - be together with Miss Mary in Heaven?

His father was weighted down with so much grief that he hardly moved. He could not be trusted to make the decisions for what Aaron wanted. Should he have a winged "death head" carved on his gravestone? After much thought, Aaron scratched down on a scrap of paper what he wanted carved on his stone:

"In memory of Mr. Aaron Root
Who died __(date)________
In ye 29th year of his age."

Hannah realized that the Reverend Mr. Edwards must be called to pray with the now-dying young man and they must call an attorney to hastily write out Aaron's "Last Will and Testament." Brother Stephen was dispatched to bring the minister from his nearby house. Meanwhile, brother Eleazar scurried down the ankle-deep muddy lanes of the town to summon attorney Joseph Hawley, who appeared an hour later with the bag of papers, quill pens, ink bottles and wax seals of the lawyers' trade.

The proud attorney awkwardly tipped his beaver hat (as gentlemen must) toward the solemn, minister Mr. Edwards. Joseph Hawley stood at the threshold, shook off the outdoor cold and grime, then entered and approached the dying man. Joseph Hawley stumbled slightly over the door jam, "shoddy, irregular carpentry," he mumbled.

A glance around the house indicated to the astute lawyer the decline and disorder here. The plaster daub was chipping, unrepaired. Unfinished food was left on trenchers. The bed linens were spotted and disorderly.

---

[23] Mary Mitchel did not marry for three years. When she did, she named her last son, Aaron (Belding). This does not seem to have been a family name with the Mitchel or Belding family lines, but maybe after Aaron Root or a distant cousin Aaron Belding who was killed in 1748?

"Mr. Hawley," said Hannah Root Strong softly, "I'm afraid we'll not be able to pay you at this moment as we paid out our last coins to Doctor Mather for the purgatives."

"Understood, Madame," acknowledged Hawley. The debt would be recorded for a later settlement.

As Joseph Hawley trod across the room to the table, he passed the immobile visage of the taller Reverend. Succumbing to a momentary urge to vindictive sin, Hawley stepped hard on the left foot of Mr. Edwards. The smirking lawyer wondered if he had truly heard a crunch of bones being displaced or just imagined it? "Oh, pardon cousin Edwards," the brash younger man uttered, thereby further diminishing Reverend Edwards with the use of their familiar relationship rather than his ministerial one.

On the walk up to the Hope Root house, Joseph had repeatedly cautioned himself to show no superiority or sneering over these Roots (cousins of his former adversaries the Hezekiah Root family) and the Reverend Mr. Edwards - who, he reminded himself, had been utterly vanquished in the appeal of brother Elisha's case to the Council of Hampshire Ministers less than a year ago. Nevertheless, Hawley congratulated himself for his brilliant legal case. Joseph Hawley reminded himself that the entire Root clan were "just the middling sort, without any distinction whatsoever," as his mother bluntly assessed. Annoyingly though, the Roots did not acknowledge their superiors. They were masters of tenacity and would not give up a fight willingly, Hawley conceded with a grumble.

In spite of his most earnest personal resolutions and fervent prayers, Hawley could not quell the fire that kindled inside him at the merest glance toward Jonathan Edwards. No 'middling' dismissal could be made of Mr. Edwards. Hawley himself had hung in total intellectual rapture at Mr. Edwards' words and analyses years ago. Emotionally, it felt like an eternity, so much had ruptured since then. Hawley's face flushed and he cleared his pinched throat. He felt his hands clenching into angry rocks of fists inside his gloves and his backbone stiffened as if it were an ironwood rod. Worst of all was his consciousness of his reaction to the Reverend. Hawley desperately wanted to feel nothing at the sight of Edwards. He tried to indiscernibly scan Edwards' deportment to judge if Edwards, too, reacted to him, but there was no visible change in the clergyman's aloof demeanor.

Imperceptibly however, the minister eased inches away from Joseph Hawley, as oil would push water aside.

The Roots' deep despair over Aaron's impending death insulated them from the icy fury swirling like a powerful magnetic force repelling the minister and attorney from each other, as they stood over the expiring man. In steely voices, the two gentlemen acknowledged each other.

"Mr. Hawley."

"Mr. Edwards."

They exchanged not another word to each other in the hour they both remained in the static house. The stagnant air lay smotheringly over their low prayers and Hawley's questions concerning Aaron's wishes for his Last Will and Testament. The sound of his quill scraping the surface of the paper grated on Joseph Hawley, who sensed his tranquil veneer being shorn off. He remained ever conscious of the sound of Mr. Edwards and Hannah Root Strong's mumbled prayers. Yet Edwards' exterior appeared as unassailable as a stone fortress. Hawley's ire stirred to hatred of Edwards' impenetrability.

"I must have silence to draft a document of such importance," the attorney commanded the minister and rueful woman. "Do you want flaws in a legal document to cause it to be rejected by the courts after this man is dead and can no longer rectify it?"

The sharp edge in Hawley's voice caused both to cease their spoken words and mumble noiselessly.

Joseph Hawley felt both power and guilt at his ability to control their reactions. He wanted to crush them down but simultaneously felt sorrow at their aching grief. He realized that this interaction would cause him hours of guilty, tormented reflection later. He would lay awake tonight and chide himself for enjoying his deliberate cruelty.

Meanwhile, Jonathan Edwards felt a sickening shock at Joseph Hawley's command to hush the words of God!

Once the *Will* was transcribed, Joseph Hawley advised them that he must have two unrelated men to witness it. Brother Eleazar Root ran to the neighbors to find a man who could legally witness it. Fortunately, Daniel King and John Miller hustled over from their nearby houses to sign their names to the parchment before Aaron succumbed.

"In the Name of God, Amen. I Aaron Root of Northampton in
the County of Hampshire in his Majesty's Province of the

Massachusetts Bay in New England yeoman being weak in Body
but of Sound & perfect mind & memory (blessed be God) do
…make & publish my Last Will & Testament…

"First I give all my Real Estate to my two brethren Stephen Root
& Eleazar Root…

"Secondly I give to Mary Mitchel Daughter of Joseph Mitchel of
Deerfield in the County aforesaid a Suit of mourning apparel
including the following particulars viz a Gown & Coat of the
best or finest Sort of black Silkcrape a black Silk Scarfe Hood &
Gauze Veil a black Velvet Handkerchief with a Lace to it, a black
pair of Silk Gloves a long black Taffety apron a Gauze fan & a
black ribbon Girdle. Also I give to the said Mary £70 in Bills of
Public Credit of the Province aforesaid of the old Tenor"

King and Miller carefully added their signatures to the bottom left side of
the Will, then stepped back from the rough table to gape around the darkened sick
room.

The sick man was in so much pain that he could no longer register
anything but his pain, which commanded the scant attention and few scattered
thoughts his brain could muster. Were they really even thoughts or merely the last
primitive sensations of a failing brain? The world surrounding him could no longer
be seen or mattered. He could think on nothing else but his searing throat and
blinding pain. "Aarrguhh," he growled out.

Then Aaron Root sat up abruptly in the bed, stared wide-eyed for his last
look at earth, and fell over dead from the cot onto the floor, trailing the bedding
linens behind his infected corpse. Hannah Root Strong rushed out the door into
the brisk March air where her hot tears froze onto her flushed face. And she fell to
the frigid ground in a seizure of grief.

After his cleansing and winding in his death shroud by his sister and
female Root cousins, Aaron's body would be stored in his pine coffin behind the
chicken coop to wait for the digging of his grave at the Bridge Street Cemetery.
Since the ground was so frozen, the Roots must pay extra for the labor. Sister
Hannah took Aaron's clothes far from the house to burn them in a stubble-strewn
corn field to avoid spreading the disease further.

Hannah Root Strong's name would be one of the next to be listed among
the deceased in the *Town Book* of records, leaving only her 75-year-old father and
brothers Stephen and Eleazar from a once numerous and boisterous family. In fact
though, Hope Root remained behind in life only physically. Any yearning he had

had to live had vanished. The deaths - one after another - of his wife, adult sons and daughters, and grandchildren emptied the stout heart of the withering old man.

Hope Root had been a staunch defender of the pure ancient ways of the true religion. He had cared not for the opinions of feint hearts who lived in fear of shame. True to their Root reputation for eccentricity, iron wills, strong opinions and unadulterated outspokenness, Hope Root had often been a bane to community leaders, civil and religious. In spring 1744, he had traveled the Bay Path to Boston to buy cochineal bugs for fabric dye and focused on visiting the Reverend Benjamin Colman to complain on the singing of new hymns (which the Reverend Mr. Colman promptly informed the Reverend Mr. Edwards of by letter). Hope objected to Mr. Edwards introducing Dr. Watts' new hymns into the Sabbath Service by standing up during the service and turning his back to the minister in the pulpit. His staggering silent protest drew every eye amongst the hundreds in the meetinghouse to his solitary figure of protest. It stunned the congregation but no one was shocked that it had been Hope Root who did it. Of course, very few agreed with him but Hope Root had always expressed his decided opinions.

His brother Hezekiah had watched Hope bleed out energy and the longing to live over the last years, so that Hope's eyes were hollow and empty. Soon Hope ate so little that Hezekiah knew he would not survive and their close companionship of almost 74 years would peter out to a desolate end. Hezekiah had urged Hope to rally for the sake of for his two living sons Stephen and Eleazer, for their church, for their right Reverend Mr. Edwards, for the lasting providence on their people, but Hope remained despondent in hopelessness. He paid scant attention to anything. Hope paid no attention to church matters anymore.

Hezekiah struggled to interest Hope how to vote in the matter of the possible dismissal of the Reverend Mr. Jonathan Edwards from the First Church, "Hope, Hope (he tried to catch his brother's eye and bring Hope into the present) …" "Hope, how goes your vote with the brethren? For the dismissal of Mr. Edwards or to save our sacred bonds? You know the Hawley faction wants Mr. Edwards dismissed because he insists on a "converting experience." Every believer should be able to recount their regeneration, as we all did. You know that those Hawleys hate Mr. Edwards. Hate him, viscerally and fervently."

Hezekiah cringed internally knowing that Hope's Timothy had been among those who did recount a converting experience, became a full church member – and then strayed so ignobly! Who could truly know the mind of another?! Or perhaps one only knew one's own mind at any particular minute? Or perhaps it was the minds of the young that were so changeable? Or perhaps the mind and heart are so fickle and inconstant, even in the face of life's greatest mystery?

Hope only replied in utter dejection, "The Lord hath dealt very bitterly with me."

When Hezekiah asked solicitously, "Brother, do you know if you have provoked God to visit these sore and grievous calamities upon thy family?"

After a significant pause, Hez Root continued tenderly, "I doubt not that you have examined thy conscience thoroughly, Hope.... I... I know thy true heart and humility always before the Lord."

This seemed as both an apology and a prod, but in the dim light of the small house's interior, every breath or twitch tremored like an earthquake. "My abiding concern is for the fellowship of the church, for Mr. Edwards and for our own eternal submission to the Lord of all. And salvation."

Aching sorrow weighted Hez's soul. "Mr. Edwards hath been a stalwart to us. He hath been our guide, our shepherd and our rock in tempestuous times. Think of his solicitousness at the deaths of dear sister Sarah and baby Esther. Think of the miraculous preservation of the church members at the lightning strike on the steeple so many years ago. Think on the deaths of the Lyman sisters or little Phoebe Bartlett's conversion. Think of all these providences, these smiles of God upon us."

The broken man gave no reply, sitting still bowed and speechless in incurable grief.

"Hope, Hope, Hope," Hezekiah sighed, "the Hawley faction will get all their people there to the vote to dismiss Mr. Edwards from this ministry!"

Finally Hope Root stirred, "And thinks you, Hezekiah, that you and your type will prevail against that horde? Them Hawleys, Stoddards, and Williams own all this county! Should you vote against their faction, they'll ruin you – and your sons. Your weaving orders will dry up. They will strangle you of work. Many of the brethren wants to stay out of it altogether and will never appear for the vote..."

Hope Root spit. He never spoke again, dying with a whimper some weeks later.

Bridge Street Burying ground, (cemetery), Northampton
Image "Bridge_Street_Northampton_080620 (20)" by melvisflickr licensed under
CC BY-NC-ND 2.0

Many were the gracious and good gifts that had been bestowed upon Betty Pomeroy. The first was her life itself. Her mother's older baby (also named Elizabeth), born two years before her, had soon gone to the grave. Betty was also blessed with a strong family linage. The rich, pious and respectable Pomeroy name commanded respect everywhere from their gun-making and blacksmithing. She had been gifted with a righteous upbringing in ye Lord Savior Jesus Christ, a quick intelligence at her lessons and the Catechism, life without hunger, schooling - expended in spite of her being only a girl, a full dower chest of linens and household goods to bring to her marriage. God's blessings and favors had been truly bestowed upon her!

As all descendants of Adam and Eve, she was born a sinner and all her efforts were for naught as it was only by the grace of God's indulgence that she was thus gifted. She reminded herself at the family's twice daily prayers, that she was a stubborn and rebellious sinner. "Oh, so vile a monster of sin am I! What shall I do to be saved? What shall I do to be among the elect?"

Betty fell asleep each night praying for guidance and for God's support for her to overcome her human depravity. "I am a stubborn, callow and rebellious sinner with a multitude of secret faults," she confessed. Indeed, as the Reverend Mr. Edwards had cautioned his parishioners, every human dangles as a spider over the flames of hell, but for God's saving grace. (She was embarrassed to have these images from Mr. Edwards' sermons in her mind in spite of her father's fervent opposition to him and the Reverend's dismissal from their church.) How she struggled to overcome her own defects! How she bowed her head with humility. She never neglected a Sabbath, a service, her daily prayers. Her soul craved redemption. How she listened with a thirsty soul to each and every word of *The Holy Book*. How she had always happily served and honored her own father, Deacon Ebenezer Pomeroy Junior. How she respected her place and those around her, greeting all with the utmost respect in the archaic fashion, "Good day, Goodwife Strong." "Good eve, Elder Lyman." She had visited the sick and delivered medicinal herbs to them. Betty Pomeroy had never dared nor dreamed of straying from the straight and narrow path. She had never engaged in the youthful frivolities or night walking of many unruly youths. No, instead her humble, uneventful life had been plain work, embroidery, tent stitch, samplers and the other womanly arts that she learned and performed well. She endeavored to choose every means of grace and had been rewarded for her dutifulness by this blessed life. But... was she truly among those saved in eternity?

Betty had been a true witness in the scandalous affair of the *Granny Book (The Midwife Rightly Instructed)* in the spring of 1744. It made her blush hot with remorse and humiliation years later to remember the life-changing, halting testimony that she and Kate Wright had stuttered out before the First Church committee of elder brethren of the church (Colonel Stoddard, Captain Lyman and her own father, the Deacon). For years, her older brother Eben refused to look her in the eyes for her naming him as one of the boys who had looked at the filthy, craven midwife's book of images of women's bodies and babes within them! Filth! Practically whoredom! (Betty shuddered at the word itself.) Betty had always done her duty. She had experienced saving grace, recounted her conversion experience before the church and been accepted into full membership in the Church, and she owed it to the church to report wrongdoing, which she dutifully did.

Betty Pomeroy was grateful for her gifts but felt a longing. It was vanity, indeed, but oh how deeply she wished for just a little more charming face and refined a figure. And frankly, she was embarrassed by her 'Pomeroy nose," planted squarely on her face as a bulky field stone amidst tiny pebbles. Granted it was the righteous soul that mattered most in life, but she would trade some of her worldly fluffery for a fair face and slender gracefulness of body. She had forsworn fancy dress and Flanders lace. She was always meek and modest of dress. No silk, no long showy hair style. As the Bible enjoined, "Strength and honor are her clothing." Her mother instructed her that it should satisfy a woman to have her husband look upon her with kindness rather than desiring more from God.

These were the pure and untrammeled thoughts of blushing maid Betty on the precipice of true womanhood. This was dutiful Betty Pomeroy as her father and Madame Rebekah Pomeroy negotiated marriage between Betty and Elisha Hawley in the autumn of 1751.

However, the mind is a place even the owner cannot always control. Thoughts develop with their own volition. Thus, although Betty dutifully accepted the proposed husband Elisha Hawley, she couldn't prevent herself from thinking of his sullied past. He had dallied with that Root woman. Betty knew that he had looked at Martha Root across the meetinghouse. Did he covet her in his heart? He had also seemed to contemplate her friend Kate Wright, while he dismissed Betty. He ignored her. It was as if she didn't exist to him at all – until they were wed.

One day she caught him staring at her beastly big hands with a shadow of revulsion. They were the hands of generations of blacksmiths, large, gawky and powerful. She sensed his physical recoil. Had her hands absorbed the omnipresent gray smutty blacksmithing dust? Had she absorbed the odor of horse and cow dung and burning charcoal they used for fuel that pervaded the shop? Had she the muscular shoulders and arms of generations of forgers of iron? Did she walk as a beast of burden carrying a weight of wood? Did he hear the heavy ring of a smith's hammer falling followed by three lighter taps on an anvil in her voice's cadence?

Regardless, her father and Mother Hawley knew what was best in their son and daughter's "helpmeet." The time had come for Elisha (and Joseph, although that is the next story) to marry, now that the Hawley sons had received their inheritance from Uncle Ebenezer Hawley. Elders knew what was best for youth. Betty said nothing when she learned of the arrangements. When Mother Hawley had informed Elisha, he flinched. Seeing his grimace, Rebekah chastised him, "What of her plain face? She is chaste and pious!"

"Not plain, mother. Ugly." Elisha corrected harshly.

"She'll be the prettiest wife in Northampton on her wedding day," Rebekah predicted confidently.

"I don't know about Northampton, but at least the prettiest wife on Pudding Lane," Elisha paused for effect. "Particularly as there are no others - since the widow Bridgman died," he finished caustically.

Brother Joe gasped in a sharp breath. Elisha was growing more careless by the day! At this rate, he would soon be audacious and irascible, almost to open revolt! No, Elisha was not there yet. He hadn't the will to oppose Mother but he was growing dangerously bold!

"Hold your tongue and throw not the first stone, Elisha Hawley! You should not be one to criticize!" her voice rebuked with the sting of a leather whip. "A marriage covenant is never to be reckoned giddily. This is not a fickle whim of love, fleeting as a shadow. Marriage is a trial from God - for you to live up to."

There was much more she could have said but she stopped herself, remembering the mental sickness of his father and fearing Elisha might be infected by it as well. The room fell silent with her stern reproach and his swallowed resentment, and dread hanging heavy over them all.

Being a family of ministerial and legal persuasion and the Pomeroys envying such, Elisha and Betty's wedding was strictly, properly and perfunctorily conducted by brother Joseph as Justice of the Peace. (Since the dismissal of the Reverend Mr. Edwards, the town had no permanent minister.) But was it dutiful Betty, her father's deacon position in the church or the Pomeroy family's wealth with which Rebekah Hawley was most enamored?

After they married on December 4, 1751, Betty was flattered when she found a highly polished looking-glass among the household items. She soon observed, however, that her husband showed more interest in gazing at his reflection in it than she did at hers! This had to be slyly detected, as Elisha only pretended to contemplate himself to comb his hair and settle his hat. He still wore his felt, tri-cornered, braided officer's hat rather than the new woolen cap that she had knit for him. He carried his wooden comb ever on his person in his pouch. Within a few weeks of their marriage, she realized that he never passed by the looking glass on the mantle in the parlor without glancing at it to regard himself and pull out his comb. She observed that if he saw her eyes on him, he immediately turned away and feigned disinterest.

Once she began actually studying him, Betty realized that her husband Elisha favored breeches rather too tight and shorter waist coasts and frocks that revealed his legs and figure! When he was in town, Betty had twice the laundry to beat out in the sun as one shirt per week could never suffice for him! He changed each week! She wore her worsted wool stockings for a month.

In honesty, Betty frequently reflected that she was more married to Mother Hawley than to Elisha. Mother Hawley crossed the fields to visit or stay with Betty (particularly in Elisha's absence) more than her own mother and sister Esther. Betty had tried to live up to the ideal "wife of noble character" of Proverbs 31: "She brings him good, not harm all the days of her life." Betty knew a good wife's qualities: strictest virtue, a gentle nature, agreeable and never harping, passable good sense, plentiful fortune brought to her marriage, a "candle burning into the night" with her hard work. Of course, she should not be meddlesome in her husband's business, nor complaining about her endless domestic duties.

At least Betty consoled herself, even if she was not comely, she was prettier than Brother Joe Hawley's chosen, Mercy Lyman. Poor Mercy, about whom Mother Hawley had harshly remarked that she has "a face like a toasting iron!" It was cruel but Betty could do nothing about that and she was grateful that she didn't live under the freezing glare of Mother Hawley's disapproval as Mercy did.

In her two slow years of marriage, Betty had spent thousands of hours silently visiting and working beside her grim mother-in-law cooking meals, hauling water, shelling peas and beans, weeding the kitchen garden, boiling the lard for soap, dipping the candles, spinning wool to yarn, feeding the animals and much more. The chores were dreary and unending. Sun-up to sun-down, there were always tasks that must be done. Ever dutiful, Betty took to her tasks in the pursuit of the ideal of the good wife: "She looketh well to the ways of her household, and eateth not the bread of idleness."

Occasionally on an obligatory visit, Mother Hawley might take the sugar nippers out of her rich-grained cherry wood sugar chest and they would sit together in the Windsor chairs and drink a hot chocolate or a mug of ale together. When Mercy, the new wife, was instructed to draw water, Mother Hawley would smile and pat the chair next to her and say, "Come, Betty. Keep me company in my sewing." Mother Hawley insured that Mercy never saw the secret drawer in her linen chest with the brass lock or how she kept the key on a deep blue grosgrain ribbon on her neck.

Dismissive, severe and superior Rebekah Stoddard Hawley could be. But Betty knew it was not for her to judge Mother Hawley. The elder woman had tried to show kindness to Betty in her own way. It was hard enough to live anywhere in the shadow of Mother Hawley in Northampton. All of western Massachusetts, lay in the shadow of Rebekah and the Stoddard family. As far away as Fort Massachusetts and West Hoosuck Plantation with nothing but endless eternal dark forests, even there the specter of Rebekah Stoddard Hawley cast a deep shade over Betty's marriage and life.

It grew more difficult as the Hawley house seemed to grow smaller with the passing seasons. On November 30, 1752, new wife Mercy Lyman Hawley had moved into the house. Betty's nervousness, edginess and impatience mounted the longer the three households clustered near each other. What an impossible predicament to hope to please her husband and her mother-in-law both, as well as subsist harmoniously with Joe and Mercy. It seemed the more she pleased Mother Hawley, the more Elisha ignored her. She resolved to find God's will for her in this labyrinth of the impossible.

It was alleged amongst the town-folk that the Hawleys were cursed. Regard Grandfather Joseph the First and Elisha's father, Joseph the Second's horrible deaths. One certainly grieved for the awful accident of Grandfather Hawley, but the perfidious act of Father Hawley taking his own life was naught but the defiler Satan! How else could one explain it?

Elizabeth Pomeroy Hawley knew too of the struggles of her brother-in-law Joseph Hawley not to hear the voice of despair (or the devil) as his father had. Many nights in the darkened house Betty knew from Mercy that Joe bumped around and did not sleep, instead burning a pine-knot torch late into the night as he sat up at his desk. What was this curse? Without his kindly wife Mercy, Joseph too might have tumbled into devilish curses and temptations.

Of her own husband Lieutenant Elisha Hawley, Betty felt little but an unknowing circumspection. There was the matter of Betty's marriage covenant, but what "covenant" for a husband to be forever and a day away? What real discourse was there between them when he preferred residing among men in the howling wilderness to the comforts of loyal wife and warm hearth? He was frequently absent at surveying or at some work away. "I cannot be so transported with the comforts of marriage as to neglect duties," Elisha excused.

Of all her trials, the most humiliating was the fact that none doubted her barrenness. Elisha had fathered a child with Martha Root. Betty recalled the Biblical verse from Psalms 72: 16 concerning fertility:

"There shall be a handful of corn in the earth on the top of the mountains; the fruit thereof shall shake like Lebanon: and they of the city shall flourish like grass of the earth."

Betty had prayed for election to the ranks of the visible saints and salvation in the "final days" but her heart inconsolably longed for a child. Although married two years, she was still without child. Wasn't it written in the Good Book that "Her children arise up, and call her blessed; her husband also, and he praiseth her." Sadly, Betty's womb and her heart were empty. Where had she failed? When would her prayers be answered? Was this a curse? Was it on her or the Hawley family? Betty Pomeroy Hawley was "a woman that feareth the Lord" so therefore, "she should be praised." The Pomeroy family had been repeatedly praised and blessed with children – until now. Until her.

At every occasion of seeing Martha Root and her doe-eyed daughter clinging to her skirts, Betty's heart was saddened. Betty knew her own barrenness was being confirmed among her friends and family who were growing increasingly unhinged with each passing month. She supposed it must be brazenly discussed by the Root women and their relatives. They must laugh at her. Tears welled in her eyes to imagine it. Her checks burned to walk into the meetinghouse and feel their eyes scrutinizing her belly to detect if there was yet any swelling there. Of course, at home Mercy and Mother Hawley needn't check anything. At a glance, their eyes inspected her washing out the menstrual rags of "her female condition." There was no hiding the emptiness of her sour womb.

One glorious fall day Betty joined the other Pomeroy women for a day working together at candle-dipping at her parents' commodious house. The Pomeroy men had slaughtered six sheep and the tallow was being used for the candles. Since the flax for the candle wicks had already been spun in a prior "work-bee," it was a full day of work boiling the tallow, rendering it and dipping,

dipping, dipping - twenty-five times - the wicks into rendered animal fat and bayberry wax for every candle to be produced. Betty hoped her share of the work-bee would enable her to take home 500 candles for the next year.

After hours of chatter around the heavy iron kettles of heated candle-wax, the older women retired for some rest, leaving the young ones. Among them was Betty's long-time confidante, "servant" girl Bathsheba, who sat as close as a whisper would want and murmured alluringly, "Oh, Mistress Betty, this heat so fatigues me. Come, sit close and hold my hand."

The enslaved woman sighed, "You seem so sad, Betty. Is all well with ye?"

"Yes, of course, Bash. What causes you to ask?"

"Just that you haven't said hardly a word this whole day. I haven't seen you smile. You hardly ate a bite of mid-day dinner. And you've hardly touched your mug of ale…" She paused languidly, "I feel a heaviness has settled on your shoulders, Mistress."

Betty Pomeroy Hawley stuttered a faint denial, "The heat bothers, that's all."

Bathsheba Negro might be a serving girl but she could well assess her mistresses (an essential survival tool for the enslaved). After the other women moved out of hearing range Bash arched her eyebrow questioningly and stared into her former mistress's eyes. Finally, Betty burst forth into a downpour of tears, racked with shoulder-shaking and hushed sobs for a full minute. The Pomeroy servant girl touched her sturdy fingers on the crying other woman's upper arms.

"Oh, poor, poor Mistress Betty. These are frowns of Providence! I knew it! Something does trouble ye… Are you ill? What is it? You can confide in me, mistress."

"My moon term comes again," Betty whispered as she turned her head in humiliation to stare away at the distance.

"Oh, I see. No fruitful seed," concluded the more knowledgeable servant girl. "Is it that ye hate your husband, Betty?"

"No, no. I swear not," adjured the frightened Betty.

"I've heard that the seeds will not mix - if the woman hates her husband," warned Bathsheba forebodingly.

"No, no, not so," poor Betty gulped.

"Well, there are foods that sweeten the womb," Bathsheba thought carefully how to proceed. A long silence ensued before she hesitatingly added, "There are the old women's tricks."

"What say you? What do you speak of, Bash?"

"Miss Betty, I've seen the old wise women… They say eating new-laid eggs fortifies the womb. So they say…" A silence hung heavy between them as each one guarded some thoughts and weighed what others to disclose. At some length Bathsheba mouthed almost inaudibly, "Some use protection against the evil ones."

"What is that? Have you seen such? Do you know of such?" murmured Betty.

"I could, I could…. I know not myself. But I could ask the old ones I know." There was a thick silence before the black woman continued. "I could ask of amulets…"

Betty grew uneasy and thought the better, "Magic spells and potions? No, Bash, not those. Never. I'm a full church member…"

"Of course, Miss Betty. No black magic! Not I, no! I, too, am a church member. I don't adhere to that at all. But I have heard that a drop of the monthly blood in the husband's drink…" Bathsheba's voice trailed off to just hot breath. "But as I said that is not for I. Not I. Not spells or potions or secret incantations."

For long seconds the air hung weighted by silence, till Bathsheba felt ready. "Satan does work on this earth. The devil lives among us. That we know. I was thinking of protections against the workings of evil. Only to ward off evil."

"How's that?"

"Some use protections to stop evil. And the womb must be balanced and sweet for a perfect babe to grow."

Betty considered further on this.

"I know women that hold close small charms or pieces of luck and good to drive away evil. To stop the devil's eyes upon them," the chocolate-skinned young woman explained.

As for warding off evil, Deacon Pomeroy's servant Bathsheba Negro, knew evil could spring forth from life with abrupt treachery. Although she had faithfully served amongst the family all the life she could recall, at the Deacon's words she could be sold away forever to the vast, wild frontiers! Thus, a scowl on the Deacon's brow could leave her in a near-sleepless state of agitation for weeks. She could be sold! Sold away from all she knew and cherished in life - all family, friends, her own sleeping pallet, her own warm corner in the attic, her precious small comforts, like the occasion cup of warm drinking chocolate or left-over puddings, the comfort of her church where she sat in the same gallery seat in the upper gallery, the quiet of the far woodlot where she could spend a few minutes of rest while collecting kindling and secretly meeting with the other "African" slaves. She could lose everything that made her life bearable as she served and waited for a blessed afterlife.

If ever they forgot this, the other blacks reminded each other that with a moment of anger they could lose everything and be sent to reside near the "savage Indians!" It was well-known that the Indians hated "black skin," who were the first killed in a raid or capture. Remember "old Frank" in the Deerfield raid? He had been first to be taken away and never seen again.

Bathsheba's eyes quickly pooled up, but in company, she could not allow herself to contemplate or show sorrow, so she blinked off the tears and turned toward Betty.

"Could you have a "sour womb" dear Mistress? Could you have a curse hanging on you?"

Betty blanched as her pale pink skin drained to sallow. Abruptly, she rose up and walked away, "Me thinks I needs the privy."

When she returned to her friend's side, the dutiful Betty muttered ever so quietly, "Bash, can you get one of those protections against evil for me?" pleaded Betty. "If only this curse could be lifted! If only I could bear a child!"

Betty's eyes flooded over in copious tears. Bathsheba said nothing more but squeezed Miss Betty's freezing hand. One week later Bathsheba profited from the occasion to deliver Betty's hardened candles and a tiny cornhusk doll, wrapped in a tightly-bound piece of red and white calico cloth. Bathsheba explained to Betty that the cornhusk baby must be given a name and worn day and night on her belly against her skin, so as to balance and then stimulate the vital humors within her barren womb and produce a child.

But wanting a child as deeply and strongly as she did, Betty could not bring herself to wear the cornhusk doll under her skirts Sabbath Day to church services. It petrified her to imagine her mother or a kinswoman touching her and accidentally discovering the charm! Resort to devilish black magic charms and she would be truly undone!

One November morning Rebekah, sister-in-law Mercy and brother-in-law Joe surrounded Betty on their walk to the meetinghouse. There was open anxiety today with the return of the Reverend Mr. Jonathan Edwards to the pulpit of the church (from which he had been dismissed three years ago) "riding circuit." The Northampton Church still had no settled minister. Every word Edwards uttered merited double scrutiny both for its petty personal and grand theological import. When, for example, Mr. Edwards had preached, "We live in a world of change, where nothing is certain or stable, and where a little time, a few revolutions of the sun brings to pass strange things, surprising alterations, in particular persons in families, in towns and churches, in countries and nations," was he secretly referencing the Hawleys and Pomeroys? Did that slight sudden cough of Esquire Timothy Dwight poke at them or was it merely a tickle in his throat? Were those Root women glaring at the Hawleys and nodding with smug self-satisfaction, rather than true contemplation of the "end of days?" Was it true, as Rebekah postulated, that the town was turning its allegiances again?

At the end of the afternoon service, the Hawley group strode down the main aisle of the church toward the door to leave. An ostentatious buzz greeted them at the back of the building where a group of the Root women and friends had gathered. Betty and Mercy recoiled in shock. But Madame Rebekah would not be cowed by anyone.

As she tried to walk past the Root group but was impeded, Rebekah hissed, "Bastard."

The sound simmered and glowed in the air of the frigid building as a hot coal on frozen snow. The poisonous word vibrated long on the darkening air, sounding as wickedness itself must. Martha Root's heart skipped a beat.

"Is a gentleman without honor indeed a gentleman?" queried Martha Bridgman Root aloud to her concurring womenfolk.

"No, no."

"Indeed not."

"No honor, no gentleman," agreed the women around her.

Undaunted, Rebekah Hawley did not even slow her march out. "A little bastard …maybe that's all the milk the cow could produce," replied Madame Hawley with sharp crispness in her voice as she glanced over at the younger Martha and the frightened girl Anne. It figures, Rebekah thought, it wasn't even a male child!

"What a prodigy of pride, malice and arrogance is she!? I've heard it said that the devil gave the world three bags of malice: one for the whole cold cruel world, one for all the degenerates of Boston and one whole bag of malice for Rebekah Hawley all by herself!" huffed Mother Martha as she stomped her way out of the wintry building, carrying her now extinguished foot-stove.

The glorious late afternoon sunset-glowing skies of stark winter went unnoticed. No one of them wondered why the bowl of the sky appeared bigger as the light descended than in the routine brightness of day? No one pondered at the daily miracle of sunlight saturating the sky with bright blues or pastel hues from palest discernible yellow to deep purple - simply by the sun's position in the sky? No one asked themselves how the sun could shine bright white at midday but splinter into different hues of buttery yellow, gold, rosy pink, vivid orange, violet, deep purple, and multiple gradations of blue depending on where the light fell? No one considered if the world was more beautiful when darkness loomed.

But the dutiful Betty lay awake in the quiet of the long night wondering whether the great God was punishing her, Elisha, Rebekah, the Roots or them all.

Many things in this world of pain and woe are hard to understand - and the 11 days that were lost between September 2 and September 14, 1752 were among the hardest. It started with the English Parliament's "Calendar Act of 1750" (or "Lord Chesterfield's Act" since he pushed for it). Everyone had known that there were problems with the Julian calendar (maybe it had worked for the ancient Romans, but no more). It was obviously askew but how to fix it without so much trouble to everyone? Negotiations with the French were much complicated by having different calendars between England on the Julian calendar and others in Europe on the Gregorian calendar.[24] It was hard to be sure what day prisoners might be exchanged or when envoys might be meeting. And worse, Englishmen and women found it confounding to plan what day to plant or remember their true birth-days, because the days and months had moved forward in the calendar. The day of the New Year (March 25, also called "Lady Day") was no longer at the spring equinox, but instead had come closer and closer to winter's darkness. Finally, the solution by the vote of the House of Lords was to change to the Gregorian calendar. Parliament dictated that they would go to sleep on Wednesday, September 2, 1752 and when the English woke up the very next day on Thursday, it would be September 14th!

In England, rumors were that there were riots and manifestations around Bristol where the common people demanded, "Give us back our 11 Days!"

In the American colonies, many grumbled that the English gentry had even managed to screw up "natural days," believing that they would somehow make a profit out of it all! Of course, the poor suspected the rich did it to them in order to have rents and loans paid sooner. Contrariwise, Dr. Benjamin Franklin of Philadelphia opined jovially, "It is pleasant for an old man to be able to go to bed on September 2nd and not have to get up until September 14th!"

In Northampton in the Massachusetts Bay Colony at Hunt's Tavern, scuttlebutt was that they must all drink enough for 11 days until the blaggard Jehiel Clark upped the ante boastfully declaring, "Why fellows, says you that you're

---

[24] The Julian calendar, by Julius Caesar and used since the Roman Empire, was insufficiently precise and advanced one day every 128 years against the solar cycle. See Footnote 6 on page 64 or http://www.history.com/news/6-things-you-may-not-know-about-the-gregorian-calendar

drinking for 11 days' worth; well, I bet you all that I can dance a jig for the 11 days!"

So inebriated were his drinking friends that they took the bet. Jehiel commenced dancing just before midnight and when they were all ready to stagger their ways' home, he asked loudly, "What's the date now, boys?"

Those remaining in the tavern commenced a furious argument over what to call that rugged dawning. "Today's Thursday, the day after yesterday, Wednesday," shouted a few still alert enough.

"Forget that, you blockheads! What's the date?!?" Jehiel yelled back.

"Blockheads, says you! Why, we'll have 'ur hide for cursing old friends!"

To which Jehiel (the genius) countered, "Boys, boys, is today September 14th? You owe me a tuppence! I danced from September 2 until the 14th! Ha-ha!"

The next day, Jehiel laughed till he fell over off his chair, having imbibed all his winnings at the same Hunt's Tavern.

Across the town, attorney Joseph Hawley glowed in the happiness that he would celebrate his nuptials with Miss Mercy Lyman 11 days earlier! "We'll become Mr. and Mrs. Joseph Hawley 11 days sooner," he crowed.

Mercy had waited many long years for Joseph's nuptial proposal. Many times she despaired that he might never amass the courage to surmount his mother's objections, but, finally - at long last - he did.

In his own quivering fervor of love, Joseph neglected to observe the deafening silence of his family. Although his younger brother Elisha, had married less than a year earlier, he was spending time surveying properties or roads rather than remaining at home with his new wife Betty Pomeroy Hawley. By the spring of 1752 Elisha Hawley occupied himself and a crew of two linemen running survey lines for the Hatfield "Three Mile Addition." Then Elisha was commissioned to work on Captain Ephraim Williams' mill at Fort Massachusetts, on the Hoosick Road from Deerfield to Fort Massachusetts, on the Pontoosuck Road and so on. When Joseph meekly probed his brother's perennial absences, Elisha explained coolly, "Joseph, I'm obliged to support my wife and my occupation is in the backlands, unlike yours." Joe's legal office was his office in the family homestead.

"Brother, you underestimate the circuit-riding of a lawyer these days. You know we are in Springfield every other session…" Joseph drew a breath. "Not to forget my travels to Boston and to meet with clients in the various hamlets and towns throughout the county. Why the travels of a lawyer are here and there and everywhere. I've hardly an antsy child's moment for reading or reflection…"

"Yes, brother, each of us to wrestle with our obstacles in order to engage our own usefulness," replied the younger brother placidly and perhaps insincerely. "Let us pray that God's strength will enable us each to our own highest ends."

Joseph thought he detected a note of evasiveness. Later he noted that even with the rising tide of dangerous incidents, Elisha slept many nights in the frontier camps he and his crew fashioned in the wilderness while Joseph hurried homeward.

While there were no specific words indicating dissatisfaction, Joe sensed a sourness and a distance between himself and his younger brother. Sometimes Joseph caught unselfconscious views of Elisha with a certain evident detachment. Joseph resolved to bridge the chasm between them. With God's grace, he would! His travels to Boston provided opportunities for him to purchase special favors for mother, Mercy and his brother's wife. Try as he might, he could not deduce what a special gift for Elisha might be… Elisha shrugged off everything recently.

Elisha and Betty's marriage had seemed ideal to Madame Rebekah Hawley. She had trusted and relied on the Deacon Ebenezer Pomeroy since the untimely and tragic death of her husband almost 20 years ago. Not only had the Deacon assisted Rebekah with her business affairs and counseled her for many years, but he was a stalwart colleague of her brother, Colonel John Stoddard. Betty Pomeroy was the deacon's daughter. Elisha was Rebekah's son. Elisha had been errant. Betty had been painstakingly upright. Betty had even reported her older brother Eben the Third to her father for his role reading Bad Books with the other Bad Boys. Of course, these ironies were deeply unsettling to Rebekah's sense of social propriety and her "pride of spirit," as were some of the Pomeroys' uncouth ways. Admittedly, Betty's uncle Seth Pomeroy was clumsy, tall, gangly, loud and somewhat dense. Nonetheless, he was much adored by many men in the town and he was a close councilor to son Joseph.

The Hawleys and Pomeroys had shared profound religious devotion and in addition deep and mounting disagreement with and outright antagonism toward their (now former) Reverend, Mr. Jonathan Edwards. If things were not completely satisfactory for Elisha or Betty at the moment, time would change that, thought Rebekah. "When she has a child…."

The Deacon cared not about emotions. Devotion to duty, religion and attention to his blacksmithing business were what mattered in his life.

Betty remained mute about her marriage, apart from perhaps to her closest confidantes.

Steeled in the conviction of her family's godliness, the righteousness of their true religion, and her determination to live for the afterlife of immortality and eternal happiness, old Madame Hawley was gnawed with wondering if the Lord was frowning upon her? Gross disappointments piled up in her brain. Her estrangement from her older sisters and disappointment with Brother John, the gruesome and notorious suicide of her husband, her joyless marriage, Elisha's infamous immorality in begetting a bastard child, Joseph's choice not to pursue the ministry (choosing law instead, as his father had done), Joseph and cousin Israel's open competition and mutual dislike and Joe's choice of a bride.

In the beginning, Joseph had tried most cautiously to persuade his mother, "I saw Mistress Lyman tonight at Deacon Pomeroy's prayer meeting."

Yet, even this strategy led his mother to reply scornfully, "Apparently young spinsters these days have much time to be out about town…"

"Why Mother, you know Miss Lyman is above any repute! Her father is the sheriff!"

Joe let this settle with his mother before adding, "They are not only eminently respectable. They are most enterprising and successful in their shop. You know they own an African serving girl…" Like all the well-to-do ministers in the Great River valley, the Lymans had a slave (a "servant for life" - as the owners preferred to discretely call them) of which his mother was both simultaneously somewhat jealous and disapproving.

"To my thinking, only the most devout and devoted daughters make a truly upright bride," the old mother announced ultimately. Joseph was dashing her last hopes upon the rocky shoals of disillusionment by not marrying the daughter of a minister!

"So, would it suit you better, Mother, if I joined that crowd pursuing one of the Reverend Mr. Edwards' daughters?"

Her answer was to tip the kettle of boiling peas into the blazing fire with a shriek. Whether it was deliberate or not was open to debate, but the result was a silent, chilled and sparse evening meal in a darkened kitchen filled with the steam of burnt legumes.

From then on, Joseph in defiance of her will, quietly and surreptitiously courted Mercy Lyman, traveling away to the town of Brookside "on business" to visit Miss Lyman at her relatives. Although Joseph would not admit it directly to himself, he had watched the example of his brother's not marrying his heart's desire - instead acceding to his mother's candidate, and Joe Hawley decided not to replicate that. One late autumn evening after a decent lull following the evening prayers, Joe Hawley announced that he would post his marriage banns at the First Church before the next Sabbath. Joseph Hawley would wed Mercy Lyman on November 30, 1752.

Mother Rebekah exhibited no emotion for some long seconds or maybe it was minutes? At last, the old woman exaggeratedly drew up her bent head and queried, "Mercy Lyman? She with the face resembling a toasting iron?"

Even the taciturn Betty gasped aloud at this remark. To which Betty hastily explained, "I beg pardon. I didn't expect such news."

Rebekah Hawley distinctly felt the accumulating disappointments of her 68 years. Rising from her unfinished food she declared dramatically, "I've lost my appetite - as well as my son."

Of course, nothing became much easier after the subdued wedding vows and the new denizen moved into the old house. In fact, the household grew more scrambled and tense. Joseph took to his legal work in his office. And Mother Hawley restricted herself to her own domains and rooms, studiously avoiding her new daughter-in-law Mercy. Rebekah was not much seen outside of her cheese-house. Although the two households resided within one structure and prayed together morning and night led by Joseph, they were divided by partition boards that Rebekah had Bridgman, the carpenter across the lane, put up.

Rebekah Hawley began planning the division of their entire familial house, properties and communal facilities, such as the parlors, the garret, the closets, the shelves, the kitchen, the well, the orchard, the buttery and barn. At one point, she started the digging of a separate new outhouse – until her sons revolted and stopped it. The sturdy and elegant old "necessary" with its barrel-vaulted plastered and white-washed ceiling (which was perfectly aired to eliminate almost all odors) obviously sufficed as their single receptacle! This refined privy was a double-seater, even having had a window installed one time when Father Joseph was feeling particularly economically flush and had unsold glass in the shop. Her sons were mortified to think that if Rebekah built her own special privy, the whole town of Northampton would be gossiping about who would use which privy and what it meant! (A prankster started to observe that "never the crap would meet.") But while Rebekah was dismissive and totally disregarded town talk, Joseph was sheepish at the thought of discussion of it. Joe could imagine those biddy hens gossiping if Elisha and Betty would be granted the privilege of discharging their bowels in the old or new outhouse! Would Joe and Mercy be relegated to a lesser one? Of course, there must be a stop put to it! The entire subject was excruciatingly disconcerting, which caused Joseph rushes of hot blood surging into his ears, blushing his body scarlet-red everywhere and producing more headaches.

Next, Joe begged Mother to have their house re-done in the new style of large, elegant and well-finished "mansion houses" with large granary, barn, chaise-house, wood house with a few acres of land adjoining, stocked with a variety of fruit trees and a fine garden (like those of local taste-makers Elijah Williams, Timothy Dwight and cousin Israel Williams). However, old Rebekah rejected the expense and extravagance - and instead subdivided the ancient house into her own and their quarters! She would not pay for any elaborate joinery, such as the carved scrolls by carpenters that others had on their built-in shelves and what-not's! Nor would she pay a shilling for exterior paint, "Not a shilling, I tell you. Not a single pine tree shilling." Forget a handsome penny for a tasteful front door. "No gewgaws. Not on my dwelling house!"

However, she did pay eight shillings for one of the Pomeroy blacksmith assistants to make a lock to her parlor and cabinet closet in which she guarded her sugar and chocolate (no new-fangled coffee or tea for her, but sugar and chocolate....). With her craving for the sweet white granules and the delicious dark powder, and knowing how dear they were from the merchants of Boston, Rebekah began wearing the key to the cabinet around her neck. She slept with the key on its cerulean-blue ribbon to be sure neither her servant girl, Hannah Colson, nor anyone else could snitch any from the sugar jar or cut grains off the sugar loaf. Even the sugar tongs and sugar nippers were locked up. She sequestered the sweet cakes and puddings, sassafras candy and other confections she baked from the rest of the family and refused to share them. Every day in the late afternoons she was seen sneaking her cup of chocolate (well doused with the intoxicating sugar elixir) into the cheese-house. She thought no one noticed her addiction but that was untrue. They all simply ignored her sweet compulsion.

Joe brought her loaves of sugar and chocolate every trip from Boston and she still bought some more at exorbitant local prices when her supply ran short. The Hawley household knew Rebekah would be beyond insupportable were she without her sugar and chocolate. Her natural crankiness accelerated like a shooting star if Rebekah were not daily sweetened. Mercy wondered whether her mother-in-law secreted some sugar in her bed?! Perhaps under the goose feather pillow? No one would know for certain until she died, since no one dared enter her chamber (except Hannah – when permitted and who was strictly observed). Mercy doubted she herself would presume to enter Rebekah's sanctum even after she died and was buried, so intimidated as she was by The Old Lady.

In some respects, Betty Pomeroy Hawley was happy to have her new sister-in-law Mercy nearby. As the newest woman in the family, Mercy would now absorb the most scrutiny and assignments. Mercy would have to get up first to light a fire, tote water from the well, get the hot water kettle heating, heat up the kitchen, lug in the firewood, bring in the milk from the dairy house and generally commence the breakfast for the household. With Mercy shouldering more, Betty could slip away to visit her mother, sisters and female cousins more often (without risking denunciation for shirking Rebekah).

Poor Mercy was left to dodge old Mother Hawley and her scathing disapproval every day. As her husband traveled with more frequency to Boston, Springfield and outlying towns for his law practice, Mercy Lyman Hawley grew lonelier. She worried about Joe's health what with the epidemics of smallpox and other distempers that recurred in Boston. She spoke less. She smiled less or not at all, until Joseph re-appeared. It seemed she ate less, too.

Joseph's soft heart ached for a solution for Mercy's increasingly bedraggled state. At last, he urged her to invite her sister Eunice Lyman Clarke over for friendly female company. Eunice and Mercy might share chores, sewing and mending, gossip and banter together. Soon, Eunice Clarke and her toddlers, Joseph and Richard, were exchanging friendly visits with Joe and Mercy Hawley. Introverted, serious young Joseph Clarke resembled Joseph Hawley as a child. Richard's boisterous behavior reminded Joe of Elisha. It was a change to have children around in the lugubrious and silent household. Joseph Hawley prayed that it might also somehow aid Mercy and Betty in their womanly ways, most especially in the mystery of conceiving children of their own. Besides, Joe Hawley delighted in Eunice's husband, Samuel Clarke and his news from the harness shop.

Most of Joe and Mercy's social visits were to the Clarke's house, simply because Rebekah was on edge around the "noisy children" and made sure everyone felt awkward and unwelcome. Besides disorder, the boys also stirred up dust, dirt and sand. So Rebekah devised special ways to express her disapproval. It seemed she had as many provocative schemes as the depth of feet in hell. In the beginning, Mother Hawley avoided Eunice and Mercy. Then, she decided to reclaim her "widow's third" of the house, including the great hearth fireplace, as she squeezed over into the space she had designated for Mercy. She pulled out the fireplace crane and shunted it out of the direct blaze of the fire so that the young women's water didn't boil for tea. Next, the old lady sputtered derisive remarks within hearing about how expensive and wasteful drinking tea was. The comments continued about the children's wild indiscipline and her sorrow and regrets about her own two sons. She started staring and glaring at Mercy and Eunice undisguised. She blew smoke from her white clay pipe into the children's faces when they accidentally got too close to her. She instructed her servant Hannah to deposit the stinkiest cheese curds on the kitchen work table for her to work on later while Mercy and Eunice tried to enjoy their cups of tea. She swore she didn't intentionally let the barn cat in the house with a live mouse, although her denial seemed neither genuine nor innocent. Similarly, Rebekah had no idea how the disgusting offal deposited on the doorstep to the outhouse had gotten there. Eunice almost stepped in it and it dirtied the hem of her dress! "Too bad that old vixen didn't partition off the outhouse as she did everything else, then she could have stayed only in her own area to deposit those turds…" muttered Eunice.

Finally, Mercy and Eunice decided to hold their tea times only when the old mother was gone from the house, although they resolved not to abandon their rights completely. When they did bring out the tea equipment and set their tea table, they assigned Hannah as a watch for when the old crone was seen coming down Pudding Lane. As "payment," servant Hannah, too, enjoyed a cup of the fashionable Boston tea laden with sugar - as well as a farthing coin. Tea was said by all the best ladies and gentlemen to be an elixir of health. Tea aided digestion against nauseous humors that offended the stomach. Some people believed it stimulated the mind, added vigor and prevented old age. "Old Mother Hawley should have consumed more tea in her youth," they chuckled.

Once the bowed figure of "The Old Granny" did appear at the top of the street ("Adzooks! Old crusty comes!"), all the women hurriedly put the tea paraphernalia away (everyone wanted to avoid her wrath). As Rebekah entered, Mercy and Eunice sat in smug silence at their own clever deception. Mercy couldn't quite suppress her satisfied little scoff.

From the peep of a smile at the corners of the young women's lips when she shuffled into the house, Rebekah sensed her daughter-in-law possessed a guilty secret. Had they plundered her sugar or drinking chocolate? "Those girls were at some mischief," deduced the old lady. "Hhhmmm, just like those old biddies in the town. Idle in work but a busybody in gossip and others' business! I don't like it at all. I'm being plotted against and overruled in my own house."

Rebekah wondered, was the serving girl an accomplice? Alternately, she speculated, had Betty missed her "monthly" and had a child begotten on her body? Had Joseph told Mercy some news that they hadn't shared with her? Or perhaps, had Jonathan Edwards been dismissed from the mission at Stockbridge? What other news could there be? Although she might not appear it, the old woman remained sharp and missed little.

Joseph Hawley, oblivious to the invisible rancor, appreciated the silence after days of blathering clients with grievances in his law office. He had many more "distractions" demanding his attention these days. Sometimes he confided to Mercy in the dark of the night, "I am surrounded by treachery at every turn, Mercy, dear child," he whispered. "Cousin Israel favors Ephraim Junior, Elisha's old commander. I know they plot to leave me out of the spoils of land speculation and military contracts. When war comes, they'll just enrich themselves and thrust me aside with the lesser crumbs. Naturally, I wouldn't in any way harm Elisha's chances with Eph, but I must watch them and be always alert. Always wary, every second. I must guard and measure my every word."

As they lay awake, Mercy heard Joe exhale a deep sigh of exhaustion.

"The world is full of wolves, Mercy. You don't know what I contend with all the day! I tell you, there are but few decent and moral men. To show you, did I tell you that old man Ephraim Senior of Stockbridge has gone totally, insanely mad? Why he woke up one morning, just weeks ago, before dawn's light and went from house to house in Stockbridge in his nightclothes! In his nightclothes! Can you believe it?!? And he was carrying a bag of every coin he could scour up, offering to buy everyone's farms and lands right then-and-there - that instant! No negotiations, no legal contracts, nothing! And why? To control the vote at the next town meeting and run out the Reverend Edwards out of town!"

His voice faltered so that she thought he might break down.

"You know that no one has opposed the Reverend Mr. Edwards more than me. You know that."

Mercy reassured him, "Without a doubt, Joseph. Everyone knows it."

It appeared that the more Joseph flourished and ascended in his law practice and in the politics of the town (he had recently been elected Moderator of Town Meetings at Northampton), the more there continued to be rancor and insurmountable contention within the church. People spoke viciously and recriminatingly. Christian spirit had evaporated entirely. They entered and departed the meetinghouse as two distinct camps, each cagily eyeing the other. The reputation of the First Church and its acrimonious disagreement with its minister had spread all the way to Boston - and beyond. Now no minister would accept their offer to settle amongst them.

Joseph's opponents in the dismissal of the Reverend were unceasing. They had tried to propose the return of the dismissed Edwards to become minister at a new church in Northampton. Second Church of Northampton? No!

Under Joe's leadership, the church brethren had again beaten back that oppositional agitation. These embittered controversies over church-town leadership and adherence to tradition continued to flare up, taking an increasing toll on Joseph Hawley. However, having led the strident and uncompromising faction in the town, it was quite impossible for him to now back away from it, become a peacemaker or articulate finesse or sophisticated discernment. When he had earnestly endeavored to retrospectively clarify his testimony against Martha Root, it had not gone well. In a letter he fretted and labored over, he wrote,

> "When I was before the Ecclesiastical Council which sat at Northampton on ye 17th day of June 1749. to determine a dispute between the first Church of s^d Northampton and my brother respecting his Obligation to marry you, In giving an Evidence to s^d Council to prove y^t you had been industrious in seeking my brothers Company for some time before you charged him with being unlawfully familiar with you, among other things I said y^t within about ye space of half a year during ye time of y^r acquaintance together, I had seen you in our street (as I judged forty several times putting a certain number for an uncertain… (Although I then spoke my judgm^t y^t on Cool consideration I must say that I suppose y^t I represented ye matter beyond ye truth and reality… Now wherein the above representation was beyond what was true in fact so far I really ~~reality and fact~~ injured you, and so far as it was beyond, what I certain knowledge ~~of~~ was true (i.e. wherein I spoke positively) so far I acted presumptively. For which I am heartily sorry…"[25]

Instead of forgiving him, the Roots were more vehemently wrathful! It had shocked and wounded him!

---

[25] "S^d" was abbreviation for "said." Y^e for the. Y^t for that. Strike-thru's are in the original. Joseph Hawley Papers, George Bancroft Collection, New York Public Library, 1750-1753, image 17 (second of two originals to Martha Root).

Poor Joseph, he could confide only to Mercy or best friend (and brother-in-law) the taciturn Samuel Clarke. Now the moody attorney began to obsess over the spiritual health of his own soul.

Ironically since Joseph Hawley was now renowned for heading the Edwards' dismissal those three years ago, he was sought to aid church dissenters against the "New Light"[26] or anti-"half-way covenant" ministers at Ware River and Cold Spring. A break-away faction at Pelham wanted Joseph's counsel for their land feud too. Every malcontent, anti-religious or unregenerate swain wanted to consult with him! Joseph Hawley was sorely misunderstood. His heart and mind felt assailed: would he be known only as an iconoclast, rather than for his subtle complexity?!

"You must never, ever, tell Mother even a whisper of it, Mercy but truly those others who are opposing their ministers do so only for their own purely venal reasons, not for principle. *I did so for the principle*," he averred. Joseph Hawley's conscience could not rest.

The voice of his dear wife cooed back in the deep night, "Of course, husband, of course." She held her breath a long second. "But are you opposing Mr. Edwards or sympathizing with him?"

"I don't know, Mercy…"

This time his voice did crack and break into a hoarse string of slow words pieced together, "Was…

… it right?

Was…

… it wrong?"

The final remark he mumbled as he fell asleep was, "I may have said something wrong and unadvisedly… maybe beyond what was true in fact and reality…"

---

[26] The term "New Lights" (versus the "Old Lights" or conservative traditionalists) developed during the Great Awakening to describe those Congregationalists who accepted revivalism, the emotional/"enthusiastic" embrace of personal experiences of sin and atonement. Wikipedia short entry: https://en.wikipedia.org/wiki/Old_and_New_Lights

Sugar nippers with sugar cone loaf. Used with permission of Susan McLellan Plaisted, Proprietress of Heart to Hearth Cookery.

A murder of crows shrieked their harsh and ominous "Caw caw caw's" back and forth to each other in their crooked dartings across the sky to their night roosts. Why did these wicked creatures bedevil humanity? Why did they carefully watch men's doings, comings and goings? The wings of the huge black birds reminded Elisha Hawley of how the wind used to flap up the Reverend Mr. Jonathan Edwards's charcoal black cloak on his way to the meetinghouse. Elisha remembered how as a boy in Northampton before harvest time he had tried to stone crows for the town's bounty of two shillings each. How satanically smart and feisty they were, slowly flapping just out of the boys' range to settle back down with their devouring eyes on people's kitchen gardens and fields! Hunted and hated they were, but clever indeed.

After so many weeks of journeying and mapping out possible roads through the dense wilderness of the Housatonic River watershed with the company of the two Indians on his surveying team, Hawley had tired of their company and their brief, trite conversations with him. He yearned for the company of white gentlemen. In the uncharted wilderness surrounding Fort Massachusetts and over to Hudson's River, the survey team had clambered over colossal boulders and piles of rocks and slogged through the calf-deep black muck of dismal swamps, all the while seeking terrain through which a road to civilization could be cut. Elisha Hawley was a man who treasured long, undisturbed silences, nonetheless, this was excessive. He prized the occasional intelligent and informed discourse of gentlemen.

Hawley pondered why nature abhorred sameness? It never seemed to be static: it was always blowing, raining, snowing, working, moving, vibrating – even pitting, scooping and sculpting land itself. No land was perfectly flat for any extended time. (Was it just to defy surveyors?!) No water lay still for long. The world was a place of constant motion, he thought.

At the new settlement of Sheffield, along the Boston-to-Albany "Great Road," the surveyors met up with civilization's representatives, the "Great Road Grand Jury." The Grand Jury was composed of twelve of the most influential and educated men from Northampton, Hatfield and Hadley who sought to resolve road routes and land disputes.

As gentlemen working at the request of the province, the Grand Jury group (Lt. Ebenezer Hunt, Lt. Obadiah Dickinson, Ensign Daniel Pomeroy,

Ensign Elisha Allis, Jonathan Ingersoll, Samuel Smith, Moses Ashley, David Bagg, Josiah Parks, Samuel Clark, Eleazer Burt and Oliver Warner) indulged in some luxuries and betook of a bit of leisure as they periodically received supplies or met an express rider passing by on the Great Road.

The Hawley crew's diminishing supply of foodstuffs had been the substandard dried rations and forest fare for too long. It would be good to relish real cooking! Hawley was thus delighted when they met up with the traveling Grand Jury in the far west of the Colony of the Massachusetts Bay.

Headed by his old commander at Fort Massachusetts, Captain Ephraim Williams Junior, the Grand Jury traveled with better accoutrements and their servants (slaves). Better yet, the Jury group carried some home comforts - even paper and some newspapers, almanac sheets of gossip and information and the local news from home. They tarried at remote taverns, like Hewit Root's Public House at the Great Bridge over the Housatonic River with the sign 'Rum, Gin, Brandy" above the door. Often these outposts were infested with lice-ridden, dirty common folk, but sometimes decent drink and food might be gotten. Importantly, there was good company and good conversation.

Analyzing the deviations of the old "New England Path" to the new road-bed of the "Great Road" involved numerous disputes, investigations and trial and error. The Grand Jury stated:

> "Then steering Westerly across ye aforesaid improvements in a
> Right line we came into ye old path about ten Rods East of a
> brook then we continued in ye Path as its now Trod by said
> Brewers house to his mill then crossing ye River at ye Bridge we
> kept said path about 60 Rods then leaving ye path to the
> Northward we kept a westerly Course by a line of Trees marked
> on three sides for ye north side of ye Road until we Reentered ye
> old path at ye foot of 6 mile hill then continuing Westward in
> said Path until we came to Sheffield bounds…"

Because none of the Upper Sheffield "taverns" were more than the inhabitants' houses with an extra one to three rooms for lodgers, the Grand Jury occupied all three of the local spots, Aaron Sheldon's, Hewit Root's and Isaac Pixley's. These were laid out stretching over the hills from the Great Meadow to the ford of the Great Bridge and then another few miles down the Great Road. Built across from the new meetinghouse (built in 1742), Hewit Root's being the central location, the gentlemen gathered there in the surrounding yard.

Well-worn copies of *The Boston Gazette* newspaper provoked most of their interest and conversation. The latest depredations of the wily Pope-ish French and their savage Indian tribal allies and reports of political and military machinations in Boston, New York, Philadelphia, Virginia and even abroad dominated the papers. As the group sat outside of Root's Public House in the yard at a long table, they read the news aloud for discussion. Was another official declaration of war coming between England and France? So it seemed from the rising drum beat of violence on the frontiers. But the orders from the provincial governors were

"To draw forth the armed Force of the Province, and to use your best endeavors, to repel force by force. But as it is His Majesty's determination, not to be the aggressor, I have the King's commands, most strictly to enjoin you, not to make use of the armed force under your direction, excepting within the undoubted limits of his Majesty's dominions."

Caution above all else! Official orders to his Majesty's military men were "not to be the aggressor."

As Massachusetts Bay provincial men, they wondered how the Virginia province had appointed a mere 22-year-old George Washington to a commission as a Lieutenant-Colonel? "Who is this Lieutenant-Colonel George Washington of the Virginia Militia?" The proverbial schoolboy-to-lieutenant-colonel-in-three-weeks it seemed! This same lieutenant-colonel seemed to have been everywhere in the news of late. What experience and judgment could he have amassed at his age?

Certainly, his family was well-placed. His brother Lawrence held a captaincy in the 43rd Royal Regiment of Foote Infantry. The family were gentlemen but were there so few seekers of commissions in Virginia that all that was required was to "mention [me] at the appointment of the officers" (the favor Washington had requested)?! Of course, there was also the requisite payment of the commission purchase price to the commander! A mere mention would be nothing among the dozens of educated, well-placed, and wealthy office or commission-seekers in the Massachusetts Bay capitol! A mere mention - even accompanied by a certain amount of the King's £ Sterling, wouldn't produce a lieutenant-colonelcy for a twenty-two-year-old at Boston, even were he Governor Shirley's son! Why Shirley's son had only received a Captain's commission! "If ever a province was debauched by a man, then it was Virginia by Washington and this ilk," someone opined.

Yes, young Lieutenant-Colonel George Washington had become the talk of the Colonies since the May 28, 1754 "Jumonville affair" when Washington's company had ambushed and killed the French diplomatic envoy, Joseph Coulon de Villiers de Jumonville out in the rocky wilderness.

Late past sundown, when the meal was finished, torches lighted and more than a few tankards of spirituous liquors drunk, Captain Eph Williams bemoaned "Oh, that my father had educated me!"

"Or perhaps you should say, Eph, 'Oh, I wish I had been born in Virginia like that George Washington!' Seems the commissions come easier and cheaper in that province than in dear old Massachusetts Bay…. And no need for an education either," corrected his cousin seated nearby in the declining evening's luminous twilight.

"Clearly."

"Indeed," mumbled several listeners in accord.

"I hear no schooling whatsoever is required there for gentlemen or commissions, neither blood nor lineage necessary. There's many in them parts who neither read nor write. Only sufficient land or currency and one instantly becomes a gentleman," chimed in another voice.

"Sufficient land, yes, one must have sufficient land," affirmed Eph distractedly. "Do you know what is sufficient in Virginia? Why those Washingtons own 10,000 acres!"

There were certainly no gentlemen of that "caliber" in Massachusetts, where land, learning and cultivation were all absolute prerequisites and expensive.

Captain Eph had always bemoaned his lack of polish. No Appleby Grammar School for Ephraim. His father, Ephraim Senior had been far too mean and miserly to educate him well. Thus, Eph attended just the local common school. As children, Eph and his brother Thomas had been left by their father and raised by their maternal grandparents after their mother died in childbirth with Thomas. Eph had always wondered what life might have been for him, had he received benevolence, such as the Appleby Grammar School and Yale College from his own surly father and manipulative, evil-tempered step-mother? Might he now have been a lieutenant-colonel like this current young toast-of-the-colonies George Washington? The perennially friendly Eph Williams Junior showed no outward resentment and studiously honored both his notorious elderly parents. However, it did bemuse him to think on what might have been.

"But what kind of cost must that commission have been for a Lieutenant-Colonelcy? And this young George Washington, only 22 years of age!" Captain Eph had muttered in an aside to his younger friend Hawley. "That would have cost more than a few farthings, indeed! A pretty penny indeed! For a Lieutenant-Colonel's appointment at that age!" He whistled, "Whew! Mighty rich that fare!"

Oh yes, indeed! Didn't they all know what hefty prices they had paid for their commissions? Lieutenant Hawley had been repaying his mother long after his own posting at Fort Massachusetts in January 1747. Oiling the wheels of patronage for commissions necessitated many small and large favors and fees along the way, from Hawley's own uncle John Stoddard, Commander of the Hampshire Militia, to paying their brashly greedier cousin Colonel Israel Williams and supplying information to their patrons. Hawley sneered to wonder when "Colonel Israel" had last slogged a scout out of Deerfield?! Had he been out on an Indian trail since Father Rale's War ended in 1727? Doubtful. And, of course, from Israel to all the other favor payments along the way up to Royal Governor Shirley!

"Certainly, all here acknowledge it is Virginia after all?! It is not the Massachusetts Bay! Why, they are worse even than those perfidious Yorkers swindlers!"

"A devil of a job being betwixt these many Yorker factions!" complained Eph at the thought of the in-fighting at Albany. Ephraim Williams was a master of comprehending the various factions vying for position and power up and down the Connecticut River and all the way to Boston. Yet it was quite another matter to sort out the intrigues carried on at the Albany Congress of 1754 as they discussed another potential war with the French. There were the wily and unscrupulous Dutch traders of the new-York province, the Iroquois Indian Confederacy of the "Six Nations," some greedy and treacherous French turn-coats who surreptitiously traded outside of French Canada, observers of a few other colonies and the puritan New Englanders! It was a witches' brew of a mix where one could never understand all of the shifting components!

"Oh, I heard plenty of that talk-talk-a-talk at the Congress in Albany in July. Gentlemen, a congress of perfidious characters indeed!" said Ephraim Williams warming up to the topic.

"Yes, fellows, quite a collection of characters! The Yorkers are an assemblage of ... of..." the loquacious Ephraim Williams searched for the right descriptor. "An assemblage of... oh, I don't know ... perhaps snakes? An assemblage of odd and devious fellows?"

He continued to his impressed audience, "Of course, there are always gentlemen of quality and education. The lieutenant governor, some of the councilors, the commander of Fort Frederick at Albany and some of the visiting delegates – Dr. Franklin, for example, although lowly-born, currently a man of much erudition."

After a pause for everyone to digest his words, he went on, "But then, the rabble – absolutely insupportable! Audacious beyond belief! Why, the Iroquois didn't arrive till almost two weeks late! And then we sat through speech after speech, translated from their crazy language. That King Hendrick Tiyanoga, for example, a fellow of no consequence whatsoever, insisted on speaking in Mohawk - even though he knows full well English! He preferred to have his friend William Johnson translate for him. Why, I saw them whispering together throughout the proceedings."

"And that Johnson! An uneducated adventurer of little consequence in his own country Ireland suddenly raised to distinction by the aid of some powerful friends - and his influence over those Mohawks!"

"The insults were well-nigh insufferable, I tell you all!" Captain Eph shook his head in exasperation before being urged on. "Begging your pardon, gentlemen, but that Hendrick proclaimed that we English are women! Women! Exactly he said, 'Look at the French, they are men, they are fortifying everywhere - but we are ashamed to say it, you are all like women bare and open without any fortifications.' Then all those Indians, sitting on their benches all shouted out, "Yo-heigh-heigh!"'"

"I tell you, we were there to discuss the question of "Whether a Union of all the Colonies is not at present absolutely necessary for our security & defense?" But instead of "burying the hatchet" between us and preparing for war against the French, there was only talk of the news from the Ohio country!"

He paused meaningfully before summarizing, "Some say young Washington attacked and murdered the French envoy Jumonville as they were sleeping. Well, Washington himself didn't strike the blow. It was, of course, that Mingo "Half-King" chief that did that. But it is said that Washington allowed the ambush of the sleeping Frenchmen carrying a diplomatic letter to the Virginian Governor. He was killed as he tried to surrender."

"And most horrendously, "the Half-King" that laid hands on Captain Jumonville, actually scooped out the Frenchman's brains and ate them! There in front of them!"

This heinous news caused universal revulsion and all fell silent.

Next, the conversation turned generally to the Colony of Virginia and the Virginians, "First, remember they ascribe to the Church of England. And their laxity of discipline? Why they tolerate all manner of cursers, swearers, blasphemers, whoremongers, harlots, fornicators and adulterers, mixing of the races, all drunkards, ranters and profaners of the Lord's Day! Recall my dear fellows, they haven't a heritage of discipline as have we. There never has been a 'City upon a Hill' among them. Honor amongst them is a matter of the right company they keep, not of personal character."

From the silence that followed, it seemed as if the summary concluded it - although it could also be deduced that no one cared to treat any further on sins more than a few of them had indulged in… Elisha Hawley winced to hear the list of deadly sins, particularly that revolting word "fornicator," which scraped his ears, mind and soul, as the Inferior Court's record of proceeding had seared his eyes:

"Martha Root Confessed herself Guilty of the Crime of
Fornication ordered to pay a fine of 25 fills of ye last Emission
and Cost. February 9, 1747/8"

He recalled with dread the vote of the brethren on his own excommunication from the First Church, his mother's sulky lamentations and almost swooning protestations. The voice of Martha Bridgman Root shouting at him five years ago was still ringing in his ears, "Woe ye Elisha Hawley, one day your foot too shall slide!"

Brother Joe had dismissed it, "'Lisha, the ministers have ruled in the Council that you are free to do as your conscience dictates. You do what ye know is right in your conscience and before God. There is nothing particularly binding on ye."

Although the affair was done and gone now, Elisha Hawley hated the word "fornicator." But, he rationalized, all had their own problems. He allayed his conscience as a little ditty Hawley had overheard one of their former obdurate soldiers sing in a tavern about Captain Eph's commission. It lilted now through Hawley's head:

"Brother Ephraim sold his Cow
And bought him a Commission;
And then he went to Canada
To fight for the Nation;
But when Ephraim he came home
He proved an arrant Coward,

He wouldn't fight the Frenchmen there
For fear of being devour'd"

They were brutal in their criticisms, those savant shirkers who hadn't seen with their own eyes a red-hot exchange of gunfire at a real pitched battle! What knew they who had never heard their kin or comrades-at-arms screech in pain or for mercy, like those loud-mouthed Bostonians! The further they had been from the flying bullets, the more people criticized, thought Hawley. These types flourished among the towns and taverns all throughout Massachusetts Bay.

Most of the Grand Jury had shorn themselves of the veneer of military life and its accoutrements when they had resigned as commissioned officers in His Majesty's Provincial Militia in the lull after the Old French War of 1744-1748. However, they were thinly shorn. Their martial instincts lay as close at hand as their long guns and officers' swords, usually at arm's length or on the mantle over the fireplace hearth. Captain Eph and those other gentlemen busied themselves now with their favorite preoccupations of land speculating and improving one's wealth and standing. Hawley too was buying and selling land some, but his other civilian occupation was surveying, until the next war lured or demanded his return to military life.

"Captain Williams, what more's in them newspapers you brought. Let's hear what's the newest news?"

"Yes, yes, I've newspapers and…." he paused for effect. "I suppose you might want to hear young Washington's Journals?" teased Colonel Eph.

"What? Do you have them?" the group queried him.

With a flourish, Ephraim retrieved a packet wrapped in a red-and-white checked calico cotton napkin and ribbon. "Gentlemen of the Grand Jury, what's your listening pleasure? I also have a July copy of the *Boston Post-Boy* newspaper, *Major Washington's Journals* and *Cato's Letters*…."

Then mysteriously he added, "Would hearing about 'Murdering Town in the Ohio Country,' 'The Mingo Half-King,' or falling into an icy river suit your pleasures?"

For the former military men, the Virginian's travel to the Forks of the Ohio River held great interest. So too, Young Lieutenant-Colonel Washington's report on a future site for a fort at The Forks:

"As I got down before the Canoe, I spend some Time in viewing
the Rivers, and the Land in the Fork: which I think extremely
well situated for a Fort, as it has the absolute Command of both
Rivers. The Land at the Point is 20 or 25 Feet above the
common Surface of the Water; and a considerable Bottom of
flat, well-timbered Land all around it, very convenient for
Building: The Rivers are each a Quarter of a Mile, or more,
across, and run here very near at right Angles: Alleghany bearing
North East and Monongahela South East. The former of these
two is a very rapid and swift running Water: the other deep and
still, without any perceptible fall."

"Nothing extraordinary in this report. Sounds very similar to my
surveying reports. Exactly my usual task: to lay out the best sites for road or fort,
and like my reports," thought Elisha Hawley. He said, "So, what is the great fussy
fandango about this young Virginian? It's the same things as I do. Who is this 22-
year-old lieutenant-colonel who's the talk of all His Majesty's colonies? Not only
was this young whip forced to surrender to the French at the Great Meadow, but
the French officer, Jumonville, was killed. Where would I be, had it been me who
mangled up such as that?!"

To Captain Eph, Hawley remarked, "Had we had such results at Fort
Massachusetts as he had at his Fort Necessity, I doubt you or I would be the toast
of Governor Shirley and Boston, much less, all of His Majesty's Colonies!"

"Most certainly not!" replied his old superior. "In the Massachusetts Bay,
as the Bible verse more likely 'the prophet without honor!' In our beloved Bay
Province, in our own towns, amongst our relatives and in our own homes we
would remain without honors! No, no, not amongst us! Prophets without honor
indubitably. Those Virginians haven't the standards we have here! Hardly."

Hawley responded, "Why even his Indian Half-King said Washington
made no fortifications there at all and said his fort was but "that little thing on the
meadow." And if we had orders 'not to be the aggressors…'"

At this, Ephraim Williams' voice grew low and obscure, "Actually, 'Lisha,
Jumonville was a nobleman from France, albeit only minor nobility, as I understand
it. However, I have heard – from very good sources, mind you - that Jumonville
was surrendering to Washington. As he was reading the diplomatic "Summons,"
the Half-King approached behind him and split open his skull with his tomahawk!"

Williams paused for it to settle in with his listeners, then continued in an
undertone. "Worse, the Half-King is said to have washed his hands with
Jumonville's brains after he split his head open!"

"What? Not so!" Hawley blurted.

"Hawley, God's truth! They say it's complete truth: no fabrication! I heard it from people in Governor Shirley's office! Why one of the French soldiers there was so terrified he ran barefooted the entire way back to Fort Duquesne at the Forks of the Ohio!"

"Unbelievable depravity!" gasped an almost speechless Lieutenant Hunt.

"Well, you read *The Journal of Major George Washington*, haven't you?" questioned Williams. "It was in all the newspapers. This whelp of a pup Washington even wrote that he found it all "charming!"

"What on earth did he find charming? The attack? The tomahawking? The brains?" demanded Hawley, still in recoil.

"Well, Hawley, that I don't know exactly but I do know he wrote a report of it and said he found it "charming." Whatever part of it it was," conceded Ephraim Williams. "It is all together completely deplorable!"

A moment later, he added, "Your beloved uncle, my great benefactor, Colonel Stoddard – may he rest in peace – would never have sanctioned such a breech! Shocking! Shocking, I tell you! Our officers in Massachusetts are true gentlemen. Such inadequacy would never happen here, never! Never! Why Sergeant Hawks only surrendered Fort Massachusetts in 1746 when they ran out of ammunition! And that when they were outnumbered 900 French and Indians to a sick garrison of 22 of us English! I wasn't there at the time, of course, you know. But my brother Tom had just left. By the grace of God…."

At the thought of how the deceased Colonel Stoddard would react, the men grew silent and speculative. Had their commanding colonel judged Ephraim Williams foolish to have been lured from the security of the walls of Fort Massachusetts to aid four insubordinate soldiers searching for a cow on that regrettable August day? Would he have reprimanded Lieutenant Elisha Hawley for lacking in valor at being dragged back to the safety of the fort after his leg wound in the skirmish on Fort Massachusetts in August 1748? Would Elisha ever have dared murmur like Washington had that he wished "to be ranked among the chief officers on an expedition" when he had not succeeded in a prior mission?! Or that Washington found bullets flying past "charming?"

Eph continued on, "Well, as far as that, I absolutely shall not now - or ever! - be considered less than men of my same rank just because they're English-born and we are Americans! You know the whole *Articles of War* passed by the

Parliament is unacceptable to free men! I esteem the services of the provincial officer to be as valuable as that of a regular British officer. Why should we Americans be of lesser worth?"

An animated conversation continued on the subject of mistreatment of provincial officers by the regular "lobster-back" red-coats. At last the group grew fatigued of which sent them all to their rests or back to their places at the other taverns. Elisha Hawley pondered the previous conversation. Who was this "cockalorum" Washington?! Who was this mere 22-year-old lieutenant-colonel from Virginia who had been entrusted with a diplomatic mission to Michel-Ange Du Quesne de Menneville, the new governor of New France, in the wilderness at Fort LeBoeuf? Things had not gone well. The French were insatiable and continued in their "intention to take possession of the Ohio country." In fact, their Captain Legardeur de Saint-Pierre even responded, "As to the summons you send me to retire, I do not think myself obliged to obey it."

Such an impudent manner! Such defiance by these French! A heathenish proposition!

Well, perhaps Washington's brashness hadn't gotten him too far. Even though he got close to Fort Duquesne mere months ago in May 1754, eventually his own immature mistakes, resulted in his retreat back to civilian life. Hawley concluded that he himself, Captain Eph, and the kid Lieutenant-Colonel Washington had all left behind their military lives. For how long, he wondered?

As he lay on his bedroll in their camp area of the Root tavern yard listening to the babble of the rowdy nearby Housatonic River over its rocky bed, it occurred to Hawley that tavern owner Hewit Root was descended from the same Root family as his former paramour, Martha. Hawley wondered if young Washington was being told to ignore a pleasing female he favored and instead introduced to less attractive "gentle-ladies" for a more advantageous marriage? Perhaps a father for whom Washington was surveying or testifying in Sessions Court on a land deal might mention his eligible daughter? From what Hawley had heard about the Virginians, it wouldn't be at meetinghouse that prospective mates would be eyeing him. More likely he would be watched for his reaction to a certain girl at one of their famous parties.

The thought of his own help-mate evoked little emotion in Hawley. Dutiful Betty might be far now from her surveyor husband but she was closely bound to her duties to his mother, her parents, her sisters, her family, her woman friends, his brother, his brother's wife, the Northampton church brethren, that larger obscure and mysterious woman-community in the town, her uncles, aunts, cousins, and so forth.

Frankly though, he didn't care much. It was easier to navigate the shoals of the wilderness and isolated men than the intertwined and tangled tongues of the towns. He felt it more comfortable to live surveying virgin land at the edges of civilization in East Hoosuck, Pontoosuck, the Hatfield Three Mile Addition, the Housatonic Road, the West Hoosic Road to Albany, the Deerfield-Fort Massachusetts Road, etc. Life was less complicated and calmer this way.

Hawley had heard of Martha Root's marriage after seven plus years of spinsterhood. It shouldn't bother him, of course. It had been eight years since their dalliance. Why should he care? It was inevitable that she would marry as had he. In fact, it was amazing that she had not married long before, as his mother had bluntly predicted when she opposed their marrying to sanction their child, "Never-mind you, she will marry another."

Hawley had stopped wondering what his life with Martha Root would have been and resolved himself to forget it all. He had almost forgotten that he had an unlawfully-begotten blood daughter. The name "Root" and the girl's name "Anne" were never spoken in the Hawley household, as was anything veering toward reminders of the Roots' very existences.

Now Martha was married to John Miller, a famously strong and tall hunter, who was honest but old (42) and uncouth. Miller was admittedly a cunning hunter and trapper of wolves especially (a nice bounty paid by the town for each one killed). But, what did Martha see in rough "Bear John" Miller? He was a man of the wilds. Admittedly, so was he himself now, Hawley realized with surprise!

Elisha Hawley reminisced on an oft-told tale of "Bear John" luring and facing down an enraged mother bear whose two cubs he had treed. How could Miller have kept his calm and aimed his shot so true into the snarling, foaming face of the bear's giant ivory incisor teeth - which were bared for Miller's face and body - 400 pounds of dark brown fury racing headlong towards him! How did he keep his focus with the space around him turned into a tumble of total, lethal tumult? Furthermore, Miller was said to have deliberately provoked the bear's furious attack by disturbing her cubs. The man was bold to reckless!

Hawley pulled and stretched on his memories to recall all he could of the older Miller man who had inhabited the far remote periphery of Hawley's own Northampton world. Mostly, it had been efficient business dealings with Miller on skins, furs and other items from which Hawley could draw no further judgments of the man.

Elisha Hawley scolded himself for brooding on Martha Root and John Miller. He must forget them and not fuss a second more over their lives. He had other pressing tasks to plan on for tomorrow's road exploration with his two Mohican scouts/surveying assistants, not to forget that he would be returning to his own wife and mother.

But surely signs abounded that a war with France and their Indians was coming, signs like the scouting missions the Virginians and the French had sent into the Ohio Country and the printed *Surveillance Reports* they had discussed. Still, Hawley couldn't but apprehend as he drifted off to sleep that the war calls that were on the winds becoming everyone's predominant preoccupation would bring him in particular special opportunities.

From inside the tavern, where the flip flavored with nutmeg was flowing freely, surveyor Hawley could hear the temporary happiness of drunken men singing "We Be Soldiers Three."

> "Here, good fellow, I'll sing you a song,
> Sing for the brave and sing for the strong,
> To all those living and those who are gone,
> With never a penny of money!"

The Miller family had fallen in prominence in Northampton's society since when John Miller's grandmother had been the only physician and surgeon in the incipient settlement of Northampton in the 17th century.

John Miller was born in 1712, in the era of the great Puritan "divines," Increase and Cotton Mather. He was a child whose timing, life, family and personality were always slightly akilter. As the eleventh (and last) child of aged parents, John was often somewhat overlooked or relegated in life's usual busy-ness. His oldest sister Sarah was 24 years old when John was born. She had already died at age 35 (and unmarried) in John's boyhood. Three older siblings John, Patience and Joseph had also died by the time John came to the age of inheritance. The losses made John Miller resolve to strengthen his inner and outer self. He must accept whatever came with little emotion.

In the 1730s, disease and death corroded the normalcy of the Ebenezer Miller family's lives. They had managed to function as a family and show kind caring to each other, until their plans for house and land inheritances were upended. Late in 1737, the "throat distemper" raged in Northampton and Hatfield. John Miller's 32-year-old brother Joseph died even before their 73-year-old father. Nineteen-year-old Aaron and their mother, too, contracted the distemper and were left incapacitated for heavy work. Worse, poor mother Sarah Allen Miller "lost her reasoning" from the illness.

The entire Miller family was thrown into such disarray by the epidemics that there was no time to alter Father Ebenezer's Last Will and Testament. Instead of the smaller lots of land in the "Old Rainbow" and "Young Rainbow" fields that would have earlier been his share, suddenly 15-year-old John was in possession of their father's house at the center of town and the lands to help support his sibling Aaron. The grief-stricken household resolved to accept the heavenly father's will while copiously weeping and wondering why they were not taken in that plague?

Thus, the child of forced early independence, disease, losses, inattention, and sudden deaths, John learned self-reliance, courage and fortitude. To others, John Miller presented a formidable face. He frequently boldly challenged men to shooting or running games in order to best them. "Bear John" Miller was renowned for his hunting and trapping in the hill country beyond Northampton. One of his methods was to scent himself with pine, cedar fir saps or sage herb so that the pungent odor muted his own scent. It was said that at other times hawks followed Miller in the forest waiting for his kills to clean up scraps afterwards. Sometimes Miller told others that hawks led him. Additionally, he was a great joker. He reveled in challenging and playing with other men, so it was hard to be sure what was true with him.

Aging slowly crept up on the outdoorsman Bear John unnoticed at first. Since he lived much of his time in the midst of unaltered nature away from Northampton town, John Miller had let years unspool without perceiving their passage. Finally, he observed that his mornings were slower. His strength diminishing. John knew that he could have calamitous misfortune descend at any moment. What then? He had no younger brothers or sisters to take him in hand and care for him. And he had to aid incapacitated Brother Aaron.

That morning John Miller didn't jump up out of his slumbers with his mind racing on ahead. Instead, he lay languorously on his bedroll in the primitive "lean-to." His mind lolled and tumbled slowly from scene to scene in his semi-wake state. He actually relished the perfect heat his body had created, thick in the insulation of pine needles and dead leaves. The subtle myriad shades of the forest became simply dark and light green. His mind meandered over the life of John Miller. "May the work I've done speak for me," he prayed.

"But what, indeed, have I done?" he queried himself. A multitude of birds singing together and to each other enlightened Miller that it was unnatural to be alone. "He that has not got a wife, is not yet a complete man."

He recalled his sickness of the autumn past with the awful bloody flux. He had prayed for rest. John longed for a woman's touch. Hard-eyed as he was, he knew only a poor old widow with a horde of children or a crippled and friendless orphan would likely be the only women in Northampton who might accept him. In point of fact, he was 42-years-old.

One Sabbath at meetinghouse, John Miller noted the bowed head of the spinster Martha Root. It flashed into his mind, "She would be a good wife to me."

Meanwhile, Martha Root had grown to think that she might be a "bride of Christ" for the rest of her life. Having been humiliated before all of the church, much of her pridefulness had been stripped away. John Miller had always been in the church community, so she knew *of* him. But when the black eyes of the fur-dressed, wild man John Miller landed on her one morning at meetinghouse, it was as if he were tracking an animal.

Decisive by nature, and now – his recognition that he had little time to squander - John Miller sought excuses to visit the nearby house of Hezekiah Root for a glimpse of "Mistress Martha Root." One time Miller purported to have misplaced his axe. Might he borrow one for a day? He promised (overly earnestly) to return it the next day. Soon thereafter, Miller needed butter. He would be happy to pay for it from Mother Martha Bridgman Root. One evening late in the winter, the frontiersman had extra tobacco. Would old Mr. Root care if John Miller joined him for a smoke in their parlor room? Miller had spoken softly of his people who, of course, Hezekiah Root knew well. This was John's explanation of how the Millers saw themselves, "We are humble people, but loving and respectful. We take care of our own."

At that discreet admission, John Miller averted his eyes and the men smoked on in silence and deep thought.

"What says you Martha to this proposal of marriage by the Miller man?" asked her father lightly soon after.

"Thinks you, Father, that he could make a serious attachment to me?" Martha Root deflected her bright glance and hung her head in abashedness. "I am simple. I'm nothing but a simple spinster …," her voice trailed off. Then she added, "…*with a child.*"

"Martha, he knows who you are, he sees who you are and what you are. Methinks if he has come, he accepts all that," the old man replied to her gently.

A gulp that stuck in her throat had to be pushed down with an ehhmum…. But what of her daughter, Anne? How to ask Miller the question of Anne, thought Martha? What could she even say without demeaning Anne or the beloved family that had buttressed her and her child throughout her trials and humiliations?

Some days later, Miller trapped a mink and came by to propose to have Martha stitch it into his new coat. "There'll likely be some of the fur left from the collar, which you might use for the little one," Miller stated quietly as he patted Anne's bent head.

Martha Root's heart surged with the deepest appreciation she had ever felt, apart from that she had for her father and mother who had sat in meetinghouse with their heads held high as she squeaked and sniffed out her confession of fornication. Anne reached out her hand to pet the luxurious rich brown fur that Miller held.

"Well," (long pause) do you think the rain will ruin the salsify?!" he said to Mistress Root with a low chuckle. "Must go," he added awkwardly.

On a March Sunday in 1754, John Miller stood most attentively before his shaving mirror and gazed intently at the image of a husky older man whose eyes darted to his own every detail. He checked himself. Was his wearing apparel cleaned? Was his hair neatly greased and in place? He had just bathed himself, only yesterday and hoped he was his most presentable (a new concern for him). He had rinsed out his mouth with vinegar and scoured his teeth white with gunpowder.

John Miller would walk together with the Root family to the meetinghouse, taking great caution to be the right distance away from - -but not too far from - Mistress Martha Root, thereby signaling their intention to marry. At the door of the meetinghouse there was tacked up for public view the banns informing anyone to come forward who knew of any reasons that John Miller and Martha Root should not be married.

Three weeks after the first posting of their banns on April 18, 1754, the new couple repeated the prescribed vows and were married under the law before Timothy Dwight, Justice of the Peace (certainly not before Joseph Hawley, the other Justice for Northampton) in the Hezekiah Root home. The new Mrs. Miller moved into a Miller house she had never seen the inside of before, but where John and his bachelor brother Aaron and their orphaned nephew Sam Fairfield all lived together. Her numerous relatives and well-wishers delivered Martha's marriage trousseau to her newly adopted home.

As she modestly unpacked and placed her own bake kettle, cooking "spider," toasting forks, cutlery, dishes, chairs, and bedding, Martha mused gratefully on the "remarkable providence" of her marriage to John Miller. In a corner of their bed-chamber, she observed the large cradle her carpenter Uncle Bridgman had made eight years ago. It had rocked her babes Anne and Esther. But she wondered, would the cradle rock future babies? Would she live up to her husband's expectations of her as a wife and mother? Could she still birth a living child? Had her womb dried up? Could she carry a growing child or would she bleed it out, as happened too often with many women when they felt the urge to pee, ran to the "necessary house" and instead experienced a rush of blood gushing out. What would her new husband say if she conceived no child? Would he blame her for not wanting it and secretly favoring Elisha Hawley only? Or would they become that childless old couple pitied by their nattering family and friends? Would they grow old in a cheerless, hushed struggling household, bereft of life, help, children and grandchildren?

Day by day, Martha Root Miller's new situation became more routine. One day Martha was in her kitchen garden picking vegetables for the noon dinner when she grabbed a squash which had but a single cap but then split and divided to produce two separate squash gourds. The Reverend Edwards was right, thought Martha, nature abounds with daily miracles! This must be how her womb birthed the twins Anne and poor baby Esther. It answered her question how she and sister Dolly (who had twins about two years after Martha did) had produced two babies birthed at the same time. She wondered why were Dolly's twins so different? Why Dolly's twins were even one male and one female!

As a line of lullaby popped into her head, without warning, Martha was whisked back to a remembrance of herself cooing and singing to Baby Esther. She sighed and dropped a flow of tears at the memory of cradling her tiny infant as the beautiful baby fought to live. But the Lord had not ordained it. Consequently, Esther lost her awful struggle to live. Was innocent little Esther rewarded in the eternal hereafter, wondered Martha?

Anne peeped up from her weeding at the far side of their kitchen garden across the orderly plot from Martha. The girl recognized the bereavement in her mother and wanted to be close. She felt confused and wanted to be protective in her mother's sorrow. Anne relished their chores together outside in spring.

Later, the still distracted Martha was brought back to the present moment by a groan of "Mother" from Anne. At their mid-day meal together with Uncle Aaron Miller (John and Sam being gone to work in the far fields), Martha hummed as she ladled a pork and apple stew, seasoned with nutmeg, into her daughter's trencher bowl. (In her diversion, Martha had ladled the stew onto Anne's fried doughnut.) With a deep sense of joyfulness and bliss in her secret places, Martha hummed softly for the rest of the day as she hauled firewood and water from the well outside.

Naturally, awareness of Martha's almost imperceptible swelling belly seeped out first into the consciousness of her womenfolk. Those hawkeyed females noted not only her singing but also her lethargy and frequent trips to the privy.

By the time the land was blanketed with layers of freshly-fallen, velvety-rich snow, John was begging Martha to excuse herself from the meetinghouse services for her health and that of the babe-to-be. The chill in the unheated structure infiltrated into one's very bones, even with their foot-warmer stoves. It was one of the frigidest winters in recent memory. Her husband feared she could contract fever after two hours of sitting motionless listening to the sermon. However, Martha insisted on attending, as she gained strength and power from the satisfaction that God had endowed this burgeoning of her belly. The Lord had seen fit to bless her and her husband. Her anticipation was calmed by the elated chatter of her kinswomen and friends, who too had just birthed or were with child. Their sisterhood of lactating and pregnant women, most of whom would be attending and visiting each other, sheltered and nurtured them all. By the time of the spring freshets flowing, Mrs. Martha Miller walked with a heavy waddle, and although her maternal happiness was overshadowed by the terrifying worry of war in the country, she felt serene and contented.

The flocks of Root and Miller women that mobbed the back of the meetinghouse cackled, called, chittered and laughed ebulliently, which made it disheartening or infuriating for the family coterie of the five Hawleys to pass through. Betty and Mercy Hawley, particularly, suffered acutely from the weekly display of fecundity - contrasted to their own shriveling infertility. All eyes curiously waited to observe some flicker of emotion from "Captain" Elisha Hawley, who was now recruiting soldiers in and around Northampton under a recent commission from Governor Shirley. Nevertheless, in spite of his presence in town sometimes, Elisha never seemed to cross eyes or cross paths with Mrs. Martha Root Miller.

Joseph Hawley found the evenings after Sabbath services particularly strained with Betty and Mercy retiring to chambers early to cry and Rebekah retiring to fume. No time felt more alone than this. Therefore, he valiantly focused on the dispatches from Boston to recruit soldiers for the summer 1755 campaign against the French and "their Indians" at Crown Point, Fort Niagara, the forks of the Ohio and the great French bastion at Louisbourg.

Beyond the Northampton church-yard and homes, the larger world trembled and fretted with rumors, news, plans and preparations for war, but Martha Root felt tranquility.

The sight of young Anne holding the hand of her mother Martha as they entered the meetinghouse usually caused Elisha's wife Betty's eyes to tear up. She bit hard on her own lips, not to spill the tears in front of the entire congregation. Betty averted her eyes from seeing "that Root woman." Elisha's former paramour Martha was now Mrs. John Miller (after seven long years in an unwedded state). Lately, however, few amongst the congregation had missed noticing the sight of Martha's again rapidly swelling belly, as Betty's barrenness persisted.

Had the Hawleys failed to observe the fact that Martha was big with child for a second time, it was displayed by the prayer request sent on a scrap of paper to Joseph Hawley as church leader the second week of June 1755. It read,

> "The families of Hezekiah Root and John Miller desire the prayers of Gods people in thanks for the safe delivery of their daughter and wife Mrs. Martha Miller of a perfect child Stephen Miller."[27]

Hawley had "lost" the first note from the Roots/Millers in the fireplace. Because he could not bring himself to mouth the words publicly, Joe had passed the note on to Deacon Ebenezer Pomeroy, but the second note was rejected by the deacon as "tinged with the tenor of pridefulness" (and very hurtful to his childless daughter Betty). Finally, a third note came the following week, at which time, Joe admitted to himself that he could dodge the issue of reading aloud this prayer request to the congregation for only so long. "Those exasperating Roots will refuse to relinquish this naughtiness until they are satisfied," he grumbled. Finally, Deacon Ebenezer Hunt read the prayer request aloud at the end of the morning Sabbath service on June 22, 1755. It occurred to Joe that the abjectness he felt over Martha Root's ripe fecundity in contrast to Mercy and Betty's lack of it might be a deliberate trial by God - or Satan, but what it meant for his ultimate personal salvation he could not comprehend. He hoped to always reflect spiritually and apply the true wisdom of the Gospel to his ways. Truly though, he was so sorely tried in all of these familial matters.

From the end of King George's War late in 1748, there had been speculation when the next conflict would begin - but it was certain there would be war. Naturally, each side utilized the peace to prepare for their next war. All sides,

---

[27] Not an actual historic document found by author. Created by author to mimic "bid prayers." For more information, see Footnote 18 on page 127.

French, British and Indian harangued, planned, held conferences and congresses, fortified, burned, murdered, skirmished and raided. The slow-burning fuses of belligerent incidents like Lieutenant-Colonel Washington's ambush of sleeping men at Jumonville Glen, and attacks on isolated settlers, guaranteed that tensions would remain at a high boil.

In London, the Duke of Cumberland decided to overwhelm the French with a strategy of a four-pronged, coordinated assault on the Forks of the Ohio (Fort Duquesne), conquering the French fortress at Crown Point (Fort Saint-Frédéric), building a fort on Lake Oswego in central New York and taking Fort Niagara and seizing the French region of Acadia (Nova Scotia).[28]

In the early spring of 1755, the famed Major-General Edward Braddock was sent to America with the 48th and 44th British Regiments to implement the Duke's plans. Massachusetts provincial officials enthusiastically raised three regiments for the Crown Point Expedition. In the west, Colonel Ephraim Williams' enlisted a regiment of 500 men, within which was Captain Elisha Hawley's company of 50 from Northampton.

In anticipation of his imminent departure, Captain Elisha Hawley set his affairs in order, including the writing of his Last Will and Testament on June 25, 1755 with his attorney brother, Joseph.

Days earlier, the church bell had pealed the call to gather Captain Hawley's Company of the Third Massachusetts Regiment on the town's Meetinghouse Hill in front of the First Church of Northampton's tall spire. (Hawley and other officers would march out later.) Almost all of the town's population of 1,000 plus souls assembled in quivering anticipation of the company's departure on the Crown Point Expedition. Major Joseph Hawley delivered a rousing convocation with considerable force and invoked divine favor on God's people. By the end of his oration, Joseph Hawley was so wearied as to be forced to sit with sweat beading on and dripping down his face. His voice had been so completely used up that he couldn't speak and was forced to gesticulate the rest of the day. The deacons of the First Church led communal prayer with every head humbly bowed asking the Lord's protection for their men and vengeance against their heartless heathen enemies, "if it be thy will. Amen." The late June air

---

[28] For a short article on the Fourth French and Indian War (called the Seven Years War in Europe), officially declared 1756-1763, see: https://www.history.com/topics/native-american-history/french-and-indian-war More comprehensive: https://en.wikipedia.org/wiki/French_and_Indian_War

of the Connecticut Valley town was humid and potent with every human thought, emotion and possibility.

Favorite psalms and cherished old hymns were sung with special reverence and passion so heartily that the glorious melodies carried across the warren of houses through the streets and paths and down to the Great River itself, where the sound hovered above the opaque blue waters. Among the psalms of Dr. Isaac Watts sung was *"And Am I Born to Die?"*

> "And am I born to die?
> To lay this body down?
> And must my trembling spirit fly
> Into a world unknown,
>
> A land of deepest shade,
> Unpierced by human thought,
> The dreary regions of the dead,
> Where all things are forgot?"

These powerful and evocative words rang long after in many heads and hearts. "A land of deepest shade, Unpierced by human thought, The dreary regions of the dead…" This description was what the soldiers knew they would be marching off into. Veritable valleys of the shadow of death lay where hideous killing and scalping lurked in bosky swamps and vine-twisted brakes of the vast untouched northern New York wilderness! So rousing and moving was the entire scene in front of the meetinghouse that several women and young girls fainted and had to be carried out of the crowd for fresh air from the sheer sensation of it all.

Amongst the throngs, Elisha Hawley caught sight of a lithe waif of a girl, big eyed in confusion and noiselessly crying beside her brawny stepfather John Miller. Miller clasped his nephew Samuel Fairfield, a soldier in Hawley's Company, goodbye and wished God's protection of him. Both men wrestled with the intense emotions of a possible forever goodbye. Young Fairfield had been recruited when the "beating orders" were marched through the town on May 2nd. He had signed up, gambling that he would not be killed or maimed and could save the signing bonus money to invest later in business or land for himself.

As the soldiers hefted their knapsacks onto their backs and shouldered their long guns, half the assembled crowd cheered and shouted goodbyes and good wishes while the other half broke into wailing and sobbing in a communal burst of pent-up emotions as sudden and powerful as a summer thunderstorm.

Sam Fairfield had packed a spare shirt and another pair of breeches, an extra pair of stockings and shoes, extra garters to tie up the stockings and his trusty sharp knife, in addition to the hearty victuals Martha Root Miller had cooked and wrapped up for him.

Then, at the head of the column of nearly 50 irregularly dressed farmer-soldiers, Ensign Elijah Smith (Captain Elisha Hawley's third-in-command) barked out orders to "Company, forward march!" Hawley's company marched out to the tight staccato beat of their drummer, which rhythm that day felt ominous. The soldiers trod down the well-rutted road out of Northampton in a proud semblance of military order till they were out of sight of the townspeople and the excited boys who ran alongside them (till the boys tired and dragged home). Following the Great River to Springfield, the soldiers then turned westward toward Westfield on to the "Great (Boston-to-Albany) Road." Every man among the company reassured himself that it was only a three-month enlistment. They hoped they would then return home, picking up their plows and tools and having done their duty, perhaps with epic stories to tell over and over for the rest of their lives to admiring relatives and friends. Each begged God to girdle them with courage, so as not to disgrace themselves as cowards.

Two days later another irritating family matter was plaguing Joe, the drafting of Elisha's Last Will and Testament.

"To my Beloved Wife…"

"To my wife…" Elisha corrected.

"To my Beloved Wife. It's always the language used, Elisha. It's the language of the law and has been for centuries. It doesn't mean anything is different or you have to change anything in your life," his brother contended.

"Is that to say that a Court of General Sessions in Hampshire County has ever refused a widow because her husband didn't write "beloved" in a Will?" Elisha insisted.

"Elisha, please! I'm the attorney-at-law here! I do know the Inferior Court of Common Pleas and the General Sessions of the Peace! Why, heavens, only one month ago, I sat in judgment there at Springfield! Can't you just let me draft up the document? We haven't time for debating English Common Law at a time like this!" Joe blurted out with growing exasperation. It was no time for them to be at odds with Elisha's departure tomorrow.

The younger brother shifted his stance into a taut, soldier-like posture looming over Joe's writing desk. Joe sensed his brother's backbone and determination stiffen. "Are you going to draft it as I've asked, Joseph?"

The older brother was close to vexation with the pressure of his only sibling's many duties yet-to-be-completed for his company and imminent exit, the necessity of obtaining all the requisite witnesses' appearances and signatures on the document, all the other minutiae to accomplish - and now he had to contend with his younger brother's stubbornness and his mother's whims as well. In the background, the clock incessantly tick-tocked away the time.

From the next chamber wafted murmurs of strained female voices touched with high tones and high emotion between lulls of uncomfortable, sodden silence. Joe quietly prayed that his mother wouldn't provoke and insult poor Mercy. Mercy was always on the verge of a gush of tears or squelched rage with mother Rebekah. Joe himself was still undecided whether mother's building a partition wall between their chambers of the house was a help or hindrance, but without doubt, it lit all the village gossips alight as the teeny sparks of a flint start bonfires. Try as he might, the aura of dignified, calm respectability always seemed to be compromised by a scandal involving someone in his family. He felt as if his life lurched from one humiliating crisis to another. At least the tantalizing smell of cooking pots on the crane over the hearth fire cheered him.

"Yes, 'Lisha, yes, of course. It is your Last Will and Testament and I will abide by your wishes, but I must of conscience point out the important rules of law governing the construction of *Wills and Testaments* and the reasons thereof."

Joe exhaled gravely, feeling constrained to fight on even the most routine details as always with his family. He placed the white goose feather quill down on the linen paper to relax his tightly cramped hand and throbbing temples. The feather nib was dulling and he would soon need to whittle the tip sharper. Without glancing up, he felt Elisha shift his posture again close over his shoulder, unyielding, pressing. This would be a long, painstaking process – word by word.

> "In the Name of God, Amen. I Elisha Hawley of Northampton
> in the County of Hampshire in the province of the
> Massachusetts Bay in New England Gentleman Considering the
> Great Fragility of Human life and being bound on the Intended
> Expedition against Crown Point Wherein I have reason to
> apprehend that my life will be brought into Special and
> Extraordinary Danger…. Do this Twenty fifth – Day of June in
> the anno Domini 1755 make and publish this my last Will &
> Testament…

"Principally I Commend my Soul into the merciful hands of
God the father …
"And I dispose my Estate with which God has been pleased to
bless me in manner following to wit

"To my Beloved Wife Elisabeth I give all my proper household
Goods and furniture, my old riding mare, and one of my cows,
which She Shall choose to have and hold possess and Enjoy
forever."

"You know it is said that the great bard, Shakespeare, left his second-best
bed to his wife?" Elisha observed wryly, knowing it would rankle Joe. He knew it
would delay his own relief from this awkwardness but he couldn't resist the
provocative aside.

"Elisha, I beg you, please! Can't we finish this in the quickest, simplest
fashion?!" rose Joe's voice.

"Simply an observation, Joseph. The quickest, simplest would simply be,
Joe, to leave all in the trust of God and the Courts of Hampshire County," he
quietly replied.

"Elisha, you are the one who wanted this proviso about the non-descent
of property should Betty, Mercy and I die without lawfully begotten issue. Do you
not want it any longer?" begged Joe both plaintively and with an edge of anger.

A few days before, Joseph Hawley's friend and fellow jurist, John
Worthington had observed critically, "I would think better than to put any
debatable or flawed *Will* into the hand of ye justices of a Court of Sessions. That
man who would do so must have less acquaintance with ye esteemed, honorable
justices than I have with such courts! That I would put an affair of importance to a
deception by a bunch of justices, instead of having it determined by a private
individual friend, that would be inconceivable!"

Worthington continued, "There being even a naked possibility of the
dying of all the legatees without children and the impossibility of giving a pecuniary
legacy with a remainder lien would lead me to omit ye most of those non-descent
caveats…"

Of course, Worthington was right, as Joe had repeatedly tried to explain
to Elisha to no avail.

Joe and Elisha cleared their throats nervously as their eyes studiously
avoided contact. Joe shifted his position in the smoothly-worn chair with great and

general discomfit. Now he could add back-ache to the head and hand-ache. Both men knew this line of argument could cross the sharp field of thistles and stones that was the existence of Elisha's ill-begotten eight-year-old illegitimate daughter Anne. The bitter fight with Anne's mother Martha Root and her family remained unabated with them calling her "Anne Hawley," in spite of Joseph's advising them of the illegality of usurping and casting foul aspersions on their honored Hawley name. Elisha had not married Martha Root. Therefore, Joseph refused to register Anne's birth in the *First Church of Christ Book of Records* under that name. As Justice of the Peace for the county and deacon for the church, Joe informed them that her legal name must be "Anne Root." She was a fatherless child (although admittedly she was a beautiful, solemn girl). Nonetheless the Root family continued doggedly to call her "Anne Hawley." Attorney Joseph Hawley felt their stubborn churlishness was aided by Elisha's refusal to say anything to denounce it.

Meanwhile Elisha mused on Martha Root Miller's now married status and happy delivery of a lusty baby boy Stephen, which he overheard from remarks of Sam Fairfield, John Miller's nephew and a soldier in Hawley's company. Stephen, was the first martyr of Christianity, whose name meant "crown" or "victory." Hawley recalled the Biblical verse at Acts at 7:55:

> "But he, Stephen, being full of the Holy Ghost, looked up
> steadfastly into heaven and saw the glory of God and Jesus
> standing on the right hand of God…"

Elisha Hawley marveled privately at the choice of this name for her baby and wondered whether the "victory" in the name alluded to Martha Root Miller's redemption by marriage and a lawfully begotten child, the safe delivery of her son after the travails of childbirth or a wish for a victory by their army in the upcoming struggle with the French and Indians that Elisha and Martha's relatives, too, were joining? Hawley wondered if Martha ever thought about him? A vision of his stroking and nuzzling her luxuriant hair in dappled light as he moved to kiss her seized his memory and he winced involuntarily. The summer smells always provoked a flood of visceral emotions and memories for Elisha.

Joe's light forced cough pulled Elisha from staring off in his contemplation and back to the present in their old house's south chamber where Joe shifted purposefully in his chair at the writing desk. "Uummh, mmmh," he murmured softly. The unfinished Last Will and Testament waited on the desk as Joe regarded Elisha like a being entirely new, unknown and unexpectedly fraught with tension and difficulty.

"I continue to want it, Joe. You know what I want written."

"'Lisha, I will not defy your will and wishes. But as your counselor and advisor, I must of necessity ask – with all due respect, of course – aah…. are you quite certain that there is no possibility … ummh… aah…."

Now it was Joseph Hawley Esquire who paused for a long hush to gaze away out the window glass until he could continue. His law practice and court representations were engraining legal speaking into his personal life. He hardly had an unscripted moment. "We must countenance any and every possibility in the writing of a Will. The likelihood of anything untoward happening is remote, of course, but every potentiality must be carefully considered. If Betty is carrying a child…"

"Joe, write the Will as I have instructed."

"I merely want to remind you that if there is any chance …." the lawyer in Joe could not relinquish any potential option and hated deviancy from tradition, law and the good order. He inserted a long pause before his desperate attempt to persuade, "It is quite unorthodox and unresolved to leave off at the end without envisioning for every clearly foreseeable potentiality."

This silent obstinacy of Elisha's upset Joe more than anything else - to leave the Will to end abruptly and without the other usual alternatives. Not including their mother would arouse no real curiosity or speculation. After all, she had already passed 70 years of age, but to use this circular logic - that if Joe and Mercy remained childless and died all Elisha's estate reverted to Betty, but only for her natural life and not descending from her. What thereafter? The sentence after Betty returned back to Joe and Mercy, after starting with Betty, Joe and Mercy! There were no other "Heirs and Assigns forever." There was no other descent. The lawyer hated the opening it left undefined for someone undeserving, grasping or illegitimate (like those conniving Roots). Both men breathed in filling their lungs with the utmost care and quietness, not budging a muscle.

"'Lisha, I would have you recall the summer 1751 and the Will of Uncle Eben Hawley: carefully thought out, deliberate, with every contingency clearly articulated. That is what I, as your counselor and advisor, urge, particularly as to the great grievous burden of reproach under which your matters are adjudged. Remember that it was Uncle Hawley's chary and meticulous Will that has allowed you your present comfortable, respectable circumstances and station. We simply urge cautiousness to preserve the 'Seisin Demesne As of Fee' within…" he continued with Elisha catching little of his language of law, ignoring any underlying emotion, "…. and of course, an estate tail or 'in reverter' is to be avoided…. Or as is said in law, 'without issue of his body' as in the jurisprudence of Sir Matthew Hale's decision of *Purefoy & Rogers*…"

"Ah yes, my "great grievous burden of reproach" must be countenanced and countered of course."

Elisha Hawley had no more patience for another of Joe's legal addresses. Elisha questioned whether he could ever be seen but through the light of his indiscretion with Martha Root? Would there ever be a day when he was not first and foremost noted for that? He was not the first, last or only fornicator. Yet in Northampton in hushed breaths behind his back, he was ever held to be "Elisha, who was excommunicated" however much his mother, brother, and in-laws tried to ignore and overcome it. Could he ever be known just as Elisha Hawley? Bitterness lined the edges of his sluggish words. "Of course, may I ever repent - for aught I know - and ever evoke the great grievous burden of my reproach…."

He held still on his lips the unspoken words, "…with Martha Root."

Instantly, Joe saw that he had once again stepped too far into the abyss between them as to that Martha Root affair. Joe reminded himself always to tread lightly on this difficult ground but their daily interactions seemed at all times to twitch with potent danger of it coming up in one context, one sight of a Root family member or any other reminder. Perhaps this was why Elisha so frequently absented himself from the house and town?

Joe sought to rectify the harshness of his words, "Elisha, it is but your too great gentleness as to legal matters that I seek to protect against. I simply seek to preserve your worldly estate and goods."

Joseph looked pallid and queasy in the June heat. He mumbled softly, "May God be pleased to so help me in subduing and correcting myself and my inward corruption. May God grant forgiveness of what has been amiss and past. May God sanctify this trial to me and give this poor man to see his pride and wickedness."

"You know, Elisha, I have tried to humble myself…"

Here a pause gaped as a chasm as Joseph Hawley struggled to pronounce the words that stung his tongue, "…before that Root woman."

Why Joe had even gone so far - after agonizing days and weeks of pensiveness, as to write Martha Root an apology in August 1750 after the dismissal of the Reverend Mr. Edwards. He had fervently prayed and contemplated how to right everything but that apology had only engendered more fury, not the forgiveness he expected!

"Indubitably what you testify as to that is true Joseph, but I cannot think it worthwhile to take much notice of what strange "Pleas and Exceptions" will be made against me. The evidences of the Will being my handwriting, my signature thereupon, your representation before the court, the legal decorum, etc. will all carry the day - should it ever be necessary." The slow prudent inaction had aggravated Elisha the soldier and he moved to dismiss himself from the overwrought company in the Hawley house. "Time is ticking away. I need to be joining up with my company. They're already ahead of me on the road and I need to get there. Captain Porter and I will be marching out early tomorrow."

Captain Elisha Hawley paused. "As I said before, 'the term of her natural life and no longer.' He reached across Joe's desk. "Here, let me sign the Will.""

The finality in Elisha's voice underscored the increasing inscrutability of the more and more distant younger brother. With that, Elisha swung the parchment to face him, inscribed his neat, trim signature at the bottom and walked out the door with nary a further word.

"Also I give my Said Wife the use and Improvement of one half
of All my real Estate during the Term of her natural life and in
Case of my said Wife Shall Survive and outlive my Brother
Joseph Hawley and any and every Child of Issue of his the Said
Joseph's body lawfully begotten and the Issue of Such Issue
Then and in Such case It is my Will and I do on that Condition
give my said Wife the fee Simple of one half of all my real
Estate. That Is to Say If my said Brother Joseph Shall die
leaving no Issue of his body lawfully begotten nor Issue of such
Issue, Living, my Said Wife, It is my Will that She my Said Wife
Should have the fee Simple of the one half of my real Estate
otherwise but only for and during her natural life the use and
Improvement of one half.

"And the remainder of that half of my real Estate which I have
herein before devised to my said Wife for life I give to my said
Brother Joseph in case he Shall Survive my Said Wife in fee
Simple and in Case my Said Brother Should not Survive my said
Wife But Should leave Issue of his body lawfully begotten or
Issue of such Issue who shall Survive and be living at my said
Wife's decease.

"In such case It is my Will that the said remainder of that half of
my real Estate devised to my Said Wife Should be taken and held
by such Issue in fee Simple That is to say ~~If there Should be but
one child of my said Brother living at ye Time of my said~~
Wife's…"[29]

And there it ended!

Joe Hawley made a conscious effort to reveal no further objection, shock
or sadness. He was at a loss for what to do and sat in forlorn bewildered
immobility. While he understood that things might have soured for Elisha with
Betty and her family, still Joe could not understand:

"It is my Will that She my Said Wife Should have the fee Simple
of the one half of my real Estate otherwise but only for and
during her natural life the use and Improvement of one half."

What this: "only for and during her natural life the use and Improvement
of one half?" Naturally, Joe understood provisions in a Will about a widow
remarrying and property reverting then, but that was not a proviso here. Elisha's
Will meant that Betty could bring nothing more to her family. But why? Betty's
uncle, Seth Pomeroy, was Elisha's military superior. Her uncle Dan Pomeroy was
Elisha's company Lieutenant. Her cousins were among his enlisted men.
Conversely, in spite of Elisha's good reputation as a respected officer and the
affection of his soldiers, Betty's brothers had not signed up with his company! Was
it continuing acrimony from that long ago "Bad Boys/Bad Book" incident in the
spring of 1744 when her brother was named among those to be investigated by the
Reverend Edwards? Was it Elisha's fornication and bastard child while Betty
remained childless? Joe dared consider upon their marital relations and if her
childless state could somehow be Elisha's fault….? The potency of the taste of
some malevolence seemed to conquer sweetness. Had there been sweet times for
Elisha? Was there something else? Joe dared not ask his good friend Seth
Pomeroy. Although they talked often freely and intensely on many topics, this was
one that Joe never broached. Joe would never have any answer as to why.

On June 26, 1755, a few days after his company's grand departure and the
completion of his Will, Captain Elisha Hawley left Northampton in company with
Captain Moses Porter and fellow officers to join up with their troops along the
Great Road.

---

[29] Actual *Last Will and Testament* of Elisha Hawley in the Joseph Hawley Papers including the
strike-out.

As each one among them scanned the Northampton Schoolhouse Common that day for a last glimpse, Hawley detected the amazing coincidence of glimpsing Anne, Martha Root's daughter (he dared not even breathe the words "my daughter" in his own head!), herding the cows out to the common field pasture in the distance. Was she watching him? He couldn't be sure. His fellow officers lined up in proper formation on the roadway.

"That is me," he acknowledged slowly to himself, swallowing hard after gazing at the girl's face and auburn hair.

Hawley sank into gloom and introspection. He moved behind to tramp alone from their small column. Thus, no one noticed that his eyes were floating with tears that he could blink back. What, he wondered, did Martha secretly whisper to her daughter about him? He supposed he would just have to think of it no more…

It had seemed as if it would never bear fruit, but at last, the assembling of the troops for the Crown Point Expedition was happening. Colonel Ephraim Williams had marched his own company of the Third Massachusetts Regiment from Deerfield to Fort Massachusetts to their rendezvous at Albany, gathering recruits along the way.

Colonel Eph and a klatch of Williams family relatives sat on logs at their regiment's campsite along Hudson's River smoking their white-clay Tippett pipes and drinking their militia-issued West Indies rum allowance in mostly contemplative silence as the dusk grew into dark around the campfire's dying embers. At the center Colonel Ephraim was not smoking due to his recent illness. He was still queasy and sat uncharacteristically morose.

Uncomfortable physical conditions and poor morale had left him with this internal complaint and bile imbalance. The army food had been very inedible. And there was much illness from prolonged living in overcrowded, filthy camps and often sleeping in the rain. Other days it was the hottest of weather, without relief (although some scalawags snuck off for a swim in Hudson's River). Discipline was non-existent. The army lacked all types of supplies from muskets to cooking kettles to salt-pork. In-fighting among the highest officers was prevalent.

Colonel Eph was ever on guard and nervously watchful about what he said to or about both his new commander General William Johnson, and his old patron General William Shirley. Eph felt he should keep muzzled, contrary to his sociable personality. It was hard to negotiate the hatred between Generals Johnson and Shirley. They despised each other openly and vengefully now. It was as dangerous as walking across slushy river ice where one might break through at any moment. The two colonial commanders actively opposed and worked against each other, although both were in his Majesty King George II's campaigns against the French. The two generals were recruiting from the Iroquois Six Nations Confederacy against each other by offering competing bounties, gifts and bribes and denouncing the other's competence and honesty. General Johnson had spent more than £10 in the last two months buying teapots, sugar, tea and punch as gifts for the Indians, whereas General Shirley was paying cash in Spanish silver dollars and supplying rum! Those persons caught between them - like Ephraim Williams - drew the ire or distrust of both sides. Poor Eph, he only wanted to use the advancement opportunity of this war, yet the utmost restraint was always necessary.

"He may know the Boston rabble, but he knows nothing of the Iroquois nature," complained Johnson about General Shirley.

"A back-stabber to my campaign which is now the primary one, now that poor General Braddock is ruined," summarized Shirley about Johnson.

Only a week before, when the officer corps (including Johnson, Shirley, and their top staffs) had dined together at Albany, military intelligences reported that General Braddock was close to taking Fort Duquesne at the forks of the Ohio. Amazingly, now Indian runners were breathlessly bearing news of the entire 2,000-plus man British army slaughtered in the woods! It was inconceivable! Impossible! Beyond belief! How could it be?!? It must be wrong! Who could credit such reports?!?

Initially, Eph Williams denounced anyone who would carry such viciously false and melancholy rumors. It must be a deliberate pernicious French stratagem to dispirit their English Indian allies! Then his Lieutenant-Colonel Seth Pomeroy confided that the reports were based on the best direct information from the front, not only from Indians but even from British sources!

Eph Williams and most of the officer corps were rattled with the news of General Braddock's stunning defeat. Somehow Seth Pomeroy could carry on every day as before, but with the Braddock news, Ephraim Williams assumed the full weight and burden of many years of fighting. Nights, he lay awake for hours. When he fitfully slept, he awoke deflated, dispirited and riddled with ceaseless plaguing worries. He resolved to settle his own affairs and write a new Last Will and Testament.

"Colonel, the men talked of you making a promise to them when you departed our old home base, Fort Massachusetts, that you would take care of them. They say you promised not to forget your old faithful soldiers so far from everyone else's remembrances?" questioned one of the ensigns.

"Well, yes, actually I did effuse too much, I suppose. Perhaps I was a-wheezing like an old bagpipe and went on and on. I did promise them never to forget them. That's a truth. But who could ever forget such as that?" replied Colonel Ephraim, turning his round amiable face to the group for assent.

"Never, no, never," chimed in Captain Elisha Hawley in agreement. "Not after all we've been through out there! After the thousands of hungry, back-breaking days and lonely, howling nights; the dangerous journeys up the Cold River valley of boulders with our packs crushing our backs; climbing up Hoosac Mountain practically to the clouds; always the worry about Indian ambuscades; the dreaded 'bloody flux' diarrhea runs to the latrines; and all the other trials! No, I could never forget our wilderness abode!"

"Hawley, you make it sound as if it was all dire and dismal? Have you no good memories of those days together? And you of all men, Hawley, who's been in the wilds all these last years!"

"Course, Eph, for certain! It's just the harshness springs to mind first. The brain remembers pain before peace. But the best music ever heard on this green earth was Micah Harrington and the boys singing out there where the sound carries forever across those beautiful, endless hills. Best discourses in my life - those nights a-talking fire-side, drinking a grog of rum with you and the men. None ever more spiritual than those prayers surrounded by the great untamed wilderness. No food ever tasted better than that roasted venison after coming in from a snowshoe scout! The wrestling matches and races we used to hold… And that Hoosic spring water, so fresh and cool in summer!"

"So much better than that swamp water in the fort well," agreed Williams. Both men silently reflected to themselves the poor siting of the fort on the swampy meadow of the Hoosic River below the "Indian ledge" rock cliff from which the attack had preceded in 1746. Elisha's uncle and Eph's benefactor, Colonel John Stoddard, had forgotten the French military genius Valbrun's maxim "heights command lower positions" and ordered Fort Massachusetts to sit where the little valley broadened. Ephraim Williams continued, breathing shallowly in remembrance of the young man, "Poor Elisha Nims died for a sip of that water! Course, that was before you got up there…"

"Is my old dog, Hunter, still on guard there? He saved our scalps from the Abenakis with his ceaseless barking before the attack in '48 in the Old French War, remember that? How are my Mohicans and the friends at Stockbridge?"

"Yup, that old yellow dog is dead, and your cat, Whiskers, too. George and Conawoca, you know, were at Stockbridge, last I heard of 'em." Colonel Eph became introspective again and paused a long moment to swallow. His thoughts drifted to Stockbridge. That lovely settlement along the rocky Housatonic River - that was to have been a model of English and Indian living together but instead became riven with bitter rivalries, jealousies and terrible fear. It was so heart-wrenching to consider on it. His mind flitted back to a pathetic picture of his cantankerous, elderly father's last days there wandering aimlessly with bags of all denominations of every nation's coins - but his fellow English settlers rejecting him! One morning "Old Colonel Eph" (the father) had presented himself to buy a neighbor's farm with an arm full of old tenor money - wearing his nightcap!

The genial Colonel Eph Jr., continued, "To be true, Hawley, there was surely good times and bad at the Fort. Those sorrowful tombstones of the folk we lost, Nims, Knowlton, Severance, little Annie. But the hardest part was leaving old John Hawks! I feared old rough and ready Hawks would bawl like a spring lamb when I said 'goodbye, faithful old friend.' With him tearing up, I feared I might as well."

The untested young men among them around the campfire pondered their own future bravery in battle, while the older men recalled the legendary story of Sergeant John Hawks and the 20 sick souls (soldiers, women, and children) "captivated" at the Fort in August 1746 and forced to march to Canada, where so many languished and died in stone-cold Quebecois prisons! Ephraim and Thomas Williams muffled a prayer to themselves thinking on that sorely-tried band. Dr. Tom had departed the Fort only the day before it was attacked – "by the grace of God!" Ephraim had been headed on his way there from Albany when the attack came. Silence prevailed, until most among the group took their leave to go to their bedrolls for the restless sleep of soldiers on campaign.

"Oh, Hawley, we soldiers are always particularly cognizant of the frailty of human life. You know, I did write a Will during the Louisbourg campaign in '46. But certainly, times have changed in the 10 years since then," Eph acknowledged. "I rewrote a newer Will. Besides, I want to make a suitable charitable or pious deed from my estate, as my reverend confessor has counseled."

"A what?" Hawley queried. Ephraim Williams' brother Tom had already heard this new urge and sat broodingly to listen again, knowing this latest whim of Ephraim's had been roiling the family.

"You know, Hawley, a minister recommends a *Bible* or flagon for the church. But I think better, something for the poor of our old Fort, like a free school… for the children of the men at Hoosic." He paused poignantly. "You and Tom and the Pomeroys have your wives and children to visit your graves and cry over your loss. They will carry on your names. But no one will visit my grave, no one will speak my name in remembrance, no one will care that I lived," Colonel Eph mused. "Granted, it is only the eternal life and resurrection into immortal glory that will matter, if it should please God to bless me in the afterlife…."

The quiet coterie smoked on in silent assent, some muttering "mmmhhmm," as Hawley mentally corrected the statement. Dr. Tom had a wife and children, Seth and Dan Pomeroy had rafts of children. However, Hawley himself had but his wife.

"Eph, you know how dearly the children love you. They could never forget you," Tom Williams pleaded almost inaudibly. "And the men, too."

The others chimed in similarly of their own accords of their affection for their affable leader. Eph then softly announced, "I endeavor to create a great and public benefit." He paused for some long, poignant seconds. "And there are all those things I must remember to set a-right, like poor Elisha Chapin, who was so despondent about his demotion from lieutenant, and the payroll owed Moses Graves, and so on. Still …" he paused dramatically, "I desire to serve some pious or charitable purpose."

All waited for what was on their commander's mind.

"I have decided to bequeath the extra - that not being set aside for my dear family and friends – for the deserving poor or a school on the frontier, like for the children of the soldiers at Fort Massachusetts."

"A most noble legacy," someone mumbled.

"Generosity most unexpected!"

An image from Hawley's childhood of a spinning wooden whorl-top faltering slowly back and forth on its point, ultimately to fall over, sprang to his mind. Hawley had noticed the Mohican children playing similar games, spinning acorns in one of their villages last summer as he traveled the Housatonic Valley with his two Indian scouts. He thought how much the spinning top was like the human life-span. Nothing lasted, nothing stayed, everything ground down to dust. It existed only for moments, faltering on a point, however long or short the moments or life. "Ashes to ashes, dust to dust," he murmured to himself.

"So, have you made a Will, Hawley?" asked Eph Williams.

"Yes, a simple, unencumbered one, without much rigamarole put into it. It was signed the day before I left – just to cover any untoward possibilities. It's the usual, half division to my wife and half to my brother," Hawley muffled.

"Of course, just as mine on the Louisbourg Expedition. One must take care to cover any theoretical misfortune, however unlikely," the Colonel concurred.

"Just so."

At the urging of General ("Handsome Billy") Johnson, Ephraim Williams had engaged the consultation of a young 20-year-old lawyer, Peter Silvester of

Albany, whom Johnson himself had used for some work, to "advise him on legalities and so on," but, in actuality, the Colonel wrote out the Will in his own hand and Silvester did little - except opine much. Williams counted the consultation as a feathering of Johnson's "courtiers'" nests (the usual political pay-offs), but it was always best to stay in the good graces of one's superiors and there was no better way than to loosen the purses liberally! More so since Colonel Williams had stayed at General Johnson's own Albany house as befitted a gentleman of Ephraim Williams' standing. Johnson had purchased the property from an old Dutchman, Henry Holland, during the winter of 1748-49. The two-story, brick building was clearly one of the best houses in Albany with good cellars, a large kitchen and a bleach yard.

While Williams had had occasions to sojourn there (as recently as a year ago at the 1754 Albany Congress of the American colonies and Indians), Albany was a foreign country for Ephraim Williams. The city was a conundrum with its bizarre composition of Dutch underlay below its English veneer. These Dutch were polite, fastidious and economical but seemed not to appreciate that it was the English who had conquered them almost 100 years earlier! Why, the Dutch carried themselves with excessive pride (as if they had been the conquerors!) and spoke their jarring Dutch language blatantly on the streets. Like the French, the Dutch built structures of stone, not wood. There were many tiled buildings with strange elements, like noting the dates of their construction on the exterior of the building. Their stone and brick houses had their rooflines gabled and iron roosters, called "weather-cocks" at the sharp peak of the roof-tops. Their doors were two half-doors together which opened at both the top and bottom (called by the English a "Dutch door").

The three-story city hall was also built of stone. The cityscape was not familiar and comfortable like Boston's. The English church at Albany was St. Peter's Episcopal, rather than Congregational churches as throughout New England. And there were the Dutch Reformed churches. The streets were either a constant mire of mud or powdery dust with pigs rooting everywhere for bits of garbage. Guarding the city was Fort Orange, another Dutch structure. Bells rang every hour from noon until 8 o'clock in evening. Even the trees on the streets of Albany were different, called "button trees."

Colonel Ephraim Williams had been wrestling over the details of who and what should constitute his Last Will and Testament for some days. First, was the Biblical injunction to care for to his "honored step-mother" Abigail -of whom he knew many spoke ill – even so far as to call her "evil." Then his beloved siblings: dear Tom and his family (whose house in Deerfield had always been a second home to Eph), Elijah, Josiah, Judith, Abigail and Elizabeth. He thought through each possibility in the Will:

"In the name of God Amen. I Ephraim Williams of Hatfield… on my march in the Expedition against Crown-point… remembering the uncertainty of it at All times, I do therefore make and publish this my last will and Testament …

Item. I give and bequeath unto my beloved brothers, Josiah Williams, and Elijah Williams, and the heirs of their bodies my homestead at Stockbridge, with all the Buildings and Appertenances thereunto belonging, with all the Stocks of Cattle and Negro Servants now upon the place, to be Equally Divided…

Item. It is my will that in Case one of my aforesaid Brothers die without Issue, then the whole of the above bequest revert to the Survivor… [or] the money be put Out to interest, and that the said Interest shall be used for Some pious or Charitable purposes, as the Propagating Christianity the Support of the poor in the County of Hampshire, or for Schools…

Item. I give & bequeath to my loving Cousin Elizabeth Williams, over and above the twenty pounds above mentioned, my Silver Cream pot and Tea Spoons.

Item. I give the remaining part of my Library not Yet Disposed of (excepting my large bible and Ridgleys body of Divinity) to my beloved brothers, Thomas and Elijah Williams to be Equally Divided between them, but in Case my brother Thomas Dies his part to go to his Son Thomas, and in Case my Brother Elijah Dies without Issue, then his part to be given to my Cousens...

Item. It is my will & Pleasure & Desire that the remaining part of lands…., Shall be Appropriated towards the Support and maintenance of a free School…

Eph Williams

Signed Sealed published pronounced and Declared by the Said Ephraim Williams as his last will and Testament in the Presence of us who were Present at the Signing.

Wm. Williams junr.
Noah Belding
Richard Cartwright

There it was: done! He knew his family would be fuming over it but he had to do it. His intuition told him that he walked on treacherous ground in Indian affairs, as well as with his own family. He had sinned. It hurt him to be judged mainly by his father's conniving land deals in the Housatonic Valley with the Indians. He had a conscience and was truly uncomfortable in discord. Further Eph knew he would need to mend his unsavory reputation amongst the new Indian allies if he hoped to rise in the esteem and favors of his new commander General Johnson. In personality type Handsome Billy Johnson was just his sort of man: he was a genial, wealthy and benevolent gentleman who was connected to important men in England, and rising in prominence there (although Johnson was dissimilar in his unconcern for social mores and reputation locally. Why Johnson had even taken an Indian squaw as his wife!).

Unfortunately, the social and political factions at Albany were as highly combustible as those at Stockbridge. At Stockbridge, the local landscape consisted of the various Indians tribes and the two white camps of Jonathan Edwards versus the Williams family. Yet one could not be oblivious to the larger world in England and Scotland that provided the financing for the Indian mission there.

At Albany, Ephraim Williams would have to make special efforts to win back the goodwill of the half-Mohican, half-Mohawk leader, Hendrick Tiyanoga. However, Eph's friendship with the sneaky unbridled Albany trader, John Henry Lydius marked Eph as a man not to be trusted amongst General Johnson's Indian advisors, particularly Hendrick.

Though the largest part of Ephraim's current consternation was General Braddock's defeat and his own place within the feud between William Shirley and William Johnson, there was also the sting of his own personal disaster at the outright rejection of his marriage proposal to his cousin Israel's daughter, Sarah. Eph remained shocked that a man as sage as Israel, military commander for western Massachusetts and Eph's direct superior (as well as being his cousin), would allow a fickle 18-year-old girl to choose who should be her husband! There was a welter of conflicting and scrambled emotions stinging him. He had felt a deep crash that made him lose his appetite for life. He had never felt so depleted before. He examined himself. He was tall and cut a dashing figure in his brilliant military uniform. Admittedly he was somewhat portly, but he wasn't such a "butter-bag" as some other forty-year-old's (he told himself). He did have to concede that he had been "bacon fed" of late, enjoying life's pleasures, unlike the typical lean and hungry common soldier. Oh, life had crept up upon him mighty speedily….

Unchained from farm seasons and attached now to the rhythms of war, Ephraim Williams wondered why time felt differently when traveling? Soon he would be on the road again. At least it helped with forgetting…. Other affairs intruded into his mind demanding attention. His great friend and Lieutenant-Colonel Seth Pomeroy had already departed Albany to the north, where the French fortress at Crown Point awaited their attack.

Seth had left at their lodgings in General Johnson's house in Albany a small wooden trunk with four fine shirts, caps, two or three white cotton handkerchiefs, a little bag of gold (hidden within a secret compartment), some English cash, his best waistcoat and jacket, his best wig, best hat, black leather boots and saddle bags. Colonel Ephraim decided to take his finery items in his chest with him on the journey north. He just couldn't be without his beloved books.

Before he had left his preoccupied, worldly-wise and world-weary friend, Colonel Ephraim Williams, Seth Pomeroy informed Eph that in the packets of incoming soldiers' mail from Massachusetts, Seth had delivered a letter in the elaborate female script of Sarah Williams of Hatfield to the new physician, Dr. Perez Marsh, the surgeon's mate to Eph's brother, Dr. Tom Williams. (It was rumored that Sarah was sweet on Marsh: Eph would have to complain to his brother Dr. Tom about allowing that young cub Marsh as his assistant!)

"Where is Marsh?" demanded Eph. But young Marsh had already gone north.

Colonel Ephraim Williams, Junior noted the sun glinting and skipping across the broad waters of Hudson's River in the soft breeze. He reminded himself to "watch particularly against those sins that a soldier's life expose men unto."

Most of its component regiments didn't start out on the Crown Point Expedition until July 1755. When the various troops (from Massachusetts, Connecticut, New York and a few Rhode Islanders) arrived at Albany, they were bogged down by lack of supplies and coordination, disunity, indecision and petty arguments which plagued the war efforts. The campaign finally reached the upper Hudson River watershed divide in September. General William Johnson, with his Mohawks allies in his train, was among the last to arrive at Lac St. Sacrement. The ever politically conscious general promptly dubbed it "Lake George."

One who had never been indecisive was the renowned Mohawk leader Tiyanoga, or "King Hendrick" as the English called him. For years he had courageously led war parties as far as Montreal through the deep and unforgivingly severe Adirondack wilderness. As recently as July 1754, he had harangued the British at the Albany Congress for their lack of martial spirits. Thus, when Tiyanoga, the Mohawks and more of the esteemed Iroquois Confederation came into General Johnson's army camp at Lake George, even the Indian-wary New Englanders cheered hurray!

At the magnificent lake, the little "West Brook" and its broad flat marsh separated the Indian encampment at the sprawling army camp recently hacked out of the unbroken primeval forests. Most of the night the endless wilds around the encampments sounded with lapping waves on the shore of the lake, the soft dragging rustle of hunkering raccoons and opossums, skittish white-tail deer grazing, far-off wolf packs howling in unison, the occasional shriek of a prey caught in its killer's death grip and the constant creaking background of billions of birds and insects. General William Johnson had issued strict orders to all soldiers: "No unnecessary shooting" so as not to alert the French enemies.

On the farthest distant Indian side of the camp, the old Mohawk head sachem and warrior hero Tiyanoga ("White Head" in the Haudenosaunee[30] language) woke before dawn in a semi-sleep, trying to gather the many strands of his restive dreams from this short night's sleep. In his dreams, he had journeyed far back in time to his youth as "Wanis" or "Long Bow," his birth name, preparing to become a great warrior. Now as he lay between the dream and wake states, his mind ticked back through the many people who had passed over to the next world. He allayed his brooding heart about the continuity of his Mohawk people, back

---

[30] Commonly termed "Iroquois" by the whites but calling themselves "Haudenosaunee."

generation upon generation long before the white people came to the American continent, beyond tales and memories even, throughout eons of time. They were "Ongwe-honwe," the "men that surpassed all other men."

The previous night as sleep eluded him, the old chief had been mired in the unanswerable questions of how his Mohawks would navigate and survive in the treacherous world of duplicitous white traders and lusting land-hungry English farmers. He was fatigued by their ceaseless demands for more and more land. One night a deal might be concluded with eating, tippling alcohol, smoking together and friendship. Soon thereafter though (perhaps the next day even), the whites would be back seeking more! The Mohicans had believed "the Great Being feeds his people in due season. We are often out of provisions and yet are wonderfully supplied. So frequently this happens that it is evidently the hand of the Great Spirit Waunthut Mennitow that doth this."

But Tiyanoga had witnessed the reduction of his once important Mohican people to a weak tribe that old white men in powdered horsehair wigs in Boston termed their "children," instead of "brothers." Tiyanoga had lived close to the whites at Fort Johnson and in Stockbridge (Massachusetts). He had listened to their silvery promises but then saw land "encroachments" one after another after another and then still another! The whites never had enough land. Their thirst for land could never be slaked! If they had the land upon which a brook cut through, next, they must have two paths to it – in case one path were to be blocked. Then they would insist that they needed more surrounding land so they could block up the brook to create a pond. The pond would need to water fruit trees which required more! They had children upon children. And on it went with the pale-face English "needing" more and more land forever…

It was just like Old Ephraim Williams (the father) at Stockbridge: first, the hoary old land-grabber and money-lover took and fenced in more land than the Mohican chief John Konkapot had agreed to sell him. When Konkapot complained, the old cranker Williams called Konkapot "a dirty old savage who knew nothing." For a man in church every Sabbath, singing loudly and praying in deepest earnestness, Old Williams lived a life of viciousness toward fellow church members including his church brethren John Konkapot. "Since our English brothers had the honor and joy of knowing Jesus Christ, their Lord, how could they be such poor Christians? Why do the white men live such vicious lives?" Tiyanoga often asked himself.

"New England people are land mad," he concluded.

On the land theft John Konkapot had complained to the Massachusetts General Court, and crochety "Old Williams" admitted to the Court that he might have "accidentally" fenced in more than Konkapot sold. Williams then argued that since the forest was now all cut down and replaced by his crops, it would be a shame to return the land to Konkapot "who was not using it at all." So once again, the white authorities allowed another land theft! "Does ye suppose a court in this land will believe a drunk Indian over a gentleman like me?" Old Williams had laughed and sneered. This ruse or some other had been recurring since the 1739 settlement of the English and Mohicans at Stockbridge, and old Ephraim William's lands now numbered in the hundreds of acres! In the end, the Massachusetts General Court reasoned further, "Why shouldn't a tract of land in a remote wilderness, scarcely worth a cent an acre, be grudged to anybody of men who were willing *to farm it*."

Still, Old Williams lusted for more land! Elderly and infirm as he was (64 years old), Old Williams was last seen in Stockbridge with fists full of money trying to buy more land – immediately with cash!

Hendrick Tiyanoga hated vicious old Ephraim Williams Senior and the rest of his covetous, land-grabbing clan. Besides his unmitigated lust for ever more land, Old Williams was cruel and manipulative. He had ignored or even encouraged beatings of the Indian children at the mission! The mission monies had been paid out to his kin as "teachers" while they forced the children to work their farms. "Spare the rod and spoil the child," old Williams had justified. Finally, when the old man gave the Mohawk children wine to drink, Tiyanoga was forced to order his people to leave Stockbridge and abandon their attempts to become educated in reading and writing and live among the whites. They hated to leave behind their good Christian friends among the whites, like the Jonathan Edwards family, but they felt compelled to move away.

How would the Mohawk people survive their own weaknesses and this engulfing surge of white peoples pressing upon them with their white powers of metals, guns, writings, large domesticated animals, fabrics and a God that mostly shielded them from sicknesses? Tiyanoga conceded that there had always been and would always be at least one weak tribesman among them who thirsted for rum or had white creditors after him for money, who would then "sell" their people's land for a taste of alcohol!

Everywhere the white people went, they left destruction and garbage. The tribes lived in harmony with their nature brothers and sisters, their "manitous." When the Iroquois abandoned a settlement, their corn fields reverted to forest. The remains of their longhouses rotted – like all living things – to loamy black soil.

But with the whites there were piles of broken glass, rusted metals, splintered and cracked wood. Forests were not shared with nature by the whites, the land was completely emptied, cleared, truncated and trampled.

As it had been with the Mohicans, Tiyanoga hoped to stop the trafficking of rum to the Mohawks and preserve their lands against cheating, theft, manipulations, divisions and speculations. He burned inside to think back to the most recent land swindle of the millions of acres of Delaware lands by that vile snake, John Henry Lydius! Once again that double-dealer had lured Indians to his place with alcohol! Days later they were shown the "white men's papers" on which the whites claimed the Indians had signed away their lands, when no one among the Mohawks or Delawares remembered anything of it! His own brother Abraham had purportedly signed that last land deal paper! Yet Abraham swore to Tiyanoga that he had not been drinking.

Hendrick Tiyanoga knew that unless the Mohawks remained strong and vigilant warriors and protected their lands, they would "become women," weak, powerless, landless and open to every exploitation by other tribes, as the Delaware tribe had become women to the Mohawks. He couldn't stand for Mohawk men "to put on petticoats!" His blood grew hot and pulsed hard at the thought.

Worse still was the white treatment of his people – hatred, humiliating words, threats, beatings and even murder. Usually the white murderers walked free with no retribution! Where was the Bible's "eye for an eye?" Such had been the case of Solomon Waunaupaugus's son at Stockbridge only two years ago! It caused his heart to ache. Where was the path through this tangle of human treachery?

Not only was there the problem of how to live with the English, but there was the diplomatic challenge of relations with their blood relatives, the French "Caughnawaga Mohawks."[31] The Mohawks were divided between their "Brother English" and those brothers that sided with the French. Despite decades long Haudenosaunee and Mohawk diplomacy to smoke tobacco peace pipes together and "be more careful before they might destroy one another," they were frequently

---

[31] In the Haudenosaunee language "Mohawk" is "Kanien'kehá:ka" or "Caughnawaga" for the British colonists. Both of these bands of Mohawk people were Iroquois who originated in eastern New York state. In the late 1600's the "Caughnawaga Mohawks" converted to Roman Catholicism and removed to the St. Lawrence River valley. This group struggled valiantly to maintain peace amongst their fellow Mohawks, French, British and Americans, especially during the American Revolution For their explanation of their history: http://www.kahnawake.com/community/history.asp Another nice summary: https://www.encyclopedia.com/history/encyclopedias-almanacs-transcripts-and-maps/caughnawaga The remaining Mohawks in New York ultimately allied with the British; see: https://en.wikipedia.org/wiki/Mohawk_people

at odds. Nothing was worse than brother-on-brother fighting! Their enemies, the French and Hurons, nipped constantly at them, trying to induce Mohawk-on-Mohawk treachery!

Tiyanoga's[32] speculations and calculations for the day ahead chased away his drowsiness. As he contemplated his preoccupations, he gazed up through the skyward length of yellow pine tree trunks that stretched tall overhead. Unlike the white men, the Mohawks had not cut down the trees but rather, camped among them. Above the elongated trunks lay the creator's countless scatter of stars. The same stars were everywhere to guide them, so reassuring, he thought, until he gulped in a breath at the surprise of a shooting star whitening a momentary bright line through the black sky! Being ever impressed by the power of omens, Tiyanoga was pleased with the luck of it! It must be an auspicious sign for the day ahead. He felt very favored and awed. Today would be one of epic actions, he sensed.

Only three days before, Tiyanoga and his most trusted counselors had met deep in the woods near "Blind Rock" with the chief sachems of the Caughnawagas to work out a way not to face off against one another, supporting their English or French brothers. Ominously, the French-allied Caughnawaga Mohawks had told Tiyanoga, "It is not in our power to comply with your request for us to stay out of any fight, for the French and we are one blood and where they are to die, we must die also."

Tiyanoga pleaded that they were foremost "offspring of one Mohawk Blood" and that the New York and Caughnawaga Mohawks were cousins, uncles, grandparents of each other. But the Caughnawaga sachems replied that the French were brothers-in-laws, cousins, neighbors. For hours, the attempted persuasions switched back and forth with neither side relenting or persuaded. Finally they parted ways in agreement only that Mohawks killing each other would be a violation of Ayenwatha's "Great Law of Peace" which must never happen. How would a fire be stopped once a fuse was lit? No one could think or say. All earnestly hoped that inter-tribal fighting could be avoided.

Yet it was clear from the increasing number of reports of his scouts out ranging the forests and runners up the Great Lake to Crown Point and down to

---

[32] Two great Mohawk sachems were baptized and called "Hendrick" by the whites: Hendrick Tejonihokarawa and Henderick Peters Theyanooguin (King Hendrick) (aka Tiyanoga herein. Note even the varied spelling of "Hendrick" in the contemporaneous sources!). Confusion over the two Hendricks prevailed from colonial times up until the present, but has thankfully been clarified by Eric Hinderaker's brilliant book, *The Two Hendricks: Unraveling a Mohawk Mystery.* Harvard University Press (Cambridge, 2011).

the "Great Carrying Place" on Hudson's River that soon all the armies of the English, French and Indians on both sides were destined to come together at war.

At that thought, Tiyanoga rolled over and touched his "Manitou-aseniah" ("spirit stones") in the deerskin pocket tied across his chest and under his left arm. The dazzling beauty of the red and clear crystals calmed and pleased him. "Garnet" and "diamond" brother Johnson called them. For the Mohawks who found them in the mountains and along their river, they had been special gifts from the "Great Creator," although many Mohawks now preferred the white men's colorful glass trade beads. Hendrick Tiyanoga was a mix of old ways and new. He chose crystals for luck, the beautiful purple and white "wampum" shell beads for decoration and English clothes and trade items to flaunt. Of course, "wampum" would always contain the greatest power and beauty for him. For weapons he carried the best English gun, a well-used Indian war club and a traditional tomahawk.

He rubbed the lucky, protective and useful crystals with his well-worn fingers. In ancient times before the white "axe-makers" came, the crystals would have chipped many a deadly arrowhead. With the whites came metal. Would he deploy his English gun today? He thought of the raiding times in "the Old French War" of 1747 when he had shot so fast that the trigger of the gun couldn't even be touched it was so hot!

As the first light began to wash above the mountainous eastern horizon the stout tattoo-faced Mohawk got up to carefully prepare himself for the Officers' Council at dawn. He pulled on his brilliant red English great-coat with its broad white cuffs of lace and rows of shining buttons up and down the front. It was resplendent! Tiyanoga peered into his looking glass mirror to carefully set his black wool tricorn hat with gold-braid edging atop his flowing white hair. Old? Yes, he was. Even with the soothing, fine suppleness of his deerskin moccasins, as soft as a mother's kiss, he increasingly felt the ravages of age. Every act took him longer and required more energy. His formerly powerful inner fire had declined. While still strong, he told himself that this should be his last campaign season. The younger heroes who would be 'born' on this campaign would lead in the future.

He chewed some dried venison before he left the Mohawk camp with his trusted counselor and Bear Clan Mohawk sachem "Thick Lawrence." Their young Mohawk warriors were starting to gather around their campfires to boil dried white corn kernels for the morning meal. Oneidas and Mohicans similarly assembled each with their fellows around as Tiyanoga and Lawrence departed the "Indian camp" to the bluff above Lake George upon which General William Johnson's elaborate white tent stood.

In the Massachusetts Regiments' camp the farmer-soldiers were similarly waking and stirring their fires to cook up their dried peas and salted pork and wondering with very serious preoccupation what this day might bring. In the few days since their arrival, thousands of English feet had worn a path through the lines of the Massachusetts soldiers' white canvas tents, jumped over the slow and swampy "middle brooklet" and climbed up the hillock to General Johnson's tent. On that trampled trail walked the three Massachusetts commanding Colonels, Moses Titcomb, Timothy Ruggles and the tall, lumbering Ephraim Williams Junior, ahead of Tiyanoga and Thick Lawrence.

Wherever they were, Tiyanoga's eye always picked out Colonel Ephraim Williams, having had daily encounters in the near past with him at the Stockbridge Mission village. Hendrick Tiyanoga knew the ways of white men well enough to understand that white men could be fast friends, but only so long as it suited them. Once it was no longer advantageous to the whites, they forgot their former Indian friends. As General Johnson said to Tiyanoga of his commanding officer General William Shirley, "From a former Friend I have reason to believe he is become my Enemy." Former friends were enemies of the worst kind. Hendrick Tiyanoga did not count Colonel Ephraim Williams as an enemy in this setting as they all were fighting the French. But he knew that Colonel Eph Williams, Junior was not much of a friend or ally to him or any Indian. Tiyanoga would be ever suspicious of "Williams-the-coyote" who, like "coyote the trickster" of Haudenosaunee myth, who could turn his smile to a snarl in an instant, particularly when it came to land or money.

As they drew into a circle around Commander Johnson's great tent, Tiyanoga and Thick Lawrence squatted near to the commanding general, while the rest of the army's white field officers crowded close to claim a seat on a cut tree stump, in order of their military rank. The officers clustered together by colonies. Connecticut men together. Massachusetts men together, and the Yorkers together. Behind them all, trying to observe everything unobtrusively, was 13-year-old Joseph Brant, the brother of General Johnson's Mohawk wife Molly.[33] As a future Mohawk hero in training, young Brant's eyes were wide as pewter plates as he took it all in. In the meantime, the General's servants scurried around among them with cups and saucers, hot water, tea, a pure white sugar cone and the sugar nippers.

---

[33] William Johnson's second wife was Molly Brant, although there were/are questions as to whether his marriages were consecrated in a Christian religious ceremony. See: Hamilton, Milton: "Sir William Johnson's wives," *New York History* 38, no. 1 (1957): 18-28. "Handsome Billy Johnson's" sexual licentiousness was notorious and it is claimed that he may have fathered up to 600 children! The *Dictionary of Canadian Biography* has good biographies of Molly and Joseph Brant, see: http://biographi.ca/en/

Colonel Williams' black servant Romano brought around dishes piled high with roasted beef chunks, bread and porridge with currants for the officers to ladle out.

"My Lieutenant-Colonel Seth Pomeroy won't be here this morning as he's terribly indisposed… Aahhh, he's in an ill state of health, I'm afraid," excused Ephraim Williams quietly before General Johnson had brought the highest-ranking gentlemen of the Officers' Council to order. Colonel Eph cringed at the remembrance of Seth's "bloody flux" (diarrhea).

The council conversation turned to the question of building a fort here to secure the lake. They had been debating this question for some days already. Should they secure their military gains by building an advanced post fort at this site on their newly secured and renamed Lake George, as they had done at Fort Lyman down Hudson's River at the Great Carrying Place? The Connecticut and Massachusetts officers only wanted to push on to fight the French at Crown Point and had no interest in New York fortifications. After much fruitless deliberation, General Johnson decided that they had to immediately address the urgency at hand that was the skulking French in the hinterlands marching to Fort Lyman.

"Gentleman," called out General Johnson. "It seems as if we are still unable to reach consensus on this topic once again." It was contrary to the Commander's social instincts and personal amiability to be argumentative. He needed to rivet the council's attention on a more urgent subject, "Gentlemen, as you may know, our Mohawk friends under Lawrence here…" Brother Johnson gestured to the Native scout Thick Lawrence. "… the scouts have discovered three French armies - each about 600-700 men - headed to menace Fort Lyman."

General Johnson gestured for the Scout Leader Lawrence to explain. Thick Lawrence was a stout, broad-shouldered powerful man. Like the other Mohawk leaders, he was deeply bronzed by the sun and richly decorated with jewels in his ears and nose, as well as tattoos and bright paint. Thick Lawrence was respected as a careful man who knew his job well. He could be trusted implicitly. He read forest signs accurately, rarely lost a man ranging the woods, would report back details of what they had discovered and why he concluded what he did. The white scouts, by contrast, on several occasions manically discovered tracks in the obscure and frightening forest, only to comprehend later that those were the tracks of their own armies!

The twenty or so English officers and four Indians at the council grew silent.

Feeling less secure in his English language abilities, Lawrence spoke in Mohawk with Tiyanoga and General Johnson translating his summary of their scouting. Since Lawrence's voice always remained flat and revealed no emotion, Tiyanoga and Johnson glanced at the thick twines of blue veins in Lawrence's neck to see if they were bulging, to suggest agitation. The Mohawk leader indicated that his several teams of scouts had been out reconnoitering every direction around the camp for days now. Finally, his scouts ranging the woods to the east had discovered the tracks of a large army leading out of South Bay of Lake Champlain. From tracks, they had determined that a French army had marched in three columns, leaving three sets of tracks. He reported, "We heard so many guns fired we could not count them."

The French seemed to be marching toward Fort Lyman. Likely these would be three different troops under different commands. Lawrence judged that each column had about 600-700 men marching in parallel towards the English fort at the Great Carrying Place.

The night before General Johnson had sent both a rider on horseback as well as runners with warnings to Colonel Blanchard and the New Hampshire troops at Fort Lyman. Some of the waggoneers told of horrifying screams and shots in the darkness down the frightening, lonely road! Someone had died piteously pleading for life in the black wilderness!

A heavy pause hung in the stationary still early morning air over the Officers' Council, until the question was asked, "Do we go after ye French army headed towards our men at Fort Lyman? Or do we leave them – our unsuspecting brethren – to die at the hands of the French without a chance?" None among them favored leaving their fellow soldiers to die.

Commander Johnson posed the next logical question, "Who goes out?"

Colonel Ephraim Williams stood up. He, too, had lain awake many hours last night, his mind churning. Eph Williams knew that this was an opportunity for glory, power and profit, to show oneself, to seize the day. "With all due respect and with your permission, General Johnson, sir, and fellow gentlemen of the council, I believe my regiment has the most experienced men, best fit to undertake this task. This is much like our experience provisioning Fort Massachusetts and the scouts we had down the road to our commissary at Deerfield. Plus, that wagon road itself is well known to my men, having had many men on the road-cutting detail. I have some of the finest gentlemen in the province as company captains." Here the tall, bulky colonel bowed to fellow Massachusetts officers, "Begging the pardon, of course, of my fellow soldiers from the great province of Massachusetts. And what's more…"

Across the faces of the two other Massachusetts Colonels Titcomb and Ruggles, eyebrows flared slightly, while both of them shifted and cleared their throats. They had both seen battle at the siege of the stalwart French stone fortress of Louisbourg in the "Late French War," whereas Colonel Eph had limited actual warfare, just "bush fighting." Meanwhile, General Johnson peered out of the corner of his eye to see his second-in-command Connecticut General Phineas Lyman rising from his seat. Lyman was clearing his throat, "Aahhh, hmmm. Thank you, Eph. I never have any doubt about the eagerness – indeed, the zealousness – of our men to engage the enemy. However, I …."

"Such a truculent boaster!" Johnson thought. Phineas Lyman, with his brash swagger, was beyond getting on the General's nerves. It was too much to endure Lyman's constant obnoxious strut through the camp with his gun fully loaded and two cartridge boxes crossed on his chest. "He's as likely to go off any minute as his Brown Bess!" And furthermore, he stopped any soldiers, not just those under his command, to inspect and correct them at his whim. It seemed he especially enjoyed inspecting Yorker soldiers and loudly demeaning their equipment, comportment and everything New York-ish!

General Johnson had vowed to himself that Lyman was not going to steal this chance to be a hero and have his name on every tongue in the colonies for saving the newly established Fort Lyman! Now General Johnson, too, rose to interrupt, "Thank you for your valiancy, Colonel Williams. Certainly, there has never been any doubt as to the spirit of the men of the Bay Colony. It is only that …"

However, Colonel Eph Williams had already commenced on his own ramble, "These French encroachments on to the land of our Majesty the King cannot be allowed to stand! This territory has been acknowledged as under the sovereignty of King George for a century since the defeat of the Dutch. My thinking is that the French can be cut off by destroying their boats at South Bay! Humiliated, for these affronts. I propose to do exactly that!"

"Yes, your outrage is clearly warranted," commented Johnson dryly. "As a Yorker myself, I feel deeply this sting of insult to our beloved colony, but Lawrence has warned that their troop strength is superior to ours. And your regiment's work preparing for the building of fortifications will be sorely needed here," Johnson rejoined.

Lyman inserted himself again, "It's nothing short of treason to tolerate their presence a day longer than necessary. They must – and will be – driven back! I will lead my regiment to answer their affront."

"General Lyman, with all due respect, and recognizing your martial gallantry, I'm afraid I simply cannot spare your work with Captain Eyre on the planning for fortifications. Colonel Williams' offer must be accepted in this instance." Consensus builder that he was, Johnson did not want all these officers getting their danders up and not then being able to back down gracefully.

"Acknowledging your regiment's contribution to the building of the wagon road, now so vital to our interests and success. Still," General Johnson paused again with feigned thoughtfulness and a slow dramatic tone. "…only the Mohawks know these parts intimately. These whereabouts are treacherous and unknown to your people, Colonel Williams, acknowledging - of course - your own many forays to Albany from Fort Massachusetts. Begging your honor, Colonel, of course."

The Commander and Tiyanoga exchanged brief glances and shared the thought that those farmers from Massachusetts constituted a quite impossible army. Most of them were so spooked by the impenetrable, multitudinously-green, mossy, thickly brakish woods that they were liable to shoot each other at any sound, as several had already done. It seemed that every tree had become a French savage to these terrified soldiers! Not to mention that the New Englanders seemed to have more officers than actual fighting men!

Waiting several seconds, Johnson announced with finality, "The Mohawks will lead this scout."

Sachem Hendrick Tiyanoga stifled his natural reaction, which was that the last officer he wanted to lead out was Colonel Ephraim Williams! He had avoided the Williams family since their venomous experiences at the Stockbridge Mission and Indian School. Unfortunately, of course, Tiyanoga could not dodge Ephraim Junior on this expedition. He would forever be on guard around Williams. Over the years, Tiyanoga had witnessed Ephraim Williams Junior's desertion of their pastor Jonathan Edwards, the Mohawks, the Mohicans and others. Further, the entire proposal appeared fraught with pointless recklessness to him. The Mohawk knew that "Brother Johnson" was a political, not a military strategist. Johnson's mind would be on all the political ramifications and alliances, but Tiyanoga was thinking about the combat side of this proposal. He was reminded of the old caution, "He who lives upon hope may die of disappointment."

Meanwhile, Colonel Ephraim Williams bit his lip. He was foiled by that Iroquois blaggard Hendrick - again! Williams wondered once more, with which side did that old white-hair really align himself: French or English? Eph recalled Tiyanoga's many insulting comments about how the English were "bare open women" as opposed to the French who were brave, fortified and built strongly of stone. It just galled the Colonel to remember the Albany Congress last year. The disrespect of the Iroquois making them wait, their rude and insolent speeches, all the while enjoying the hospitality of His Majesty's government's food, drink and their specially constructed Indian village lodgings outside of Albany. Colonel Eph vowed he needed a good stiff shot of rum before he marched with that old huff-and-bluff Hendrick Tiyanoga!

Behind the Commander the low rasp of Tiyanoga was heard speaking to Thick Lawrence in their odd vowel'y Iroquoian language. Immediately, some of the Englishmen grew uneasy hearing the sing-song tongue they couldn't understand. After a few words between the two Mohawks, Tiyanoga boldly intruded commandingly, "Brethren, you desire us to speak from the bottom of our hearts, and we shall do it. We renewed that "Covenant of Friendship" between us. It brightens the chain that binds Mohawks and English. It forges a good understanding of peace and friendship which we may cultivate and continue forever." Here he paused and extended his arms, "Look about you and see your Indian friends… We stand with our English brothers. We came when you renewed and brightened the ancient Covenant Chain of Friendship between us. Neither thunder nor lightening can break this friendship!"

The Mohawk sachem waited for affirmation around the circle of Englishmen, "Yes, yes, yes, indeed, undoubtedly, yes" went the nods and murmurs.

Then the flashy, cocky chief peered around himself and grabbed a handful of sticks from the wood pile. He stepped into the middle of the circle of men confidently. The English officers held their breaths, turning to gaze questioningly at each other. The proud sachem slowly pronounced, "But to send 500 men?"

The old man paused dramatically, then continued with a flourish, "If they are to be killed, they are too many!"

Once again, the chief waited for his audience to take in his potent words, "But, if these 500 are to fight against the French army, they are too few!"

In the center of the circle of officers he held up a stick dramatically announcing to the assembled, "Separated, they break easily."

With that the old chief cracked the stick in half and held it aloft. Following with another gesture, he produced a small bundle of twigs, saying, "But together…" Now, he demonstrated how he could not snap the twigs. "Together, they are strong, unbreakable!"

The white officers at the council tried to glance surreptitiously at each other. The ostentatious old Indian was right. Now, how would General Johnson react to this advice - or had the two of them already plotted out this strategy? The general demurred with a "Hmmm, indeed." Johnson consented, accepting the Mohawk's sage advice. He drawled out his words, slowly, "Yes, Colonel Williams' your regiment alone is not enough…"

All eyes turned to General Phineas Lyman who was rising pompously again. However, not noticing his superior, Lieutenant-Colonel Nathan Whiting interjected confidently, "The Connecticut boys are always ready to do their duty." Although speaking only in his normal tone, Whiting's voice as usual was so loud he was clearly audible far beyond the officers' circle. Those near him always had an urge to cover their ears when Whiting spoke. "My regiment is prepared to give ample revenge for the injuries of the villainous French!"

"Yes, indubitably, Colonel Whiting, thank you."

The suave Commander agreed hurriedly. Next General "Handsome Billy" Johnson rose to his full six feet of height. He had dressed for his leading part, wearing a magnificently vivid red waistcoat, ordered from the New York City merchants of Colden and Kelly, with more than 100 white and gilt buttons up and down the front, back, and wrists. Everything about him commanded respect from officers, the common sentinel and native warriors. Swinging a tomahawk above his head, General Johnson summarized, "Gentlemen of the Council, the Mohawks have taken up the hatchet!"

He turned to Tiyanoga for assurance, who nodded in emphasis.

The Commanding General continued, "I ask you, will Englishmen be driven like sheep before the French? Or are we ready to fight off the encroachments of the French so that we may all live in bright sunshine? We will go after the French and we will be strengthened by conquest!"

A loud chorus of assent resounded heartily around the circle.

"So, gentlemen, are we in concurrence to send the Third Massachusetts and the Second Connecticut?" summarized Commander William Johnson quickly. He added, "…along with King Hendrick's Mohawks."

No one noticed the dour look on the face of General Phineas Lyman, who had - once again - been pushed aside by the sensational Commander Johnson and Colonel Ephraim Williams, who would have his old village and church adversary Tiyanoga scouting out ahead of him.

By this time, the sun was rising glaringly in the sky. A breeze had come up from the south, causing the excited dancing of millions of leaves at the highest treetops in the imposing forests around the camp. A flock of petite gold finches skipped in flight across the open meadow cleared for the camp. Abruptly, things and people jolted into action as orders were given for the drums to beat "to arms." A staccato "rat-a-tat-tat" echoed loudly, bouncing off the rocks and the extensive sheet of water that was the lake, as if the sounds were claps of thunder. There was activity, noise and movement everywhere. Shouts were heard throughout, "A scout is to be sent out to intercept the French dogs!"

"A scout is going out!"

"The Mass boys and Mohawks are marching to Fort Lyman." (Naturally, this infuriated the Connecticut soldiers who felt their role forgotten.)

King Hendrick Tiyanoga and Colonel Ephraim Williams were now at the center of action. Their names were being hailed everywhere across the camp. Their soldiers were jittery with either trepidation or anxious anticipation – or any combination of both. Some of the Mohawk men ran back to their camp for their looking glasses, war paints, clothing, feathers and other articles. Everywhere men were running and readying. Every single thing seemed to be moving, vibrating, pulsing.

Old Tiyanoga stood barking commands in the Iroquoian Indian language. His friend Commander William Johnson regarded him for a long moment, realizing that the man Johnson had met almost 20 years ago had a thinning lock of gray hair then but it was totally white now. It was tied at his back. Tiyanoga was conspicuous among the young Haudenosaunee "bucks." General Johnson grasped that Tiyanoga was an old man, corpulent. Johnson pulled at his arm, "Brother, iateno," he murmured. "Take my pony."

General William Johnson barked to his aide-de-camp, "Double the daily ration of rum! And give the men their ration before they go out! Let 'em drink to the King's health!"

Begrudgingly, with a glance at Johnson, Tiyanoga nodded and turned to continue his orders in Iroquoian to the rapidly gathering horde around him. He held up a smoothly luminous wampum belt of purple and white polished shell high above his head for all to see. All the Iroquois murmured in reverence. Two young Mohawks lifted him onto a 32-pound cannon's carriage, where he stood and proclaimed, "Are you ready to hear me?!"

For a few long seconds, Tiyanoga surveyed the throng around him: Indian and English. All waited in anticipation for what they knew would be memorable. All took in the sight of the statuesque old man, his face lined and tattooed with a half sun, in his blazingly colored garments. At the edge of the crowd Massachusetts Lieutenant-Colonel Seth Pomeroy sat anemically watching, as he still felt as if he might lose his guts again, wanting desperately to join the occasion yet feeling too nauseous. The Mohawk sachem commanded attention as a natural superior. Pomeroy thought, "How bizarre that General Johnson dresses often times like an Indian yet King Hendrick wears English clothes? Truly, he is magnificent!"

Before addressing his men, Tiyanoga shouted to the whites, "Now I tell my mind and ask my brother Mohawks, Oneidas and all other Haudenosaunee, if they still honor the Chain of Friendship with our English brothers and if they will accompany me going out on this march to the fort?"

The sachem switched speaking from English to Iroquoian, that wordy, musical language. All the while he gestured and incanted as if it was magic – and the Iroquois, most especially the Mohawks were spell-bound in rapture at the eloquent stream of his words. He jumped down, strutted and stalked. He jumped up on another one of the cannons to raise himself higher and gestured prominently with his arms. He reached to the sky and all around. He gushed words. His face was an exhibition of all the possible human emotions flowing like liquid over his visage. There could not have been a more natural orator in ancient Rome or Greece.

At the end of his speech, a whooping cry resounded from the throats (maybe originating in the guts) of more than 200 native men. Tiyanoga began the "War Song" which set all the Mohawks, Oneidas, Mohicans, the few Senecas and Onondagas and anyone else to join in energetically. It truly stirred the heart. Sickly Lieutenant-Colonel Seth Pomeroy scanned admiringly from his log at the edge of the camp (where he could quickly run away to empty his angry bowels).

"Find and catch the enemy in their retreat or at their bateaux and engage them!" went the cry among the common soldiers.

Captain Elisha Hawley had been sitting by his campfire re-reading his brother Joseph's letter and wondering whether Joe would, in fact, travel up to inspect the army here at the camp? At the realization that they would be moving out, Hawley hastily scribbled down a last line in his reply

> "I am this minute a going out in Company with 500 men to see
> if we can Intercept 'em in their retreat, or find their canoes in the
> "Drowned Land."

The captain folded the letter, grunted and signaled his fifteen-year-old drummer Benny Stebbins to beat the "call to arms." Immediately Bennie felt his heart beating as loudly and quickly as his drum sticks. Five-hundred men of the Massachusetts Third Regiment began scurrying from their campfires to line up on the rising ground where the wagon road emptied into the camp.

Now it remained for the Mohawk warriors to be dressed and ready to march out. They needed to paint themselves with verdigris and Chinese vermillion paint mixed with bear grease. They were still carefully checking their looking glasses to see if their appearances were in order. Thick Lawrence caught a glimpse of his beloved life-long friend Tiyanoga deeply intent on conversing with brother "Warraghiyagey" General William Johnson.

The sun had risen over the colossal mountain squatting directly to their east. Impatient Ephraim Williams gave the order to "fall in" and the order was repeatedly barked out along the straggling, irregular lines. Behind them racing to get in order was the Second Connecticut Regiment with Lieutenant-Colonel Nathan Whiting shouting his orders here and there almost loud as the roar of an earthquake.

A wild cheer of "Huzzah!" erupted when Ephraim Williams led his spirited company up the slope at the head of a long column of hundreds of marching soldiers. In the distance, the sun flashed and danced off the magnificent "queen of lakes."

Chapter 25
A Bloody Morning Scout
On the Military Road, South of Lake George, September 8, 1755

The extended line of marching soldiers slowed to a stop on the wagon road just a few miles south of the army camp at Lake George in the murky ravine to Fort Lyman at the Great Carrying Place on the upper Hudson's River.

Most of the 500 jumpy Massachusetts provincial soldiers glanced around, plopped down their knapsacks and stretched out on any available spot astride the newly cut military road or on a rock or fallen log along the gurgling Rocky Brook to await the Connecticut regiment and the Mohawks. Some men pulled out their wooden canteens, while others ran over to the clear sandy-bottomed rivulet for a drink. Surprisingly, some soldiers were already unwrapping their luncheon food-stuffs, although it was just mid-morning.

"King Hendrick" Tiyanoga reminded himself again that it was this very hillock which was the dividing of the waters between Hudson's River (the river whose waters flow both ways[34]) that flowed south and those waters that flowed north to the French domain of Lake Champlain.

Soon the Iroquois warriors scampered over or filed past the seated Massachusetts soldiers to the head of the column in the usual single-file of the native scouts, one line on both sides of the road to spread out wide in advance of the regiments. Even a flock of Canada geese would post sentinels to vigilantly watch for predators. Unfortunately, in the ravine, the vertical rock walls blocked their ability to flank out. Within this gloom-infested, inhospitable ravine the mountainsides narrowed to the tightest space. At one point it was merely rods across, tightly packed with rocks, trees, giant boulders, and impossibly thick brush, leaving hardly any space for a shoulder-to-shoulder column of marching men. Little sunlight penetrated this primeval forest. So deep were the shadows that the floor of the forest looked black (instead of a brown tan to taupe) with only few flecks of illumination widely sprinkled. The Massachusetts men hated this dusky, mossy gorge enclosed on both side by two looming mountains but no other route could be found between them. The little valley provoked a sense of entrapment and extreme risk.

Within a minute or few, Tiyanoga was ahead astride General Johnson's chestnut Narragansett Pacer pony leading the Iroquois scouts out short rods on the freshly-cut road. He was distinguishable in the dim light in his scarlet jacket with

---

[34] The Hudson (then called "Hudson's River") is a tidal river with the ocean tide's water running into it all the way up river to Albany as the bulk flows down river to the sea.

246

gold-braid, buttons, bright white ruffled holland shirt and long tail of flowing white hair. Hendrick's figure was the brightest object in the obscure, melancholic landscape. Behind him lagged two lines of half-naked, painted warriors, mostly Mohawks. Only two hours before they had whooped and howled war cries, but now silently tensed every muscle as their venerable chief reined in and paused the horse. The old man gazed around, then back at where his warriors were tracking behind him.

A single voice shouted out in the compressed silence.

Captain Elisha Hawley, Ensign Stratton, Captain Ingersoll, Major Ashley and a handful of officers came up beside Colonel Ephraim Williams at the sound of the voice ahead of them. Elisha Hawley's heart started pounding. The furious staccato hammered stridently in his ears. All his training and experience told him of danger and treachery. His nerves were so overexcited that it felt as if his entire body might soon combust and explode of the tension.

There followed the sound of further incomprehensible human voices.

"Hendrick told me a minute ago, "I smell Indians,"" said Colonel Williams in a harsh low tone. "The Mohawks, the Caughnawagas .... Something with King Hendrick.... I hear Hendrick. Them Indians is a-talking...." They all strained to listen, although none of them understood any of the strange Iroquoian language.

"But what was that to mean?" asked Major Ashley in desperate exasperation.

"Precisely, I don't know," replied the twitchy Colonel. "But then he just walked his pony on ahead. Precisely indeed. He said nothing more! Did he mean prepare for "bush fighting" or that he goes ahead to scout? He can't be too far up the road.... Do any of you know if he's sending out flankers? Did you hear any orders to his men? These Indians are inscrutable, capricious. I've lived with 'em many years. Most particularly the Iroquois League. They play both sides.... They play us English and those French," continued the Williams with deep worry furrowing his aging face. He reached reflexively for his gold pocket watch. Then he recalled that he had given it to his brother Tom that morning.

"Flankers? I think not. That swamp is impenetrable…" offered Major Ashley with glance off to their left. "Why the bush there is chest high, even those deer couldn't run through there."

"But that deer herd running by us," murmured Hawley. "… was very… ah… preternatural. Very odd, most very odd and abnormal."

"Do you see Hendrick?" asked Major Ashley, gazing down the road, past the piles of brush and axed trees along the sides. "It's all mighty, mighty…. ah, eh… ah… preternatural, as you said, Captain."

The clutch of officers stood with muscles strained in the dank woodland, smelling the vegetative musk of time-immemorial forests, feeling the length of each breath stretched. Each man's eyes scanned around them, although none had yet drawn their ramrods, cartridges or musket balls. They instinctively held themselves from the slightest movement. The air quivered with a hidden electricity as the entire column of 1,000 men behind the officers also stilled their breaths to hear. The absence of noise was bewildering. It seemed as if every forest creature had ceased to move as well. Minutes slowed down to long seconds, while a thousand men waited and watched.

But as a boom of thunder hides within a ponderous storm cloud, suddenly a single musket shot rang out far in front with the clarity of a church bell peal!

Then, as instantly as a bolt of lightning thwacks the air, a volley of bullets erupted around them, piercing the narrow vale with a thunder of hell, breaking open directly over their heads! The sound blasted into their ears, ricocheted off the rock walls and continued to reverberate around the tight ravine. Burning hot lead balls filled the air, flying everywhere! Elisha Hawley turned his gaze from side to side as he tried to track the direction of the fire, only to realize that the direction was indistinguishable because the killer lead balls peppered the air everywhere, swarming like a thousand enraged hornets' nests! There were even hot stinging balls sizzling from behind him! Musket balls whizzed past, so close that he felt their searing air waves roll by him. He instinctively dodged and recoiled.

"Damn traitorous Mohawks!" cursed the Colonel.

The choking smoke of hot gunpowder clogged the stagnant air, making it hard to breathe and impossible to distinguish anything. From the tangle of vegetation down to their left came another deafening roar of shots! A wall of flames and clouds of blue-gray sulfurous smoke filled the air. Hawley could discern objects or men only in a very, very compact circle around himself. Even the men near him appeared hazy in the vaporous smoke.

Ahead, where Hendrick and the Mohawks had led the column, there were more volleys of firing accompanied by terrible noise, acrid tangy smoke and flashes of light. Muskets boomed with hideous Indian war-whoops and white men's shouting ringing in between.

Their regiment's orders had been to scout out to find the French and "intercept them in their retreat" but these blasting salvos announced that the French and their Indians had found 'em first! Elisha Hawley thought that this is what must have happened to the massacred army of General Braddock on the Monongahela River just two months ago! Now it appeared that Colonel Williams' regiment had themselves stumbled into a waiting ensnarement by the famous French general, Baron Jean-Armand de Dieskau, who they had heard was on the march from the French Fort St. Frédéric. This must be the French general whose motto was "Audacity wins!" Truly audacious! Their French enemies were not at Fort Lyman, in the "Drowned Lands" or in retreat at all. They were here and now and ambushing them! Who had scouted out whom? Who "intercepted" whom? It was devilish irony!

What was this? Elisha Hawley's thoughts clunked leadenly in his head with the overwhelming chaos all around. He fought to understand this uproar and think what to do next. Why was it so hard to think? Why was everything so slow and heavy? Was the torpor in his head from the rum (No, that was an hour ago!) or was it the heat and closeness? Why was it so hard to focus? He angrily struggled to think. He had never had to think about thinking before. He fought to keep his brain from screaming and shutting down. He wasn't afraid, he reassured himself. He was an officer. The right action was to deliberate rationally, then order the men. He must have an officer's "presence of mind."

"I knew it!" he thought to himself. "I knew there were too many things that signaled wrong. The deer herd was startled. The forest was too quiet. The scouts should have been out front earlier, they should have been climbing up the terrain and in that swampy morass. Why didn't I bring the dog? Did the Mohawks betray us? Why didn't I put it together before? I should have known! I did know! Why didn't I think more?! I knew things were wrong! Remember the *Hints for a Commanding Officer* to not let anything ruffle your temper. Be always cool, happen what will. Now which way? What now?"

Ahead of him, Captain Hawley saw the lubberly figure of Colonel Eph Williams. Eph had turned toward the ridge line of rocks uphill to their right. He dazzled in his brilliant scarlet coat, studded with rows of brass buttons, snowy white shirt, leg garters, and officers' gorget glinting at his neck. He had powdered his hair, but did not wear his wig with the rigors of the march today.

"Charge men, as behooves real Englishmen!" the Colonel shouted into the din of weapons discharging. "Charge this way!" he screamed, pointing up the steep, rocky slope of the West Mountain, rising up sharply from the road floor. Surrounding them were his and Hawley's companies, packed in a huddled confused mass of rank human fear.

Suddenly a line of Canadian fighters in soft deerskin leggings and a number of Abenaki Indians with their long French muskets primed and at the ready rose up from the ridge of rough and jumbled rock boulders before the Third Massachusetts companies! Had it not been for the confusion in his brain, Hawley could have made out the brilliant paints streaked across the Indian grimacing faces. In another time he could have seen which ones wore waist-shirts and which were naked; whether they wore doeskin leather, linen breeches or loincloths; or even if they sported beaded straps of cartridge boxes across their chests. They were that close! A wave of shot slammed into the unsteady Englishmen. Again, reverberations from the shot rang in their ears. Terrific heat, blinding smoke, tremendous noise and hot flying balls were just a few paces off, practically in their faces! Almost the instant the words were out of Colonel Eph's mouth, a musket ball thudded into his forehead, creating a round red smear of blood there. Hawley's stomach reeled and pitched at the sight of the spurt of blood from his friend's forehead, the roll of Eph's terrorized-and-then-uncomprehending eyes, the jerky flailing of his extended arms and the prolonged "Oooouuufffff!" of his lungs' final exhalation. The light in his eyes was extinguished instantly, although they remained in a wide-open stare. Then he dropped down completely lifeless, as a passenger pigeon shot out of mid-air - dead, dead, dead - in the split of a second!

Hawley gasped to watch it. "Bloody ghastly! Audacious!" flashed the thought through his brain. From vibrant living, breathing man to stone-cold stillness in the flicker of a second. Slain with his musket in his hand. Cut down in mid-action. Maybe the Colonel was in mid-sentence or mid-thought? Did his death thought get snatched by the devil or fly to the angels Hawley wondered? He had witnessed the Colonel's instant death from within arm's length! How long had it been - minutes or only seconds ago - that Colonel Williams had stood in the middle of the road consulting with Hawley, Ensign Stratton, and Major Ashley?

"Charge!" Hawley yelled at the top of his lungs into the din.

Ensign John Stratton hurriedly dragged the Colonel's dead body aside to a spot underneath a thick pine tree. The Colonel lay still bleeding into the dirt, but Hawley hadn't a moment more to think about his commander and friend of almost eight years with the overwhelming tumult surrounding him. Ephraim Williams was gone, as a puff on the air.

On every side, over Hawley's head and even down at his legs, the consuming fire of death was claiming man after man. Here and there around him, he saw men face down in the dirt and others on rock boulders or amidst the fallen pine needles thrashing and howling in contortions of torment. Twigs and leaves would occasionally rain down, shredded amidst the calamitous shooting everywhere. Time was distorted as each second dragged out into an eternity. He saw the glint of a gun barrel here and there but had no time to warn his men!

Behind him he heard a soldier cry out, "Lord what shall I do?" before he was mangled by a ball to his face. Blood spewed forth on everyone near him. The sentinel dropped down amidst the verdant woodland, writhing and wallowing in his deep maroon blood. Another man stood paralyzed with the back of his head a bleeding mess and his brains exposed! Had he been shot by his own men or the Abenakis and Canadians? Hawley wanted to vomit but instead gagged and retched up horrible tasting bile.

Hawley had pulled the leather cover off his "Brown Bess's" trigger lock, but had not yet fired a single shot or even ripped open a paper gunpowder cartridge with his teeth. To his utter astonishment, Private Sam Fairfield screamed behind him, "Captain Hawley's hit!"

"Captain Hawley's hit!" repeated one of his company's soldiers somewhere around him.

"Hawley?" Elisha Hawley thought. "I am Hawley!"

"Hit. I am hit? What?!"

Then, a realization smacked his consciousness that he, Elisha Hawley, had truly been hit. "Hawley's hit!" Suddenly puzzlement and panic seized his malfunctioning mind! He had been hit by an ugly, cruel ball. He had been hit! "Audacious!" he thought again on this bloody day.

His next thought after the beastly lead ball ripped through his body from his left lung to somewhere inside up near his shoulder, was that he didn't feel pain. Curious. It was most curious. He felt a sticky, warm moistness spreading unstoppably across his upper body. He gazed down at his chest below the proud, sparkling gorget to the horror of a blackened hole through his handsome blue coat with scarlet lapels and flourishes of brass buttons. On his milky white linen waist-shirt, a dark burgundy stain of blood seeped, growing wider across his chest.

As soon as he could see the wound and think about it, he would do something to arrest any more bleeding. He must know how badly he had been hit?

He burned with anger at the affront of it. But he realized he must try to order his mind. It was critical now that he think clearly!

It might have been some seconds that had passed, although he felt as if he could no longer register time. Perhaps it had been two minutes? Or ten? Or then again, perhaps it was eternity? Perhaps it was a lifetime? Perhaps it was his lifetime?! Perhaps it was the end of his lifetime?! He fought with himself. "Think, Elisha! Think carefully! You are an officer and a gentleman. You must lead the men. Keep good order!"

Behind him Captain Hawley heard a chilling shout, "Every man for himself!"

Looking around him, Hawley was then seized with the hideous awareness that he was far out in front of the rest of the officers and men of the regiment! He was almost alone on the stony hillside of tall pines. Turning around, he saw most of the 50 soldiers of his company running like the herd of deer, jumping over rocks, tree stumps or branches, brush other men, anything in their path of terror! They seemed to sprint faster than any mortals he had ever seen. But for some unlucky ones, rocks, tree roots, brush and a hundred other objects grabbed and tripped the frantically running men. Elisha Hawley realized he was being left behind. He was an officer whose company was disappearing, except for the injured who lay squirming around with piercing howls - or the dead in horrifying positions on the ground.

Elisha Hawley stood motionless for the longest moment in his life. Around him in the ravine was mortal mayhem and disorder. Everything and every man moving was in furious sound and motion. Some men were running. Some men were fighting hand-to-hand. Some were loading their long-barreled weapons. Some firing Brown Besses, trade muskets or flintlocks. Some hurling tomahawks and pulling out glinting knives. Hawley saw some soldiers being hit by the ubiquitous musket balls flying everywhere through the thickly heated, compressed air. His ears were assaulted by crashing, discordant and dreadful cacophony such as he had never before experienced. Each second split into hundreds of ticks, as his sodden brain struggled to recall, focus, consider and order. It was total, consuming, catastrophic evil - condensed and distilled into a battle to the death!

Some of his men in the midst of the melee were fighting on. Somewhere near him, the voice of his Lieutenant, Daniel Pomeroy shouted to the disappearing company, "What then? Shall we run?!"

One of their men shouted back, "Yes! This ain't about courage, Dan! This is about surviving!"

Hawley saw "ole Dan" extract the ramrod from his musket, pour in gunpowder, drop in a .75-caliber lead ball and steady himself to aim. "Well, I'll give them one more shot before I run!"

But as Dan stared down the barrel of the long musket he himself had forged in the Pomeroy gun shop in Northampton, one of the Abenaki warriors only paces away was two seconds ahead of him in the same process and shot Lieutenant Dan straight through the middle of his forehead! Thus, old Dan's outrage was deflated by the deep grunt of air involuntarily forced out of his dead body. Dan Pomeroy's long groan was but a momentary dull, deep agony, as he must have been dead as it escaped. In a long second or maybe two he, too, had fallen to the ground before Hawley's eyes! "Dastardly devil," thought Elisha Hawley of the Canadian Indian who had mowed down another of his comrades-at-arms.

Precipitously, Hawley remembered that the whizzing balls around him could hit him again! As he turned, Hawley saw Private Tom Fairfield grabbing under the shoulder of his cousin Sam. Hawley reached out an arm. "Fairfield, help me," he croaked weakly, but the two Fairfields were already gone before he said it.

Now pain surged over his body down to a cellular level that shrieked for all of his attention! It cleared his mind of any other thought whatsoever. It became a herculean, conscious struggle to breathe. It seemed to him that time had slowed down for his brain to experience every split ticking second of this trauma. Was this what it felt like to die? Would he soon fall over dead, too? He was exhausted by the intensity of his focus and by the effort it extracted.

As he felt himself falling to his knees, an arm scooped under his. What was this? Who was this?

To his utter amazement, he realized from the bright red garter tied around his forehead that this must be one of King Hendrick's Mohawk warriors picking him up!

Hawley turned to stare at the Mohawk. Although last year he had traveled for weeks at a time with the Stockbridge Indian Jacob Hunkamugg laying out the Albany Road, Hawley was not prepared for the shock of being up so close to a lean "war-faced" Mohawk painted in broad stripes of red, yellow and white with dots. One half of the man's face was painted one way, the other half had different colors and patterns. Hawley had never been so near to the face of another person, glaring

so intently into their eyes (except so long ago lying under a tree with Martha Root).
The men's faces were only a foot apart! It was jarring!

Hawley stared at the smooth, brown plane of the skin on the man's head.
He stared into the Mohawk's abstruse brown eyes, as the man did the same to him.
The whites of his eyes had enlarged. There Hawley read surprise, perhaps as great
as his own? Maybe this man, too, didn't expect this disaster to befall them? How
Hawley wished he could ask the man what had happened: did you see who fired
that first lone shot? Were we attacked? Was the attack by your "Brother
Caughnawagas?" By the French? Canadians? By the Abenakis? Had they been
betrayed? What was the true situation ahead, down the road? Who was dead and
who alive there?

The Mohawk sported brightly-colored beads, interspaced with the ivory
and brown/black of porcupine quills. Silver jewels dangled from his ears and nose.
The pungent tang of bear grease, with which he had rubbed his body paint,
pinched at Hawley's nostrils. Hawley thought the Mohawk looked hideous and
grotesque, but felt thankful and humbled by the help of this inscrutable man. Why
had the Mohawk stopped to help a pale-faced English soldier like himself? Hawley
knew he would not have stopped to help a "savage Indian" he saw along the road.
He felt shame to remember his own run back into the security of Fort
Massachusetts seven years ago. In that ambush, he had not looked for anyone else.

"Ohronte! Ohronte! Tiyanoga ohronte! Taragiorus ohronte! Moses the
Song ohronte! Kaheoana ohronte!   Ohronte! Haudenosaunee ohronte!
Kanien'keha ohronte!" wailed the Mohawk at the top of his lungs.

"English, English," shouted Hawley, understanding nothing but only that
it was something bad, very bad.

"Dead, dead. Tiyanoga dead. Taragiorus dead. Moses the Song dead!
Great Turtle dead! Mohawks dead! Many dead!" the Mohawk shouted back.
Hawley felt the breath and sputum of the other man on his own face.

"Sasnoron Ronkwe! Hurry, run, white man!"

In front of them, irregular Canadian militia and Abenaki Indians were
standing, yowling and starting to run towards them with tomahawks, hatchets and
muskets at hand! Hawley understood that they must run, but wondered how this
warrior would be able to carry him out of this death trap while running for his own
life? He noticed that the Mohawk carried his musket in his right hand. At his belt
his tomahawk was tied at the ready. His left arm had slid under Hawley's. He felt
the pounding blood of the Mohawk's hot body next to his own faintness. Sweat

poured off his skin and onto Hawley. The Mohawk's muscles were as stretched tight as a bow string pulled to its limit, while Hawley was losing strength. Hawley couldn't sort out whether what he was seeing was a living nightmare around him or a reality? What was happening to the world?

"Sasnoron Ronkwe! Hurry, white man!" screamed the Mohawk into his face.

Hawley must not have moved or reacted because he next heard the Mohawk shout, "Seni'nikonhraién:tas ken? Understand, white man? Hánio! Hánio!"

The Mohawk warrior's eyes were opened wide enough to hold every emotion in the world. His eyes blazed at Hawley as he shouted again, "Hánio! Hánio!"

Whatever the Mohawk was saying, Hawley understood it must be "run." Around them everywhere shouts and cries rang out above the general clamor. Far and wide around them, Hawley could hear the "Indian yell" so terrifying to the white men. The incessant blasting roar of gunpowder igniting, rang out and reverberated through the turbid air.

Against every probability, Hawley found himself leaning on and running alongside the Mohawk. Part of his mind thought it must all be a most terrible dream. How he could be running? Each time he was sure he would collapse, the Mohawk would dodge behind one of the mammoth pitch-pine trees, pulling Hawley with him. The Mohawk crouched down quickly and instinctively loaded his musket, aimed and shot to their rear. Hawley hadn't the strength to glance back to see the Mohawk's accuracy. Scratching branches of trees and brush flailed, pulled, pricked and tugged at Hawley's clothes and skin from all directions. Flying balls whizzed and streaked through the air. In front and all around them were frantic men in crazed fright running for their lives. Behind them, pursuing them through the forest, would be the vicious, murderous French and their Indian allies.

Bizarrely, above the terrible clamor, Hawley recognized the booming voice of Lieutenant-Colonel Nathan Whiting of the Connecticut Regiment which had marched behind them, "Halt, men! Halt! Steady now, lads. Cover the retreat! Remain steady! Stay steady!"

Very occasionally along their path, Hawley noticed that a few soldiers had thrown down their firearms, knapsacks, or even clothing to better run - no better sign of military bedlam than a soldier casting away that which makes him a soldier, his protection. Hawley wondered if there were any of them shooting to keep off the enemy? Were they firing into the trees, air or ground?

Somewhere along their run back towards the camp on the tree stump-clogged, congested road, Hawley saw Daniel Granger staring incredulously at his left hand where three fingers hung by the skin, dangling and spurting blood – although almost entirely detached. He appeared not to know what to do. Micah Harrington of Colonel Williams' company was stumbling along dragging his bleeding right leg where a ball had torn through the upper thigh and come out the back. His breeches were shredded around the gaping, gushing mess. His leg was but a slab of useless flesh now. He cried most hideously, "I shall die, I shall die."

Hawley thought, "Run Harrington, Run!" But he had no strength to say anything. He only tried to cling to the Mohawk.

At another place on the road were Sergeant Caleb Chapin and his sons Joel and Ezekiel of Colonel Williams' company, who had stayed closely together in their trajectory of flight. When the father was shot in the back, his strength failed and he couldn't rise despite his sons' pleading and woeful urgings. The old soldier lay in agony commanding his sons to leave him and run, saying, "Go, go! Save yourselves. Your lives are more useful. Go! Take care of your mother. Go, go, go at once. God bless you all. Good-bye. Goodbye, my sons."

Hawley and the Mohawk saw the Chapin brothers screech in indescribable anguish, peer at each other in a deep wordless understanding and then fall in step with them running.

As they ran and ducked back down the rock-strewn woods and along the rutted road, they passed Hawley's friend Captain Moses Porter with whom he had sung hymns only last night!

The two captains, Hawley and Porter, had spent countless hours together in deep and earnest conversation. In many ways, Elisha Hawley had felt Moses Porter was the brother whose strings of existence vibrated in deep harmony with his own, more now than his own birth-brother Joseph. Porter articulated what Hawley himself thought as Hawley thought it, but had trained himself never to speak aloud. Hawley and Porter were often the last two officers remaining as the camp's evening fire coals glowed faintly, late into the summer nights. There they sat in complete absorption, pouring out their thoughts to each other in hushed voices.

Moses Porter had but a single offspring, a daughter, like Hawley's own unacknowledged one, born eight years ago. Each and every time they conversed, invariably, every topic interconnected with Porter's home life. If they commenced recollecting their purchases of their new military clothing and equipment, Moses soon turned to his daughter Betty's demand to try on "Papa's hat." If they started talking of the final sermon at meetinghouse before they marched out on this Crown Point Expedition, Moses talked about stroking Betty's long hair as she sat raptly on his lap. When Captain Porter showed Captain Hawley his gleaming sword, his next breath sketched his wife Elizabeth and little Betty's awestruck reaction to it. Porter described one incident or another of his adoring wife and the beautiful child "Papa Porter" practically idolized, such as kissing their creamy, smooth faces as they fell asleep or warming their chilled fingers and toes when the ladies came home from a wintry visit in the carriage. Porter's descriptions of his profound love for his wife Elizabeth and little Betty gave Hawley a glimpse into a happiness Hawley had been denied. With each of Porter's raptures, Hawley fell completely silent. It gnawed at him and some nights he lay sleepless with tears in the dark. Yet he yearned for Porter's recounting of his private paradise.

Now here was poor Moses Porter tied to a giant tree and surrounded by beastly French Indians butchering him alive! The warriors had stripped him of most of his fine clothing. One young warrior already preened in Moses' splendid gold-braided officers' coat as he slashed at the tormented man! With a crowd of the Caughnawagas hacking at him, Porter was being lacerated everywhere on his person by tomahawks crashing down and sinking their iron teeth into his bodily pulp. His face was contorted with deep lines of agony and his eyes were bugging out of their sockets. Porter's ghastly, unnatural shrieks and the high-pitched howls of the attackers filled Hawley's ears, crowding out his own dreadful moaning. The sounds alone would be enough to drive one insane! They were the sounds of unendurable suffering, as if all of hell's curses on humanity had descended to the spot. The sight of blood pouring out of countless slices in his skin caused Hawley to retch as if he would vomit. How many more moments could poor Porter even stay alive?

Hawley's own body was so jumbled and wracked in the run that he felt a burning sting as if being shot again and again by the bullet lodged deep within him. The French lead ball grated and scraped his insides with each breath, with each jounce! It smashed, nicked and stung with each footstep or budge. He urgently longed for all the movement and jolting of his wound to cease! Just let him sit down and die, but he couldn't say it to the Mohawk. He sensed he could never get back to the army camp. It was too far and he was too weak now. Every step sent searing burns flaring across his lungs and upper body. His shins and leg muscles felt as if each step poured scalding water over them. He felt his eyes closing in exhaustion and a deep hungering to be released from this agony. His mind closed in, so that he could see nothing of the world around him. Only pain registered, nothing else, and that was shutting down his consciousness.

He mustn't lapse into unconsciousness. It would certainly mean death! It required all the strength he had to hold open his eyelids. His eyelids felt as heavy as stones in water. "Don't succumb to death, Elisha!" he urged himself.

To his Mohawk helper, he mumbled, "No, no, can't. No. No more."

It had only been overpowering fear and a Mohawk with a half-shaved head, a painted face, eagle feathers down his back and a silver charm dangling at his nose that had enabled Hawley to run at all. As the circle of his focus shrunk down to only his own excruciating pain, Hawley no longer saw the brutal, hectic world around him or the Mohawk at his side. He felt his eyelids going down and darkness conquering, but Hendrick Tiyanoga's words echoed in his head, "Depend upon it, we are true to you, and mean to join you. Wherever you go, we will be by your sides. Our bones shall lie with yours."

"Why, sir, it's so much smaller than our balls," observed Billy Williams, Dr. Thomas Williams' assistant, with some incredulity, as the surgeon dropped the blood-covered lead ball into a tin cup with a sharp clink. "It appears to have a greenish colored cast."

"Smaller, yes. It's only a .62-caliber, while ours are 75, but it's still big enough to bring down a big man," remarked the middle-aged doctor wryly.

"A big man, like me," interjected Private Sam Fairfield lying on a bedroll nearby. "Depending on where the small ball hits."

Luckily for him, Fairfield had suffered but a surface wound on his arm, which the doctor's assistant had washed and dressed in linen. Yet Fairfield had felt its dull throbbing throughout an extended, violent night of nightmares and alarms at the army camp at Lake George. As he awoke Fairfield had tried to place himself. Where was he and what had happened? Each time he awoke, he was drenched in sweat.

"True indeed, soldier," replied Dr. Tom. "You were with Captain Hawley's company. Weren't you in the column that marched out yesterday on that bloody morning scout?"

"Yes, sir. I was."

"What's your name, Private?"

"Samuel Fairfield, sir."

"Fairfield, if you were there with Hawley, did you see my brother Colonel Ephraim Williams fall?"

"Yes, sir, I saw it. It was the most awful, terrible nightmare of a day I ever seen and probably will ever see, or so's I hope," replied the tall, lanky soldier bleakly, reclining on a dirty blanket on straw in the recently-built store-house.

"Billy, where is that warm water and cognac to clean out Captain Hawley's wound?" barked the doctor.

"R-r-right here with it, Doctor Williams," stuttered the young assistant.

"That water's stone cold," the doctor rebuked the orderly as the delirious Elisha Hawley tried to roll and thrash on his cot but without much strength, all the time moaning and gasping. "Remember, gently, Billy!"

"Doctor Williams, it was hot when I brought it from the fire. I cain't help if it cooled down now," explained the chastised assistant. "I can't touch any lighter but for not touching at all."

"All right, Billy. You just have to remember that these men are in dying pain - the pains of death! The pain that drives a mind insane. You have to feel what they feel and do your utmost!"

"Yes, sir. I will endeavor to do better." Poor Billy had joined the army on the old adage, "If you wish to be a physician, follow the army." He never anticipated it would entail this!

The doctor turned back to Sam Fairfield again. "What did you say your name was, soldier?"

"Fairfield."

"Yes, Fairfield. The Hawleys are family to me. And we haven't the time to care for Captain Hawley properly. The ball's been extracted from his left shoulder but I can't care for everything he needs, what with all the other wounded men - and only Billy, Marsh and me to care for them all…"

"And that's not even to mention General Johnson and the French General Deesescow or whatever, the 'gentleman' is called in his crazy language," inserted Billy Williams in disdain.

"Billy, it's not for you to question the General's orders," scolded the doctor. "You are here to serve, remember that," he turned back to where Sam Fairfield lay. "Now Fairfield, I am instructing you to care for Captain Hawley until we can move him to an officers' tent. He needs to be fed, and fed very, very carefully because he might easily ingest food or drink into his lungs, so I want the utmost care. Understood?"

Doctor Thomas Williams consciously drew in a deep breath, then continued with precision, "I'll have a lemon or orange sent over from General Johnson's headquarters. You are to give it to Hawley to suck on. Food will be toast and boiled turnips mushed down."

The doctor paused for a few long seconds to lower his voice and stress the importance of the next words which he spoke in the lowest audible tone.

"Listen, Fairfield. I have a few opium pills from Dr. Sydenham in England. These are very precious and I can't share them with the common soldiers. They are too dear and I have but few. Hawley will face unendurable pain as he dies. When he grows too restless, you will need to give him one of these opium pills sweetened with three teaspoons of white sugar in a glass of French wine at nightfall. Do you understand me, soldier?"

Young Billy Williams averted his eyes as the wizened doctor slyly deposited three tiny black pills in Fairfield's palm.

"Do not lose them. Do not waste them."

Fairfield suddenly realized that he was being left in charge of the wounded officer, due to his own improving strength. "Aahhh, sir…"

"Listen, Farley…"

"Fairfield."

"Yes, all right, Fairfield. This man is mortally wounded and he needs succor! Also, I want you to carefully feed him a tea of sassafras and willow bark daily."

Fairfield tried to interrupt, "Doctor Colonel, sir, I haven't any experience in doctoring. None at all. I don't esteem myself too particularly suited for it and, further, I haven't any sassafras or willow bark and I…."

"Never mind that, Farley, I'll leave them with you. Then, I want you to place a poultice of comfrey root to slow down the imbalance of humors which would cause the possibility of infection on his chest, but absolutely being most meticulous not to get it within the injury or the lungs. Do you understand?" He paused and mentally reviewed his own instructions. "And, not to worry, I'll have my assistant Billy give you the poultice."

"By your leave, sir, Captain Hawley … well, aah, my Uncle John Miller is married to Mistress Martha Root, Captain Hawley's… uhhh, uhhh…" Sam Fairfield felt deep shame and wondered how he could explain the terrible problem of the bad-blood between the Root and Hawley families since Elisha Hawley had refused to marry her or acknowledge their child, and Joe Hawley had testified that Martha "was a woman of the town!" It deeply humiliated him to bring it into his mind. It was something he never wanted to think on, much less speak about.

"Farley, I haven't time for incidentals or countryside noise like what Captain Hawley did or didn't do before. I know his story, but this man is dying and I'm ordering you, as a good soldier of King George II, to obey my directions for his care. I haven't time now for any fickle dispositions. This is war, man! Do you comprehend that, soldier?"

"Yes, sir. Understood," Fairfield swallowed the acid that had accumulated on his tongue. Here he was, with the shock of his own mangled arm. It occurred to him that he couldn't move it well. His entire body felt weak and stiff. It didn't move as it should. How bad was it? Would he be able to work? What would become of him, if he should lose his arm or couldn't move it?!

Added to his worries for his own health and future, here he was beside the ravager of his uncle's wife! He had been ordered to care for that man with the tenderness Hawley had never shown for her! How would he go home and tell Uncle John this?!? He felt sickened to his stomach and totally exhausted.

"All right, then, one more thing, and I regret it. I'm sorry but it must be done. Hawley needs to be cleaned; he's lying in his own filth. I can't have it!" said the doctor. "Here is what it means: you will have to clean him… his ahh… excrement …and aahhh… anything else…"

Of a sudden, Sam Fairfield realized he'd had now had added the job of emptying the Captain's chamberpot! It was demeaning beyond anything!

The crusty doctor continued in solicitous earnestness, "Tomorrow I'll need you to be up, if you are able. Look Fairfield, it wasn't the job you enlisted for with Captain Hawley, granted that. But in war, one might have to do anything and you're going to have to do this. I know this nursing and cleaning filth is a woman's job, but there aren't any women around to handle this, since when they were ordered away from the camp. You've got to do it! I've already assigned Colonel Williams' Negro boy, Romano, to help with this, and the other officers also. So Romano will help you. He no longer has anything to do now that he doesn't attend to my brother…." The doctor paused for a moment of private sorrow as he turned his head aside, but it was just a short pause to swallow agonizingly.

It quickly flitted through Fairfield's mind that he was being relegated to work with a "servant for life," like the African boy! It was one thing to serve as a soldier in Hawley's company with black men like John Bush and Peter Ladrue, who at least were real men, but now this denigration to be working like a slave or woman! It was stunningly insulting.

The doctor read the thought as it registered on Soldier Fairfield's face and sought to direct him, "I want Captain Hawley well cared for as he dies. You're the only man here convalescing from his company who is capable," the doctor's voice became muted and etched with both pleading and growling. "We've already cleaned your wound with rum and bandaged it with linen strips. It will heal in time. But half your company is dead or gone. No one knows... They's that are alive are needed on the front! Lemuel Lyman there," he gestured to another blood-smeared, immobile human lump nearby, "has a bullet in his chest. Only reason he's not dead is the ball hit three of his fingers, pierced his leather vest, went through three shirts, and his bullet pouch before it went in! Providence only knows if he'll survive the extraction of the ball. Therefore, you see, Fairfield, I've got to count on you because I've got the French Baron Dieskau and General Johnson to attend to, besides all these men. But Fairfield," Thomas Williams' eyes bored into Samuel Fairfield's. "I promise you'll be compensated for it. The Captain's brother, Major Hawley, will make it up to you. I'll see you get good food and everything else you'll need and you won't needs be foraging around for food or anything... Do I have your word of honor, Mr. Fairfield?"

Fairfield felt almost as decision-less in this demand as he had on that blood-soaked morning when they marched down the road into the French trap. Dr. Thomas Williams stood waiting impatiently for the soldier's reply. Fairfield cringed to think of the hours he would spend beside Hawley watching his breaths and sputters, his falters and his rallies, the rattleclap of his certain death. Fairfield felt he had already endured much witnessing of death and grief weighing on him. And to throw out the "slop bucket" as well!

"Sir, I... I'm ...I..." muttered out Fairfield, as he searched for another excuse.

"Thank you, Fairfield. You'll have my appreciation and God's blessing for your mercy," the doctor sighed with relief. "So tell me please, Fairfield, what you saw when my brother Colonel Williams died. Tell me the truth, soldier. It's the truth of my brother's death that I want to know, not some kindly notions or some prattling tittle-tattle. Tell me truly what happened there. I need to know how my brother died..."

"Yes, sir. Well, you know when we entered that ravine, we all felt a gloominess, something amiss. I know the woods well. I've lived in the woods outside Northampton town with my uncle many a-year, but this was unnatural. Too, too quiet. Entirely too quiet and motionless. It spooked us all."

Soldier Fairfield had found his voice again and took a deep breath, "Why, we had cleared that road only a week ago, so we knew it well enough. I remember that wall of rocks down by the little brooklet. It rises up straight from the ravine floor as if it was a chimney put there, although much, much taller and broader, admittedly. They's the perfect spot for killing! Even when we was cutting the road, the men hated that place. So dark, not a ray of sunshine lights on the ground anywhere! Impossible to see your own shadow! The brakes and brush in there's so thick you could walk by a man within touching distance and yet not see him at all. Especially not an Indian. You cain't see one rod off the sides of the road, it's so dark there. Pure bush fighting."

"Yes, all right, Fairfield. I know about the French and their Indians lying in wait for the regiment. I know about the French General's trap. The French General's told us about that. I've been treating him at General Johnson's tent, as I told you. That French general keeps saying 'I almost had 'em in the bag.' He keeps saying to that one who speaks their language. So, I know that. But after they started firing on old Hendrick and his Mohawks, what happened then?"

"Everything happened then, sir! Pure everything - direct from the gates of ahhh, aahhh, errr, hmmm, Hell itself, if you'll pardon the cursing language. Begging you pardon, sir, but it was hell on earth! Hell-fire couldn't be hotter! Within no time whatsoever. I heard some voices of the Indians, because the forest was so still, we could have heard a butterfly whisper! The Mohawks had just started to lead the vanguard. They had just gone out in front of us...."

"What do you mean, they had just gone out? Didn't they have flankers out?" interrupted the doctor. "What about an advance guard? No scouts out in front and to the sides?"

"Colonel, don't you remember we marched in the lead? The Connecticuters and Indians followed us out of the camp." This time it was Sam Fairfield who caught Tom Williams full-bore in the eyes.

"The Mohawks came up from behind us at the brooklet, there, down the road. We were down the road to Fort Lyman. I'd say about three miles or so."

Sam Fairfield continued his narrative, "With all due respect, Doctor, I thought you said you knows the road? There's no room there for flankers! The little valley floor there is only but feet wide. They's no space whatsoever! None. Ain't nobody, not even the best Indian scouts that can flank a sheer rock wall!

That rock there stands as straight up as a tombstone marking a grave! The Indians had just only got ahead...."

Doctor Williams' eyes seemed to glaze over and he stared off for a few seconds.

"Who should have put out the flankers, Doctor Williams? The colonel or the chief? They wasn't talking but for just a second. 'I smell Indians,' says he, the chief sachem. I don't even think the Colonel said anything to him. Course, I don't know precisely...."

Dr. Williams' eyes relit, "Wait. Tell me again. My brother didn't put out flankers?"

"Well, ah.... no," replied Sam Fairfield fumbling in his own mind to think on it. "The Colonel didn't order out flankers as we paused. We was waiting by the stream for the rest of 'em. How it happened.... aahhh..."

The soldier struggled to order all the myriad physical and mental details of the morning's traumatic bloody march down the military road.

"Sir, I know the Colonel was in charge of us, but the Indian chief was General Johnson's man... and it was the General who gave the orders."

Fairfield felt a heavy weight upon himself, "Course, I don't know. I'm only a common sentinel." His voice trailed off in the deep desolation of sad remembrance.

"Did no one give the orders for flankers?" questioned the Doctor intently.

"Who to put out the flankers then? The old Indian rode out ahead, but it were the Colonel in charge of the scout and we was behind.... Aahhh, I don't know such, Doctor. I'm just a common soldier."

"Well, of course, the Colonel was in charge. How could it be an Indian in charge of a white man?! I think not, soldier," corrected Dr. Williams with ice at the edge of his voice.

"Well then, yes - or no. I don't know. Colonel Williams didn't order out Hendricks' Mohawk flankers as they passed us, leasts so far as I know," stated Fairfield in summary. "But further...."

The heavy air between them absorbed some long seconds of silence.

"… But further, the Mohawks had just passed by us at the creek there. We were sitting by the brook when the Indian scouts just went by us on either side. They had just gone ahead – AND," the soldier paused again.

"… And, sir, remember the land there! There was just room to pass by. The rock walls are close in there! Some of 'em had to step over and bumped some men. Those Indians was just passing on ahead and we were not yet moving out. I don't even know how far they had gone on ahead. I didn't see. You couldn't see. But, for a fact, it weren't too, too far, because it weren't too long after they passed us. There was some confusion then, as a herd of deer ran at us. Deer ran right at us! The time is jumbled in my mind; I couldn't say how long it was. Then, we was just about resuming. I think we was getting up to march …"

"Hummm..," murmured the doctor lost in a train of too many thoughts.

"There was just a single gunshot, which rang out clear. I'll remember it forever, that sound so loud and pure in that valley of death. It felt like a cannon blowing up! Then, boom! Boom! Everywhere, boom! No warning whatsoever, just the boom of five thousand guns going off at once! There was blazing guns everywhere! From everywhere, sir! Absolutely everywhere, from every side, all around - except us! We was like a log at target practice, sitting pretty for them to shoot at!"

Soldier Fairfield became reflective in the remembrance and didn't speak for some moments. He struggled with a hard knot in his throat and his eyes welled up with bulbous tears. Fairfield turned aside as he stifled a tremoring breath laden with emotions.

"I'd be lying dead there with my brains bashed out by a tomahawk and a piece of my scalp as someone's souvenir, if not for my cousin, Tom. 'Twas he that got me back to camp."

A silence settled amongst them as Fairfield blew his nose and wiped off his face.

"Tom saw me and said, 'Sam, they's blood all over ya!' He grabbed me as I was standing like a dumb beast. That's when we came in. I mean we came back to camp… I just didn't want to be scalped alive.…"

Picking up his tale of trauma, Sam Fairfield noted, "Me and the Captain, too. And maybe many more. I don't know how I got back really. I don't know how I run. 'Tis only the great, good Lord that preserved me.… 'Twas an Indian that brought Hawley in, I remember that…. But what happened with the French General? What happened with the battle? Did we whoop 'em?"

Billy Williams picked up the tale, seeing Doctor Williams' dark scowl.

"Yeah, we routed 'em. Chased 'em back down that dark, bloody road, we did," Billy informed him. "But, that ain't to say they's all gone. They's skulking around in the woods to come again. All the troops are on high alert. Sentries – day and night – in case of another attack. It could happen anytime…."

Doctor Tom Williams pushed on the conversation. He had already heard multiple accounts of the column's disaster and his brother's death. In spite of what he might hear from this soldier's account, he had to know about his lost brother, Colonel Ephraim, whom they had all loved for his warm good humor and endless stories of his travels and life. He still couldn't believe it! He kept turning to look for Eph – then reminding himself that Eph was dead. He thought to himself, "I'll ask Eph," then remembered that Eph was dead. How had he truly died? Was it an honorable death?

"Fairfield, did you see the Colonel? Did you see how my brother died?"

"Yes, sir, I did."

Fairfield considered, then continued carefully, "After all that firing started, there was no seeing anything with the smoke and din and all. I couldn't figure where our Indians or our other companies was, who was shooting at us, where they were? I mean, of course, they was the French and their Indians, but where they was we couldn't see," his memories and the telling of it unwound at a slow speed as he paused and paused again to clear his head and think.

"Our company was right behind Colonel Eph's. When he heard the firing ahead, the Colonel knew what it was. He pulled out his sword, fast as a flash of gunpowder in the pan and pointed up the hill to the rocks. He gave us some order, but I cain't recall what it was right now."

At this memory, Fairfield choked up and could only stutter out the next part of his story, "We couldn't even unshoulder our muskets…."

"…before a blast came at us from right above! Right in front of us, right in our faces!"

Fairfield struggled mightily to hold back tears. He did not want to cry like a woman! Perhaps he didn't realize some tears had escaped and streamed down his aggrieved face.

"There wasn't a moment, not a second, sir, before the colonel was hit by a ball. I saw it. I saw him. There wasn't any chance… We couldn't load and fire! We couldn't even unshoulder and get out our cartridges!"

Almost inaudibly, Fairfield said, "Your brother was a great man, sir. He was killed without a chance…. I don't think he felt a thing. One minute he was charging up the rocks … then not even an instant later… He fell dead almost right in front of us! He didn't say a thing…. Just… just, died … A brave man." He paused. "He was a great leader. He led his men…. I-I-I was one of them."

Doctor Williams interrupted to choke out a quiet question, "Was my brother Eph shot through the head?"

"Yes, he was, sir. It were an awful, terrible sight! I swear to you, I saw that ball go in and go clean through and come out the back…" Fairfield's shoulders shuddered. This retelling was agonizing. It was hard to bring to mind the sight of macabre violence to a man - and then tell his brother how that man had died. Fairfield swallowed hard but neglected to note how Colonel Eph had rolled back his eyes and threw out his arms wide as he fell back. "It was his destiny, sir. It must have been predestined by the Lord, because that's how it happened…. Further, sir, I cain't say more."

As Sam Fairfield had told all that he could tell at that time, Doctor Thomas Williams had heard all that he could then hear. The doctor stood up and turned so swiftly, the scarlet lining on the tails of his officer's waistcoat swung out behind him. The bowl of cooled spring-water overturned onto the dirt floor of the log house. He said nothing in parting but left with an image of a red-hot musket ball burning its way through the skull and brain of his beloved older brother. He bit his lower lip sharply for composure. He could weep like a woman in his own tent tonight.

"The Colonel was a great man. He led bravely on such a day as was never seen before! It will never be forgotten, Doctor Williams," muffled the doctor's assistant Billy Williams.

As they walked out of the rough and rude wooden hut, Dr. Thomas Williams mumbled to no one, "Yes, yes, General Dieskau, you 'almost had 'em in the bag.'"

Tonight he would pack up his dead brother's chest of books and personals. Tomorrow he would return to care for the three ghastly wounds of the French general who had ensnared and killed his brother.

Young assistant Billy Williams uttered bitterly, "The devil be your doctor, Frenchman Dieskau!"

September 13, 1755 had dawned a lovely autumnal day. It started refreshingly cool with the promise of a gently warming sun in which to linger in the rich goldenness and the satisfaction of a bountiful harvest. The air moved just subtly enough to caress, but not so much as to disturb. Cats had come out of farm outbuildings and barns to stretch themselves on heated rocks and dry grass. The meadows were decorated with scatterings of white, yellow, golden and deep purple wildflowers. The first few dazzling orange and red maple leaves at the tops of trees quivered in testament to the coming autumn. The earliest changing leaves gleefully trumpeted the glorious blaze that would color the timbered countryside and hills the next month.

However, that restful night before the Sabbath, Northampton's peace had been shattered by the pounding of racing horse's hooves and hectic, hoarse shouts late in the night. The meetinghouse bell clanged and clanged repeatedly for long minutes, signaling urgent news. The shouts had been joyous: "Victory at Lake George!"

"The French Papists are routed!"

"The French and Indians are defeated by our gallant troops!"

"Praise the Lord Our God! Victory!"

"Battle fought at Lake Sacrament!"

The news had been mostly swelling, glorious. Hearts and minds sighed in boundless gratitude that the dreaded Abenaki and Huron Indian nations were pushed back and kept at bay from the New England frontier - at least temporarily.

But while it was that victory which all the province of the Massachusetts Bay had ardently prayed for, not all the news had been rejoicing. Many households in Northampton afterwards donned mourning black crepe. The courier crying the news of the battle at Lake George brought detailed reports of the dead and wounded, hundreds of them! The families, who were gathered at the meetinghouse for the news were a study of deepest dread. When the names were read out, the wailing commenced.

Thus, about midnight at the outskirts of the town the Hawley and Daniel Pomeroy dwelling-houses in the pitch-black town were rudely awakened by insistent, sharp rapping on the heavy oak doors with the news of deaths in their families. "Captain Elisha Hawley is mortally injured and will soon be dead," cried the messenger. "Lieutenant Daniel Pomeroy dead!"

The groggy Joseph Hawley slurred out, "The evil I feared has come upon me."

He ran to the "necessary" house latrine behind their home to spill out his guts. His devoted wife Mercy followed behind him weeping, "Joe, Joe, let me help you. Joe, Joe, come and sit. Joe…"

Within the house, old Rebekah Hawley sat up in her bed and was crying out, "What is it? What is it? What has happened? Tell me!"

When she was awakened with the news, Joseph Hawley's sister-in-law, Betty Pomeroy Hawley's face was ashen: pale gray as burnt-out embers. Her eyes darted franticly as she struggled to understand what it all meant for her? Conversely, Joseph's eyes appeared to be dead: empty, nothing sparked within. Meanwhile, Mother Rebekah Hawley retreated to her cheese-making house. She had not come out since. No one dared approach her: she must be inconsolable.

Hampshire County had suffered the worst loss of men in the current memory. Among the grieving families were the best (wealthiest) bloodlines in Northampton area, Williams, Ashley, Porter, Pomeroy, Hawley. The officer corps had been decimated! Now the debilitating pallor of shock and grief descended like a fall's frost, freezing hearts with anxiety or loss.

Their companies had marched off spiritedly from Northampton for the Crown Pointe Expedition only two months ago. They were young men, some boastful, some gay about the adventures to come, some worried, but all sharing in the excitement and hatred of the French and Indian enemies. Now some were injured and those remaining hardened by war, like the fire-hardened picket-poles around the perimeters of their frontier forts.

As the subsequent morning of September 14, 1755 emerged, a brilliant gold-dust of pollen sprinkled the giant leaves and the soil around the late-season sunflowers. Their weighty heads of seeds bowed lower each day. Stubs of corn stalks presaged the coming winter. At the line between the western hills and sky, angry storm clouds scuttled in warning of possible cloudbursts.

Already predisposed to melancholia (and hypochondria), Joseph Hawley had instantly taken to his sick bed at the news, moaning and writhing. If he was out of their bed, he was in the outhouse. The noise of the racked retching and blubbing could not be suppressed.

"I fear for his life," sobbed his wife Mercy Lyman Hawley to her sister Eunice Lyman Clarke who had come in haste to the Hawley homestead. "Out of the question that he could survive such an arduous travel to the death-bed of Elisha in that forlorn and far-away place! He cannot! Doesn't anyone value his life who would stand-in for him?"

Mercy's face was buried on Eunice's shoulder. "How can he travel in such a state? His constitution will not support it," she bawled, wiping her dripping nose on her apron. "Someone else must go. I cannot support him dying along the road alone and abandoned!"

Joseph Hawley's brother-in-law and best friend, saddle and harness maker, Samuel Clarke, listened in pained sorrow and guilt as his wife and sister-in-law twined their arms around each other. Could he not alleviate this tragic situation? Who could comfort the dying Captain and blot away his seeping blood (if he lived long enough for anyone to arrive)? Oh woe, woe!

Later, Sam Clarke, cursed silently to himself: why, oh why, had he thought to volunteer to go on this possibly lethal mission in place of Joseph?! It had been a moment of pity and lapsing judgment! Now here he was riding off on the Boston-to-Albany Old Bay Road towards the war front! It was the ugly brutishness of fighting he thought he himself had hitherto avoided by hiring out his servant to perform the required militia services for him! He had business and a family! In spite of that, a vortex of war had sucked him in! Instead of civilian work in Northampton, now his personal errand was to care for the mortally-wounded Captain Elisha Hawley at the scene of the great battle. Already he was surrounded by the detritus and disorder of war on the increasingly congested road. As he was riding toward the battle scene, other travelers on the road were hurrying away.

A welter of emotions struggled inside Clarke's breast: a part of him resented Joe's sickness and inability to make this awful journey himself to his brother - for whom there was no hope for recovery! Instead, Joe's beloved brother Captain Elisha Hawley would get himself, Samuel Clarke, brother-in-law of brother's wife to nurse and console him.

Clarke felt a gnawing worry when a whoosh of air lifted a flock of thousands of blackbirds. The flight of the birds swept and flowed across the sky like a wave of rushing water. Clarke grumbled, "Cursed crows!" They reminded Clarke of looming death. Thousands more infernal passenger pigeons, with their chilling red eyes, were roosting in the distant woods at the edge of town where there were so many pigeons that the woodlot pulsed with their gossipy chatter. They called back and forth incessantly to each other.

It occurred to Samuel Clarke that crows taking to their dark beating wings might portend the flight of souls out of this world. Thousands of crows with their heartless caw-caw-caw couldn't be a favorable omen… If they did portend damned souls, was Elisha Hawley among them? The saddler Clarke shuddered down a frightening chill with this notion fleeting across his mind. "Lord God forbid!" He thought of Captain Hawley dead or lying at the point of death. If already departed this sad earth, was Captain Hawley doomed to the fires of damnation? Clarke worried that his brother's mortal wound and the battlefield scene might drive Joseph Hawley into madness.

Clarke felt for his saddlebags to assure himself that he still carried the St. John's wort seeds, melilot bulbous paste, fragrant spikenard oil, and bottle of French cordial - medicines that Dr. Mather had prescribed for Captain Hawley. Clarke recalled the Biblical verse from John 12:4: "Then took Mary a pound of ointment of Spikenard very costly, and anointed Jesus' feet, and wiped his feet with her hair, and the house was filled with the savor of the ointment."

Samuel Clarke shuddered to ponder where the dead Lazarus is raised up. What would Clarke discover when he arrived at the army camp at Lake George? Would Clarke have to anoint a puss-oozing Elisha with the dark sweet oil of spikenard from the blue and white Delft glass vial or apply a poultice of crushed St. John's wort seeds to a chest crusted with wine-colored, dried blood and bodily humours? Seth Pomeroy had written describing one soldier – still alive – that they had carried back from the battlefield with his brains spilling out of his half-blown off head! Sam Clarke gagged back a burp and felt a cold shiver ripple down his spine.

Elisha Hawley's soul indeed had its sins. The smell of the old scandal with that Root woman lingered like a sour whiff on the air, not consciously perceptible, but still there deep in the recesses of memory. Elisha Hawley had refused to confess his sins before the Reverend Mr. Edwards. He had refused to marry Martha Root. Oh, New England had strayed from its fore-fathers in sinful ways!

Clarke continued on the Bay Path Road, past Springfield and turned westward toward Albany. From there it would be northward to wilderness. He would travel up river to Fort Lyman. Then on to Lake George and the now-storied ravine of the Military Road where the "Bloody Morning Scout" had occurred and where Captain Elisha Hawley had been mortally wounded a week ago. The news contained in Seth Pomeroy's letter echoed in his mind, "Hawley is alive but no hope for his life."

Further, Hawley's wife Betty's uncle, Dan Pomeroy, had been Hawley's lieutenant and was now listed among the supposed dead. It was being told in the town that Dan Pomeroy had not wanted to enlist with Hawley (he was, after all, 40-years-old). Presciently Lieutenant Dan had remarked to his brother Major Seth, "I know I must go and I must die."

Clarke prayed for the traveler's blessings of a good road, safe traveling companions and a warm inn with unspoiled food and commodious liquor supplies. But instead, he endured sleeping at "houses for common entertainment" (i.e., rowdy taverns) or barns on the arduous, unruly road to Albany. Food was whatever was available, not suitable for a poor plowman even! Sam was, by necessity, forced to consume any fare that came to hand – however filthy and disgusting. Worse still, it was terribly costly. Sam Clarke ended up rubbing shoulders with dirty soldiers who might be diseased with the "bloody flux" or worse - smallpox!

Dangers lurked everywhere. There were always those who would gladly waylay a solitary traveler far from home: soulless, greedy robbers or Indians, eager to scalp, who might lay camouflaged amidst dark, tangled bushes and swampy morasses of slimy, pulsing green water.

Poor Samuel Clarke spent three protracted days of jostling ride with uncivilized conditions and nightmares of being scalped by half-naked, painted Indians in the worst bedbug and lice infested sleeping spots. On the road, it was constant annoyance by gnats and ever-present mosquitoes. Clarke prayed for his own return to his dear family, muttering on the crowded turnpike, "I pray God for my undeserving, miserable soul. Preserve me for my family and your service, God."

When he arrived at the straggly, degenerate army camp beside Lake George, no one had time for Samuel Clarke or visitors of any kind. It was in a state of virtual anarchy. Clarke was unable to get anyone take him directly to Captain Hawley. They were too busy with their own commotions. He walked through rows of tents, asking soldier after soldier for the Third Massachusetts regiment's location? Finally, Clarke managed to find the Third Massachusetts' tents in the camp. He had never seen so many men together in his life. There were thousands upon thousands here with more arriving and departing each hour! At last, by great good luck, he spied the Physician's Aide from Deerfield, Billy Williams, to whom Clarke insisted, "Hello there, young Williams, take me to Captain Hawley, I say."

"Sir, I'm on an errand for Dr. Williams, I haven't the time."

It was only Clarke's refusal to release Billy from his desperate grasp that got the attention of the frazzled young man long enough to point out the storehouse where some of the dozens wounded in the battle were being attended to. "There, over there, in that log storehouse beside the western creek there. That's where our men from Massachusetts are mostly."

Billy paused to think clearly and added, "But I doubt if Doctor Williams is there now. He's probably caring for the Baron Dieskau at General Johnson's headquarters, the big tent up there on the rocky bluff."

The young man pointed a short distance up an incline to the highest spot overlooking the stunning azure lake. Billy Williams began to explain about the Frenchman, "You know, sir, our troops took the French general captive at the end of the battle? He didn't merit it, of course, cursed papist Frenchie! But we saved his life from the Mohawks who wanted to kill him on the spot in revenge for the death of their King Hendrick. Perhaps you knew Hendrick? He lived in Stockbridge."

This brought Clarke back to the moment. "Look Williams, it's the sick house I need. Where is Captain Elisha Hawley of Northampton with the Third Massachusetts regiment formerly under Colonel Ephraim Williams? Until Colonel Williams's untimely and awful demise, that is…."

"Poor Colonel Williams…." Billy Williams paused to look away to the distance. "With luck, perhaps you can catch the surgeon's mate, over there at the sick house. This time the young assistant pointed down to a clear, narrow brook immediately in front of the low ground that ran into the dazzling lake. "Anyway, if you want Captain Hawley, I'm supposing he's in there - if he's still alive."

As he trudged to the storehouse, Sam Clarke prepared himself for the disgusting stench. Nonetheless, when he entered the dark log cabin, nothing could have prepared him for the overpowering miasmas of decay, pus, sour urine and excrement that assaulted him! The stench was suffocating and assaulting! Men were lying everywhere on blankets, bedrolls, straw or on the mud of the ground. The sounds of moaning and crying assaulted his ears. "Where's Captain Hawley, man?" Clarke demanded of the only young man standing inside the ammunition storehouse.

"Captain Hawley… Hawley… aahh, let's see," puzzled Perez Marsh as he spun around the dimness of the dirt-floored building to inventory the groaning soldiers laid out across the floor. (Wanting to learn to be a physician, Marsh had enlisted as the regimental doctor's aide but never counted on this much experience!) "Ah, I think that's the Captain over there against the wall," Marsh scurried about from yowling soldier to keening soldier.

A tense Sam Clarke swallowed the acidic bile that pushed up from his revolted stomach into his mouth and up his nostrils. It took an immense effort to swallow. When had he developed this pounding ache across his forehead and urge to puke? It had descended upon him the instant he walked from the glaring sunshine outside into the nauseousness of a filthy, raw slap-stick storehouse where he felt trapped like a cornered rat! "What is this filth?! he barked."

"I'm sorry, sir, but the men haven't cleaned this room yet."

"Is this being cleaned? It appears never!"

"Well, yes, almost every day there's a crew that takes out the refuse and brings in clean straw," explained Marsh somewhat sheepishly. "But, in truth, these men are not as meticulous as the women were. Unfortunately, the camp women were all sent down to Fort Lyman a week ago. It's actually very hard to get any work done whatsoever these days."

"Is this Captain Hawley?" demanded Clark to no one in particular, but to everyone around him.

"Why, man, where are his accoutrements? Where is his sword and officer's gorget? I suppose his only effects here - not stolen - are his Bible and books?" Clarke demanded. "What is this disgusting rag he's sleeping upon? This is inadequate! Who is the officer in charge here?"

Clarke received no reply as Marsh had turned to other whimpering or wailing men and was across the room ordering some others to fetch water and rum, and otherwise struggling to manage the ghastly scene of disorder, dirt and cataclysmic suffering.

"I say, is this Captain Elisha Hawley? Tell me," the saddler Clarke demanded as if to his apprentice boy.

A bright-eyed man on the next bedroll, with an ugly bullet track across his arm answered, "Yes, that's Captain Hawley."

"Joe? Joe?" the foul, fatigued Hawley gasped, blinking to open his eyes and trying to raise himself from the crusted bedding. The wounded man weakly spit out a fine spray of spittle and blood droplets across Clarke's face as he talked.

"Captain Hawley, no, no, it's not your brother Joseph. It's me, Sam Clarke, Mercy's brother-in-law. Joe was ill…. too ill to be able to come here. He couldn't make the journey," Clarke stammered. Clarke felt distaste. He was lying and despised being in this position. Clarke had left Joseph Hawley "convalescing," when the Major was actually in bed in self-induced misery and grief. Joe was convinced that he was dying and had been giving Mercy his last wishes when Sam Clarke was with him three days ago. Clarke knew from Joe's prior bouts of hypochondria that Joseph Hawley would recover from this physical ailment, but never from his melancholia.

"Captain Hawley, I've come on behalf of your brother Joseph and your mother. They wanted you to have every attention in your dying days. Yes, every circumstance and attention befitting an officer of your station. Why, see, I've brought salve and poultice from Dr. Mather for you."

Hawley blinked and struggled mightily to think - and even more so to sputter out the words, "Joe, Joe? Eph is gone, dead. Joe, … Eph is g-g-g-one, gone, gone!"

He paused to audibly try to suck in breath. After a long minute, he continued with his urgent message, "Gone, I tell you! Joe, Eph is s-s-s-hot through the forehead!"

This toil at speech caused beads of sweat to break out on Hawley's sallow face. "He had just turned to me, Joe. I stood there. "Hawley…'" he said. Then he turned. He called out, "M-m-men, charge!'"

"I saw them… Canadians…" Seconds passed.

"They rised up just there - in front of us." By now, the dirty man was glistening with sweat and spittle. "They shot him. I-I-I saw him fall…. Ole Dan Pom… too."

His chest rose and fell shallowly, with the ripped open shirt crusted with blood and pus. In spite of the effort, he labored on, "Shot through the head, clean and clear as daylight. His eyes looked at me. Then he just fell over still staring."

The half-insensate man continued painfully stumbling along in his recounting of an event no one wanted to hear, although his words were no longer comprehensible and he was becoming drained.

From across the smothering airlessness of the storehouse, another grimy soldier bellowed, "Give 'em some more rum so he'll stop cryin'! Else, give it to me so I don't hear 'im!"

To which another man retorted, "Stop that you! He's an officer and a gentleman. He gets rum and brandy! And, he ain't cryin'. He's dying."

Clarke hated being here in this God-forsaken place. Oh, dear Jesus, how he hated this place! He grappled with how to make things simple and clear for the ruined Captain Hawley before him, "No, Captain Hawley. It's me, Samuel Clarke. Remember me? Your sister-in-law Mercy's sister's husband? I've come instead of Joseph … to aid you."

"Joe? Where's Joe?" After a pause, he added, "Mother?"

Clarke had known this would be difficult. Best to turn to another topic but he searched his mind for what to say in such an awkward situation. As he sat blankly, Elisha Hawley suddenly seemed in earnest. "I am…" he struggled to speak with whatever air his punctured lungs could pump. "… a dead man."

"Captain Hawley, yield yourself to God! Lay hold of his covenant! Beseech Jesus Christ, his holy spirit. Pray for saving grace, whether you deserve it or not," Clarke counseled. He felt flustered and panicked with the responsibility to know how to handle this horrible situation.

Hawley struggled on to speak with powerless rasping breaths. Clarke averted his eyes from the torn linen shirt through which the blackened ragged musket ball hole exposed ugly innards. A few drops of spittle dripped to Hawley's grizzled blood-flecked chin. Samuel Clarke pondered how the man was still alive and had been possibly thought able to survive? How? How? It required monumental effort for Hawley to try to speak and produced only a hair's wisp of a murmur and excruciating grimaces of pain on the Captain's flaccid discolored face. Clarke recoiled at the thought of moving his face closer to the oozing man's lips to hear anything he might utter.

A sudden shadow blocking the door caused Sam Clarke to startle and turn quickly with his own musket. It was the regimental physician, Dr. Thomas Williams. Clarke noted the great changes in the doctor's depleted demeanor, probably wrought by the battle.

"Mr. Clarke, what are you doing here?" queried Dr. Williams. "Where is Joseph Hawley?"

"Ah, Dr. Williams, hello," stumbled Clarke, "Joe was most terribly indisposed as to be completely unable to travel."

Clarke paused. "Dr. Williams, sir, so good to see a face from home in these heathen lands! I am gladdened to see you here!" Clarke sighed deeply. "Doctor, I am under very particular obligations to the Hawley family for Captain Hawley's faithful, most comforting care in these singular difficulties and troubles. I have given my promise to the family."

Impatiently, Dr. Williams said sternly. "Certainly, Mr. Clarke. But I ask you not to overexert him. He hasn't the strength and it will only hasten his death."

"I seek not to provoke him, rather I am trying to console him in his final hours," offered Clarke stiffly.

Reflecting a moment, Dr. Williams added brightly. "We will be most relieved to have your aid and assistance here Mr. Clarke. You see we are so overwhelmed with caring for the injured men. Besides these here, there are three other storehouses overflowing with wounded and dying others."

Elisha Hawley flickered his eyelids and stirred again to awareness. He mumbled a series of incomprehensible syllables.

"What was that?" Clarke asked. "Hawley, what? What say you? I can't understand."

After a long silence a nearby voice spoke, "Sirs, I can understand him. He's spoken to me in the last days."

It was Sam Fairfield, a common soldier, recuperating on a close-by bedroll.

"Then, man, what said he?" demanded Sam Clarke impatiently.

"Well, in the beginning when he looked as dead for the first few days, he asked over and over, 'Where is my Mohawk?'"

"Say what, man? Precisely, what is that supposed to mean?" demanded the unnerved Clarke.

Fairfield resumed his retelling, "Meaning that Hawley was carried back to camp by a Mohawk. In the retreat from that bloody morning scouting, he came back with one of the Mohawks."

"That's of no import to me now. What of importance said he?"

"He told me, 'Tell Martha I'm sorry….'" replied Fairfield quietly. He paused (as Hawley had also in his mumblings), "I wasn't the man I wanted to be."

"That's nonsense!" retorted Clarke animatedly. "He's hardly able to articulate a thing, much less, sputter out all of that! As always, 'the first casualty of war is truth,' as they say. Don't bother me, man, with your imaginings! This man is dying and I'm sent here on an important mission from his brother."

"Mr. Clarke, my brother Colonel Ephraim Williams was one of the first casualties of this war - after the Mohican King Hendrick, that is. So too were Captain Hawley and the other dead officers. Don't tell us about the casualties of war!"

"Begging your pardon, Doctor. I am deeply sorry about your loss. No harm meant - none at all - of course. And sir, the entire province of Massachusetts lauds the heroic death of your brother the Colonel. He died a brave Englishman in service to His Majesty King George and his country. A true patriot of our country, who fell as becomes an Englishman. He died in opposition to an anti-Christian power, those Popist French and heathen Indians. Of utmost heroism, clearly. His heroic death is a great public loss."

"He was shot through the head while rallying his men," said the Doctor with a hard, astringent note peeling off the undertones of his dull voice. "Death makes a mockery of heroism and dignity, Mr. Clarke."

"My deepest condolences, Doctor. May he live in glory with our Lord," added Clarke lamely. He wondered, "And the Captain? Did he kill any Indians or French?"

The tall Doctor intensified his glare and stated with undisguised impatience, "Mr. Clarke, Captain Hawley, Lieutenant Pomeroy and their ensigns hadn't a moment to even prime their muskets before they were shot. The enemy vastly outnumbered and entrapped 'em." The Doctor's voice was slowing and cracking.

"Yes, yes, certainly, Doctor. I' m just under very great distress here."

Clarke abhorred the idea of returning to Northampton to relay to Joseph and Rebekah Hawley that Captain Elisha had said, "Tell Martha I'm sorry." This message would certainly have to be squelched. It would never get out of this hell's gate of a camp! Clarke resolved that he must relay a noble story of Captain Hawley back home - even if he had to invent it himself.

"Fairfield here was also out on that bloody morning scout in my brother's regiment. Both he and the Captain were carried in from there. Fairfield's a member of Captain Hawley's company and he's been lying here for almost a week. He might know a thing or two."

Clarke stiffened. "Dr. Williams, I was strictly instructed to care for Captain Hawley by his brother and mother and to retrieve his belongings, not to listen to the ramblings of every dirty soldier between Northampton and Crown Pointe!" huffed Sam Clarke.

"Then Mr. Clarke, you can find his tent and provisions up front towards the lake where, I hope, it hasn't been pilfered. Last I heard Lieutenant-Colonel Seth Pomeroy had secured the personal belongings of the deceased officers. Check with Lieutenant-Colonel Pomeroy," said Dr. Williams as he moved on with his assistant to the next wounded soldiers to examine, cut out infections, top them with a jolt of rum and dress their bandages.

Sam Clarke shook off the damp despondence that had invaded his soul. He felt that the impenetrable shadows of death might be lurking at every dark edge within the room. "Yes, I believe you are right, Dr. Williams. I'll be going to Captain Hawley's tent. Quite right, sir. One other matter, Doctor, if I may? Where will I find the gravediggers and the burying grounds for the officers? I'm instructed by his brother and mother to assure a proper Christian burial with all honors due to an officer. A coffin and a cross, of course."

There was no reply. Now alone again, Clarke mumbled to Hawley, "Captain Hawley, we must patiently and quietly submit to ye will of God in everything, knowing that if we belong to God, it will be but a very little while before we shall have all our tears wiped off from our eyes and we shall meet with all our dear relations and friends and never be separated any more. The Lord prepare you for your change that you may be ready for death," he paused and then realized that he should add a caveat, "when it should come. You must be ready to pass from earth to…. aahhh, heaven."

Clarke's voice trailed off. Again, Sam Clarke had to pause to wonder if indeed Hawley was headed to heaven? Perhaps this horrible disfigurement and looming, inevitable death was the start of the journey to hell? One could never know, but it was certain that the effects of sin were profound. Elisha Hawley, of course, had been excommunicated by their church.

"What did it all mean?!?" Clarke speculated to himself. Was Hawley saved or condemned? It was all too tangled and sticky a web for Sam Clarke to evaluate. He would think no more on this onerous topic.

Samuel Clarke stared at the grubby, pathetic figure of the once-proud, strong Captain Elisha Hawley.

Finally however, Clarke's complete fatigue and rising hunger caused him to consider on the situation he found himself in. He doubted he could ever sleep amidst all these strangers – Indians, Yorkers, Dutch, Germans and others in this cursed camp with the constant upheaval of thousands of men and animals crowded together on a denuded, muddy camp space engulfed within a vast eternal wilderness. There was ceaseless noise, hubbub and alerts for further deadly attacks. All knew that the French and Indians were skulking about in the woods just outside their camp at the ready to happily scalp and kill pitilessly! A full-scale attack could come at any time!

How long would it be before Captain Hawley would die and release Clarke from his responsibility to remain here to care for him? There was much to do. Clarke must have a coffin made, instead of the common soldier's "winding sheet." He would get someone to carve a wooden cross and cut Hawley's name into it. A grave in the officer's burying ground on the west hill must be dug. Clarke would oversee a proper Christian burial. Thank God, Hawley's body had not been desecrated by a denuded circle of missing hair and skin that was evidence of a scalping. The family would be grateful for that which every New England soldier earnestly prayed to avoid.

As he was leaving the sick house Clarke glanced back to see the face of death on Elisha Hawley. The Captain lay staring straight ahead in a dulled stupor. Hawley was numbed to the crazed frenzy of life around him. Some moments he appeared to smile wanly, dreamily and pensively as he lay oscillating between life and death.

"Next time….," he moaned faintly.

Private Samuel Fairfield choked down tears. He realized that Captain Hawley would not have a "next time" in this world.

The intervals between the Captain's feeble breaths grew longer and longer, so that Sam Fairfield wondered each time if that one was Hawley's last? About 7:00 in the early evening of September 24, 1755 the faint bubbles of air flecked with dried blood ceased. Captain Elisha Hawley was dead.

Tomorrow morning his body would be carried out of the sick house/storage house and buried with whatever gravitas his brother's brother-in-law Samuel Clarke could muster up. Then Clarke would be on the Military Road away from Lake George.

Chapter 28

At the Bar

Springfield and Northampton, August 28, 1759-February 13, 1760

August 28, 1759 was court day in Springfield.

The spectators had convened early at the "town house" for court day before the justices of the Hampshire County Court of Common Pleas. Magisterial Chief Justice Israel Williams was the last to arrive, so that his grand sweeping entrance could be witnessed and appreciated by everyone. Justice Williams was called the "Monarch of Hampshire" by many who hated his arrogance and increasingly presumptuous manipulation of governance and land speculation for his family's profit. Israel Williams had returned to his court position after the "Hampshire Justice Revolt" against the appointment of Charles Phelps as a justice last year by Governor Pownall. The notorious Justice Williams wore his pricy and highly stacked curled wig, black robe and his usual ill-tempered impatience and aggravation at having to tolerate court day riff-raff and rabble.

Justice Williams had been buttressed by his fellow justices who (apart from Phelps) happened to be Williams family members or relatives by marriage, in refusing to accept the commission of Phelps – then Governor Pownall informed them of his absolute right as their duly appointed Governor of the Massachusetts Bay Colony to appoint his own justices – or conversely, to withdraw them. Thus, with that realization, the justices' uprising of Hampshire fizzled.

Justice Williams' cousin, Prosecutor and sometimes Judge, Joseph Hawley was in a more foul mood. Attorney Hawley sensed the day would be onerous, not only for the verbal lashes he would likely feel from the hated Chief Justice, but also for facing off against Defense Counsel Charles Phelps, another of Hawley's main antagonists over the years.

Most of Joseph Hawley's daily world seemed pitted against him lately. Why even one yeoman, from a far-out settlement in which Hawley had a contested land deal, had the insolence to write him,

> "Sir, let me be so free with you as to tell you that I look upon
> you to be in a very dangerous situation & circumstance when
> you wears that very threatening aspect. Why, for you, to tell me,
> that if I refuse a compliance with your court suit, you hope it
> would please God that I live… Why sir! Sir, I'm practically
> speechless. Sir, a gentleman doesn't wear such a threatening
> countenance!"

284

"Now I even have yeoman farmers telling me -ME! as a gentleman - how to behave!" fumed Esquire Joseph Hawley to his wife Mercy, normally meek and obedient.

It absolutely astonished Joe when she answered back, "Did he have reason?"

His spouse did not wait for his answer, but walked abruptly back over to the hearth fire and turned away from him. No more words were exchanged that evening or into that night, as both of them simmered their personal grievances with strongly flavored rancor.

Mercy Lyman Hawley was furious that her husband had issued a warrant and was bringing before the county court her own sister's husband for prosecution! She had scoffed, such prosecutions, as fornication, were becoming increasingly rare these days. The arguments over his filing of the White Horse Tavern presentment complaint with the Hampshire County Inferior Court of Common Pleas had nagged at Joseph Hawley and corroded his home-life, as well as his peace of mind for weeks.

Mercy was in a dark and obscure fugue, thinking of her husband prosecuting her brother-in-law and younger cousins. Mercy tormented herself, thinking of all the bitter recriminations, reproaches and whispered gossip circulating in the Lyman and Pomeroy families (with whom the Lymans had frequently intermarried and who were also charged) as well as around the Northampton and Hadley communities. Oh shame! What mortification for the mild-mannered Mercy! For shame and worry over their "daily bread" and reputations, Mercy could not peer into the eyes of kinswomen Betty Pomeroy Hawley Lyman, Mindwell Lyman Pomeroy, Eleanor Lyman Pomeroy, Esther Pomeroy and the others. She cried in silence at home, muffling her tears as she went about her daily chores although her bleary red eyes betrayed her anguish. Her life had been shorn of reassuring regularity and precious honor. The thought of her relatives criticizing and blaming her and her husband caused Mercy to avoid her kinswomen's gatherings.

Consequently, it seemed she pulled her hair tighter into its knot within her mob cap. The household's meals were singed more frequently. Their conversations at meals were abrupt, terse and sharp. The silences were elongated and cumbrous with the only distractions the loud and jarring snaps of pine wood knotholes in the fireplace. The hearth fire burnt low more often. Mercy was rolling over in bed to fall asleep with her back to Joseph each night. She was distanced from her husband and her birth family both.

Joseph Hawley wondered sorrowfully if this distance between him and his wife would be permanent? They had been so lovingly doting on each other before… Regardless of his personal discomfit or inconvenience, as a representative of the civil authority for the county, Officer of the Court Hawley felt compelled by his moral obligation and legal responsibility to uphold the law and good order - even when prosecution entailed sanctioning a relative by marriage. Of course, he regretted that the culprits were Mercy's and sister-in-law Betty's blood relatives. Despite his proclaimed purely ethical stance, the prosecution was no way acceptable to Mercy.

Joe knew that his mother Rebekah was also agitated. Esquire Hawley was unsure how much of the quagmires, squabbles and rumors of this distasteful case his mother had actually heard since she didn't engage with anymore much, particularly not with anyone under seventy years old. These days Rebekah Hawley spent her days in her buttery building behind their unadorned mansion house. Alone with the cheese wheels, she sputtered to herself about the decline of true virtue, respect for authority and the rise of worldliness in modern times. Old Mrs. Hawley had warned her besieged attorney son about the lack of strict punishment, "Now-a-days, a man falls asleep in the meetinghouse belfry - with his hat on! - on the Sabbath day! – and he receives practically no punishment for such lack of deference to God and authority!"

The crochety old woman snorted out her disgust and continued on, "Where is the holy watchfulness over one's neighbors? Instead of holy watchfulness of each other, today there's "chambering" (bundling) and wantonness in public houses, wickedness on the night of the Sabbath, folly and lewdness at harvest time, excessively nipping too much alcohol, vanity, the snares of evil company, girls going far from their fathers' houses, an affection for liberty rather than family governance, a fondness for freedom, carousing and dishonoring God! Swilling and swaggering with great bravado." Joseph and Mercy knew she could recite a chorus more of modern evils.

"There are no morals, I tell you! None at all! None! All the world's gone to the dogs and the devil! There will be hell to pay for it! Hell-fire, hell-fire to them that defy and desecrate! Strict punishment for 'em."

Augmenting the tribulations was Betty Pomeroy Hawley, brother Elisha's "relict" (widow) with her maneuverings and negotiations. Following the death of her husband Elisha Hawley, Betty had spent less and less time with the Hawleys and more and more time with her siblings, particularly across the Great River in Hadley and Hockanum. Worse, Betty's siblings and in-laws aligned now with the religious controversies and personalities of the dismissed Reverend Jonathan

Edwards. It reminded Joseph Hawley of his own role in the dismissal, a chapter in Hawley's life that he regretted and was ashamed of.

Unlike her mother-in-law, Rebekah, Betty Pomeroy Hawley had neither interest nor capability for managing a farm, house and business – her household was enough. Betty was an appealing young widow, as she brought no children into a remarriage. In addition, she was attractive financially: not only was her father well-off with the Pomeroy blacksmithing and gun-smithing, but Betty had inherited one-third of Elisha's estate. Further contrasting her from her mother-in-law, Betty had no taste to remain alone the rest of her life.

Normally, a widow retained her ex-husband's estate. Most Wills dictated that she retain her "widow's third" only until she remarried. It had been Joseph himself who wrote up Elisha's Last Will and Testament; thus, he knew that if Betty remarried, she should then legally be stripped of her inherited holdings. Yet, with their deep and ensnaring ties to the Pomeroys, Joseph and Rebekah dared not disenfranchise Betty.

Phinehas Lyman had been widowed by the death of his wife in February 1759. He was seriously impeded in his business by the care of his three very young sons. Phin's own mother was dead and he had no sisters able to live-in and assume the care of his household. Neither could any woman in the family of his in-laws. How could Phin handle his farm, deal making and purchasing land with Eben Pomeroy, the younger Charles Phelps, the Hadley town selectman Oliver Warner and the Bostonian merchant John Hancock? Betty's wealth fit nicely into these prospects, as well as meeting Phin's need for a home-maker and mother to his boys. So, after almost four years of widowhood, Betty Pomeroy Hawley remarried the similarly widowed Phinehas Lyman, a relative of Mercy and Betty's brother's wife.

Joseph Hawley hated the hurly-burly of speculations, deals and markets: it was all so crass and crude. However, he was aware he was being left out of immense profits and sidelined in commerce. Additionally, a twinge of jealousy and inarticulatable grief crushed and pommeled the heart of Joseph Hawley: the remarriage of his brother's widow hurt. Elisha was joining the ranks of the forgotten departed with the departure of his widow. Betty was leaving her former husband Elisha to the dustbin of death.

Betty's brother Eben Pomeroy III owned the White Horse Tavern in Hockanum, just south of Hadley. Joseph had heard wild tales of cavorting, wicked dancing and similar debauchery at the tavern across the river from Northampton, for which Joe had issued a court summons.

The morning session of the Inferior Court of Common Pleas on August 28, 1759 began with the cases continued from the last term being called up one after another:

Jacob White and John Ingersoll,
James McCrister of Enfield versus Joshua Taylor,
Nathaniel Downing versus Bailey Austin,
James Smith versus Stephen Stockwell,
etc., etc.

First was an estate appointment; then, debt judgments never executed and the appointment of two referees for a dispute. Defaults were entered against persons who failed to appear. Next, were debts unpaid for grinding nuts not delivered or for a side saddle (and other commodities); a trespass on land; uttering a profane curse ("By my Savior I have so much wheat!"); more debts, and more debts. Thomas Gilbert sought to have the debt case against him dismissed because it labeled him as "Thomas Gilbert Gentleman" instead of "Thomas Gilbert Esquire." (This was denied.) One defendant arrived four minutes late (at the Justice's prior approval) and was informed that a judgment had already been entered against him to which the impudent rogue shouted, "Kiss my arse in the face of this honorable court!" When threatened to be dragged up front and fined further, he quickly and humbly begged the pardon of the Justices "for me being much in drink."

"May God pardon me…" he apologized with a strong slur in his voice. "… as well as your Honorables." Once he staggered out onto the packed dirt street, he was cursing the justices again as he dodged traffic.

One defendant testified that he could not appear at the prior court session due to his horse being a mile-and-a-half away from him. As a final clincher for his argument, he added, "And that's as good an excuse as any!" The Chief Justice did not think so and ordered judgment against him - plus court costs.

As the day and the cases dragged on, the spectators grew disinterested, restless, hungry and thirsty. Toward the hearing of the last cases before the mid-day dinner break, another yeoman farmer was heard griping, "Damn the Court! Curse the Court! Haven't we waited long enough on them? A pox on them! It's time to retire to Parsons Tavern! I wants some victuals and drink. I wish these grandees would come to my mill right now. I would put them between those millstones or under the water wheel. They treat us like a cursed old horse. They have no business with our affairs. We know of no such body of men!" He finished by calling the justices "puppies" and stomped out the door to the tavern's sign.

Parson Tavern
Entertainment for Men and Horses

Within seconds, they heard the ringing of the tavern bell for the 3:00 pm dinner and that most welcome call, "Victuals ready!"

"Yes. Yeah!"

"Hear, hear!"

"For one and all!"

"Let us out of here," hostilely grumbled the crowd at the back while Chief Justice Israel Williams steamed and stewed as he watched the throng of men (and a few of the rowdier women) stream out of the court house. He, too, was fatigued of the day's disorderly pleadings and wanted to get to some rum noggin, small drink, spruce beer, Madera wine or even a bowl of flip. As soon as the morning's session finished, the justices retired to their private room at Parsons' to dine and deliberate.

When the afternoon's session resumed again after the meal for the General Sessions of the Court of Peace, the atmosphere was languid and much relaxed. Both the audience and justices would nod off during the boring case arguments on highway rights of way or being wickedly absent from Sabbath worship but would awaken for the real amusements such as the fornication cases – with everyone hoping for some particularly loquacious witnesses to testify about how they might have seen some couple engaging in their dirty deeds! In the testimonies on Eben Pomeroy's public house, the White House Tavern "misrule and disorder" case, some would talk about the mixed gathering of boys and giddy girl maiden "tipplers." That would be tantalizing! What common man wouldn't relish the spectacle of the Chief Justice's struggle to maintain his composure and the decorum of the courtroom (who was so jeering of their personal struggles)? Who wouldn't enjoy the hypocritical silence of Deacon Ebenezer Pomeroy Junior (father of the innkeeper and one of the rowdy young men) next Sabbath in Northampton: he who had lectured so sternly once upon a time on "family governance?"

The spectators perked up immediately when the case of "Hawley Esquire and Informer versus Pomeroy"[35] was summoned by the sheriff. Joseph Hawley left the justices table on the dais to move down to the prosecutors table and called his witness, an Informer unknown to most of the Hadley and Hockanum people.

---

[35] Hampshire Co Court of General Sessions of the Peace, Lib E/Vol 6, Pg 200/652. Online: http://credo.library.umass.edu/view/pageturn/mums704-i5862/#page/200/mode/1up

The Informer peered around warily. He perceived the disfavor of the onlookers. Therefore, he commenced quickly in a low voice relating how Esquire Hawley had asked him to go imbibe at the White Horse in Hockanum and would pay him for information.

"Let's get to the matter at hand, rather than peripherals," groused Hawley who was growing uncomfortably warm and sweaty. "Tell us what actually happened, man."

"Well, sir, I was at the White Horse, as you asked me…"

"Sir, the Court is not interested in the inconsequential details! Can you just testify to what happened with the crime?" cried Joseph Hawley in raw aggravation.

"Wait, let the man tell his story, Mr. Hawley," beseeched recently-appointed Defense Attorney and new Justice Charles Phelps. "I would find enlightening all the gory details of the affair."

"So, as I says, sir, the honorable Mr. Hawley asked me to go to the White Horse in Hockanum to spy if his brother-in-law's brother-in-law, Mr. Lyman, was there a-drinkin' as he'd heard."

"Pray which Mr. Lyman?" interrupted Attorney Justice Mr. Phelps again. "Undoubtedly you know there's many of them."

"Well sir, I knows not all the Lymans. I does know there's some, but Mr. Hawley pointed out to me the gentleman he was interested in."

A low mumble of discontent and audible "hisses" rolled forward from the back of the courtroom. Joseph Hawley fidgeted at his table and shuffled the parchments in front of him. "That Phelps is way too zealous in politics," griped Hawley to himself. "He should stay out of it."

"Again, I ask, can you tell us which Mr. Lyman?" prodded Phelps further.

"Yes, Mr. Phinehas Lyman, who lives thereabouts. That Mr. Lyman just married to Mr. Hawley's brother's widow," the Informer plodded on. "So naturally I went there as asked to look around and see what goes on there."

Here Phelps interjected, "And Mrs. Innkeeper's brother-in-law."

"What?" asked the surprised Informer.

"Oh, you didn't know? responded the Defense Attorney. "Yes, in these parts, it's all a family affair: Mrs. Mindwell Pomeroy, who kindly served you, is also the sister of Defendants Caleb and Heman Pomeroy, sister-in-law of Defendant Eben Pomeroy's sister's wife, cousin of Phin Lyman, as well as Lyman's wife's sister-in-law in the next case. Plus, her sister is married to her husband's brother."[36]

"You won't be expecting me to keep them all straight! They's too many ties that bind for a poor sop like me to remember."

"Yes, challenging indeed, even for one in the midst of it. Did you too perchance imbibe spirituous liquors at the White Horse?" Phelps wondered aloud.

"Beggin' your honorable's pardon, Mr. Justice, but who goes to a public house and doesn't drink there?"

A great guffaw arose from the court audience.

"Indeed, indeed."

"It would be most inhospitable not to join in," agreed the crowd.

"Besides, sir, t'would look most suspicious if I didn't have a gill or two of rum with the other folks. So, course, I had me a drink or two with the lively crowd there. It was like an obligation to be amenable and friendly."

"Would you please tell us about the going on's there?" probed Attorney Hawley impatiently, hoping to speed up this agonizingly slow statement by the Informer.

"What I seen there was shocking to my own eyes and mind! It weren't but a few drinks into the evening that someone brought out a fiddle and started playin' some right lively tunes. Such as "The Fly," or "Nottingham Ale, and…"

"To the point, man!" pleaded Mr. Hawley.

---

[36] Besides the aforementioned convoluted and interwoven relationships, Charles Phelps' step-mother Catharine King Hitchcock Phelps Lyman married as her third husband, the father of Defendant Elijah Lyman (who was also the husband of Mercy Lyman Hawley's sister Eleanor) and Phinehas Lyman. See Benjamin H. Hall. *History of eastern Vermont, from its earliest settlement to the close of the eighteenth century.* D. Appleton & Co. (New York, 1858). Pg 690.

"Oh yes, sir. With that, them boys and girls began a-singin' and dancin' and merry-making right lively. Yup, right lively indeed!"

"Well, man, were they both young men and women together? Can you tell us how long this mischief making went on?" questioned Attorney Hawley.

"Oh yes. Yes, indeed sir. They carried on and on into the late night. Past midnight I would say. But most shocking of all, beyond those fripperies, was that those coquettes and young bucks went upstairs together where they's night chambers!"

He paused and blushed, "Uuuhh-umm, I suspect to carnally know each other, as they might say. Them young mistresses was definitely of lascivious carriages. Me thinks there was dissipation and "naughty dalliances.""

"The informer is a "lying Dick!" came a cry from an unidentifiable male within the mass of seated people packed on the benches in the back. The courtroom seemed to explode at once with voices all speaking at the same time — all indistinguishable words and phrases in the morass of noise.

"His dick would surely know about lieing and lying!" chortled someone else in the back.

"Quiet! Quiet! Quiet in this honorable courtroom!" shouted Israel Williams in an attempt to return control and decorum. "There'll be no more indecent publication of such distasteful details, no more obscenity before this august court! Mr. Hawley, have you completed your prosecution yet?" asked the scandalized Chief Justice in a sharp tenor. "Let me warn that we will tolerate no further lustfulness here."

"Yes, Justice Williams, I am confident the prosecution can rest now," Joseph Hawley replied uneasily.

The Chief Justice turned angrily to Defendant Eben Pomeroy the Third who hastily confessed to the crime. "The Court finds Ebenezer Pomeroy guilty."

A voice interrupted, "Not more than a farthing fine!"

Clearly the innkeeper was guilty. The Informer testified so. Chief Justice Williams had to levee some punishment of course. The sentiment of the people with whom the jovial Pomeroy was popular was clear though. The other justices cleared their throats with slight coughs or "uhm's" as they shifted awkwardly in their chairs and averted their eyes. Most were relatives of friends or friends of relatives and friends of the defendants. It was most knotty indeed. A long, empty, clumsy pause hung in the dense summer air.

"Fined ten shillings lawful money, plus costs of court," ruled the Chief Justice.

Audible relief passed over everyone as a tense moment vaporized. Now they were all anxious to move on to the following cases, including the issuances of liquor licenses for the subsequent year. One of these was that approving the same Ebenezer Pomeroy of Hadley to be an "innholder, retailer, and common victualler for the ensuing year." The crowd began departing.

The trial and confession of Innkeeper Pomeroy should have ended the actions in the White Horse Tavern case the prior August, but on Tuesday, February 12, 1760 once again, they were back in court arguing. Another Grand Jury indictment had been brought this time against the rowdy, frolicking youths. Knowing he could not count on incriminating testimony from Innkeeper Pomeroy or other Hadley residents, Prosecutor Hawley had hired the outside Informer. The local chatter forewarned the prosecutor that local sentiment favored the youth.

Joseph Hawley Esquire was assailed from all directions again. For the past months, his wife had been stone-cold to him after he brought the case of his ex-brother-in-law Eben Pomeroy and brought the prosecution of Mercy's and Phinehas' cousins and brothers-in-law among the youthful offenders at the White Horse Tavern. The attorney in Joseph had meekly – and vainly - argued the importance of law and morality at the supper table as his wife sat without speaking a single syllable. His mother sat smirking and occasionally interjecting her agreement, "Yes, indubitably." Finally, Mercy announced to Joseph that she didn't want to hear any more of it and dashed from the table in tears.

Joseph Hawley burped up some foully bitter-tasting bile as he thought of who would be his opponent in the White Horse Tavern case at the bar. The attorney for the defendants would be Charles Phelps, conceited, loud, so obtuse as to not recognize his inferiority, a brick-layer-turned-lawyer. Hawley reflected that these days a dirt-crusted yeoman looked at the tavern copy of *Every Man his Own Lawyer* or *Gilbert's Law of Evidence* and imagined he could argue before the court! People simply did not recognize their places and act so! This was especially true of the too tall, gangly, ostentatious Charles Phelps.

"Oyez, oyez, oyez! All rise!" bellowed the court bailiff. "All manner of persons having business to do before this honorable court of His Majesty's Justices, draw near and give your attendance. If anyone have any plaint to enter or suit to prosecute, let them come forth and they shall be heard. Silence is commanded in the court upon pain of imprisonment. God Save the King!"

At the back of the Northampton court house, late-comers were still shuffling into the court session. It was packed with a large but groggy audience, as a hogshead barrel is stuffed to the top with salted pork. All the court gawkers hoped these sessions would be interesting and provide plenty to talk about when they went back to their homes, favorite tavern or after the church service.

"Quiet! I say, quiet! This Court is in session!" shouted Chief Justice Israel Williams. This day the imposing Justice Williams acted with caution not to inflame the audience, as they might jeer him, like they had the time "his ole majestic Judge Hinsdale" came to court drunk and fell off his chair while pronouncing someone guilty.

As the Inferior Court of Common Pleas was called, an ill-looking man approached the justices, his face peppered with the ubiquitous red spots of measles and requested relief from arguing his case for illness.

"Don't approach this bench, man!" exclaimed the Chief Justice. "Yes, yes, out with you till next session at Northampton." Israel Williams grasped his lace-edged handkerchief dipped in snuff to his nose. Before the next case was called, he thought he ought to remind everyone who was in charge and why, "We are here to conserve the peace and dignity of His Majesty, the King, and this honorable court. There'll be no disturbing of the peace or brawling here."

Thinking about disturbing the peace, the Chief Justice swallowed hard as he glimpsed Charles Phelps. Israel Williams wanted to smack his overly-powdered periwig off Phelps' pettifogger head! The mere presence of such an interloper as Phelps was an insult to the dignity of *my court*, thought Israel Williams. "We know what is best for us here. We know how things are done. I will crush down that recalcitrant rogue," vowed Israel Williams to himself. As the Monarch of Hampshire, Israel had been plotting to insure the next elections at Hadley didn't select Phelps for a single town office - not even hog reever. He would use his connections to remind any inhabitants to whom they owed allegiance and their votes in the next public town meeting!

The Chief Justice warned, "We are a Sessions Court of Hampshire County, Mr. Phelps, not of Boston or elsewheres. We administer the law here as we see it and as has been our history and traditions. We tolerate no vane babbling or specious argumentation. I'll not abide it!"

Among the first cases at this session were two of drunkenness. One defendant appeared disordered already, to which the chief justice asked if he was sober enough to testify and argue his innocence? He replied, "Begging your Honor's pardon, but my mind just won't work right now. I'm not drunk yet. I'm just too nervous here in Court."

"Come back after the dinner break when you're in your right mind," Justice Williams cautioned the besotted man.

Next came a pair of neighbors with the defendant complaining, "He has made and spread a shameful and distrustful story about me, in saying that I drinked a number of barrels of cider for him in two months, I do hereby certify to the public that what he has said is a downright lie!"

So that everyone could participate in the spectacle, those people who had arrived early to claim the best seats in the front passed back the words spoken to those in the rear by repeating and repeating to those behind them. For the justices, it sounded as if there was a murmuring echo throughout the courtroom. By the end of the sessions, their heads would be splitting. The justices on the bench sighed deeply, discharging all the stale used-up air that they could exhale. What was needed was a blast of cool, refreshing intelligence, not dullards like these defendants and this audience.

A slight mumble arose from the crowd. It didn't originate from an individual but from the group, as the court watchers smiled in delight. This would be no boring litany of cases of low-level disputed debts. Today there would be dramatic speechifying and bold accusations. Attorneys Phelps and Hawley would tangle on the next case. Would Justice Israel the Monarch rule in favor of his hated cousin Hawley? Or would his animosity for Phelps supersede that? What testimony would there be on the White Horse Tavern cavorting case against the young Pomeroys and Lymans, Hawley's brothers-in-law? Some among them had heard tell of the boys and maids going upstairs together after their bar-room frolicking! At midnight, no less! Such depravity!

When the Attorneys Hawley and Phelps were summoned for the matter of "Deos Rex versus Wright and Others"[37] the young tipplers from the White Horse Tavern included Noah Wright Junior, Samuel Persons, Elijah Lyman, Heman Pomeroy, Oliver Lyman, Jonathan Allen, Hezekiah Russell and Caleb Lyman, the mood in the room was extremely unpredictable.

---

[37] Hampshire Co Court of General Sessions of the Peace, Lib E/Vol 6, Pg 254-5 of 652 (page 123 as written on top left corner of bi-fold)

Joseph Hawley presented and stood unmoving droning on, "On the sixth of August last, Innkeeper Ebenezer Pomeroy acted contrary to law and against the peace of the town of Hadley. He was unfit for the business and employment of an innholder by reason that he doth not keep "Good Rule and Order in his House." In stilted legal language the lawyer intoned, "Young people of the town of Northampton – of both sexes were together – into the night. They were singing and dancing and reveling in his establishment, the White Horse Inn."

There followed explicit testimony about unpatriotic songs, mocking their social superiors, lewd behaviors and bowl after bowl of rum punch, cider and beer – the usual tavern fare.

"Do you wants me, sir, to … eeuhhum… go into the humpty-bumping I heard upstairs?" inquired Hawley's embarrassed Informer witness.

At this lewdness, Chief Justice Israel Williams slammed down his gavel on the table and bawled out, "Absolutely not! There'll be no such grossly indelicate testifying in this honorable courtroom! Are we finished with this mockery, Mr. Hawley?"

"One more thing," interrupted Defense Attorney Charley Phelps exasperatingly to the Informer. "Would you know of those who went up chambering might be lawfully married and staying the night on their way back to Northampton or which might be Hockanum neighboring people?"

Its effect worked to provoke prosecutor Joseph Hawley's righteous indignation at the law-breakers. Hawley paused to take a breath before summing up. "Singing, dancing, fiddling one whole night and into the next, past the midnight hour! You have heard the testimony and their guilt of the crime charged is clearly evident. The Grand Jury should be fully satisfied with the testimony to bring a finding of guilty, in the name of His Majesty the King and this province."

"Your Honor, I object," interjected Esquire Charles Phelps who clearly enjoyed belaboring the case and listening to his own arguments. "We must hear all the testimony. Why, if a dog gave birth to pups in an oven, we wouldn't consider them biscuits! We must know exactly the nature of the accusations."

The courtroom crowd erupted in a roar of laughter at the outlandishly dramatic Phelps (but actually understanding this analogy). "I'd be more fully satisfied to hear tell of the appetites and coquetries of those young disturbers of the peace," sneered one in the audience.

Hawley heaved a sigh of relief. His part was over.

But Attorney for the Defense, Charles Phelps was just commencing his performance. Phelps was well known as a bagpiper of a talker. He could go on for hours with highs and lows of voice and flourishes of hands. His face captured one's attention by innumerable expressions of every discrete or powerful emotion, particularly set against his flaming red hair, possibly deliberately slightly disheveled to give an aura of carelessness?! His clothes were flamboyant, making an impression he cultivated and relished. His entire body drew notice from its power and strength as a brick-layer, to his height which was well over six feet tall. In addition Charlie Phelps was a whirl of motion, in constant movement pacing the echoing wooden floor. Who could look away?!

Phelps questioned the prosecutor's Informer as to Justice Prosecutor Hawley's monetary payment to him, eating at the prosecutor's motivation, "What tidy sum will you be paying your Informer to testify against my client, Mr. Hawley?" pondered Phelps aloud.

"Who's being interrogated here, Mr. Phelps? I'm not subject to your questions!" objected Joseph Hawley.

All could feel unease and the broil of anger rising amongst the audience. Esquire Phelps was emboldened, "I recall you testifying that it was Mr. Phinehas Lyman who was the gentleman that Mr. Hawley had pointed out to you to spy on, correct? The same Phinehas Lyman married to the widow of Mr. Hawley's brother?"

"I wouldn't know about that, sir."

"Oh, you wouldn't? Have you forgotten your testimony last court session?" asked Phelps coyly. "Well, fortunately, I would know and the answer is yes." He suspended his questioning for effect. "Yet Mr. Phinehas Lyman is not here among those charged, is he?"

Phelps stopped for a long minute in the middle of the courtroom (which he understood that he now commanded) to display a series of facial expressions to the crowd. "But Mr. Phinehas Lyman's brother is here. And Innkeeper Eben and Mindwell Pomeroy's brothers is here. And Mrs. Betty Lyman's brother is here."

"Did you not wonder about that? Did you not wonder why? Did it not occur to you that perhaps Mr. Joseph Hawley might not have his own motives of jealousy or greed or vengeance or whatever, perhaps a motivation more than mere protecting the morals of our towns? Perhaps Mr. Phinehas Lyman owns and is possession of property formerly owned by Mr. Hawley's brother or Mr. Elisha Hawley's widow-relict?!" questioned Phelps.

Joseph Hawley jumped to his feet in outrage. His entire head - ear to ear - was painted a vivid scarlet color, "How dare you, Phelps?! This is scandal! This is beyond the bounds of civilized courtroom behavior! I object. I absolutely object!"

At this insinuation, the Chief Justice, too, had sprung up to attempt to intervene but a hiss emanated from the back of the room. Judge Israel Williams felt a flash of intimidation and annoyance before such a mob of angry, indignant country people. "Order! Order!" he shouted.

When some measure of orderliness was restored (after a 15-minute recess during which many ran to the Red Tavern to refresh and be amongst the first to spread the news of the courtroom sparring), Israel Williams warned the audience and attorneys, "If there is any further calamity, this court will be sequestered and closed to the public. No fisticuffs or unruly passions!"

He wanted to threaten them all more, but worried about another explosion of rage. "Phelps, you are hereby warned against incitement. Do you understand?" The chief justice swallowed consciously. He could not pronounce "Mr." in front of the name Phelps.

Charles Phelps did not answer. As big, bold, and brash as he was, he had supreme confidence in himself and would enjoy a physical fight even more than a legal one. However, he did lower his voice as he needed to finish his case in order to be paid. Now was the time to strike for his kill.

"As I was saying, these simple fresh yeomen – these common youthful men, who were never Prosecutor Hawley's objects of interest - are here today charged before this honorable court and the King's justice - simply for having a diversion from their heavy daily labor – and perhaps for Mr. Hawley's revenge?! Is it not true? Do they not deserve to quench their well-earned thirst on a hot August evening?"

Charles Phelps, eccentric, social gadfly and provocateur extraordinaire, stood front and center again. He reminded himself to deliver his lines, which he had honed and practiced for days, with coolness and precision.

Hawley scowled thinking, "There's even not a crossroad out there in Hockanum among those farms, but first thing they do is build a tavern – and fill it probably every night!"

"Mr. Gentleman Hawley, you are but a stooge of power and oppression, not good governance for the province and king. These honest plowmen are but youth of this community who engaged in a night of mirth. This Justice of the

Peace who brings this case claims he is all about law and order and public morality. But I remind the good citizens of the Grand Jury that this is a court - not our beloved church. Bring your moral case to the meetinghouse, Mr. Hawley, not the courthouse."

With supreme sarcasm, Phelps added, "You know well how to …. As our dear deceased Reverend Mr. Edwards would attest were he still amongst us!"

There was a collective gasp. Everyone present understood the reference to Hawley's agitations against the Reverend Edwards prior to his June 1750 dismissal. Some were taken aback at Phelps' boldness in the face of power.

"You sir…" Hawley paused in frustrated anger bubbling up. He was near apoplectic. "First, you are not a "sir". You are but a dressed-up mason and the son of a common laborer!"

"And you, sir, your father was but a cattle drover," replied Phelps caustically.

Hawley renewed his vitriol, "Secondly, Phelps, you seek to mollify the mob with liquor. It's a dishonor. I saw you buying drinks during the recess at the Red Tavern to buy their allegiance!"

"You bought the testimony of the Informer!"

Hawley shouted, "Shut your maw, Phelps, you blow-hard! You do but fill-in *Writs* and you do that poorly!" Joseph Hawley prepared for a renewed sudden gust from Phelps.

"Honored Justices," announced Phelps calmly and all the more dramatically in the face of Hawley's steaming anger, "You know that Mr. Pomeroy has conceded and acknowledged the sale of a mug of "sangaree" to each and every one of the defendants. Mr. Pomeroy doesn't run a mere disorderly grog shop. He makes the best punch in the County, not stingy with the rum, molasses, or sour cherries!"

Someone in the audience murmured, "Rum! Glorious rum!" At which a chuckle and general approval circulated. The Chief Justice instructed sternly, "Quiet!"

Phelps continued, "Duly acknowledged that some young persons did commence to dance a minuet within Pomeroy's tarry-house when he went to the cellar to replenish the stock. He knew not what transpired while the Informer was there guzzling of the house's generosity."

"A minuet, ha!" thought Hawley, "… more likely a wild jig."

"Gentlemen of the Grand Jury, those poor youth gathered at the White Horse after a day's hard toil – our own valiant militia men not long returned from battles against the dreaded enemy - then come home and at haying and harvesting, only relished rest, a beverage and good company. Just a short respite with a mug of cider or beer. Do these youth not merit a dismissal of this complaint?"

"Sirs," Phelps stared at the Grand Jury with the deepest most subterranean earnestness. "Fellow citizens of the Grand Jury," again he paused. "Can the Court in truth characterize these youths as "ale-guzzling rascals?!" These are your neighbors and friends! More accurately, this was but a gathering of family. Why look here: these men are brothers or husbands of Innkeeper Pomeroy and his brother-in-law Mr. Phinehas Lyman! The women therein were many wives and daughters cooking and serving up."

Finally, Charles Phelps ceased any further argument as to the evidence of the case and instead shocked the Court by calling for the Grand Jury to quash the presentment.

The short and leaden February afternoon was fading into evening. If the case wasn't completed soon, they would have to be lighting torches for a night meeting and all going home in the treacherous darkness. The Grand Jury resented that it was already half a year since the original complaint had been filed. These White Horse cases were dragging on. They should not have been difficult cases to prove. One might call legions of the best witnesses of elevated character to prove the charge of "Misrule and Disorder." It was not as if taverns weren't esteemed by most honest people to be places of "riot and reveling." Further, the town tithingman could have been reliably summoned to describe the fiddling and dancing in a chamber full of young fellows and girls, a wild rabble of both sexes, drinking flip and toddy and drams…. Conversely though, Hockanum was but a tight-knit back-water, not the bustling Hadley Commons.: Like the crowd, the Grand Jury felt soured.

Immediate silence descended as the Jury Foreman Daniel White rose stiffly from his chair and announced, "Having fully heard the parties, viz, Mr. Charles Phelps and the Prosecutor for our Sovereign Lord the King, and having fully considered the same, we do hereby determine the said presentment complaint ought to be quashed and the defendants go free without delay."

Loud shouts of "Huzzah!" came from the crowd.

At the defense table, Charles Phelps shook hands and congratulated the eight discharged fledgling defendants. Without a doubt the men would reassemble at the White Horse to celebrate tonight over a spiritous beverage.

Joseph Hawley Esquire promptly gathered his writing implements, law books and parchments into his leather knapsack. He hastened to the door as he wanted to avoid encountering Phelps at the back of the courtroom but, of course, Phelps enjoyed his ability to intimidate with his immense size. The giant tried to place himself in Hawley's path on the way out of the town-house. In their physical nearness with their blood thumping within, angry words were guaranteed to ensue and did indeed follow.

"Ever the snooping intermeddler, Mr. Hawley. Prosecuting common citizens for the same deeds you excuse in the powerful…" needled the confrontational Phelps loudly to all within hearing. "…and excuse in your own family!"

"Phelps, if you have an accusation, make it directly," retorted Hawley indignantly with a challenging glare.

"Yes, I have one, Mr. Hawley. And this is it: you have destroyed the reputations of innocents like that of a faithful, devoted man-of-God, who labored many years to bring countless souls to true salvation, our former pastor, the deceased Reverend Mr. Edwards! Why? Because he insisted on true personal conversion, not a lame substitute and because he defended a woman misused. You dared insult the character of my wife's sister, Mistress Martha Root, a full church member and upright virtuous woman whom you called "a woman of the town!" Then, with complete bald-faced hypocrisy, you charge Moses Howe of Belchertown for the same fornication which you denied by your deceased brother! And now, you accuse a humble innkeeping family who seeks only to make an honest living, slaking the thirst and hunger of travelers. And why? Perhaps because his sister, the widow of your deceased brother, has chosen to marry another man! It's nothing against Mr. Pomeroy. It's that his sister won't bear the loneliness of empty widowhood for the rest of her natural days!" answered Phelps with deliberate coldness in the face of Hawley's heat.

There was paralyzing shock! Phelps was brazen to recklessness!

Around them angry adherents of Pomeroy's tavern were shouting, "Come here you dog and fight!"

"I've got a pitchfork that I'll show you!

"I'll knock that dunce's brains out! If they's any in there?!"

"Prosecuting a poor widow and the youth. The devil himself wouldn't be that cruel!"

Joseph Hawley felt his fury surging up within. Betty Pomeroy Hawley was definitely not a 'poor widow!' Her father was one of the most powerful and wealthiest men in Northampton, far more than Joe's brother or widowed mother. Besides, it was clearly settled law in the province: widows inherited "the widow's third" *unless they remarried.* It had been so settled for years. It had been so for his own mother and all the other women in the town, in the colony, practically back to the establishment of the Massachusetts Bay Colony.

With Betty married to Phinehas Lyman, then he could support her out of *his* competency! Why should it be his brother's estate to provide for the wife of another man? Why, the wife of Captain Moses Porter was avowed to remain a widow and mourn him for her life, although she too was young. Same was true for Rachel Pomeroy, wife of Lieutenant Dan Pomeroy. And even further, why should the heirs of that Phin Lyman (even if he was kin to Mercy) inherit the property and sweat work of his dear deceased brother? The property should revert to Hawleys, not to Pomeroys and Lymans. Joe felt certain Deacon Pomeroy must be exerting pressure on his mother on behalf of his daughter. There were the morals and good order of his beloved town of Northampton as well…

Another thought clutched Joseph Hawley's imagination. Would Betty produce children by Phin Lyman?! Perhaps birth sons she had never birthed for his brother Elisha?!

The galling boom of Charlie Phelps' voice seized Hawley's attention and yanked him back from reverie to the immediate present. "Or perhaps the widow Mrs. Betty Hawley Lyman refused to relinquish her widow's property rights and dower?" accused Phelps.

Joseph Hawley felt as if his head would implode! Such lying, libeling and spreading false news to the injury of another gentleman's reputation warranted punishment (although the fine for slander was only a maximum of twenty shillings). Still, he should sue that monster Phelps for slander! This base fellow Phelps deserved nothing short of a pillory! Although much shorter and less vigorous, Hawley jumped to assault Phelps, but was held back by the justices around him, their powdered wigs flying off several heads. Ruffled lace cuffs were ripped off. Older men of the Jury gathered to separate the groups and call for calm,

"Gentlemen, gentlemen, no blows within the townhouse! To your homesteads, everyone. This is enough for one day."

In the scuffling, unnoticed by all, a pickpocket circulated collecting pocket bags of coins that many men had tied too loosely on their breeches or belts. The thefts wouldn't be noted until they all arrived home.

Joseph Hawley burned with the shame of it all. How dare Phelps reference their colonial militia before him? Phelps knew well that Hawley's beloved only sibling Elisha had died commanding his company of militia at Lake George. Phelps knew, too, that Hawley had sent a private letter of contrived apology to Martha Root years ago. What more did she want?! Yet so cheeky was this blaggard Phelps! To accuse him of prosecuting a case against Pomeroy merely because he didn't want the widow Betty to remarry Phineas Lyman wasn't true! His true concern was public morals, which were so declined these days! Phelps' words echoed in Hawley's mind as he listlessly plodded home. "What a bane on the public discourse. That Phelps is so combustible he can't get along with anyone. I can't tolerate him!"

Joseph Hawley felt hated, misunderstood, aggrieved and oppressed by deep melancholia and in an extreme depressive state.

That night the grateful Mercy Hawley secretly rejoiced that her brothers and brothers-in-law had not been severely sanctioned, although her satisfaction was tempered by the emotional devastation of her husband. In terror of his melancholy tendencies, she pleaded with Joe to think no more on the irascible Charles Phelps, but to no avail.

Phelps' accusations and his own feelings of guilt played on Joseph Hawley's mind throughout his sleepless night and many of those after. He tossed off his bedsheets and rolled from side to side without repose. Joseph shed tears that rolled down his hot face as he thought back on the deceased Jonathan Edwards and the one calamity after another that had befallen the Edwards family since they were forced out of Northampton. The excruciating death of Edwards by smallpox, Sarah Pierpont Edwards, their daughter Esther Edwards Burr and her husband Aaron Burr. Next, Hawley reflected on the Hawley family's own scourges in Elisha's mortal wounding and painful death, Elisha's widow's and Joseph's own wife's sterile wombs, his mother's venomous obsessions and his declining prominence compared to that of his cousin Israel Williams. Would he die forgotten and unmissed?

Joseph Hawley agonized if he himself had been misused by the devil and had acted unbeknownst, unintentionally harming others, as well as himself? The catcalls of the angry crowd rang through his head like a clanging bell. Where did he, Joseph Hawley, stand in God's graces?

Names are only sounds we give to someone, some place or something, yet we imbue them with so much significance.

"Anne Hawley" was the name the girl was called by her family. It was who her mother and family had told her she was. These two names – "Anne" and "Hawley" - were recognizable enough in Northampton. Neither was distinct nor particularly unusual. Yet together, the two held special power. The two names seemed to have a unique inflection within her family. It was spoken firmly, decidedly. Outside the confines of their home, it had a sharp edge and some people actually flinched when the name was pronounced. "Anne Hawley" wasn't said in the same flat and non-descript voice as every other name, if it was uttered at all. It was pointedly not spoken by some persons. Others chose to ignore the full name and just say "Anne" stopping after it, as a thought stifled curtly.

At a young age, Anne realized the explosive force of the two names together. One day, her mother walked her to the Northampton common school and turned her over to the schoolmaster. Anne did not hear all their words, but his tone informed her that he and her mother, Martha Root, had quarreled.

"Is it in *The Book*?"" challenged the master, referring to the official vital records book, *Record of Publishments in the Town of Northampton*. Of course, he knew Anne's birth had not yet been documented, due to exactly this dispute.

"No," admitted Martha, "but neither is mine. Yet I am always called by the name Martha Root."

"And since you are a Root, so I shall call her Anne Root."

"No, meaning not Root, but that what I am called is not recorded therein." She recognized that he comprehended the issue and chose to ignore her point which she continued to insist on – accepted or not.

"Well, I cannot but call her by what the clerk for the town has recorded in the *Book of the Town*. That's what the church and the town accept," the schoolmaster retorted. He was growing annoyed and losing patience with the quarrelsome spinster Root woman. "Mistress, I'll not contend with ye on the issue. I have scholars to attend to here. Take your arguments up with Mr. Hawley, the Town Clerk."

Henceforth, the schoolmaster always pronounced "Anne Root" as a resolute statement of his position, rather than being about calling on Anne as a scholar child. It set the girl at some disquiet, embarrassment and discomfort. However, she knew to grit her teeth, ignore insult and stand proudly. She had seen such scowls before. Right then, she realized "Anne Hawley" possessed strength and defiance. "Anne Root" somehow was a condescension. In the beginning, it confused her exactly as to why.

One Sabbath in meetinghouse, seeing a bare-faced glare, Anne muttered timidly to grandmother Big Martha, "I don't like those people." She averted her eyes.

"They're the Hawleys," her grandmother replied tartly. "Old lady Hawley is a witch."

"Martha!" huffed old Hezekiah, Anne's grandfather. "Not in the Lord's house!"

"Husband, neither can I lie in the Lord's house," Big Martha snorted.

Throughout her minority Anne witnessed other incidents when her name was repeatedly and vociferously challenged. "Anne Hawley" versus "Anne Root." Simple names which commanded robust reactions. Anne observed that her mother might write "Anne Hawley" on a scrap of paper for some purpose (such as a prayer request to the minister) but it was still announced as "Anne Root" by the deacons. She knew her dead twin sister was documented in *The Town Book* as "Esther, daughter of Martha Root." Anne absorbed that she was alone in this name distinction in the town.

Over time though, Anne grasped some of the forces attached to her name. She also appreciated that she would never completely grapple with all of the feelings engendered by her name to different people. She did discern that her mother would never talk much on it. Pointedly, her mother would state with forceful finality, "Your name is Anne Hawley. Enough said."

A cousin finally enlightened her in a clandestine whisper, "Why do you think you don't have a father? Elisha Hawley is your father. He denies it. No one believes that though. That's why you are Hawley."

Anne ultimately did comprehend that this was why she and her mother lived with her Root grandparents until her mother married John Miller and they went to live with him and his self-effacing "Uncle (Aaron) Miller," and the kindly and fun "Uncle (Sam) Fairfield."

As the years passed, the magic passion in her name dissipated. It wasn't until October 12, 1766 that she saw the name "Anne Hawley" inscribed on an official document. Finally, her nuptials to William Guilford were written slowly, carefully and deliberately in the *Town Book*. The sight of the script of those letters on the lifeless page almost danced and shouted! It produced a surge of emboldening confidence through her body. She fought her urge to well up with tears. No one else would understand her amplifying emotions. There is a profound mysticism and potency in the act of writing a name on paper to exist beyond one's life, forward into time forever in the permanence of an official record. Power, heft and premeditated, deliberate choice are conveyed by names. Anne Root Hawley felt the gravity of this more than anyone.

Besides the seriousness of her name, Anne felt its connectivity – those intended and those denied. Thus, the publishing of her wedding banns to William Guilford was not as simple as every other young couple's. In a sense it was a statement of pride to claim one's own identity and it was a finality, following the deaths of old Madame Hawley and her grandfather Root in January and June 1766.

At this same time Anne Hawley Guilford prepared to join the society of mothers. She was expecting a baby in January 1767. Her own mother Martha Root Miller had just lost a baby – dead as it was born. Was Martha experiencing her change of life and reaching the "woman of years" category? Anne's eyes pooled with tears at the merest whisp of thinking of her mother aging and living without her. Martha had been at the center of every day of Anne's life. How would Anne balance and fill that hole one day?

Martha's stillborn late baby loss was not unusual as "Sister Susannah," Sam Fairfield's wife, had lost her pregnancy at the same time. These losses were hardest for those women who were showing their maternal condition, as by then, their babes within had "quickened" to feel real inside to them. Many times, almost-mothers-of-lost-"embryos" could only console themselves by keeping company with sisters in spirit, the mutual singing, the solace of mindless occupying work (like sewing bees, corn husking) and prayer (together or alone). They rotated their women's gatherings to different houses. What is the nature of these souls, Martha pondered? "Life is but a vapor," she sighed as tears wetted her pillow linens.

Yet, with four other children under age 12 in their house atop "Miller Hill," the endless chores of a home and farm and Anne departing to form a new household, Martha felt she didn't have one minute's rest or time to grieve for a fetus that never was birthed a living "perfect child." The never-ending tasks of hauling water and firewood, tending the fire, preparing food, cooking, baking, making butter and cheese, food storing, cleaning, washing, sewing, mending, flax threshing, soap-making, candle-making, spinning, weaving, gardening, childcaring, comforting, mediating between childhood disputes, reading the Bible to children, teaching the older ones their A-B-C's, milking the cows, feeding the chickens, doing farmyard chores and etc., etc. occupied every minute of every day until the release of sleep. Some respite came from exchanging work with other women like Sister Susannah. So Martha could spin and weave fabric for "Sam Fairfield's Shelter" (as his tavern was called) and Susannah could share her baking or look after 6-year-old John Miller Junior and the toddler 3-year-old "li'l Martha."

For the men, life was a buzz of activity all the time as well. Days, twelve-year-old Stephen and his ten-year-old brother Cyrus worked alongside their father at the farm tasks, dragging away branches of massive trees, clearing the land, pulling out and piling up stones, chopping wood and hauling it, plowing, planting, scaring away birds, weeding, tending to the orchard, feeding animals, cleaning up from animals, assisting with the maple syrup boiling, berry picking, snow shoveling, etc. and the dangerous, dirty, smoky job of potash making. "That is what hell is," the father advised his sons as they gazed at the booming, bellowing, blazing, thundering, roaring combustions in their potash pit which burned for weeks. Never imagining having children until only a few years ago, father John Miller now cherished his. The boys were assigned jobs that kept them close-by so they could observe and emulate him but away from the most perilous tasks.

John Miller and nephew Sam Fairfield were able to enjoy the respect of their age and statuses as long-time residents of their hill-town of Williamsburg. Although John had little appetite for the company of groups (he was mostly silent and solitary), as an older man among younger ones, the crowd listened when he spoke at town meetings. He was elected with Sam to town offices.

When Anne and William's first child, William, was born in January 1767, both were relievedly grateful that they didn't have to experience the public humiliation and inconvenience of appearing before the Hampshire County Inferior Court of Common Pleas in Northampton or Springfield on a fornication charge as Anne's mother, Martha Root had. Since 1763, there hadn't been a presentment in Hampshire County, such cases having unobtrusively evaporated from the scrutiny of the civil authorities. Instead of "spinsters" and midwife's testimony about a woman's "travails," now-a-days, the justices worried about "bastardy." More men were denying patrimony and the women had no recourse but to fall on the town for "poor relief." Anne clamped her teeth together at the thought.

Even the old crimes of hunting "the king's (i.e., wild) deer" or the cutting of white pine trees on unowned land (the "pine laws") became rare prosecutions in these times, as the vast majority of cases in the Hampshire Courts were over who-owed-whom-what-debt. Morality concerns had been pushed aside by money concerns. Happily for the Guilfords now, the courts were mostly "debtors' court."

Anne reflected in her introverted moments whether she felt like a "bastard?" Could her precious baby William, for whom she had risked her own life in childbirth, have been labeled a "bastard?" Does a label help or doom someone in who they grew up to become? Anne had always suspected a buried differentiation or unique quality in/for herself. Anne posited that the controversy over her name had affected her life. One time she was shocked when an out-of-towner supposed Anne's name to be "Anne Miller" thinking it because John Miller was her father. It made her speculate how she might have been indistinguishable from every other of her cousins and friends had she been born Anne Miller.

Nonetheless a new conundrum was presented when proud new father William Guilford needed to register the birth of his infant William. Where should it be recorded (besides in their family Bible)? The "Hatfield Three Mile Addition" where they lived was not recognized as a town by the Province of the Massachusetts Bay and thus they had no official clerk or *Town Book*. Anne and William would have to journey into the town of Hatfield, where the hated Israel Williams and his clan ruled as monarchs over all matters civil and ecclesiastical. A trip into town normally presented a nice opportunity to sell one's potash, get credit and pick-up supplies at the Williams family store. (Yet, it was at infuriatingly low prices that they sold their goods and high prices to buy supplies. Better to go into Northampton.) Puritanical, archaic Israel Williams or his son, puritanical, archaic Israel Williams Junior would pronounce how to register their child's name. Perhaps Israel Williams would dictate that baby William would be decreed as "William Root" or "William Hawley" or "Bastard William" instead of "William Guilford?" It infuriated Anne and William that Israel Williams held such power over their child's naming.

Anne and William knew how deep was the hatred for old Israel Williams of Hatfield by their elders.[38] They recalled someone vowing, "Death is too mild a punishment for that most vile villain! I'd relish seeing the greatest judge of Providence rule to condemn the Hampshire Judge to hell forever!"

---

[38] Israel Williams was a Loyalist to the British during the American Revolution while he lived at Hatfield. This, and his life-long arrogance and self-service, resulted in vigilante actions (including frequent violent threats) against him and his son. A mob from Williamsburg marched to his house in July 1774. Israel and his son were kidnapped from their home, had a mock trial and "smoked" in an outhouse in February 1775.

"Even Satan will cry then," responded another old-timer. "Satan don't want him!"

"We've bled under that old dog's treacherous yoke far too long! We're not free men under his tyranny. We're just beasts of burden to labor for his enrichment! It's insufferable!"

But the Guilfords could not reckon what to expect on their own small personal name issue? Therefore, the young couple waited to record it in the *Town's Book* later. With so many pressing tasks at hand on their farm, in William's shop, with her infant son and for their incipient household, there was never time for non-pressing affairs, like the legal registrations.

Once "Williamsburg" was legally organized as a town from the old Hatfield Addition by the province in May 1771, William Guilford mentioned it to the first elected Town Clerk, John Nash. The diligent Nash had loyally commenced inscribing: "The Record of the Births and Deaths of the Inhabitants of the Town of Williamsburg" in the first volume of the new *Town Book*, back-dating to 1763 for "Rebeckah Daughter of Lt. Abijah and Prudent Hunt his wife born 7th March 1763." Nash painstakingly deliberated on how to organize the book? Should he record it in alphabetical order or chronologically? Should he leave spaces to in-fill late-comers or errors? If so, how much space? But finding advantages on all sides, he decided to simply start the first few pages, which could be corrected or altered later. Nash labored at the tedious work for five pages until he put down his quill at the page with Jonathan Warner's daughter's birth. "Wife, what the name of Mr. Warner's wife?" the clerk called to his own wife from his desk in the parlor to her kitchen.

Hearing no reply, he sighed. "Darnation," he thought. "I know it's something unusual and difficult…. Aaahhh-something? Hhhmmm, Ef-what? Maybe not Eff-? Ephah? Euodia? It's from the Hebrew but an unusual Old Testament name, dissonant to the ear these days. Oh, well, I'll add it later…"

John Nash was forced to continue writing another page as he had much to do. He proceeded on logging in names and dates until he was stopped again at William Guilford's son's birth: "Hhhmm, Guilford's wife: is her name Anne or Abigail?"

He hesitated, "Confound it, I'm not thinking properly." John Nash felt a flash of nausea and heat pass over himself. "This is bringing on a headache," he noted to himself. He pushed himself on though, "Guilford's wife. Now what is

her name? I know it's something common and normal, but what? Hannah?
Sarah? It's not Elizabeth…"

From the kitchen came his wife's calling, "Mr. Nash, it's time to go to
Hatfield! The horses are hitched up!"

Resignedly, John Nash conceded that he couldn't complete these entries
now and would have to finish them later. He put down his quill, capped the ink
bottle, wiped a handkerchief across his beaded forehead and grabbed his hat for the
trip. Spontaneously, Nash decided to have his farm-hand ride along – just in case
his queasiness didn't abate and he had to do some heavy lifting.

When asked to go, the laborer, who had barely a tooth left in his entire
head, ran up to his room in the attic, where he grabbed his best shirt and a fellow
farm-hand's wooden dentures. "Going into town," he asserted aloud. "Myself
going to town, gots to look presentable to go to town. Good ole Henry won't
mind if I just borrow his teeth for this special occasion," the hired-hand reasoned.
With a clean shirt on (washed only last week), the man fairly dashed back down the
back servants' stairs and out the door to the cart.

On the ride over the rocky hills and down into the verdant Great River
Valley, Mrs. Nash noticed a flush spread across her husband's face and neck, "Mr.
Nash, are you feeling unwell?"

By the time they arrived at the Smith relatives, John Nash had vomited
and begged leave of his hosts to lie down. A few hours of weak denials of how he
didn't feel too very bad, the dreaded red pustules were erupting everywhere on his
flaming body. The house was soon thereafter quarantined for smallpox.

Some days later, John Nash's coffin was carried to the Hatfield Hill
Cemetery at night with the town constable walking in front of the corpse warning
any inhabitants who might not yet have heard, "Hear ye warning and admonition
that ye may be in danger of infection!"

Consequently, none crossed the path of the short train of the grieving on
their way to bury the fever-cooked corpse of John Nash.

Back at the Nash house in Williamsburg, the *Town Book* lay on the desk
exactly as the clerk had left it - never to have Anne Hawley Guilford's or Eglah
Warner's names inscribed in it.

As every book finishes with "The End," so every human life finishes with death. There is struggle and that is the story. Within the story, happiness swells and ebbs away. So too, with sadness, trials and tribulations, labors and loves. The answers that make each story unique concerns the when's, how's and what's of each life. When did the events happen in each lifespan and in the larger social history? How did events unfold? And what has one done in betwixt the birth and death?

The bookends of John Miller's four-score-long life were his birth in the late Puritan era of British dominion and his death in the burgeoning republic of the United States of America. He lived through seven ferocious wars and through the growth of the population to hundreds of thousands of people in the Bay Colony; through dramatic changes of society, material life (from log cabins to mansions), technology and culture. He lived through a tumultuous decade of dazing tariffs and laws (Stamp Act, Sugar Act, Quartering Act, Currency Act, Townsend Revenue Acts, Tea Act, Boston Port Bill, Massachusetts Regulating Act, New England Restraining Act, etc.) and protests against them, American boycotts, embargoes and rebellion, which culminated in the American Revolution. Then came the wearisome struggle to establish the fledgling, struggling country, the United States of America. The new state was beset by further rebellions and tax crises to near ruination; and finally, the successful creation of a bold system of democratic self-governance with an elected "President." John Miller was born an English colonial subject but died a free, participating American citizen.

John and Martha Root Miller lived full lives of loves, losses, wars, dangers and sacrifices. Their sons, relatives and friends had bravely marched off in the late 1770s in the grand American struggle for liberty and to defend their freedoms against the encroachments of tyranny and taxation without representation. Miller sons Stephen, Cyrus and John Junior faced the "invincible" British "red coat" Army when they were but raw countrymen dressed in homespun clothes and carrying their own muskets and supplies. The cost of their liberties was high. Nephew Lieutenant Elihu Root, the only child of Martha's deceased brother Simeon had lost his health to "camp fever;" then died sunk down by his gun and knapsack into the chilly depths of the Connecticut River in April 1779. Elihu was but one of many.

There had been fearful epidemics and unremitting hunger for the civilians in those treacherous years and near-starvation for the soldiers. In far-away North

Carolina, John Miller Junior fought often wondering how he escaped dying in the (American) Continental Army as he saw fellow soldiers fall. They had had to forage and scour the landscape for anything they could find to eat or drink. In one stretch, after days without any nourishment whatsoever, they ran to a stream and gulped, till some died of having too much water too fast. Of course, one expected sleeplessness, the terror of being under gunfire, ill-treatment even by one's comrades and superiors, illness and injuries… But the conditions they endured crushed many valuable and cherished lives.

Besides their sons, innumerable other Miller and Root family members played their parts including Captain Sam Fairfield, John's nephew and amongst their dearest family, and Martha's brother-in-law Charlie Phelps. They had paid dearly for their new country with the lives, blood, health, their hard-earned work, wealth and deprivations of their men and the untold hardships upon the women and children at home. This whilst the local, wealthy Tory "river gods," aristocratic families that controlled and dominated the economy and amassed great fortunes (like Israel Williams),[39] shirked, fled and otherwise sought to protect their ill-gotten wealth and influence patronage advantages. For long years the yeoman had suffered the sting of the English lords and American river gods!

After the astonishing defeat of British General "Gentleman John" Burgoyne on October 7, 1777, there had been British "lobster back" soldiers camped in their own town and countryside, just across the Mill River at Sam Fairfield's Shelter (inn and tavern). Hessian mercenaries had marched to the west at Kinderhook, New York and south at Springfield. There was conflict, threats, dangers and fear all around.

There had been myriad other trials, large and small. Martha had sewn a coat to be donated to the "minutemen" surrounding Boston, as well as stockings, breeches and shirts. That clothing was delivered to Boston by Captain Fairfield. They had boycotted the Williams store in Hatfield, refusing to buy British goods. There had been constant revolutionary debates. How could all free men make their way in the world without local monarchs or gentry, such as the Williams kin, dictating to them and taking the fruits of their labors. Northampton had been envisioned at its founding as a settlement "knit together as one." Instead, it had

---

[39] The river god families "came to dominate local business and politics, ran the local militias and chose the ministers." For the New England Historical Society 's definition and examples: https://www.newenglandhistoricalsociety.com/river-gods-connecticut-river-valley-create-world/ Many of these "gods" and ministers owned enslaved peoples.

become as corrupt as the English aristocracy, a distillation of increasing concentration of wealth and power on top of more wealth and power by the "imperial" families of the valley.[40] The founding settlers of Northampton would have disavowed it! Such back-sliding! Such excessive pride and lack of Christian charity! Indeed, these were the reasons their forebearers had left England! In nearby Hatfield, so obsequious had the townspeople become to the Israel Williams family that the church members rose and remained standing when the Williams entered and departed the meetinghouse – as if King George and Queen Charlotte had paraded in! The congregation remained standing until "Monarch Israel" and "Lady Sarah Chester Williams" were seated. "Are these the acts of free and equal men?" grumbled John Miller in conversations. "Or is this enslavement? I was born for liberty, to live by conscience freely before God!"

Soon town meetings changed their practices and instituted Committees of Correspondence,[41] true representation by secret votes, rebelling against their old grandee "rulers," who had been perennially voted in (like the Williams), and erected a "liberty pole" on village greens across the county, province and country.

There were many stories of stirring debate, about boycotting British imported luxuries; refusals to buy calico and fabrics, sugar, tea or such; necessitating substitutions or more back-breaking labor. "Only Massachusetts can tax Massachusetts citizens, not a far-away Parliament who know us not!" the citizens asserted. How many tales might John and Martha have told of the years of anxiety, impoverishment, hunger, the threat of the loss of people's farms and land for debt and lack of cash currency, imprisonment for even shillings worth of debt, forced quartering of British soldiers into citizens' homes and market depressions when there was no money to pay taxes, while the state didn't pay its own debts!

---

[40] On Northampton's disproportionate land distribution and concomitant wealth skewing, "When the new settlers divided up land, they did it according to status and wealth. The wealthiest 10 percent along the Connecticut River got between 30 and 40 percent of the land. The poorest 50 percent got 10 to 20 percent of the land." Again see: https://www.newenglandhistoricalsociety.com/river-gods-connecticut-river-valley-create-world/
[41] "Committees of Correspondence" were the colonies' coordinating and communicating mechanisms. They were organized, first in Boston, before the Revolution, to share ideas and plan opposition. Joseph Hawley was a member of the Northampton Committee. When he resigned from the national Committee, he was replaced by John Adams (second President of the US). See: https://www.history.com/topics/american-revolution/committees-of-correspondence

John and Martha had lived through monumental history being made but surely, they would rather have lived peaceful, humble lifetimes with family and devoted to God.

By 1792, eighty-year-old John Miller was fading. The only possible conclusion was that his physical and spiritual journey through life approached its end. As a sage had observed: "The young *may* die, the old *must* die."

Third son John Junior and his wife Hannah had taken over John and Martha's farm and house high atop the magnificent hill commanding a view over an undulating arboreal ocean. Down the steep and heavily forested "Miller Hill" and across the glittering, boisterous Mill River lay the road to Hatfield where the tavern of Captain Sam Fairfield was situated. Over the next hill lay the impenetrable wooded valley of Unquamuck Brook. Up the pebbly clear Mill River to the center of the town of Williamsburg rising onto the southern hill, there were the homesteads of son Stephen and grandson Aaron. Beyond were the houses of Anne and William Guilford and their sons. Throughout the surrounding hills were the farms and workshops of son Cyrus, in-laws, nieces, nephews, cousins and their families, all were beginning to flourish. Their farms and the town now provided some rising comfort and surety, after all the years of sacrifices. Providence was smiling on John and Martha Root Miller after so many turbulent events.

Martha gratefully extolled, "I do think that there never was a man more truly kind to a woman than you have been to me, Husband."

In April 1792, as the maple sugaring weeks ceded to the gushing of spring freshets, Martha Root Miller sat watch by husband John's bed. He faded in and out of consciousness. Martha dabbed her weepy eyes and sensed the death angel invisibly approaching him. "Wait for me, Husband. Don't go yet," she pleaded softly. It was more to herself than him.

But the depleted John rolled his enfeebled body with great effort to face her. He desired his whisper to be heard, "Not to fret, Martha. God's holy will must be humbly submitted to…"

He groaned and tried to roll again, but lacked the strength. "Your children are near, even if I go far," he gasped harshly. "You'll always have a bed and a candlestick. Not to worry… no worry, my Martha."

Thus, Martha lost her help-meet, her rock, her companion of years who had built a life with her, as life inevitably dribbled away from the elderly John Miller. Each death in her life was a departure that took a piece of her heart with it, but she reminded herself how much heat and light a single candle threw.

Martha knew that one day, it would be her turn. It did not matter to her how many years in the future that would be. She prayed to die with dignity and feeling the presence of her Savior near-by. She hoped for fortitude in her second days of "travail" (the first travails being when she was brought to bed with her babies). Over the course of her life, she had served her family and friends well. She had been a founding force in organizing a church for them at Williamsburg. Although the Reverend Edwards had taught that corrupt and wicked humans could never earn their salvation by good works, she darest hope that she and John would be among "the elect." One Biblical piece of that salvation was forgiveness as the verse at 1 John 1: 9: "If we confess our sins, he is faithful and just to forgive us our sins, and to cleanse us from all unrighteousness." As the Lord had commanded and her pastor had taught, Martha Root had forgiven Elisha Hawley. Nevertheless, however much she tried, she could not forget Joseph Hawley's continued denial of Anne's paternity. She deliberated to set her house in order in all other aspects before her spiritual journey.

Thirteen years after husband John died, Mrs. Martha Miller entered her own final decline and decay. As she was 85 years of age, most of her siblings and in-laws, age-mates of early Northampton society and almost every one of her contemporaries had died years before. There were but a handful in the entire Great River Valley and hill-towns of her same advanced years left. Everyone around Martha was younger. None could imagine the world Martha Root had been born into, when their puny frontier settlements existed remote from civilization. None of the youngers really grasped how the people of olden days had acted, talked, dressed, believed or lived. None could understand how cataclysmically the times, people and the physical world had been transformed. An emptied aloneness hollowed Martha out. A subdued witness of colonial life, she waited for her call to depart.

The autumn of 1805 brought a good harvest, fast upon the golden days of summer. The summer past Martha's oldest granddaughter Hadassah had assisted her fewer times to sit out in the sun or be helped to the outhouse. The winter of 1805 to 1806 approached, harkened by frosty mornings of iced-over buckets and leaden grey skies. The lure of a sluggish cozy bed was irresistible to her dwindling energy and worn-out body. She rose from her bed less and less, even to sit upright. The early melty snows had fallen and evaporated, then fallen again with a building crescendo and descent.

Martha gazed out the window to the rolling hills tumbling out across the earth to the farthest horizon line. It occurred to her that nature abhors flatness. Even in the Connecticut Valley, where the fields were their flattest, still there must always be swells of hillocks or the slightest of dips undulating the earth. As water rarely remains motionless but must ever move, so the earth is up and down and around and on and on. Here on her husband's own land in the hills, nature played with bigness and challenged them with vast expanses of mountains, woods and creatures. The Millers overlooked limitless blue-to-purple hills after more forested hills. How many days after days had her men spent trying to tame this wilderness? Thousands upon thousands of trees her husband and sons had axed, felled and burned for their heat or to produce potash for cash money or clear the land for crops.

Martha Root Miller spent more of her days now staring out or dozing. This is a preview of the great eternal rest, thought daughter Anne, her daughters-in-law and grand-daughters (Hadassah, Electa, Betsy, "Little Martha," Sally, Polly, Phydena, Hannah, "Stephen's Martha") who gathered at her side to read aloud from her worn Bible or poems of Anne Bradstreet or Martha Brewster. It was the winter of Martha Root Miller's life and New England winters linger slow and long. As the poetess had written,

> "Surely it is winter with me
> and though frosty – yet kindly."[42]

Elderly Martha Root Miller had no desire to speed her winter to its end. Her days were as plodding as watching herself grow old had been. Being wrapped in warmth and the reassurance of care, the ebbing of time was a pleasure to savor. At times she lay between sleep and wake, unsure in which she really was at any moment. Sometimes she thought she was awake hearing and smelling - but realized she was lying down and her eyes were closed. Perhaps only her mind was awake? Or perhaps she dreamed she was awake? Maybe her mind was traveling over landscapes of her life and not awake? Some of these thoughts were about events, she knew had not been, but might have. Some were not really thoughts at all. Some were more accurately a smell wafting across her brain, a fleeting presence, a sentiment or momentary consciousness.

It occurred to Martha that one didn't even truly know what one carried within oneself. Dreams were the proof of this. Dreams seemed so real in the moment, but are composed like the substance of spiders' webs that cling lightly, sometimes without even the puff of a memory, and disappear at the touch of wakefulness.

---

[42] Martha Wadsworth Brewster "A Mother's Guiding Poems for Her Children," 1757. Available on the National Humanities Resource Center:
http://nationalhumanitiescenter.org/pds/becomingamer/ideas/text4/brewsterpoems.pdf

Martha woke again from a dream of her three lives. There was the dream of her days with Elisha Hawley, which recurred rarely, but occasionally. Her rapturous love for Elisha had given her a strange sensitivity to his nearness. She had been able to sense him nearby without even seeing or touching him. She had glowed with joy to detect his presence. When she woke from these pale but complicated dreams, there remained the suffused serenity of being in a tranquil wooded glade cradled in loving arms.

But John Miller was her devoted husband. Because of John Miller, her life had been blessed (even though she was so undeserving). She no longer wanted or thought much of Elisha Hawley. Martha was no longer even sure what Elisha Hawley's face had looked like: he was only a background. He had suffered tremendously at his end. It did occur to her that she had never heard her husband pronounce the name Elisha.

Then there were the dreams of her younger life from childhood to herself as a wife. Those dreams were now populated with so many people dead and gone on to other worlds. Her husband, her parents, baby Esther, her sisters, neighbor women, relatives, friends – even old rivals – lived in these. More dead people lived in Martha Root Miller's mind and memories than in her dwindling every day waking world. Half of her life was lived in dreams and it was the better half now. It was the world where she still had energy, zest and vitality as she was sapped of life-force in the waking world.

This was the one of the three that contained most of the lessons and meanings of her life. In this one were her unshakable religious convictions. Her Lord and Savior had brought her to this acceptance. This was her deepest well-spring that fed everything else. Most important was the cautious hope of grace and salvation.

There were also the dreams of her American life in a new country with so many transformations. Frail, ancient Mrs. Martha Root Miller, 85 years of age, a respected "relict" of the founder of Williamsburg village, was harbored in a safe, enveloping circle in her last days in their farm-house. She dreamed of being surrounded by hundreds of children in a place unknown, but familiar and soothing.

As her days numbered on, the harsh realities of daily life barged in to her consciousness less and less. Fewer visitors trudged up the hill. Voices and faces around her were fewer and fewer. Martha wanted to submit herself completely to her Lord's fate for her with complete submission.

Finally, her world shrank down to encircle her bed. In a deep delirium she dimly heard the muted voices of her loved ones. It seemed they were crying but everything was veiled in a cloaking fog. It was confusing, but not frightening. Why did people keep saying goodbye, she puzzled?

Martha knew that one of her future dreams would be to turn from the past into a blinding bright light of a next world.

The End

<u>Epilogue</u>

Now for the last and later actions.

Mr. John and Mrs. Martha Root Miller finished the days of their lives as respected and valued citizens of Williamsburg, Hampshire County, Massachusetts. They had a large network of three sons, a daughter, many grandchildren and a vast coterie of relatives and friends surrounding them.

Martha's daughter Anne Hawley Guilford and her husband William Guilford lived out their lives productively in Williamsburg. Anne died at age 71 in 1818; William at 70 in 1814. Both in Williamsburg. As noted, they raised sons, William[43] (Chapter 29), John, and Ebenezer. Anne and William lost at least two unnamed, unbaptized infants.[44] Sons John and Ebenezer Guilford proceeded to produce 16 sons and daughters who lived to adulthood. Eventually Anne and William's great-great-grandchildren numbered in the hundreds. Some of this multitude of descendants stayed in or near Williamsburg (Massachusetts) but many others spread across the United States to California, Connecticut, Indiana, Iowa, Michigan, New York, Washington and perhaps other states.

John and Martha's eldest son Stephen Miller farmed in Williamsburg but relocated with his family and his sister Martha Miller Wright's family to the wilds of Middlebury, (far western) New York at the start of the War of 1812 (when Stephen was 60!). The author believes Stephen was forced by liquidity insolvency to sell his farm about 1810 to "the miser Oliver Smith."[45] Stephen died in New York in 1834 at age 78 with 12 living sons and daughters and maybe 80 grandchildren!

Captain Samuel Fairfield remained a tavern keeper and farmer in Williamsburg, as did John and Martha Miller's younger sons. Sam died in Williamsburg at 72 with six surviving daughters and sons. He is noted well in town histories.

---

[43] William's death recording in the *Williamsburg Town Clerk's Book*, Volume 1, page 9 (or page 26 of 1155) online at: https://www.ancestry.com/imageviewer/collections/2495/images/40143_271049__0001-00025?pId=4530066 is illegible due to the page edges breaking off. Email communication from Eric W. Weber, President, Williamsburg Historical Society, to Mary Lane February 14, 2021. It is likely that William died quite young and thereby left no other church or civil record.

[44] Email communication from Eric W. Weber February 14, 2021.

[45] Oliver Smith's fortune established Smith College in Northampton, Stephen's cousin's (Charles P. Phelps') son, Theophilius Phelps, was the lynch pin of the Smith Charities controversy; see: https://en.wikipedia.org/wiki/Elector_Under_Will_of_Oliver_Smith

Brick mason and self-made attorney Charles Phelps, Martha Root Miller's brother-in-law and husband to Martha's sister Dorothy Root, as well as legal representative in the negotiations with the Hawleys (Chapter 13), died in Marlboro, Vermont in 1789 aged 71. Later records and letters indicate that Charles was "a warm supporter" and agreed with the conversion experience principles articulated by the Reverend Edwards.[46] Throughout his life, Charles Phelps was frequently at odds with the established order and general consensus and had an unusual career of long activism, including against the foundation of the "pretended state of Vermont!"[47] Like Ephraim Williams Junior, Charles Phelps Senior tried to establish a college in his area with the endowment of his personal library.[48] Charles and Dolly, left six adult offspring and multiple grandchildren, at least two sons having been educated at Harvard College.[49]

Timothy and Simeon Root and Oliver Warner, the three major attributed culprits in the "Bad Boys/Bad Books" affair of spring 1744 (Chapter 3), confessed their sins before the church, as scraps of their confessions were discovered in the papers of the Reverend Jonathan Edwards.[50] Martha's brother Simeon married and fathered one son. Simeon died in 1752, perhaps in an epidemic.[51] Oliver Warner, a hatmaker and land speculator, became propertied, esteemed, served on the 1754 Grand Jury (Chapter 20) and was elected as Selectman in Hadley multiple times.[52] Although married, he had no children.[53]

The Reverend Mr. Jonathan Edwards was dismissed from his position as minister of the First Church of Northampton on June 22, 1750 by a vote of 200

---

[46] Like his brother-in-law Hezekiah Root Junior, Charles Phelps lived outside of Northampton during the 1750 Edwards dismissal. Root Junior is mentioned favorably in the Diary of another Edwards' supporter, Reverend Edward Billings of Cold Spring. (Belchertown). Also see Joseph Hawley letter to Elisha Hawley of August 11, 1749; Dow, "Bucking the Tide," in Bibliography.

[47] Peter Dow has labeled Phelps' career as "complex and, indeed, perplexing." Dow, "Bucking," Pg. 12 of 209. In the Bibliography following this section, see publications by Dow and Graffagnino. The Charles Phelps Papers at the University of Vermont contain papers from ~60 legal actions involving Charles Phelps Senior: https://scfindingaids.uvm.edu/repositories/2/resources/1268

[48] For brief biographies of Charles and sons Charles and Timothy, see: https://vermonthistory.org/documents/findaid/PhelpsCharles.pdf or footnote below.

[49] Phelps, *The Phelps*, Pg 294-5.

[50] Thomas Johnson, "Young Folks Bible," pg 51 in Bibliography. Formerly at the Andover Newton Theological Seminary, now at Yale University's Beinecke Center: https://archives.yale.edu/repositories/11/resources/11376

[51] Root, *Root genealogical*, Pg 117.

[52] Judd, *History of Hadley*, Pg 450.

[53] Warner, Lucien C; Nichols, Josephine Genung. *The descendants of Andrew Warner*. Tuttle, Morehouse & Taylor Co. (New Haven, 1919), Pg 92.

male "full members" to 23.[54] The Edwards family moved to the Indian Mission at Stockbridge until 1758 when Edwards accepted the presidency of the College of New Jersey, now Princeton University. He and daughter Esther Edwards Burr died as a result of a failed smallpox inoculation in March and April 1758. [55] His wife died six months later. Other tragedies befell the family thereafter, although many Edwards descendants were very accomplished and noteworthy.

General William Johnson was awarded £5,000 and made a baronet by King George II following his "victory" at the day-long Battle of Lake George on September 8, 1755 (Chapter 25).[56] One frank biographer quipped that, "Never was such an insignificant encounter so generously rewarded."[57] Throughout the French and Indian War, Sir William continued as a British military commander in New York state. "Handsome Billy" Johnson died of a stroke in July 1774 at age 59 at his home, Johnson Hall in Johnstown, New York. At the time, he was one of the three largest land owners in British America due to land gifts from Native Americans. William Johnson had two "consorts," including the Mohawk leader Molly Brant.[58] Johnson left 14 acknowledged children.[59] William's son, Sir John Johnson, led Loyalist forces in the American Revolution and fled to Canada.[60]

The Battle of Lake George (Chapter 25) has been termed "the darkest day in Mohawk history" because of the bloody Mohawk-on-Mohawk fighting. Mohawk casualties in the battle have been estimated at 20-30%.[61] Immediately after the battle the Mohawks withdrew to mourn their dead, quietly leaving their white allies to return to their home villages.[62] The matriarchal Iroquois women

---

[54] Various sources. Trumbull, *History of Northampton*, Vol 2, Pg 223 gives the number as 200 to 20. See Bibliography following for full citation.

[55] See https://en.wikipedia.org/wiki/Jonathan_Edwards_%28theologian%29

[56] See Hamilton, O'Toole and Shannon in my Bibliography or for an online brief biography: https://en.wikipedia.org/wiki/Sir_William_Johnson,_1st_Baronet

[57] Julian Gwyn in the *Dictionary of Canadian Biography*, IV (1979). See: https://en.wikipedia.org/wiki/Sir_William_Johnson,_1st_Baronet

[58] On Molly Brant: https://en.wikipedia.org/wiki/Molly_Brant

[59] See: https://en.wikipedia.org/wiki/Sir_William_Johnson,_1st_Baronet

[60] https://www.battlefields.org/learn/biographies/sir-john-johnson

[61] Mohawk Nation member Darren Bonaparte gives a total of 60 lost of 300 total involved in the Scout, but most accounts number the Mohawk scouts under Tiyanoga at 200. Bonaparte, "The Darkest Day in Mohawk History," on *Wampum Chronicles*, online at: http://www.wampumchronicles.com/darkestday.html

[62] Historian Barbara Sivertsen has written, "In all, 32 of Johnson's Indian allies were killed or missing and 12 were wounded….to the Mohawks it was a disaster. Not only had they lost their greatest speaker and another influential sachem, but in all twelve of their principal men had fallen in the battle. They had also involved themselves in war with their Caughnawaga relatives, a war which would become increasingly bloody in the years to come." Sivertsen, *Turtles, Wolves* Pgs 175, 177.

decided that the Confederacy would no longer be drawn into internecine warfare on behalf of the French or British.[63]

Ephraim Williams Junior died in the "Bloody Morning Scout," the first of the three skirmishes in the Battle of Lake George (Chapter 25). His then-recently-written Last Will and Testament (Chapter 23) donated his sizeable estate to the establishment of a "free school" in the town of West Hoosac, not far from Fort Massachusetts (Chapter 16). The Will stipulated as a condition that the town be renamed "Williamstown." Instead of complying with the specifications of Ephraim's Will, Israel Williams (Chapter 29), other Williams family members and friends (including Joseph Hawley) tried to establish "Queens College" in Hatfield (which was successfully opposed by Harvard College).[64] Finally, "Williams College" was chartered by the state of Massachusetts in 1795 in Williamstown.[65] Bequeathed from the estate of a slave owner, Williams College's first graduates were required to speak on female education and the barbarity of the slave trade in 1795![66] Williams College actually spurred the development of Amherst College through one of its several student rebellions (and then, along with Harvard, opposed that institution)! The tiny-but-eminent college's mascot is a colonial called "Eph" and a purple cow!

No other records of confessions are known to exist for the First Church of Northampton under the Reverend Mr. Edwards, so we do not know that Martha Root confessed to her fornication in church (Chapter 9, 11), although I presume this from her confession at the Inferior Court of Common Pleas, her personal and family history of religious devotion and the later Edwards' employment of Martha's sister Hannah Root. Conversely, Elisha Hawley appealed his excommunication (Chapter 15) and won. The Hawley brothers' letters express continued opposition to the Reverend Mr. Jonathan Edwards until 1754. This, plus, the lack of mention in Northampton historiographies and the lack of documented reference anywhere else leads me to presume that Elisha did *not* confess to fornication with Martha in church or the court(s).

Elisha Hawley and Elizabeth Pomeroy had no descendants (Chapter 18). Elizabeth ("Betty") Pomeroy Hawley was widowed on September 24, 1755 when her husband Elisha died. She remarried 'after some years of widowed life'[67] to

---

[63] Parmenter, Jon. "After the Mourning Wars, Pgs. 39-76.
[64] Brown. *Colonial Radical.* Pg 91-2.
[65] See Wikipedia: https://en.wikipedia.org/wiki/Williams_College
[66] For more on its fascinating history and customs, see the Williams College website https://williams68.org/memorabilia/history/
[67] No marriage record found online but obviously after the death of Phinehas' first wife Joanna Eastman on February 5, 1759. Clark, *Historical Catalogue*, Pg 63.

Phinehas Lyman, a second cousin of Mercy Lyman (Joseph Hawley's wife) and Mindwell Lyman (Betty's brother Eben Pomeroy's wife, see Chapter 28) who lived across the river at Hadley. Elizabeth and Phinehas had no children, but as Phin's children by his first marriage were about aged 3 to 9 years when they married, the re-married couple would have raised his three sons. Tragically, two of Phin's sons committed suicide by hanging themselves at ages 29 and 36 (before the deaths of Phin and Betty).[68] Six months after the death of Joseph Hawley, Phinehas and Betty sold Elisha Hawley's real estate.[69] Phinehas died unexpected of illness in Orange, Vermont in April 1792. His surviving son Dr. Timothy Lyman died only four months later. Betty died less than nine months after Phinehas at age 64 in Hadley, where she is buried. Betty Pomeroy Hawley Lyman had inscribed on her tombstone that she was the "consort" of Phinehas, without mention of her first husband Elisha Hawley. Tellingly, Betty Lyman also had chiseled in: "The memory of the just is blest."

Rebekah and son Joseph Hawley (the Third) lived their lives out in the homestead on Pudding Lane[70] in Northampton. Rebekah Hawley died at age 81. While she certainly was literate, Rebekah apparently left no documents or letters, besides those recorded in Hampshire County deeds or records and one receipt at Historic Northampton. Did she *never* write to her son Elisha during the periods when he was stationed at Fort Massachusetts or otherwise out of Northampton, so that not a single letter or note survives? She frequently sent Elisha packets of salve and butter. Considering the force of her personality and the fact that she ran her husband's and own businesses, I doubt that she never wrote a letter. Northampton historian and editor Sylvester Judd traveled the Connecticut River valley interviewing many persons to collect oral histories in the early to mid-1800s. Discretely, he regales us only with the aside that 'many infamous stories were told about the Mother Hawley' but he (maddingly) doesn't divulge them.[71]

The Hampshire Gazette of June 15, 1852 states in its retrospective biographical article "The Mother of Maj. Hawley" that "Her hand-writing was decent, and some of her letters were extant a few years since."[72] There is no note of where these letters were, what happened to them or whether the author saw them. The same article mentions that "There was not a more ardent, bold and patriotic man engaged in the cause of the revolution [than Joseph Hawley]; yet at

---

[68] Boltwood, *Genealogies of Hadley*, Pg 92.
[69] From an untitled document dated September 2, 1788 in the Hawley file in collection of Historic Northampton.
[70] Now called Hawley Street.
[71] Unnamed author [probably Sylvester Judd], "The Mother Hawley", *Hampshire Gazette*, June 15, 1832, unpaginated.
[72] Unattributed article, *Hampshire Gazette*, June 15, 1852 (Northampton).

times, dejection of spirits overwhelmed him, and he gave up all for lost, and burnt his letters and other revolutionary papers."[73]

Joseph and Mercy had no "issue of their body" (children/descendants) to carry on their genetic heritage and name; thus, neither did Rebekah (apart from Elisha's alleged but never acknowledged daughter Anne Root Hawley Guilford, who as aforenoted has hundreds of descendants) (Chapter 19). Joseph and Mercy "adopted" Samuel and Eunice Lyman Clarke's oldest son, Joseph Hawley Clarke, although most of their property was gifted to the town of Northampton.[74]

Mercy Lyman Hawley, like Rebekah and Elizabeth, left no trace of her existence beyond her gravestone. She and Joseph also had no children, but "adopted" Mercy's sister Eunice's son, Joseph Hawley Clarke.[75] One wonders what sacrifices poor, patient and beleaguered Mercy made to maintain Joseph the Third's sanity? Mercy died in Northampton at age 77, almost 20 years after her husband. Her tombstone is a demure shadow set off behind the rest of the Hawleys.

Attorney, Joseph Hawley the Third (1723-1788) was "melancholic" or so severely depressed as to withdraw almost completely from normal life. He is reported to have spent hours sitting, smoking and staring. According to Northampton historian James Russell Trumbull, Joseph Hawley "burned papers" during one of his melancholic attacks.[76] On October 2, 1764 Joseph Hawley obscurely referenced some kind of breakdown in a memorandum in his *Johnson Dictionary* margin that he had had become "Incapacitated to Judge in Moral or religious matters, lost to all the business of my profession."[77]

Joseph Hawley served on the "Committee of Correspondence" for Northampton prior to the American Revolution, although he relinquished his position to John Adams due to his debilitating depression.[78] Hawley did lead the

---

[73] Authorship unattributed but possibly Sylvester Judd? IBID. Also Trumbull, *History*.
[74] Believed not to have been a "legal" adoption. After Joseph Hawley's death, the bequest to the town was attacked by peripheral Hawley relatives - but not Anne Hawley Guilford. For the actual litigation, see Tyng, "Hawley et Al." *Reports of Cases*, Pages 9-43 Bibliography.
[75] Named "Joseph Clarke" at his birth on October 8, 1749 but called "Joseph Hawley Clarke" on his tombstone. The Massachusetts Adoption of Children Act in 1851 was the first in the United States but too late for this situation.
[76] See Trumbull's *History*, Vol II, Pg 542-3 in Bibliography or Brown's *Joseph Hawley*, Pg 94.
[77] Trumbull. *History of Northampton.* Vol II, Pg 542.
[78] Committees of Correspondence were clandestine organizing and communication networks proposed by Samuel Adams in the decade before the American Revolution. The seminal work on Joseph Hawley is E. Francis Brown's *Joseph Hawley* in Bibliography. Or see the "Biographical/historical Information" tab of "Overview" of the Joseph Hawley Papers,

Northampton examination of the Massachusetts Constitution of 1780 as Moderator.[79] He argued for the application of rights to *all* men; thereby further securing the Bay State's opposition to slavery.[80] One issue that did rouse Joe was his fierce opposition to the 1780 Massachusetts Constitution's religious oath of allegiance.[81] Hawley particularly attempted to disestablish the Congregational Church from state government.[82] That conviction likely grew from his life experiences, such as those that informed my stories herein. We who treasure the separation of church and state owe him a debt of gratitude for this.

As Joseph left behind a collection of more than 100 sermon notes, letters, and documents, amongst which there is not a single scrap by Rebekah and only three letters by Elisha.[83] It is likely that it was Rebekah and/or Elisha's correspondences (and perhaps some incriminating or suspect of Joseph's own?) that might have been burned.

It seems inexplicable that the Hawley Papers contain copies of his brother Elisha's brief and inconsequential correspondence from Colonel Ephraim Williams Senior in 1749, from Eph Williams Junior, William Williams, John Williams, but that there is *only one letter written from Elisha* to Joseph during the same year, the year in which Joseph appealed Elisha's excommunication.

Manuscript and Archive Division at the New York Public Library. Online: http://archives.nypl.org/mss/1360#bioghist

[79] Morison, Samuel Eliot. "Joseph Hawley's criticism [sic] of the constitution [sic] of Massachusetts," in Mary Catherine Clune. *Smith College Studies in History.* Vol III, No 1, October 1917. Pg 11. Online: https://archive.org/details/josephhawleyscri00hawlrich/page/10/mode/2up

[80] IBID. Pg 12.

[81] IBID. Pg 41-43.

[82] IBID. Pg 42, footnote 21.

[83] The family's *Account Book* is at the Hampshire Room for Local History of the Forbes Library in Northampton, Massachusetts. The Joseph Hawley Papers at the New York Public Library contains those of the Joseph Hawley families, including his father's notes on sermons (in Latin) and a few documents and some Elisha's letters, a couple of his documents and his "Journal of the Crown Point Expedition." The Joseph Hawley Papers were purchased by George Bancroft, the "father of American history," who "approached his subject philosophically, molding it to fit his preconceived thesis that the American political and social system represented the highest point yet reached in humanity's quest for the perfect state. He placed great emphasis on the use of original sources, building a vast collection of documents and hiring copyists to translate materials from European archives." Per Encyclopedia Britannica at: https://www.britannica.com/biography/George-Bancroft-American-historian Bancroft donated the collection to the New York Public Library.

Joseph Hawley's specific references in his own letters to letters of Elisha makes clear that Joseph received and possessed some by Elisha that are not now in his Papers or anywhere else to be found. An example of such was Joseph's March 11, 1750 letter that says: "You desire in your last (viz. ye 16th of last month) to be informed of our ministerial concerns…"[84] Of course, there is no letter of February 16th in the current Hawley Papers. In fact, there is only *one* letter of Elisha's from 1747-1750! The pertinent question is whether this is simple loss/misplacement (certainly conceivable after 272 years) - or was it deliberate destruction? Furthermore, this lack of Elisha correspondence is more notable because of Joseph's frequent urgings of Elisha to write more, contained in multiples of Joseph's letters on important topics: "P.S. If you don't design to be down [to Northampton from Fort Massachusetts] soon you will write to me how you would have y^r land disposed of & also what disposition you want made of y^r oats-."[85]

What was not burned were copies of three noteworthy items:

1. The May 16, 1748 financial agreement signed by Enoch Lyman, Charles Phelps and Martha Root;
2. Two drafts of a letter of apology to Martha Root (August 1750); and
3. Two pieces of correspondence regarding/resembling an apology to Jonathan Edwards.

It is striking that neither Joseph nor anyone else from the Hawley family signed the May 16th, 1748 financial agreement for £155. Should we attribute this to Joseph's (since he was managing "your affair" in Elisha's absence at Fort Massachusetts) lawyerly reticence to admit to anything? Would such hesitancy have been due to worry about self-incrimination of his client/brother? Or perhaps Joseph himself (for perjury)? Or might Joseph have doubted Elisha's innocence? Could it be all of these? My own conclusion is that Joseph Hawley strongly suspected his brother's guilt but more strongly schemed to escape admitting his guilt: "I would Do, what I knew ~~God~~ was right in Conscience and before God, ~~by~~ if there was anything [scrap of paper pasted here obscuring word] knew of, that was particularly binding that, Nobody else knew of."[86]

---

[84] Hawley Papers, 1750-1753, image 1. https://digitalcollections.nypl.org/items/bef86d60-e7ab-0132-4ea6-58d385a7bbd0#/?uuid=bef86d60-e7ab-0132-4ea6-58d385a7bbd0

[85] IBID.

[86] Strike-thru's in original. Joseph Hawley to Elisha Hawley, Dec 23, 1748 in Joseph Hawley Papers. Viewable online at: https://digitalcollections.nypl.org/items/121f7170-e7a7-0132-95a3-58d385a7b928#/?uuid=1714b840-e7a7-0132-3c2f-58d385a7b928&rotate=0

Throughout the rest of their correspondence, Joseph would be concerned for the "spiritual

These three items reveal that Joseph Hawley wanted those succeeding him to know of his repentance and resolution of these issues (by his reckoning). Similarly with his published apology in the *Boston Evening-Post*, characterized as an "ingenuous confession" by contemporaneous Massachusetts Governor and historian Thomas Hutchinson. During Edwards' lifetime, Joseph admitted privately and quietly; however, Hawley's denunciations and false accusations against Jonathan Edwards and Martha Root were loud and public. Joseph Hawley had practically publicly called Martha Root a prostitute. Similarly, and although not the only responsible party, Hawley publicly agitated against Edwards thereby contributing to the family's loss the head of household's position and financial support. By purging his documents, Joseph Hawley altered this small corner of history and our understanding of it. We can only be cognizant of it and try to analyze and compensate for it.

Completely captivating to me is that we could conceivably now resolve the 274-year-old paternity question for Martha Root's twins, Anne and Esther! Was Elisha Hawley their father or not? The most absolutely incontrovertible proof would be the DNA results of Anne Hawley Guilford's descendants compared to those of another known Hawley family line (since Elisha, Joe, and Rebekah left no descendants). It would of necessity be a collateral family line, which could easily and indisputably include, exclude, or label as inconclusive Elisha Hawley's alleged paternity. The Hawley Society has compared some DNA results to trace their family lineage back in England. Therefore, some results are certainly publicly available.

Perhaps DNA evidence already exists on one of the popular genealogical websites to settle this old controversy conclusively? Unfortunately, this evidence is not my own genetic material as I am a descendant of Martha Root's through Stephen Miller (Anne's half-brother), so I cannot access it currently. However, because my fascination with these acts and my sense of justice/truth, I will continue searching for an answer. I hope to learn of it someday as Sally Hemings' descendants have with Thomas Jefferson!

---

health of [Elisha's] soul" (a worry he never expressed in letters to his wife Mercy) and offered many recommendations on religion and practice.

Bibliography

Abbatt, William. "Old Great Barrington," *The Magazine of History with Notes and Queries.* Volume XXIII (Poughkeepsie, and Tarrytown, NY, July -December 1916). Pages 173-184.

Account Book #0-015. Manuscripts, Small Collection, Box 1 (donated by Professor Winthrop H. Root, Williams College Library # 120038). Sawyer Library, Williams College, Williamston, Massachusetts.

Adams, Charles Francis. *Some phases of Sexual Morality and Church Discipline in Colonial New England.* John Wilson and son University Press (Cambridge, 1891)

Allen, Ethan. "Ethan Allen's Description of his Capture by Peter Johnson," Appendix G in Lois M. Huey and Bonnie Pulis. *Molly Brant: A Legacy of her Own.* Old Fort Niagara Publications. (Youngstown, NY, 1997).

Allen, Willard S. *Genealogy of Samuel Allen and Some of his Descendants.* Privately Printed (Boston, 1876).

Allosso, Dan. *An Infidel Body-Snatcher and the Fruits of His Philosophy: The Life of Dr. Charles Knowlton.* Stay Outside the Box Publishing (2013).

American Antiquarian Society (1877); "January 27th, 1778 Letter from John Glover to General George Washington", in Proceedings of the American Antiquarian Society Volumes 70-75, pg. 58, Charles Hamilton: Worcester, Massachusetts on: http://greensleeves.typepad.com/berkshires/2011/05/documenting-the-route-of-prisoners-from-burgoynes-army-between-saratoga-and-boston-in-1777.html

American Genealogical Biographical Index. Godfrey Memorial Library, comp.. *American Genealogical-Biographical Index (AGBI)* [database on-line]. Provo, UT, USA: Ancestry.com Operations Inc, 1999. Original data: Godfrey Memorial Library. *American Genealogical-Biographical Index.* Middletown, CT, USA: Godfrey Memorial Library. Vol 149, page 311 "General Column of the "Boston Transcript".

Ancestry.com. *Massachusetts, Town and Vital Records, 1620-1988* [database on-line]. Provo, UT, USA: Ancestry.com Operations, Inc., 2011. Original data: Town and City Clerks of Massachusetts. *Massachusetts Vital and Town Records.* Provo, UT: Holbrook Research Institute (Jay and Delene Holbrook).

Anderson, Fred. *A People's Army: Massachusetts Soldiers and Society in the Seven Years' War.* W. W. Norton & company (New York, 1996).

Anthropology Lover. "Native American Face Paint; Customs, Colors, Designs" on-line: https://anthropologylover.wordpress.com/2013/02/09/native-american-face-paint-customs-colors-designs/

Argentine Productions. "George Washington Remembers" (video, 2005) from the book by Fred Anderson, *George Washington Remembers: Reflections on the French and Indian War.* Rowman & Littlefield Publishers (2004).

Author unattributed by Ashfield Historical Society. "The Belding Legacy," in the *Ashfield Historical Society Newsletter.* June 2019, Pages 4-6.

Author unknown. *Hampshire Gazette & Northampton Courier* (newspaper), "Prof Sears on the Life of Major Hawley," unpaged, November 19, 1914. Later published by Lorenzo Sears in *The Magazine of History*, May 1915. Volume XX, No 5, unpaginated. Article entitled: "Joseph Hawley The Counsellor of Boston Patriots."

Author unknown. "An Inventory of the late Colº. Ephraim Williams cloath[e]s & put on board the Sloop/Special Walter Griswold Master", dated December 2, 1755 at Albany. Thomas Williams Papers, New York Historical Society.

Author unknown. *Memoires de la Societe Historique de Montreal, Campagne de 1755*. TYP. C. A. Marchand (Montréal, 1900). « Détail de la Marche de M. le Baron de Dieskau campé sous le Fort St Frederic avec 3000 hommes et de l'Attaque du camp des Anglois au nombres de 3000 pres du Lac St Sacrement par 1500 François (Ecrit de la main de M. de Montreuil). » In French original: "Le 31 Aout, M. le Baron de Dieskau fut informé que 4000 anglois étaient campés sous le fort Lydius construit de cette année près de la rivière d'Orange, à sept lieues du lac St. Sacrement. » [Translated by Mary Lane]

Baller, Bill. "Kinship and Culture in the Mobilization of Colonial Massachusetts." *The Historian* 57, no. 2 (1995): 291-302. http://www.jstor.org/stable/24448978

Barber, John Warner. "Historical Sketch of Bernardston, MA" in *Historical Collections Relating to the History and Antiquities of Every town in Massachusetts with Geographical Descriptions*. Warren Lazell Publisher (Worcester, MA, 1848).

Barshinger, David. *Jonathan Edwards and the Psalms, A Redemptive-Historical Vision of Scripture*. Oxford University Press (London, 2014).

Beall, Ortho T. "Aristotle's Master Piece in America: A Landmark in the Folklore of Medicine," in The *William and Mary Quarterly*. Vol. 20, No. 2 (Apr., 1963). Pp. 207-222. Online at: http://www.jstor.org/stable/1919297

Benedict, William A. (Rev.) and Rev. Hiram A. Tracy. *History of the town of Sutton, Massachusetts, from 1704 to 1876, Grafton til 1735…* Published for the Town, Sanford & Company (Worcester, MA, 1878).

Bielinski, Stefan. "A Middling Sort: Artisans and Tradesmen in Colonial Albany." *New York History* 73, no. 3 (1992): 261-90. http://www.jstor.org/stable/23181879

Billing, Edward. Diary of the Rev. Edward Billing of Cold Spring (Belchertown, Mass.) and Greenfield, Mass., 1743-1756. 1 vol. manuscript 14 cm Interleaved in Nathaniel Ames' *An Astronomical Diary or an Almanac…1743-1752; 1754-1756 and Shepherd's Poor Job, 1753*. Historic Deerfield collections.

Black, Ralmon Jon. "3 Hatfield Street: Built by Captain Samuel Fairfield" for Williamsburg Historical Commission & Society. 2002.

Black, Ralmon Jon. Unpublished "Ancient Road Records of Hatfield", notes copied from the *Judd Manuscripts*, Forbes Library, Northampton, Massachusetts.

Black, Ralmon Jon. "Williamsburg 1st Grants" (A work in progress). Unpublished work from author to Mary Lane via email, 9/16/2016.

Black, Ralmon Jon. "Colonial Asheries: Potash, an 18th Century Industry: Inroads for Change in the Land: the Exploitation of America's Hardwood Forests: Local History Unrecorded and Forgotten." Williamsburg Historical Society (self-published, 2008).

Black, Ralmon Jon. Electronic mail to Mary Lane. March 29, 2017; April 1, 2017. Personal conversations with Mary Lane, various dates.

Black, Ralmon Jon and Eric W. Weber. Personal conservations with Mary Lane and explorations of Miller land sites in Williamsburg, Massachusetts.

Blake, Henry T. *The Battle of Lake George (September 8, 1755) and the Men who Won It.* Publisher unknown (New York?), undated. https://archive.org/details/battlelakegeorge00blakrich

Bloch, Ruth H. "Changing Conceptions of Sexuality and Romance in Eighteenth-Century America," *The William and Mary Quarterly*, Vol. 60, No. 1, Sexuality in Early America (Jan., 2003), pp. 13-42. Omohundro Institute of Early American History and Culture. https://www.jstor.org/stable/3491494

Blodget, Samuel and Henry Newton Stevens. *The Battle Near Lake George In 1755: a Prospective Plan With an Explanation Thereof by Samuel Blodget, Occasionally At the Camp When the Battle Was Fought.* London: H. Stevens, son & Stiles, 1911.

Blodget, Samuel. *A Prospective-Plan of the Battle near Lake George on the Eighth Day of September, 1755.* Facsimile reprinting Montgomery County Historical Society (Fort Johnson, NY, undated).

Boltwood, Lucius M. *Genealogies of Hadley Families, Embracing the Early Settlers of the towns of Hatfield, South Hadley, Amherst, and Granby.* Metcalf & Sons (Northampton, MA, 1862).

Bonaparte, Darren. "The Darkest Day in Mohawk History" and "Old Mohawk Words" on website: http://www.wampumchronicles.com/

Borin, Matthew. "History of Ephs parallels that of Amherst Lord Jeffs," in *The Williams Record*, February 10, 2016.

Bouton, Nathaniel. *Provincial Papers, Documents, and Records relating to the Province of New Hampshire (From 1749-1763).* James M. Carter State Printer (Manchester, NH, 1872). Vol. VI. https://openlibrary.org/books/OL5708048M/ Provincial_papers._Documents_and_records_relating_to_the_province_of_New-Hampshire

Bouton, Nathaniel. *Provincial papers. Documents and records relating to the province of New-Hampshire, from the earliest period of its settlement: 1623-[1776].* John B. Clarke State Printer [for New Hampshire] (Manchester, NH, 1869).

Bridgman, Burt Nichols and Joseph Clark Bridgman. *Genealogy of the Bridgman Family Descendants of James Bridgman 1636-1894.* Clark W. Bryan Printers (Springfield, Mass, 1894).

Bridgman, Thomas. *Inscriptions on the grave stones in the grave yards of Northampton, and of other towns in the valley of the Connecticut, as Springfield, Amherst, Hadley, Hatfield, Deerfield, &c.* Hopkins, Bridgman, & Co. (Northampton, Mass, 1850).

Brook, J. "The Life of Hawley." Amherst College, History Department Thesis (1992).

Brooks, Robert R.R. editor, et al., with Henry N. Flynt. *Williamstown: The First 250 Years, 1753-2003.* Williamstown House of Local History (2005).

Brown, David C. "The Keys of the Kingdom: Excommunication in Colonial Massachusetts," in *The New England Quarterly*, Vol. 67, No. 4 (Dec., 1994), pp. 531-566. Online: https://www.jstor.org/stable/366434

Brown, E. Francis. *Joseph Hawley, Colonial Radical.* Columbia University Press (New York, 1931).

Brown, Jerald E. *The Years of the Life of Samuel Lane, 1718-1806: A New Hampshire Man and His World.* University Press of New England (Hanover and London, 2000).

Browne, William B. *The Mohawk Trail: Its History and Course.* Reprinted by Elder Printing Co. (North Adams, Mass, original copyright 1920).

Buchanan, John, edited by Paul Kopperman. *Regimental Practice: An Eighteenth-Century Medical Diary and Manual.* Ashgate Publishing Company (Burlington, Vermont, 2012).

Bumsted, J.M. "A Caution to Erring Christians: Ecclesiastical Disorder on Cape Cod, 1717 to 1738," in *The William and Mary Quarterly.* Vol. 28, No. 3 (Jul., 1971), pp. 413-438. Online: https://www.jstor.org/stable/1918825

Campanile, Robert. *The Mohawk Trail.* Arcadia Publishing (Charleston, SC, 2007).

Carlisle, Elizabeth Pendergrast. *Earthbound and Heavenbent: Elizabeth Porter Phelps and Life at Forty Acres, 1747-1817.* Scribner (New York, 2004).

Carroll, Brian D. "I Indulged My Desire Too Freely": Sexuality, Spirituality, and the Sin of Self-Pollution in the Diary of Joseph Moody, 1720-1724" in *The William and Mary Quarterly*, Vol. 60, No. 1, Sexuality in Early America (Jan., 2003), pp. 155-170 Online: https://www.jstor.org/stable/3491499

Castle, Ian. *Fort William Henry 1755-1757: A battle, two sieges and bloody massacre.* Osprey Publishing (Oxford & New York, 2013).

Caulfield, Ernest. "A History of the Terrible Epidemic, Vulgarly Called the Throat Distemper as it occurred in his Majesty's New England Colonies between 1735 and 1740." Presented at the Beaumont Medical Clue (December 1938) in the *Yale Journal of Biology and Medicine.*

Caulfield, Ernest. "The Pursuit of a Pestilence" in American Antiquarian Society *Proceedings*, April 1950. Pages 21-52.

Chafee, Zechariah. "Colonial Courts and the Common Law." *Proceedings of the Massachusetts Historical Society* 68 (1944): 132-59. http://www.jstor.org/stable/25080378

Chamberlain, Ava. "Bad Books and Bad Boys: The Transformation of Gender in Eighteenth-Century Northampton, Massachusetts" in David Kling & Douglas A. Sweeney,

Jonathan Edwards at Home and Abroad: Historical Memories, Cultural Movements, University of South Carolina Press (2003). Pgs. 61-.81.

Chamberlain, Ava. "Edwards and Social Issues," Pages 325-344, in *The Cambridge Companion to Jonathan Edwards,* edited by Stephen J. Stein. Cambridge University Press (Cambridge, 2007).

Chamberlain, Ava. "The Immaculate Ovum: Jonathan Edwards and the Construction of the Female Body," *William and Mary Quarterly,* Vol. 57, No. 2 (Apr., 2000), pp. 289-322. https://www.jstor.org/stable/2674477

Chamberlain, Ava. *The Notorious Elizabeth Tuttle: Marriage, Murder, and Madness in the family of Jonathan Edwards.* New York University Press (New York, 2012).

Champney, Wendy. *The Forgotten Ledge of Fort Massachusetts.* CreateSpace Independent Publishing Platform (2016). Also, personal conversations, on-site visits October 29, 2016.

Chandler, Abby. "At the Magistrate's Discretion: Sexual Crime and New England Law, 1636-1718 (2008). *Electronic Theses and Dissertations. 114.* Online: http://digitalcommons.library.umaine.edu.etd.114

Chandler, Abby. "And the author of wickedness Surely is most to be blamed": The Declaration of Debora Proctor," in *Legacy.* Vol. 28, No. 2, *Women and Early America.* (University of Nebraska Press, 2011), pp. 312-329. Online: http://www.jstor.org/stable/10.5250/legacy.28.2.0312

Chandler, Abby. "From Birthing Chamber to Court Room: The Medical and Legal Communities of the Colonial Essex County Midwife." *Early Modern Women* 9, no. 2 (2015): 109-38. https://www.jstor.org/stable/26431318

Chandler, Rev. Samuel. "Extracts from the Diary of the Reverend Samuel Chandler," in *The New England,* by John Ward Dean. J. Munsell (Albany, 1863). Pages 346-54.

Chandonnet, Ann. *Colonial Food.* Shire Publications (Botley, Oxford, U.K. 2013).

Chauncy, Charles. *A Second Letter to a Friend; Giving a more particular narrative of the defeat of the French army at Lake-George, By the New-England Troops, than has yet been published...* (Published by Edes and Gill, Boston, 1755).

Cheever, Susan. *Drinking in America: Our Secret History.* Hachette Book Group (New York, 2015).

Chernow, Ron. *Washington, A Life.* Penguin Books (New York, 2010).

Chused, Richard H. "Married Women's Property and Inheritance by Widows in Massachusetts: A Study of Wills Probated between 1800 and 1850," in 2 *Berkeley Women's Law Journal.* 42 (1986). Online: https://digitalcommons.nyls.edu/cgi/viewcontent.cgi?article=1278&context=fac_articles_c hapters

Claghorn, George S. *The Works of Jonathan Edwards: Letters and Personal Writings.* Volume 16. Yale University Press (New Haven and London, 1998).

Clark, Delphinia L. H. *Phineas Lyman, Connecticut's General.* Connecticut Valley Historical Museum (Springfield, MA, 1964).

Clark, Peter. Letter of Peter Clark of Salem to Ebenezer Pomeroy, April 4, 1750. Beinecke Library, Yale University Online: https://findit-uat.library.yale.edu/catalog/digcoll:3909167

Clark, Rev. Solomon. *Antiquities Historicals, & Graduates of Northampton.* Stram Press of Gazette Printing (Northampton, 1882).

Clark, Rev. Solomon. *Historical Catalogue of the Northampton First Church 1661 -1891.* Gazette Printing Company (Northampton, 1891).

Clements, William L. *The Journal of Major Robert Rogers.* American Antiquarian Society (Worcester, Massachusetts, 1918).

Coe, Michael D. *The Line of Fort: Historical Archaeology on the Colonial Frontier of Massachusetts.* University Press of New England (Lebanon, NH, 2006).

Coffman, Ralph J. *Solomon Stoddard.* Twayne Publishers (Boston, 1978).

Cole, Richard C. "An Eighteenth Century Rhode Island Adventurer" in *Rhode Island History,* Volume 53, Number 4. Rhode Island Historical Society (Providence, 1995). Pages 103-119.

Coleman, Lyman. *Genealogy of the Lyman family in Great Britain and America; the ancestors & descendants of Richard Lyman, from High Ongar in England, 1631.* Joel Munsell publisher (Albany, NY, 1872).

Colonial Sense, the website for all things Colonial. "*New England Weather* 1744 Earthquake" from website: http://www.colonialsense.com/Society-Lifestyle/Signs_of_the_Times/New_England_Weather/1744_Earthquake.php

Committee on Historical Localities. *Historical Localities in Northampton.* Gazette Printing (Northampton, 1904).

Conger, Vivian Bruce. *The Widows' Might: Widowhood and Gender in Early British America.* New York University Press (New York and London, 2009).

Conroy, David W. *In Public Houses: Drink and the Revolution of Authority in Colonial Massachusetts.* University of North Carolina Press (Chapel Hill & London, 1995).

Cooper, James Fenimore. *The Last of the Mohicans.* Barnes & Noble Classics (New York, 2003).

Copeland, David A. "Fighting for a Continent: Newspaper Coverage of the English and French War for North America 1754-1760." On-line: http://www.earlyamerica.com/review/spring97/newspapers.html

Corbin Collection. Vital Records of Northampton.

Corbin, Lottie S. "The Story of Betty Allen." Daughters of the American Revolution papers. Online: http://www.massdar.org/BettyAllenStory.html

Coughlin, Michelle Marchetti. *One Colonial Woman's World: The Life and Writings of Mehetabel Chandler Coit.* University of Massachusetts Press (Amherst & Boston, 2012).

Covey, Barbara L. *Rebecca Kellogg Ashley 1697-1757 From Deerfield to Onaquaga.* Heritage Books (Westminster, Maryland, 2008).

Cowing, Cedric B. "Sex and Preaching in the Great Awakening," *American Quarterly* 20, no. 3 (1968): 624-44.

Crawford, Michael J. "The Spiritual Travels of Nathan Cole," *The William and Mary Quarterly* 33, no. 1 (1976): 89-126.

Cronon, William. *Changes in the Land: Indians, Colonists, and the Ecology of New England.* Hill and Wang (New York, 1983).

Dalacker, Svenja. "Burying the Afterbirth: The Archaeological Record of Modern Placenta Burial Vessels," in *The Society for Historical Archaeology Newsletter,* Fall 2017, Vol 50, No 3. Pages 13-15.

Darling, Anthony D. *Red Coat and Brown Bess.* Historical Arms Series No. 12, Museum Restoration Service (Alexandria, NY, 1993).

Daughters of the American Revolution. *Early Northampton.* Published by the Betty Allen Chapter, DAR (Northampton, 1914).

Day, Richard Edwin. *Calendar of the Sir William Johnson Manuscripts in the New York State Museum.* University of the State of New York (Albany, 1909).

Dayton, Cornelia Hughes. *Women before the Bar: Gender, Law, and Society in Connecticut 1639-1789.* The University of North Carolina Press (1995).

Deming, Phyllis Baker. *A History of Williamsburg in Massachusetts.* The Hampshire Bookshop (Northampton, 1946).

Demos, John. "Old Age in Early New England," *American Journal of Sociology* 84 (1978). Pages 248-287.

Demos, John. *The Unredeemed Captive: A Family Story from Early America.* Vintage Books (New York, 1995).

Devlin, Jane [Transcribed by]. "Register of the Deaths in Northampton [Hampshire Co., MA] From the First Settlement of the Town In 1653 to Augus 1824 Copied From the Town Records & from the Records of Deac. Ebenezer HUNT, Rev. John HOOKER Rev. Solomon WILLIAMS, Doct. Eben HUNT & Doct. David HUNT Northampton: 1824." Online: http://dunhamwilcox.net/ma/northampton_ma_deaths.htm

Diamond, Jared. "The Arrow of Disease," in *Discover* magazine. October 1992.

Dictionary of Canadian Biography, generally: http://biographi.ca/en/ For "Tiyanoga" (aka Theyanoguin or King Hendrick) see online:
http://www.biographi.ca/en/bio/Tiyanoga_3E.html

Doolittle, Rev. Benjamin. "A Short Narrative of Mischief done by the French and Indian Enemy of the Western Frontiers of the Province of the Massachusetts Bay" in *The Magazine of History with Notes and Queries*, Extra Numbers 5-8. William Abbott (New York, 1909). Volume II, Pages 203-223.

Donahue, Brian. *The Great Meadow: Farmers and the Land in Colonial Concord.* Yale University Press (New Haven & London, 2004).

Dow, Peter E. "Bucking the tide: Charles Phelps and the Vermont land grant controversies, 1750-1789/." Masters Theses 1896 - February 2014 for University of Massachusetts - Amherst, History. Paper 1465. On-line: http://scholarworks.umass.edu/theses/1465

Drake, Samuel Gardner. *A Particular History of the Five Years French and Indian War in New England and Parts there Adjacent.* Samuel G. Drake (Boston, 1870).

Drew, Bernard. "The Engineer and the Ashley Falls Bridge," in the *Berkshire Eagle*, November 10, 2012. Unpaginated. Quoting Engineer/Author David L. Costello. "The Mohawk Trail Showing Old Roads and Other Points of Interest." Self-published (1975). Online: https://www.berkshireeagle.com/stories/the-engineer-and-the-ashley-falls-bridge,280408

Drew, Bernard A. "Grand Jury Trekked Westward in 1754". Printed in *The Berkshire Eagle* (newspaper). July 21, 2012.

Drew, Bernard. *Henry Knox and the Revolutionary War Trail in Western Massachusetts.* McFarland & Company (Jefferson, NC & London, 2012). Quoting the *Boston Gazette*, 31 May 1748, 3 and *Stockbridge, 1739-1939* by Sarah Cabot Sedgwick and Christina Sedgwick Marquand.

Drew, Bernard A. Personal conversation, emails, and location tour August 11, 2018 by Author/Assistant Editor, Bernard Drew at Great Barrington, Massachusetts.

Duffy, John. *Epidemics in Colonial America.* Louisiana University Press (Baton Rouge, 1971).

Dunn, Elizabeth E. "Grasping at the Shadow:" The Massachusetts Currency Debate, 1690-1751," *The New England Quarterly* 71, no. 1 (1998): 54-76. doi:10.2307/366724.

Dwight, Abigail to Abraham Booker Letter dated Nov 10, 1755, Williams College, Special Collections. Pg 1.

Dwight, Benjamin W. *The History of the Descendants of Elder John Strong of Northampton, Mass.* Joel Munsell Publisher (Albany, NY, 1871). Volume I.

Dwight, Richard Henry Winslow Collection, Williams College Library, Archives and Special Collections. Volume 50, 1744-1911.

Dwight, Timothy. *Travels in New-England and New-York.* Printed by William Baynes & Son (London, 1828). Volume III, Letter III, Pages 344-356.

Earle, Alice Morse. *Home Life in Colonial Days.* The MacMillan Company (New York, 1910).

Earle, Alice Morse. "Old-Time Marriage Customs in New England," in The *Journal of American Folklore*, Vol. 6, No. 21 (Apr. - Jun., 1893), Pages 97-102. Online: https://www.jstor.org/stable/533294

Earle, Alice Morse. *The Sabbath in Puritan New England.* Charles Scribner & Sons (New York, 1891).

Earle, Alice Morse. *Stage Coach and Tavern Days.* The MacMillan Company (New York, 1901).

Eckert, Allan W. *Wilderness Empire.* Bantam Books (New York, 1969).

Eckert, Richard Scott. ""The Gentlemen of the Profession: The Emergence of Lawyers in Massachusetts 1630-1810." Dissertation, University of Southern California (History), 1981.

Edwards, Jonathan. *A Faithful Narrative of the Surprising Work of God in Converting Many Hundreds of Souls in Northampton, and the Neighboring Towns and Villages in New-Hampshire in New England.* Revised from the Boston Edition of 1738.

Edwards, Jonathan. "The Nature And End of Excommunication by Jonathan Edwards" in Henry Rogers, *The Works of Jonathan Edwards, A.M., with an Essay on his Genius and Writings.* Ball Arnold & Company (London, 1840). Pages 118-122.

Effingham de Forest, Louis. *The Journals and Papers of Seth Pomeroy, Sometime General in the Colonial Service.* Published by Society of Colonial Wars (1926).

Egleston, Nathaniel Hillyer. *Williamstown and Williams College.* Judd and Detweiler Printers (Washington, D.C., 1884).

Egleston, N. H. "An Old Fort, and What Came of It," from *Harper's New Monthly* (magazine), September 1881. (Reprinted by North Adams Historical Society as *Old Fort Massachusetts*, 1991, containing both "An Old Fort" and Rev. John Norton's *The Redeemed Captive*.).

Ellis, Joseph J. *His Excellency George Washington.* Alfred A. Knopf (New York, 2004).

Ellsworth, Patricia Laurice. "Hadley West Street Common and Great Meadow: a cultural landscape study" (2007). Landscape Architecture & Regional Planning Masters Projects. 44. Retrieved from https://scholarworks.umass.edu/larp_ms_projects/44

Emery, Joshua, "Earthquakes 1638 to 1883 in the New England States and in the British Possessions North of the United States and East of the Rocky Mountains" in Henry Harrison Metcalf, John Norris, et al. "The Granite Monthly, A Magazine Devoted to New Hampshire. Vol VII, No 1 (October 1883), Pages 188-190. Online: https://books.google.com/books?id=GSVRAQAAMAAJ&pg=PA190&lpg=PA190&dq=june+3,+1744+earthquake&source=bl&ots=EUnKsd77Vf&sig=wbyqOve3Wn0fXhPs2pPmAW1SG-Y&hl=en&sa=X&ved=0ahUKEwjP1-21iZ_bAhVqFTQIHQxvD7kQ6AEIPzAD#v=onepage&q=june%203%2C%201744%20earthquake&f=false

Everts, Louis H. *The History of Connecticut Valley in Massachusetts (with Illustrations and Biographical Sketches).* Press of J.B. Lippincott & Co. (Philadelphia, 1879).

Fairlie, Susan. "Dyestuffs in the Eighteenth Century," *The Economic History Review*, New Series, 17, No. 3 (1965): 488-510. Online: www.jstor.org/stable/2592624

Fitzpatrick, Ellen. "Childbirth and an Unwed Mother in Seventeenth-Century New England," in *Signs*. Vol. 8, No. 4 (Summer, 1983), Pages. 744-749.

Fitzgerald, Monica D. "Drunkards, Fornicators, and a Great Hen Squabble: Censure Practices and the Gendering of Puritanism," in *Church History*, Vol. 80, No. 1 (March 2011), Pages 40-75. Cambridge University Press on behalf of the American Society of Church History. Online: https://www.jstor.org/stable/41240523

Fitzgerald, Monica D. *Puritans Behaving Badly Gender, Punishment, and Religion in Early America.* Cambridge University Press (Cambridge and New York, 2020).

Flaherty, David H. "Crime and Social Control in Provincial Massachusetts," *The Historical Journal* 24, No. 2 (1981): 339-60. http://www.jstor.org/stable/2638790

Flaherty, David H. "Criminal Practice in Provincial Massachusetts," in *Law in Colonial Massachusetts 1630-1680*. Vol. 62, Pages 191- 242. Published by the Colonial Society of Massachusetts. Online: https://www.colonialsociety.org/node/914

Forbes Library (Northampton, Massachusetts). "Seating Plan of the main floor of the 1737 Meetinghouse."

Foster, Mary Catherine. *Hampshire County, Massachusetts, 1729-1754: A Covenant Society in Transition.* PhD Dissertation for the University of Michigan, Department of History, Ann Arbor, 1967.

Foster, Thomas A. *Sex and the Eighteenth-Century Man: Massachusetts and the History of Sexuality in America.* Beacon Press (Boston, 2006).

Frazier, Patrick. *The Mohicans of Stockbridge.* University of Nebraska Press (Lincoln, 1992).

Founders Online. "George Washington's Professional Surveys," *Founders Online* National Archives, https://founders.archives.gov/documents/Washington/02-01-02-0004 [Original source: *The Papers of George Washington*, Colonial Series, Vol. 1, 7 July 1748–14 August 1755, ed. W. W. Abbot. Charlottesville: University Press of Virginia, 1983, pp. 8–37.]

Gale, R. R. *A Soldier-Like Way: The Material Culture of the British Infantry 1751-1768.* Track of the Wolf, Inc. (Elk River, MN. 2007).

Gallup, Andrew editor of "Jolicoeur" Charles Bonin. *Memoirs of a French and Indian War Soldier.* Heritage Books (Westminster, Maryland, 2007).

Gélis, Jacques. *History of Childbirth: Fertility, Pregnancy and Birth in Early Modern Europe.* Polity Press (Cambridge, United Kingdom, 1991).

Gerstner, Edna. *Jonathan and Sarah: An Uncommon Union (A Novel Based on the Family of Jonathan and Sarah Edwards (The Stockbridge Years 1750-1758)).* Soli Deo Gloria Publications (Morgan, Pennsylvania, 1995).

Gerzina, Gretchen Holbrook. *Mr. & Mrs. Prince: How an Extraordinary Eighteenth-Century Family Moved Out of Slavery and into Legend.* Amistad Publishers (New York, 2008).

Gifford, George E. "Botanical Remedies in Colonial Massachusetts 1620-1820," *Colonial Society of Massachusetts.* Volume 57 (1980), Pages 263-288.

Godbeer, Richard. *The Sexual Revolution in Early America.* The Johns Hopkins University Press (Baltimore and London, 2002).

Graffagnino, J. Kevin. "Vermonters Unmasked: Charles Phelps and Patterns of Dissent in Revolutionary Vermont," in *Vermont History* 57/3 (Summer 1989). Pages 133-159.

Graham, Judith S. *Puritan Family Life: The Diary of Samuel Sewall.* Northeastern University Press (Boston, 2000).

Gray, James. "Letter [of James Gray] to John Gray Srgt July 11, 1755 att Fort Massachusetts," in Thomas Williams Papers, New York Historical Society, New York.

Gray, Lauren Davis. "Birthing The New Birth: The Natural Philosophy of Childbirth in the Theology of Jonathan Edwards," Electronic Theses, Treatises and Dissertations. Florida State University (2009). Paper 4024.

Greene, Nelson. *The History of the Mohawk Valley, 1614-1925.* The S. J. Clarke Publishing Company (Chicago, 1925).

Garvin, Donna-Belle and James L. Garvin. *On the Road North of Boston: New Hampshire Taverns and Turnpikes 1700-1900.* University Press of New England (Hanover and London, 1988).

Goodwin, Gerald J. "The Myth of "Arminian-Calvinism" in Eighteenth-Century New England." *The New England Quarterly* 41, no. 2 (1968): 213-37.

Greenlee, Ralph Stebbins. *The Stebbins Genealogy.* M.A. Donahue (Chicago, 1904).

Griffin, Dusty. "The 1746 Attack on Fort Massachusetts" lecture for the Williamstown Historical Society, given October 9, 2014. On-line video: http://www.williamstownhistoricalmuseum.org/featured-slider/1746-attack-fort-massachusetts/

Grigg, Susan. "Toward a Theory of Remarriage: A Case Study of Newburyport at the Beginning of the Nineteenth Century." *The Journal of Interdisciplinary History* 8, no. 2 (1977): 183-220. *JSTOR,* www.jstor.org/stable/202787

Guerty, P. M., and Kevin Switaj. "Tea, Porcelain, and Sugar in the British Atlantic World," *OAH Magazine of History* 18, No. 3 (2004): 56-59. http://www.jstor.org/stable/25163685

Gunning, Sally Cabot. *The Widow's War: A Novel.* Harper Collins (New York, 2007).

Hale, John G. (Surveyor & Civil Engineer). Map of Boston and Vicinity From Actual Survey. Boston: Published by John G. Hales Proprietor, & by J. Melish, Philadelphia, 1819.

Hall, David D. *Worlds of Wonder, Days of Judgment: Popular Religious Belief in Early New England.* Harvard University Press (Cambridge, Massachusetts, 1989).

Hambleton, Else L. *Daughters of Eve: Pregnant Brides and Unwed Mothers in Seventeenth Century Essex County, Massachusetts.* Routledge (London, 2013).

Hamilton, Milton W. *Sir William Colonial American, 171-1763.* Kennikat Press (Port Washington, NY and London, 1976).

Hampshire Court of General Sessions and Inferior Court of Common Pleas. On-line: http://www.library.umass.edu/spcoll/umarmot/

Hampshire Council of Governments Records. "A Book of Records of Acts of the County Courts holden at Springfield & Northampton in the County Hampshire," and "Inferior Court of Common Pleas and Court of General Sessions of the Peace," Volume 5 (1746-1757).

Hampshire Council of Governments Records (MS 704). Special Collections and University Archives, University of Massachusetts Amherst Libraries, MS 704. Vols 6, 7 (Lib E, F). Online: http://credo.library.umass.edu/view/pageturn/mums704-i5862/#page/174/mode/1up

Hampshire Council of Governments. *Inferior Court of Common Pleas and Court of General Sessions of the Peace.* Vol. 08 (Lib. H), 1764–1766.

Hampshire Council of Governments. *Inferior Court of Common Pleas and Court of General Sessions of the Peace.* Vol. 09 (Lib. G), 1766–1767.

Hampshire County, Massachusetts. *Inferior Court of Common Pleas and Court of General Sessions of the Peace.* Lib D, Volume 5. 1746-1757. Online: http://credo.library.umass.edu/view/pageturn/mums704-i4657/

Hampshire County Probate Court, "Mr. Hezekiah Root's Will", Ent. Lib F, fol 306/7; Box 124-36, July 1, 1766.

Hartog, Hendrik. "The Public Law of a County Court; Judicial Government in Eighteenth Century Massachusetts," in *American Journal of Legal History.* Vol. XX (1976). Digital repository of Indiana University, Maurer School of Law. Online: http://www.repository.law.indiana.edu/facpub/1920

Haskins, George Lee. *Law and authority in early Massachusetts: a study in tradition and design.* Archon Books (New York, 1968).

Hates, John G. "*A Plan of the Town of Northampton in the County of Hampshire,*" Pendleton's Lithography (Boston, January 1831). Reprinted by Historic Northampton.

Hawley Account Books. Local History Collection, Forbes Library, Northampton, MA.

Hawley, Elisha. "Last Will and Testament," filed October 14, 1755, Hampshire County Probate and Family Court, Northampton, MA. Box 69-34.

Hawley, Elisha. "Last Will and Testament," dated June 25, 1755 in *Probate Records for the County of Hampshire ~ [Massachusetts], Liber D, Begun November 14th 1753 Finished May 9ᵗʰ 1758 - --*, Page 136. Transcribed from *Massachusetts, Wills and Probate Records, 1635-1991*, Image 155 of 690. Online: https://www.ancestry.com/interactive/9069/007705552_00155/608014?backurl=https://www.ancestry.com/family-tree/person/tree/50650150/person/13499851418/facts/citation/343707732640/edit/record#?imageId=007705552_00155

Hawley, Elisha S. *Historical Sketch of Major Joseph Hawley of Northampton A Reprint from The Hawley Record 1300-1890*. Press of E.H. Hutchinson (Buffalo, 1890).

Hawley, Elisha and Joseph. "Letters" and "Papers" in the Joseph Hawley Papers, Bancroft Collection, Manuscript Division, New York Public Library. Online: https://digitalcollections.nypl.org/collections/joseph-hawley-papers#/?tab=navigation&roots=36f6db50-e6dc-0132-8019-58d385a7b928

Hawley, Elias S. *The Hawley Record*. E. H. Hutchinson (Buffalo, N.Y., 1890).

Hawley, Rebekah, Joseph Hawley, and Elisha Hawley. "[Untitled] Indenture Tripartite," probated September 24, 1759. Book 2, pages 17-18, *Hampshire County Land Records*.

Hervey, William. *Journals of the Hon. William Hervey, in North America and Europe, from 1755 to 1814; with order books at Montreal, 1760-1763*. Publisher Bury St. Edmonds, Paul & Mathew (1906). Online: https://archive.org/details/journalsofhonwil00inherv

Hendrix, Scott N. "The Spirit of the Corps: The British Army and the Pre-National Pan-European Military World and the Origins of the American Martial Culture, 1754-1783." PhD Dissertation for the University of Pittsburgh (2005). On-line: http://d-scholarship.pitt.edu/10438/1/hendrixsn_etdpitt2005.pdf

Hill, James. "The Diary of a Private on the First Expedition to Crown Point 1755," Wellesley College Special Collection. Online: http://repository.wellesley.edu/msam6/index.3.html

Hinderaker, Eric. *The Two Hendricks: Unraveling a Mohawk Mystery*. Harvard University Press (Cambridge, Massachusetts, 2010).

Hinderaker, Eric and Peter C. Mancall. *At the Edge of Empire: The Backcountry in British North America* (Regional Perspectives on Early America). Johns Hopkins University Press (Baltimore, 2003).

Historic Northampton. "Map of the Home Lots of the First Settlers of Northampton." (Also reprinted in James Russell Trumbull, *History of Northampton*.)

Hochstetler, Laurie. "Making Ministerial Marriage: the Social and Religious Legacy of the Dominion of New England," in *The New England Quarterly* 86, No. 3 (2013): 488-99.

Hopkins, Mark. *Historical Sketch of the Congregational Church at Belchertown from its Settlement 114 Years*. Published by Hopkins, Bridgman & Co. (Northampton, 1852).

Hopkins, Samuel. *The Life and Character of the Late Reverend, Learned, and Pious Mr. Jonathan Edwards, President of the College of New Jersey: Together with Extracts from his Private Writings, and Diary.* C. Dilly (London, 1785).

Horton, S. (2009). "Of Pastors and Petticoats: Humor and Authority in Puritan New England," *The New England Quarterly, 82*(4), pgs. 608-636.

Hoyt, Epaphras. *Antiquarian Researches Comprising A History of The Indian Wars.* Ansel Phelps (Greenfield, Mass, 1824).

Huey, Lois M. and Bonnie Pulis. *Molly Brant: A Legacy of her Own.* Old Fort Niagara Publications (Youngstown, 1997).

Hutchinson, Thomas. *History of the Province of Massachusetts-Bay from 1749-1774.* John Murray (London, 1828). Volume III. eBook: https://babel.hathitrust.org/cgi/pt?id=nyp.33433113859676&view=1up&seq=417

Iannaccone, Laurence R. "Why Strict Churches Are Strong," *American Journal of Sociology* 9, No. 5 (1994). Pages 1180-1211. Online: http://www.jstor.org/stable/2781147

Jarvie, Jean. *Stories from Our Hills.* Originally Published by the North Adams Historical Society (1926). Reprinted by Adams Specialty & Printing Co. (Adams, Massachusetts, 2013).

Jennings, Francis. *Empire of Fortune: Crowns, Colonies, and Tribes in the Seven Years War in America.* W.W. Norton (New York, 1988).

Johnson, Thomas H. "Jonathan Edwards and the Young Folks Bible" in *New England Quarterly* 5 (January 1932). Pages 37-54.

Johnson, William [Sir]. *Letter.* "Camp at Lake George, Sept 9, 1755. To the governours of the several colonies who raised the troops on the present expedition." Eighteenth Century Collections Online. Gale (document # CB3327290295). University of Michigan.

Joseph Dwight Collection, William Clements Library, the University of Michigan. Various letters of varied dates in regards to military affairs.

Judd Manuscript, Northampton series, Forbes Library, Northampton. Volume I, Page 493. "Rebekah Hawley."

Judd Manuscripts, Volumes III, IV, "Massachusetts" in the Forbes Library, Northampton, Massachusetts.

Judd, Sylvester and Lucius Boltwood. *History of Hadley, including the Early History of Hatfield, South Hadley, Amherst and Granby, Massachusetts.* Metcalf and Company (Northampton, 1863).

Kalm, Peter with translation by John Reinhold Forster. *Travels into North America; Containing its Natural History and A Circumstantial Account of its Plantations.* T. Lowndes printer (London, 1771).

Keith, H.F. "Early Roads and Settlements of Berkshire, West of Stockbridge and Sheffield" in *Four Papers*, by the Berkshire Historical and Scientific Society. Published by the Society (Pittsfield, 1886).

Kellogg, Lucy Cutler. *History of the town of Bernardston, Franklin County, Massachusetts: 1736-1900.* Press of E.A. Hall & Co. (Greenfield, MA, 1902).

Keysser, Alexander. 1974. "Widowhood in 18th Century Massachusetts: A Problem in the History of the Family." *Perspectives in American History 8 (1974).* Charles Warren Center for Studies in American History, Harvard University (Cambridge, 1974). Pages 83–119.

Kimnach, Wilson H. and Kenneth P. Minkema. "The Material and Social Practices of Intellectual Work: Jonathan Edwards's Study," in *The William and Mary Quarterly*, Vol. 69, No. 4 (October 2012). Pages 683-730.

Kling David and Douglas A. Sweeney, *Jonathan Edwards at Home and Abroad: Historical Memories, Cultural Movements.* University of South Carolina Press (2003).

Kopperman, Paul E. *Braddock at the Monongahela.* University of Pittsburgh Press (Pittsburgh, 1977).

Krueger, John W. *A Most Memorable Day: The Battle of Lake George, September 8, 1755.* North Country Community College (Saranac Lake, NY, 1980).

Krutak, Lars. "America's Tattooed Indian Kings." Online: http://www.vanishingtattoo.com/tattooed_indian_kings.htm

Labine, Eleanor. "We Live at this Fort Well: Revisiting the 1748 dinner of a future Revolutionary War General" in *Muzzleloader* magazine. January/February 2017. Pages 63-70.

Lacey, Barbara E. "The World of Hannah Heaton: The Autobiography of an Eighteenth-Century Connecticut Farm Woman," *The William and Mary Quarterly* 45, No. 2 (1988). Pages 280-304.

Lane, Mary M. "Whatever Happened to Martha Root?" in *Jonathan Edwards Online Journal.* Volume 4, No. 1 (2014). Yale University, Jonathan Edwards Studies. Online: https://jestudies.yale.edu/index.php/journal/article/view/144

Lanning, Anne Digan. "When will Foolish Tipplers be Wise?" in *Historic Deerfield*, Autumn 2002. Pages 21-24.

Leavitt, Judith Walzer. *Brought to Bed: Childbearing in America 1750-1950.* Oxford University Press (Oxford and New York, 1986).

Leckie, Robert. *A Few Acres of Snow: The Saga of the French and Indian Wars.* John Wiley and Sons Publishing (New York, 1999).

Lewis, Theodore Burnham, Jr. "The Crown Point Campaign 1755," in *The Fort Ticonderoga Bulletin.* Vol XIII, No 1 (December 1970). Pages. 19-88. "The Bloody Morning Scout," Pages 49-57.

Lincoln, Charles Henry. *Correspondence of William Shirley: Governor of Massachusetts and Military Commander of America 1731-1760.* MacMillan Company (New York, 1912). Volume 2.

Live Science: https://www.livescience.com/8350-canadian-earthquake-felt.html

Lombard, Anne S. *Making Manhood: Growing up Male in Colonial New England.* Harvard University Press (Cambridge, MA, London, 2003).

Lowell, John. "A sermon occasioned by the much lamented death of Col. Moses Titcomb: who fell in battle near Lake-George, September 8, 1755" (funeral sermon). Press of E.W. Allen (Bookstore of Thomas & Whipple, Newburyport, Massachusetts, 1806).

Lydekker, John Wolfe. *The Faithful Mohawks.* Cambridge University Press (Cambridge, 1938).

Lyman, Payson W. *History of Easthampton: its Settlement and Growth, its Material, Educational, and Religious Institutions.* Trumbull and Gere (Northampton, 1866).

Main, Gloria L. "Naming Children in Early New England," *The Journal of Interdisciplinary History* 27, No. 1 (1996). Pages 1-27. Online: www.jstor.org/stable/206471

Main, Gloria L. "Widows in Rural Massachusetts on the Eve of the Revolution," in *Women in the age of the American Revolution,* edited by Ronald Hoffman and Peter J. Albert. United States Capitol Historical Society (Charlottesville, 1989). Pages 67-90.

Major, James. Personal conversations, site visit to the "Bloody Morning Scout" location on the Warren County Bicycle Trail, and personal collections of French and Indian War objects and discoveries.

Manning, M.M. "Treatment of War Wounds: A Historical Review," published on-line Feb 14, 2009. Online: https://www.ncbi.nlm.nih.gov/pmc/articles/PMC2706344/

Mante, Thomas. *The history of the late war in North-America and the islands of the West Indies.* W. Strahan & T. Cadell (London, 1772).

Marsden, George M. *Jonathan Edwards, A Life.* Yale University Pres (New Haven, 2003).

Marsella, Paul Donald, "Criminal Cases at the Essex County, Massachusetts, Court of General Sessions, 1700 – 1785," (1982). Doctoral Dissertations 1341, University of New Hampshire. Online: https://scholars.unh.edu/dissertation/1341

Marsh, Dwight Whitney. *Marsh Genealogy: Several Thousand Descendants of John Marsh of Hartford, Connecticut 1636-1895.* Press of Carpenter and Morehouse (Amherst, MA, 1895).

Marsh, Perez. Letter of Perez Marsh to Sarah Williams, dated September 26, 1755 in *The Drums of Ephraim Williams, A Brief by a Former Teacher at Williams College.* William A. Pew. Privately printed by Newcomb & Gauss (Salem, Massachusetts, 1925).

Massachusetts Daughters of the American Revolution, Betty Allen Chapter. *Early Northampton.* Published by the Betty Allen Chapter DAR (Northampton, 1914).

Massachusetts Court Records: Court "Court Records Book A, 1664-1812", Pages 48-51. (per note on front inside page: "contained in Court Records, Vol. 1 of Registry of Probate Northampton, Hampshire 1664-1686"). Online: https://archive.org/stream/CourtRecordsBookA1664-1812#page/n11/mode/2up

Massachusetts Court records for Hampshire County. *Inferior Court of Common Pleas & General Sessions of Peace*, May 19, 1747 session at Northampton. Vol 5 (Lib D), Pg 26 (right hand side, showing as second half of 2 page 26's). Also, see February 9, 1747/8 (Julian calendar) at page 27-31 and May 17, 1748 at page 31-39. Online: http://credo.library.umass.edu/view/pageturn/mums704-i4657/#page/69/mode/1up

Massachusetts Historical Commission. "Reconnaissance Survey Town Report: Williamsburg." (Boston, 1982).

Massachusetts Land Records 1620-1986, Hamden County. *Massachusetts Land Records 1620-1986*. Deeds 1759-1761, pages 17-21. Online: https://www.familysearch.org/ark:/61903/3:1:3QS7-99ZH-L3H8?i=57&wc=MCBL-W6X%3A361612401%2C361689201&cc=2106411

Massachusetts Land Records 1620-1986. *Massachusetts Land Records 1620-1986*, "Tripartite Indenture," Hampshire County, Book 2, Pg 17(right side)-19, 26-7. Online: www.FamilySearch.com

Massachusetts Land Records. *Book No. 2 for Recording of Deeds in the County of Hampshire, 1759-1761* (Actually found under Hamden County) Massachusetts Land Records, 1620 -1986. Online: https://familysearch.org/pal:/MM9.3.1/TH-1951-36378-23960-9?cc=2106411&wc=MCBR-DPT:361612401,362427401 Page 323-4. Online: https://familysearch.org/search/image/index#uri=https%3A%2F%2Ffamilysearch.org%2Frecapi%2Fsord%2Fwaypoint%2FMCB2-866%3A361612401%3Fcc%3D2106411

(Province of) Massachusetts. "Plat [Map] of Two Hundred Acres of Land laid out at Hoosuck to satisfy a Grant made by the General Court to Capt. Ephraim Williams in which is Included Ten Acres, reserved…" in Massachusetts Archives *Maps & Plans*, #679. Volume 46. Page 279.

Massachusetts Probate Records, *Hampshire County,* Vol 7 (1745-1752), Pg 269 (277 of 367 in online display).

(Province of) Massachusetts. *Massachusetts Provincial Laws 1692, Chapter 18,* "An Act for the Punishment of Criminal Offenders."

Massachusetts, Town and Vital Records. "Records of Publishments in the Town of Northampton from July 3ᵈ 1630 to [undated]." Online: https://www.ancestry.com/interactive/2495/40143_270308_0070-00077/7644226?backurl=https://www.ancestry.com/family-tree/person/tree/4639504/person/6920662218/facts/citation/100179164642/edit/record

Massachusetts Town and Vital Records 1620-1988. *Massachusetts, Town and Vital Records 1620-1988*. Ancestry.com Publishing (Provo, Utah, 2011). Page 362/2680.

Massachusetts, Town and Vital Records 1620-1988. *Massachusetts Wills and Probate Records, 1635-1991*, Hampshire County. Volume 3, Pages 421-2 of 689. Will of Joseph Root Sr. at: https://www.ancestry.com/interactive/9069/007705549_00421?pid=628325&backurl=https://search.ancestry.com/cgi-bin/sse.dll?_phsrc%3DBlb1567%26_phstart%3DsuccessSource%26usePUBJs%3Dtrue%26indiv%3D1%26db%3DUSProbateMA%26gss%3Dangs-

d%26new%3D1%26rank%3D1%26msT%3D1%26gsfn%3Djoseph%26gsfn_x%3D0%26gs
ln%3Droot%26gsln_x%3D0%26_89004261_int%3D1711%26_8A004260_ftp%3DNort
hampton,%2520Hampshire,%2520Massachusetts,%2520USA%26_8A004260%3D4488%26
MSAV%3D1%26uidh%3D1y5%26pcat%3D36%26fh%3D0%26h%3D628325%26recoff%
3D%26ml_rpos%3D1&treeid=&personid=&hintid=&usePUB=true&_phsrc=Blb1567&_p
hstart=successSource&usePUBJs=true#?imageId=007705549_00421

(Province of) Massachusetts. *Massachusetts, Wills and Probate Records 1635-1991*, Hampshire County Probate Records, Volumes 11-12, 1767-1777.

(Province of) Massachusetts. *Massachusetts Wills and Probate Records 1635-1991*, Hampshire County. "Last Will and Testament of Ebenezer Miller." Volume 5-6, 1729-1745. Pages (in book on upper right-hand corner 246-7) 233-4 of 539. Online: https://www.ancestry.com/interactive/9069/007705550_00233/482328?backurl=https://www.ancestry.com/family-tree/person/tree/4639504/person/-842144129/facts/citation/502047363958/edit/record

(Province of) Massachusetts. *Massachusetts Will and Probate Records*, Hampshire County. "Last Will and Testament of Ebenezer Pomeroy." Volume 11-12, 1767-1777.

(Province of) Massachusetts. *Massachusetts Will and Probate Records*, Hampshire County. "Last Will and Testament of Elisha Hawley." Volume 8-9, 1753-1761. Pages. 155-6.

Massing, Michael. *Fatal Discord: Erasmus, Luther, and the Fight for the Western Mind.* Harper Collins Publishers (New York, 2018).

Matossian, Mary K. "The Throat Distemper Reappraised," in the *Bulletin of the History of Medicine.* Vol. 54, No. 4 (Winter, 1980), pp. 529-543. The Johns Hopkins University Press.

Matossian, Mary Kilbourne. *Poisons of the Past: Molds, Epidemics, and History.* Yale University Press (New Haven and London, 1989).

McAnear, Beverly. "Personal Accounts of the Albany Congress of 1754," in The *Mississippi Valley Historical Review*, Vol. 39, No. 4 (Mar., 1953). Pages 727-746. Oxford University Press on behalf of Organization of American Historians.

McCleery, Jennifer Reagan. "A Profile of the Northampton Minority," in *Jonathan Edwards Online Journal.* Yale University, Jonathan Edwards Studies. Volume 7, No. 1 (2017). Online: http://jestudies.yale.edu/index.php/journal/article/view/251

McDermott, Gerald R. *One Holy and Happy Society: The Public Theology of Jonathan Edwards.* The Pennsylvania State University Press (University Park, PA, 1992).

McManus, Edgar J. *Law and Liberty in early New England: Criminal Justice and Due Process 1620-1692.* University of Massachusetts Press (Amherst, 1993).

McNamara, Martha J. ""In the Face of the Court…": Law, Commerce, and the Transformation of Public Space in Boston, 1650-1770," *Winterthur Portfolio* 36, No. 2/3 (2001): 125-39. Online: http://www.jstor.org/stable/1215306

Mellen, Paul F. "Coroners' Inquests in Colonial Massachusetts," *Journal of the History of Medicine and Allied Sciences* 40, No. 4 (1985). Pages 462-72.

r

Merrick, Jeffrey. "Patterns and Prosecution of Suicide in Eighteenth-Century Paris," *Historical Reflections / Réflexions Historiques* 16, No. 1 (1989). Pages 1-53.

Miles, Lion. "The Red Man Dispossessed: The Williams Family and the Alienation of Indian Land in Stockbridge, Massachusetts 1736-1818," *The New England Quarterly*, Vol. 67, No. 1 (Mar., 1994). Pages 46-76.

Miller, Aaron F. "The Day and Account Books of Elijah Williams: A Case Study of Mid-Eighteenth-Century Material Life in Western Massachusetts," *Valley Advocate*, February 12, 2012. Online: https://valleyadvocate.com/2012/02/17/the-day-and-account-books-of-elijah-williams-a-case-study-of-mid-eighteenth-century-material-life-in-w-ma/

Miller, Amelia F. and A. R. Riggs. *Romance, Remedies, and Revolution: The Journal of Dr. Elihu Ashley of Deerfield, Massachusetts 1773-1775*. Pocumtuck Valley Memorial Association (Deerfield, Massachusetts, 2007).

Miller, Arthur Scott. *Diaries, 1862-1890*. University of Denver Library, Miller and duPont Families Papers.

Miller, Harry. "Potash from Wood Ashes: Frontier Technology in Canada and the United States," *Technology and Culture* 21, No. 2 (1980). Pages 187-208.

Miller, John Sears. "History of the Miller Family 1842," unpublished manuscript. Later published in *The Wyoming Reporter* (newspaper), September 2, 1931, page 1, columns 2-5. Also reprinted in the *Wyoming County Times*, September 10, 1931, page ?, columns 1-3. Online at www.fultonhistory.com

Miller, Marla R. *Entangled Lives: Labor, Livelihood, and Landscapes of Change in Rural Massachusetts*. Johns Hopkins University Press (Baltimore, 2019).

Miller, Marla R. *Rebecca Dickinson: Independence for a New England Woman*. Westview Press (Boulder, Colorado, 2014).

Miller, Marla R. "The Needles Eye: Women and Work in the Age of Revolution." University of Massachusetts Press Books. (2006) 2. https://scholarworks.umass.edu/umpress_books/2

Miller, Perry. *Jonathan Edwards*. Meridian Books (New York, 1959).

Miller, Perry. "Jonathan Edwards' Sociology of the Great Awakening," *The New England Quarterly* 21, No. 1 (1948). Pages 50-77.

Minkema, Kenneth P. "A Chronology of Edwards' Life and Writings." Published online: https://edwardseducationblog.files.wordpress.com/2013/10/je-chronology.pdf

Minkema, Kenneth P. *Documents Relating to the Elisha Hawley-Martha Root Case*, unpublished work shared with Mary Lane.

Minkema, Kenneth P. *Documents Relating to the Elisha Hawley-Martha Root Case*, "Some Reasons, Briefly Hinted At," unpublished work. Shared with Mary Lane.

Minkema, Kenneth P. "The Edwardses: A ministerial family in eighteenth century New England," Ph.D. dissertation, University of Connecticut, 1988.

Minkema, Kenneth P. "Hannah and Her Sisters: Sisterhood, Courtship, and Marriage in the Edwards Family in the Early Eighteenth Century," in the *New England Genealogical and Historical Register*, 146 (January 1992).

Minkema, Kenneth P. "Jonathan Edwards on Slavery and the Slave Trade," in *William and Mary Quarterly*, 54 (October 1997). Pages 823-834.

Minkema, Kenneth P. and Richard A. Bailey. "Reason, Revelation, and Preaching: An Unpublished Ordination Sermon by Jonathan Edwards," in *The Southern Baptist Journal of Theology* SBJT 3/2 (Summer 1999).

Moffett, Edna V., and James Hill. "The Diary of a Private on the First Expedition to Crown Point," *The New England Quarterly* 5, No. 3 (1932). Pages 602-18.

Mongeau, Beatrice, Harvey L. Smith and Ann C. Maney. "The Granny Midwife: Changing Roles and Functions of a Folk Practitioner," in *American Journal of Sociology*, Vol. 66, No. 5 (March 1961). Pages 497-505.

Moody, Josh editor. *Jonathan Edwards and Justification.* Crossway Books (Wheaton, Illinois, 2012).

Morgan, Edmund S. *The Puritan Family.* Harper & Row Publisher (New York, 1966).

Morgan, E. (1942). "The Puritans and Sex," *The New England Quarterly*, *15*(4), 591-607.

Morgan, Edmund S. *Visible Saints: The History of a Puritan Idea.* New York University Press (New York, 1963).

Morison, Daniel. *The Doctor's Secret Journal: A True Account of Violence at Fort Michilimackinac,* edited by George S. May. Fort Mackinac Division Press (Detroit, 1960).

Moses, Robert. "Diary of Robert Moses during the French and Indian War." The Gilder Lehrman Collection, The Gilder Lehrman Institute of American History, New York, NY.

Munsell, Joel. *Men and Things of Albany Two Centuries Ago.* (Read before the Albany Institute April 18, 1876).

National Geographic [documentary television series, 2011] (Dr. Xanthe Mallett). "The Decrypters: The Last Mohican." Aired March 29, 2012.

Native Languages of the Americas online: http://www.native-languages.org/

New England Historic-Genealogical Society from *Hampshire County Recorder's Book.* "Border Indian Massacres in Massachusetts 1703 to 1736," in the *New England Historical and Genealogical Register.* Samuel G. Drake Publisher (Boston, April 1855). Volume IX. Pages 161-164.

New England Historical Society. "The Great Throat Distemper of 1735." Online: https://www.newenglandhistoricalsociety.com/great-throat-distemper-1735/

New York State Museum. "The People of Colonial Albany Live here!" website: http://www.nysm.nysed.gov/albany/index.html with indexed on-line biographies of William Johnson (#8489, by Stephen Bielinski), Peter Silvester (#1064 by Stephen Bielinski).

Nichols, Franklin Thayer. "The Organization of Braddock's Army," in *The William and Mary Quarterly*, Vol. 4, No. 2 (Apr., 1947). Pages 125-147. Published by Omohundro Institute of Early American History and Culture.

Niles, Grace Greylock. *The Hoosac Valley, Its Legends and Its History.* G.P. Putnam's Sons (New York, 1912).

Nobles, Gregory Hight. *Politics and Society in Hampshire County, Massachusetts, 1740-1775 The Rural West on the Eve of the Revolution.* Ph.D. dissertation. University Microforms (Ann Arbor, 1979).

North Berkshire Register of Deeds, *Proprietors Book*, East and West Hoosuck Lots, Williams Land Grant.

Northampton Town Papers, 1753-4 Tax Assessments. Forbes Library, Northampton, Massachusetts. Microfilm roll #146.

Northampton Town Records 1653-1754. "A List of Polls & Estates as Presented After Correction & Amendments 1748." Massachusetts Town and Vital Records 1620-1988. Online: https://www.ancestry.com/interactive/2495/40168_270297__0020-00177?pid=76985713&backurl=https://search.ancestry.com/cgi-bin/sse.dll?indiv%3D1%26dbid%3D2495%26h%3D76985713%26tid%3D50650150%26pid%3D13397377755%26usePUB%3Dtrue%26_phsrc%3DBlb2750%26_phstart%3DsuccessSource&treeid=50650150&personid=13397377755&hintid=&usePUB=true&_phsrc=Blb2750&_phstart=successSource&usePUBJs=true&_ga=2.187190568.1825309924.1569458591-1768399619.1508594087#?imageId=40168_270297__0020-00177

Norton, John. *The Redeemed Captive, Being a Narrative of the taking and carrying into Captivity of the Reverend Mr. John Norton When Fort Massachusetts Surrendered to a large Body of French & Indians Aug. 20, 1746.* (Boston, 1748).

Norton, Mary Beth. ""The Ablest Midwife That Wee Knowe in the Land": Mistress Alice Tilly and the Women of Boston and Dorchester, 1649-1650," in *The William and Mary Quarterly.* Vol. 55, No. 1 (Jan., 1998). Pages 105-134.

Norton, Mary Beth. *Liberty's Daughters: The Revolutionary Experience of American Women, 1750-1800.* Little, Brown & Company (Boston - Toronto, 1980).

Nylander, Jane C. *Our Own Snug Fireside: Images of the New England Home 1760-1860.* Alfred A. Knopf (New York, 1993).

Oberholzer, Jr., Emil. *Delinquent Saints: Disciplinary Action in the Early Congregational Churches of Massachusetts.* Columbia University Press (New York, 1956).

O'Callaghan, E.B. *Documents relative to the Colonial History of the State of New York.* Weed, Parsons & Company Printers (Albany, 1855). Volume 6.

Old Bailey. "The proceedings of the Old Bailey; London's Central Criminal Court 1674-1913." Online: https://www.oldbaileyonline.org/index.jsp

O'Toole, Finan. *White Savage: William Johnson and the Invention of America*. Macmillan Publishers (New York, NY, 2005).

Paladin Communications, Michael Foster and Robert Matzen. "George Washington's First War" [documentary television series]. Pittsburg, Chicago, 2006).

Paladin Communications, Michael Foster and Robert Matzen. "When the Forest ran Red" [documentary television series]. (Pittsburg, Chicago, 2007).

Pagan, John Ruston. *Anne Orthwood's Bastard, Sex and Law in Early Virginia*. Oxford University Press (New York, 2003).

Pargellis, Stanley McCrory. *Military Affairs in north America 1748-1765*. D. Appleton-Century Company (New York, London, 1936).

Park, Charles E. "Excommunication in Colonial Churches." Transactions of the Colonial Society of Massachusetts, Vol. 12 (1908-9). Pages 321-32.

Parkes, Henry Bamford. *Jonathan Edwards, The Fiery Puritan*. Minton, Balch & Company (New York, 1930).

Parkes, Henry Bamford. "Morals and Law Enforcement in Colonial New England," *The New England Quarterly* 5, No. 3 (1932): 431-52.

Parkman, Francis. *A Half-Century of Conflict: France and England in North America*. Little, Brown & Company (Boston, 1898). Volume 2.

Parkman, Francis. *Montcalm and Wolfe: the French and Indian War*. Little, Brown & Co. (Boston, 1910).

Parmenter, C. O. *History of Parmenter, Mass. From 1738 to 1898*. Press of Carpenter & Morehouse (Amherst, Mass, 1898).

Parmenter, Jon. "After the Mourning Wars: The Iroquois as Allies in Colonial North American Campaigns," in *The William and Mary Quarterly*, Vol. 64, No. 1, (Jan., 2007). Pages 39-76. Published by the Omohundro Institute of Early American History and Culture.

Patten, Matthew. *The Diary of Matthew Patten of Bedford, N.H. From Seventeen Hundred and Fifty-Four to Seven Hundred Eight-Eight*. The Rumford Printing Company (Concord, NH, 1903).

PBS Home Video. "A Midwife's Tale" [documentary television series]. (2005).

PBS Home Video. "The War that made America: The Story of the French and Indian War" [documentary television series]. (2005).

Peale, Frederick Clifton. *Forbes & Forbush Genealogy: The Descendants of Daniel Forbush*. Published by the author, Rand McNally Printers (Chicago, 1892).

Pocumtuck Valley Memorial Association. "Bill of sale for J Romanoo", accession #L00.075.

Pollack, Rosemary. "The Influence of European Medical Texts on Colonial New England Medicine: The Contributions of Dr. Thomas Williams and Elihu Ashley." Online: www.medicinae.org

Pomeroy, Ebenezer. *Account Book* [household and tavern accounts from the White Horse Tavern, Hockanum, Hadley, Massachusetts]. Unpublished, privately held, microfilm #2175 at Dubois Library of the University of Massachusetts Amherst.

Pomeroy, Seth. *Journals & Papers* in Forbes Library, Northampton, Massachusetts.

Pomeroy, Seth. "Letter to the Governors of the several Colonies," of September 9, 1755.

Pool, Robert. ""Give us our eleven days!" The English calendar riots of 1752," from *Time's Alteration: Calendar Reform in Early Modern England.* (UCL Press/Taylor & Francis, 1998).

Premo, Terry L. *Winter Friends: Women Growing Old in the New Republic, 1785-1835.* University of Illinois Press (Champagne, 1990).

Preston, David. "When Young George Washington started a War," in Smithsonian magazine, October 2019. Online: https://www.smithsonianmag.com/history/when-young-george-washington-started-war-180973076/

Reed, Samuel W. "A Copy of a Journal kept by James Gilbert, of Morton, Mass in the Year 1755" in *The Magazine of New England History.* Vol 3, No 2 (April 1893). Pages 188- 195. Online at: https://books.google.com/books?id=CskUAAAAYAAJ&pg=PA150-IA2&lpg=PA150-IA2&dq=journal+of+james+gilbert+in+magazine+of+new+england+history+III+1893&source=bl&ots=EN5XL50CEE&sig=9T-TUdc4P9whAl6lEzz-FWPE05Q&hl=en&sa=X&ved=0ahUKEwiQ9fDFytXVAhXBjVQKHVvsA9UQ6AEIKDAB#v=onepage&q=journal%20of%20james%20gilbert%20in%20magazine%20of%20new%20england%20history%20III%201893&f=false

Reid, Stuart. *Redcoat Officer 1740-1815.* Osprey Publishing (Long Island City, NY, 2008).

Rensselaer-Taconic Land Trust. "Thro' a Country Not Well Settled: the Albany Road of 1752-1773." (1999). PDF Online: https://www.renstrust.org/images/portfolios/Albany%20road%20of%201752-1773.pdf

Roberts, Robert B. *Encyclopedia of Historic Forts: The Military, Pioneer, and Trading Posts of the United States.* Macmillan Publishing Company (New York, 1988).

Roeber, A. G. "Authority, Law, and Custom: The Rituals of Court Day in Tidewater, Virginia, 1720 to 1750," in *The William and Mary Quarterly*, Vol. 37, No. 1 (Jan., 1980). Pages 29-52.

Rogers, Henry. *The Works of Jonathan Edwards, A.M.* Appleton & Co. (New York, 1835). Vol I.

Romer, Robert. "Higher Education and Slavery in Western Massachusetts," in the *Journal of Blacks in Higher Education*, Winter 2004/2005. Online: https://rhromer.people.amherst.edu/MISC/JBHE-final-Slavery.pdf

Root, James Pierce. *Root Genealogical Records 1600-1870*. R.C. Root, Anthony & Co. (New York, 1870).

Royster, Paul editor. *The Journal of Major George Washington (1754)*. Digital Commons@University of Nebraska – Lincoln: http://digitalcommons.unl.edu/cgi/viewcontent.cgi?article=1033&context=etas

Ryan, Kelly A. *Regulating Passion: Sexuality and Patriarchal Rule in Massachusetts 1700-1830*. Oxford University Press (Oxford and New York, 2014).

Schafer, Thomas A. "The Miscellanies" in *The Works of Jonathan Edwards*, Volume 13. Yale University Press (New Haven, 1994). No. 3. Page 200.

Schmotter, James W. "The Irony of Clerical Professionalism: New England's Congregational Ministers and the Great Awakening," *American Quarterly* 31, No. 2 (1979): 148-68.

Scholten, Catherine. "On the Importance of the Obstetrick Art": Changing Customs of Childbirth in America, 1760 to 1825," in *The William and Mary Quarterly*. Vol. 34, No. 3 (Jul., 1977). Pages 426-445.

Scribner, Vaughn Paul. "Imperial Pubs: British American Taverns as Spaces of Empire, 1700-1783," University of Kansas dissertation. Online: https://core.ac.uk/download/pdf/213402588.pdf

Sederholm, Carl. "The Trouble with Grace: Reading Jonathan Edwards's "Faithful Narrative."" *The New England Quarterly* 85, No. 2 (2012). Pages 326-34.

Selig, Robert and Wade P. Catts. ""In the Morning We Began to Strip and Bury the Dead:" A Context for Burial Practices During the American War for Independence." Online: http://w3r-us.org/wp-content/uploads/2019/04/Volume-3-FOC-2018.pdf

Severance, Reverend John F. *The Severans Genealogical History*. R. R. Donnelley & Sons Company (Chicago, 1893).

Shammas, Carole. "Child Labor and Schooling in Late Eighteenth-Century New England: One Boy's Account," *The William and Mary Quarterly*, Vol. 70, No. 3 (July 2013). Pages 539-558.

Shannon, Timothy J. "Dressing for Success on the Mohawk Frontier: William Johnson, and the Indian Fashion," in *The William and Mary Quarterly*, Vol. 53, No. 1 (Jan, 1996). Pages 13-42.

Shannon, Timothy J. *Indians and Colonists at the Crossroads of Empire: The Albany Congress of 1754*. Cornell University Press (Ithaca, 2000).

Sharswood, George and Henry Budd. "Hawley v. Northampton", *Leading Cases in the Law of Real Property in the American Courts*. M. Murphy Law Bookseller, Publisher and Importer. (Philadelphia, 1885). Vol II. Pages 378-421.

Shaw, Charles Lyman. "Hawley Papers" in *Daily Hampshire Gazette* (Northampton, MA). Nov. 24, 1893.

Sheldon, George. *History of Deerfield, Massachusetts: The Times When and the People by Whom it was Settled, Unsettled and Resettled.* Press of E.A. Hall (Greenfield, MA, 1895). 2 volumes.

Shipton, Clifford K. *New England Life in the Eighteenth Century: Representatives Biographies from 'Sibley's Harvard Graduates'.* The Belknap Press of Harvard University Press (Cambridge, MA, 1963).

Sivertsen, Barbara. *Turtles, Wolves, and Bears: A Mohawk Family History.* Heritage Books (Bowie, Maryland, 1996).

Sklar, Kathryn Kish. "Culture Versus Economics: A Case of Fornication in Northampton in the 1740's", *Michigan Feminist Studies.* The University of Michigan Papers in Women's Studies (Ann Arbor, 1976).

Sklar, Kathryn Kish. "To Use her as His Wife: An Extraordinary Paternity Suit in the 1740s," in *Women and Power in American History*, edited by Kathryn Kish Sklar and Thomas Dublin. Prentice Hall (New York, 2002); Volume 1, Edition 2. Pages 73-91.

Smith, Daniel Scott. "" All in Some Degree Related to Each Other": A Demographic and Comparative Resolution of the Anomaly of New England Kinship," *The American Historical Review* 94, No. 1 (1989). Pages 44-79.

Smith, Daniel Scott. "Continuity and Discontinuity in Puritan Naming: Massachusetts, 1771," in *The William and Mary Quarterly.* Vol. 51, No. 1 (Jan., 1994). Pages 67-91.

Smith, Daniel Scott and Michael S. Hindus. "Premarital Pregnancy in America 1640-1971: An Overview and Interpretation," The *Journal of Interdisciplinary History*, Vol. 5, No. 4, *The History of the Family*, II. MIT Press (Spring, 1975). Pages 537-570.

Snow, Dean R. "Searching for Hendrick: Correction of a Historic Conflation," in *New York History.* Vol. 88, No. 3 (Summer 2007). Pages 229-253.

Society of Colonial Wars in the State of New York. *An Account of the Battle of Lake George September 8, 1755.* Committee on Historical Documents (New York, 1897).

Society of Colonial Wars in the State of New York. *Daniel Claus' Narrative of* his *relations with Sir William Johnson and Experiences in the Lake George Fight.* Printed by the Society (June 1904).

Sommer, Elisabeth. "A Different Kind of Freedom? Order and Discipline among the Moravian Brethren in Germany and Salem, North Carolina 1771-1801," *Church History* 63, No. 2 (1994): 221-34.

Spargo, John. *The Epic of Fort Massachusetts: An Address delivered at the Dedication of the Replica of Fort Massachusetts August 19, 1933.* Vermont Historical Society. The Tuttle Co. (Rutland, VT. 1933).

Spear, W. F. *History of North Adams, Mass. 1749 – 1885.* Hoosac Valley News Printing House (North Adams, Massachusetts, 1885).

Spring, Leverett W. *A History of Williams College.* Houghton Mifflin (Boston, 1917).

Starbuck, David R. *Excavating the Sutlers' House: Artifacts of the British Armies in Fort Edward and Lake George.* University Press of New England (Hanover & London, 2010).

Starbuck, David R. *The Legacy of Fort William Henry: Resurrecting the Past.* University Press of New England (Hanover & London, 2014).

Stein, Stephen J. "For Their Spiritual Good": The Northampton, Massachusetts, Prayer Bids of the 1730s and 1740s," *The William and Mary Quarterly* 37, No. 2 (1980): 261-85.

Stinson, Susan. *Spider in a Tree.* Small Beer Press (Easthampton, Massachusetts, 2013).

Stockbridge Library. *Deeds of our Past: Stockbridge Indian Lands and Colonial Bonds.* Catalogue book to accompany Library exhibit, July 15, 2021 to January 8, 2022. Online: https://stockbridgelibrary.org/wp-content/uploads/2021/07/Exhibition-catalog-booklet-7_12_21.pdf

Strange, Alan D. "Jonathan Edwards And the Communion Controversy in Northampton," in *Mid-America Journal of Theology,* 14 (2003). Pages 57-97. Online: https://www.midamerica.edu/uploads/files/pdf/journal/14-strange.pdf

Sullivan, James. *The Papers of Sir William Johnson.* The University of the State of New York (Albany, 1922). Volumes I, II.

Sweeney, Douglas A. *Jonathan Edwards and the Ministry of the Word: A Model of Faith and Thought.* Intervarsity Press (Downers Grove, IL, 2009).

Sweeney, Kevin Michael. "Mansion People: Kinship, Class, and Architecture in Western Massachusetts in the Mid Eighteenth Century," in *Winterthur Portfolio,* Vol. 19, No. 4 (Winter, 1984). Pages 231-255. Online: http://www.jstor.org/stable/1180948

Sweeney, Kevin M. "Meetinghouses, Town Houses, and Churches: Changing Perceptions of Sacred and Secular Space in Southern New England, 1720-1850," *Winterthur Portfolio* 28, No. 1 (1993). Pages 59-93. http://www.jstor.org/stable/1181498

Sweeney, Kevin Michael. *River Gods and minor related Deity: the Williams family and the Connecticut River Valley, 1637-1790.* University Microfilms International (Ann Arbor, 1989), Yale University Ph.D. dissertation (History, 1986).

Symmes, William. "Testimony of Williams Symmes of Winchester," July 11th (?), 1750, Deerfield, in Israel Williams Papers, Massachusetts Historical Society, Boston.

Taylor, Charles J. *History of Great Barrington (Berkshire County), Massachusetts.* Clark W. Bryan Publishers (Great Barrington, Mass., 1882).

Taylor, Robert J. *Western Massachusetts in the Revolution.* Brown University Press (Providence, R. I., 1954).

Temple, Josiah Howard and George Sheldon. *A History of the Town of Northfield, Massachusetts for 150 Years.* Joel Munsell Co. (Albany, NY, 1875).

Thomas, M. Halsey. *The Diary of Samuel Sewall 1674-1729*. Farrar, Straus and Giroux (New York, 1973).

Thompson, Roger. *Sex in Middlesex: Popular Mores in a Massachusetts, 1649-1699*. University of Massachusetts Press (Amherst 1989).

Todish, Timothy J. *The Annotated and Illustrated Journals of Major Robert Rogers*. Purple Mountain Press (Fleischmanns, New York, 2002).

Town and City Clerks of Massachusetts. *Massachusetts Vital and Town Records*. Provo, UT: Holbrook Research Institute (Jay and Delene Holbrook). *Williamsburg Town Clerk's Vital Records*, Book I. Online at www.Ancestry.com

Town of Northampton (Massachusetts). *Record of Publishments in the Town of Northampton from July 3, 1820 to."* Massachusetts Town and Vital Records. Online: https://www.ancestry.com/interactive/2495/40143_270305_0052-00076/4432686?backurl=https://www.ancestry.com/family-tree/person/tree/4639504/person/6114976510/facts/citation/502192521007/edit/record#?imageId=40143_270302_0044-00001 [Note that although dated July 3, 1820, contains marriage intentions from 1820 at the beginning, then records earlier marriages, at page 287 of 2680).

Travers, Len. *Hodges Scout: A Lost Patrol of the French and Indian War*. Johns Hopkins University Press (Baltimore, 2015).

Trumbull, James Russell. *History of Northampton, Massachusetts, From its Earliest Settlement in 1654*. Press of Gazette Printing Company (Northampton, 1898). Volumes 1, 2.

Tunis, Edwin. *Colonial Living*. Johns Hopkins University Press (Baltimore and London, 1999).

Tyng, Dudley Atkins. "Hawley et Al. v. Northampton," *Reports of Cases Argued and Determined in the Supreme Judicial Court of the Commonwealth of Massachusetts*. Little Brown & Company (Boston 1839). Vol VIII. Pages 9-43.

Ulrich, Laurel Thatcher. *The Age of Homespun*. Alfred A. Knopf Books (New York, 2001).

Ulrich, Laurel Thatcher. *A Midwife's Tale: The Life of Martha Ballard, Based on Her Diary, 1785-1812*. First Vintage Books (New York, 1991).

Ulrich, Laurel Thatcher. *Good Wives: Image and Reality in the Lives of Women in Northern New England*. Random House (New York, 1987).

Unattributed. *Hampshire Gazette*. "Old Times," November 26, 1834.

Unattributed source. Original untitled, signed document dated May 16, 1748 in Joseph Hawley Papers, George Bancroft Collection, NY Public Library (main branch).

Unknown for Austin Community College. "Massachusetts Marriage Ways: The Puritan Idea of Marriage as a Contract". Online: http://www.austincc.edu/jdikes/Marriage%20Ways%20ALL.pdf

Unnamed author (probably Sylvester Judd), "Ebenezer Pomeroy II," *Hampshire Gazette*, May 18, 1880: microfilm. Forbes Library, Northampton, Massachusetts.

Unnamed author "S.J." (Sylvester Judd?), "The Mother of Major Hawley," *Hampshire Gazette* [newspaper], June 15, 1832. Unpaginated.

Unsourced. *Plan of the Town of Northampton in the County of Hampshire surveyed under direction of the Selectmen, Boston.* Pendleton's Lithography (Boston, January 1831).

Unsourced. "The Excommunication of Joseph Ash," *The South Carolina Historical and Genealogical Magazine* 22, No. 2 (1921). Pages 53-59. http://www.jstor.org/stable/27569553

Untitled. "Receipt of Mrs. Rebekah Hawley [of] the hands of Mr. Ebenezer Pumroy," Boston, dated November 20, 1735. Historic Northampton collection.

Urban, Sylvanus. *Gentleman's Magazine and Historical Chronicle* Printed by D. Henry and R. Cave (London). Volume XXV (25) for the Year MDCCLV (1755). Pages 252-256, 519-20 (November 1755).

U.S. Federal Censuses for the years 1790, 1800, 1810 for the state of Massachusetts, town of Williamsburgh. Online www.Ancestry.com

Van Rensselaer, Cortlandt. "An Historical Discourse on the Occasion of the Centennial Celebration of the Battle of Lake George, 1755," (Originally printed by L. Johnson & Co., Philadelphia, 1856. Reprinted by the Warren County Historical Society, New York, 2005).

Vermont Wills and Probate, Orange County. "Last Will and Testament of Phineas Lyman." Volume 1, 1792-1838.

Viets, Henry R. "Some Features of the History of Medicine in Massachusetts during the Colonial Period (1620-1770)," *Isis* 23, No. 2 (Sep., 1935). Pages 389-405.

Walett, Francis G. *The Diary of Ebenezer Parkman, 1703-1782.* American Antiquarian Society (Worcester, Massachusetts, 1974).

Walton, Josiah. "Military Journal, June – October 1755," reprinted in the *New England Historical and Genealogical Register.* V (1851). Page 42.

Watkins, Walter Kendall. "Lake George Expedition 1755," in *Year-book of the Society of Colonial Wars in the Commonwealth of Massachusetts: constitution and by-laws, addresses and original papers, list of members, etc.* Printed for the Society (Boston, 1897, 1906). Publication #8.

Webb, Anne Baxter. *On the Eve of Revolution: Northampton, Massachusetts 1750-1775.* University Microfilms (Ann Arbor & London, 1979).

Weber, Eric. Electronic mail with Mary Lane on topics, such as location of Miller and Guilford houses, graves and other Williamsburg topics, various dates between 2013-2021.

Weber, Eric. "Old Village Hill Cemetery tour" online presentation to Williamsburg Historical Society. Online: https://www.meekins-library.org/ckfinder/userfiles/files/ OVHC%20Tour%2C%20reduced%20size.pdf

Weiser, Conrad. *Journal of Tour to the Ohio, August 11 – October 2, 1748.* Online: https://archive.org/details/con00radweisersjouweisrich

Welch, William Lawrence, Jr. "River God: The Public Life of Israel Williams, 1709-1788." University of Maine, Ph.D., dissertation 1975.

Wertz, Richard W. and Dorothy C. Wertz. *Lying-In: A History of Childbirth in America.* Yale University Press (New Haven and London, 1989).

West Williams, Stephen. *The Genealogy and History of the Family of Williams in America.* Printed by Merriam & Mirick (Greenfield, 1847).

Wheeler, Rachel. *To Live upon Hope: Mohican and Missionaries in the Eighteenth-Century Northeast.* Cornell University Press (Ithaca and London, 2008).

White, Carolyn L. "Personal Adornment and Interlaced Identities at the Sherburne Site, Portsmouth, New Hampshire," *Historical Archaeology* 42, No. 2 (2008). Pages 17-37. www.jstor.org/stable/25617494

White, Joseph, Edward Weeks, Boldero Canning. *Address and Poem Delivered Before the Society of Alumni of Williams College [Williamstown, Massachusetts].* T. R. (Boston, 1855).

Wickham, Parnel. "Conceptions of Idiocy in Colonial Massachusetts," *Journal of Social History* 35, No. 4 (2002). Pages 935-54. http://www.jstor.org/stable/3790617

Williams, Abigail. *The Social Life of Books: Reading Together in the Eighteenth Century.* Yale University Press (New Haven, 2017).

Williams College Archives and Special Collections in the Sawyer Library [Williamstown, Massachusetts], "Ephraim Williams Artifacts." Viewed by author in March 2015.

Williams, Elijah. "Day" and "Account Books" 1746-1762 (photocopies of originals) in the Pocumtuck Valley Memorial Association Library, Historic Deerfield [Massachusetts].

Williams, Ephraim. *Account book.* Williams College, Sawyer Library acquisition # 120038, gift of Professor Winthrop H. Root, PhD.

Williams, Ephraim. "Muster Rolls," Massachusetts Historical Society, Boston, Massachusetts.

Williams, Ephraim. "Letters" and "Papers" in the Israel Williams Collections, Historic Deerfield [Massachusetts].

Williams, Ephraim. "Last Will and Testament" from Williams College website: http://archives.williams.edu/founding/will1.php and Thomas Williams Papers in the New York Historical Society, New York, New York.

Williams, Israel. Letters of/to William Shirley, Letter of John Worthington Sept 3, 1755. Israel Williams Papers, Massachusetts Historical Society, Boston.

Williams, Israel. "Papers" file for 1748-9 in Massachusetts Historical Society. Boston.

Williams, Israel. Israel Williams Papers: "A True Acct. of those killed Wounded and missing of Col⁰ Williams's Regiment In Action Sept 8, 1755", Letter of Seth Pomroy to My Dear & Belovᵈ Wife, dated Sept 20 (or 10?) 1755, etc. in the Massachusetts Historical Society, Boston.

Williams, Israel. Israel Williams Papers: "Muster Roll of the Company in His Majesty's Service under the Command of Ephraim Williams, Junr---Captain, viz." for March 12 to Dec 10, 1749 in Israel Williams Papers in Massachusetts Historical Society, scanned copies.

Williams, John. *The Redeemed Captive Returned to Zion or The Captivity and Deliverance of Rev. John Williams, Deerfield.* H.R. Huntting & Co. (Springfield, [Massachusetts] 1908).

Williams, Thomas. Letter of Dr. Thomas Williams to Mrs. Esther Williams, Sept 26, 1755 at Camp at Lake George. Thomas Williams Papers, New York Historical Society, New York.

Wiley, Harvey W. "Early History of Rum in New England," in *Beverages and their Adulteration Origin, Composition, Manufacture, Natural, Artificial, Fermented, Distilled, Alkaloidal and Fruit Juices.* P. Blakiston's Son & Co. (Philadelphia, 1919).

Winiarski, Douglas L. ""A Jornal Of A Fue Days At York": The Great Awakening on the Northern New England Frontier," *Maine History* 42, 1 (2004): 46-85. https://digitalcommons.library.umaine.edu/mainehistoryjournal/vol42/iss1/4/

Winiarski, Douglas L. "New Perspectives on the Northampton Communion Controversy I: David Hall's Diary and Letter to Edward Billing," *Jonathan Edwards Studies* 3, No. 2 (2013). Pages 282-94.

Winiarski, Douglas L. "New Perspectives on the Northampton Communion Controversy II: Relations, Professions, and Experiences, 1748-1750," *Jonathan Edwards Studies* 4, No. 1 (2014). Pages 110-45.

Winiarski, Douglas L. "New Perspectives on the Northampton Communion Controversy III: Count Vavasor's Tirade and the Second Council, 1751," *Jonathan Edwards Studies* 4, No. 3 (2014). Pages 353-82.

Winslow, Ola Elizabeth. *Jonathan Edwards, 1703-1758.* Collier Books (Gloucester, Mass., 1940).

Winslow, Ola Elizabeth. *Meetinghouse Hill 1630-1783.* The Macmillan Company (New York, 1952).

Woodward, Samuel Bayard. "The Story of Smallpox in Massachusetts," *Annual Oration 1932.* Online: http://www.massmed.org/About/MMS-Leadership/History/Thyuyuie-Story-of-Smallpox-in-Massachusetts/#.XinZEchKhPY

Wright, Wyllis E. *Colonel Ephraim Williams: A Documentary Life.* Berkshire County Historical Society (Pittsfield, MA, 1970).

Yeager, Jonathan M. "Samuel Kneeland of Boston: Colonial Bookseller, Printer, and Publisher of Religion," *Jonathan Edwards Online Journal.* Vol. 5, No. 1 (2015).

Zemsky, Robert. *Merchants, farmers, and river gods: an essay on eighteenth-century American politics.* Gambit (Boston, 1971).

Zuckerman, Michael. *Peaceable Kingdoms: New England Towns in the Eighteenth Century.* Alfred A. Knopf (New York, 1970).

1723 Deed from Thomas Sheldon to Joseph Hawley II. Joseph Hawley Papers, Bancroft Papers, New York Public Library, New York, New York.

ee

ff